"Jack," she breathed.

"You came," he said. "I didn't really believe you would. I kept watching for the police...."

She stared, barely recognizing him. "You're hurt."

"Some. I think it's okay." He eyed her. "Lend me some money, Eve." His tone was harsh, as if he hated himself. "A couple hundred dollars. I'll—"

"Money? Jack, I'm taking you straight to the hospital. This is crazy. You can't—"

"No hospitals," he said fiercely. "No hospitals or doctors. Now, don't make me beg. Some money, that's all I need."

Eve stared at him, thinking frantically. "Listen to me," she finally said. "They'll kill you, Jack. Some dumb cop will spot you and..."

Suddenly Jack grabbed her chin and forced her to look him in the eye. "Eve," he said sharply, "you're not in charge here. Not anymore. I'd rather die here and now trying to find out who murdered Allison. I'm not going to rot for years in prison and then let them stick a needle in my vein."

"Jack..."

"No. Just shut up and listen. This is my gig now. All I need is some money, a little time, that's all. I know that by being here, you're putting yourself in jeopardy. I know you could be disbarred for this. Just lend me the money and drive off."

Eve took his fingers from her chin and shook her head. "No. I won't leave you. No," she said adamantly. "The system failed you once, I failed you. I won't do it again."

LYNN ERICKSON

The ELEVENTH HOUR

MIRA

ISBN 1-55166-426-7

THE ELEVENTH HOUR

MIRA and the star colophon are registered trademarks of MIRA Books.

Printed in U.S.A.

This book is dedicated to Burton Baldridge,
lawyer and architect.

"…informed public opinion about the death penalty is, in fact, anything but informed…the American people are largely unaware of the information critical to a judgment on the morality of the death penalty… if they were better informed they would consider it shocking, unjust and unacceptable."

—Justice Thurgood Marshall
in the Furman decision, 1972

PROLOGUE

It started to drizzle a few minutes after the graveside service began.

Jack Devlin lifted his gaze to the pewter sky and took a heavy breath, thinking that nowhere else on earth could a sky leak so much dampness. He recalled with sudden clarity Allison's statement on their first visit together to the Low Country of South Carolina. "I hate it here. I'm always sticky."

His stare fell again to the cherrywood coffin that rested before him in the Charleston cemetery. How ironic it was that Allison would be buried in the rain on this oppressively sultry May morning. In the bosom of her family.

"The Lord is my shepherd, I shall not want..." Jack heard the minister intone, but the next words of the familiar psalm were lost on him.

He was vaguely aware of Allison's son, Ben Richards, opening an umbrella and holding it over them, of other umbrellas opening and spreading blackly above bent heads. He could feel the limpness of his dark suit and sweat dampening his shirt collar.

"Yea, though I walk through the valley of the shadow of death," the voice droned on, "I will fear no evil, for thou art with me..."

Weeping willows bowed over the stone monuments in

grief, and steam was beginning to rise from the curving drive that wound its way through the elegantly tended family plots. Jack watched ghostly wisps drift up off the pavement like a cartoonist's version of souls. Allison's soul?

Then the moisture began to drip from the hanging moss on a centuries-old live oak. The moss reminded Jack of ancient tattered scarves, gray-green, dissolving in the rain. It tapped monotonously on the umbrella that Allison's son held above them. Jack felt a terrible constriction in his chest.

Allison, he thought. This couldn't be happening. His mind fled the dripping cemetery and returned to the same questions that had been twisting in his head like a dagger for days. *How had this happened? Who had done it? Why?* Nausea rose in his throat, followed by a hard anger. Anger and determination. Her death would not go unavenged.

"Dear Lord," the minister was saying, "we now deliver to you the soul of Allison Wickwire Devlin...."

Allison Wickwire Devlin. Even in death, Jack realized, she was still and always would be a Wickwire. Before she'd married Jack—when she'd been Allison Richards—she'd used the Wickwire family name. Allison *Wickwire* Richards. Her twenty-three-year-old son was, of course, Ben Wickwire Richards. There was no escaping the Charleston family. And when Jack had tried to convince her mother, Venetia, to bury Allison in Aspen, near her home, Venetia had sharply denied the request.

"My daughter will be laid to rest with her family," the older woman had said three days ago. And then she'd hung up the phone.

Jack shifted his gaze to Venetia and Trevor Wickwire, Allison's parents. Trevor was staring glassy-eyed at the coffin, but Venetia was staring coldly at Jack.

Just then Jack became aware that next to him Ben was stifling a sob. He reached over and carefully touched Ben's arm, sharing his grief. No one else made a sound; not a single murmur or sigh could be heard above the endless dripping of the rain in the lovely old cemetery.

The minister finally closed his Bible and began to move quietly among family and friends, shaking hands, touching shoulders beneath the field of umbrellas that had sprung up like hovering ravens' wings.

"Come back to the house with us." Jack heard a catch in Ben's voice. "Please, Jack, I want you there."

But Jack couldn't. He would never again enter the stately East Bay Street mansion. He wouldn't miss it, either. The few times he and Allison had visited her family, he'd been acutely uncomfortable. It had been in that grand brick and white-columned antebellum house that Venetia had called him a mongrel.

No one in the extensive family had much use for him. Or for anyone else who was not Old South. The Wickwires were a close bunch of blue bloods. After the Civil War they'd shut themselves off from the turmoil in the country and concentrated on the survival of the family business—textiles. By the turn of the century, the textile business was flourishing, supporting the entire family. It still was. And only a handful of Wickwires ventured far from the protection of Charleston society. Allison had been one of those few exceptions.

"Just for an hour," Ben was saying to him. "You don't even have to talk to Grandmother if you don't want to."

Jack turned away from the coffin and put a hand on Ben's shoulder. "I can't, Ben. I need to be here for a while by myself." He was aware of the group dispersing now, heading to awaiting cars and limousines. No one had spoken to him. He hadn't expected anyone to. Of course, they all knew about the divorce.

"All right," Ben finally said. "The limo's waiting. I'd better get going. Can I call you at your hotel tonight? We could have dinner."

Jack mustered a smile. "Sure. Call me. I'd like that." Then Ben was gone, ducking beneath the hanging moss and striding toward the lead limousine that would deliver him and his grandparents to the family home.

Jack stood in the rain alone and watched the cars weave slowly through the cemetery until one by one they disappeared behind a wall of azaleas and magnolia trees that buffered the site from the road. Then he turned back to the coffin. The polished cherry gleamed dully in the rain, and he stared at it, his vision blurred. He was unaware of his surroundings, unaware of his wet hair and damp shoulders, of the water puddling around his shoes. All Jack could think about was Allison in that coffin.

It was only a week ago—no, less than that, he realized— that she'd been so alive in their...*her*...Aspen home. Alive and vibrant—and furious. He'd stopped by at her request to sign the divorce papers. The papers *she'd* insisted on. But on that last day of her life, she'd blamed him for the failure of their twelve-year marriage. She'd claimed he was more interested in his career as an architect than he was in her. The usual fight. Allison wanted him free to travel, free to attend all her charitable social functions. Essentially, she wanted him to live off her wealth, a trophy husband. And Jack could never be that.

"Goddamn it, Allison," he'd said in the sweeping living room he'd designed, "let's not do this. We can still make it work."

"Oh, it can work, all right," she'd replied, "if you'd just stop taking on new clients. I don't know anyone else who works as hard as you."

"There's nothing wrong with hard work," he'd growled.

The argument had worsened. They'd never actually yelled at each other before. But they did that day. Uncharacteristically, both of their voices had risen, and Jack had felt as if he were going to burst with anger. He'd finally given up and stormed out past the cowering live-in caretakers, Allison throwing a ridiculous, desperate accusation at his back.

"Damn you, Jack! Don't sign the papers! I'm still going to cut you out of the will!"

As if he cared. And she knew it. It had just grown too

ugly, too painful. And that futile threat was the final thing he'd heard her say.

The live-in couple had found her body the next morning, very close to the spot where Jack had last seen her alive.

Jack stared at the coffin and took a breath. He whispered, "I'm so sorry, Allison. I'm so damn sorry."

He never knew exactly how long he stood there that morning. He only knew that he was drenched to the skin when the groundskeepers arrived to inter the coffin.

"Hey, we can come back," one of the men offered.

But Jack shook his head. It was time to go.

He turned away finally, his chest leaden. He had something to do now, though, something more important than his job, than anything he'd ever done. He had to see that Allison's killer was brought to justice. Irony again, he thought—Allison had finally managed to pry him away from his career.

He thought about Ben, too, hoping his stepson did call about going to dinner, though most likely Venetia would insist her grandson stay at the family house after the wake. Still, it would feel right to be with Ben tonight, Jack was thinking when he looked up and through the drizzle saw three men standing near the curb where he'd parked his rented car. They looked...official.

Jack dismissed them from his thoughts and walked down the gently sloping path. Unseeing, he passed dozens of stone markers, all old Charleston, dignified and understated monuments to the Low Country's finest citizens. Allison had been born one of them, but she'd thrown off the family shroud and moved west, to the mountains, to freedom. But she was back now, wasn't she? Back with the clan forever, stranded in a curiously grand design of pride and dignity that was meaningless to most of the world.

An infinite sadness filled Jack. Allison would not have wanted this.

He left the crushed seashell path and cut a diagonal toward his car, the ground sucking at his shoes, the air so heavy it was hard to breathe. Even on the Hawaiian island of Maui, where he was born and raised, the air was never this close. At least, he had no memory of this discomfort. Or maybe it was Charleston, a place he'd never felt welcome.

Jack stepped onto the road and automatically reached into his coat pocket for the car keys, again becoming cognizant of the three men; they were moving toward him. He put the key in the lock, heard the pop of the four doors. And then he looked over the roof of the car toward the sloping hillside and Allison's gravesite. Something inside him knew he'd never come here again. He needed to remember her in life, not like this, he was thinking when a voice broke his reverie.

"Devlin? Jack Devlin?"

Jack gathered himself and turned. "Yes, I'm Jack Devlin," he began, and that's when he noticed one of the men had flipped open a wallet, displaying a badge.

"Detective Wirth," the man said, "Aspen police." Then he nodded at the other men. "This is Lieutenant Fulton and Sergeant Lowery from Charleston."

Jack merely stared at them, unable to fit his mind around the meaning of their presence here. Aspen. A detective from Aspen. "What's this all...?"

"We're arresting you for the murder of your wife, Allison Devlin."

Jack let out a sudden, humorless laugh. "What?"

"You have the right to remain silent," the Aspen detective said. "You have the right..."

And then another one, Lowery, maybe, produced a set of handcuffs.

Jack just stared. It was as if he'd gone out of his body and was gazing down on the whole scene, not really there at all. He never even felt the handcuffs being snapped on his wrists or realized they were leading him toward a car parked down the road.

When he spoke, it might as well have been someone else in his body. "This is a mistake. This is crazy."

"Uh-huh," one of the men said as he opened the back door of the vehicle, then put a hand on Jack's head and ducked him into it.

"Look," Jack said, "you've made a terrible mistake. Really." He saw the iron grill separating him from a uniformed driver, a shotgun mounted on the dashboard. *My God!* he thought. *This can't be real!*

He turned toward Detective Wirth, who'd slid in next to him. "Listen, you've got the wrong man. You should be out looking for the one who killed her. I had nothing to do with it."

"Yeah," Wirth said, "sure. That's what they all say."

Jack looked at him, unseeing, thinking that this was a joke, that someone was playing a real bad joke on him. The trouble was, Jack Devlin wasn't laughing.

PART I

The Public Defender

ONE

"I still can't believe it," Frank Iverson said.

"For God's sake, Frank, believe it," Jack Devlin replied. "What is this, a reversal of roles?"

Frank sighed, a big man with a leonine head and a receding hairline.

"Look," Jack said, "I know you're a good lawyer, the best. But you can't control a jury. It happens."

Frank's head snapped up and he glared at Jack. "I don't know how you can be so goddamn magnanimous. They found you guilty of murder in the first degree."

Jack gave a short laugh.

Frank stood up in the tiny interview room of the Pitkin County Jail, very aware of the window that put them both in plain view of the booking desk. "Damn, I hate this room," he said between his teeth.

"So you've said for the past year," Jack replied dryly.

Frank scrubbed his thinning hair with a meaty hand. "Okay, okay, we'll get this decision reversed, Jack. I swear we will."

"Can't say I'd mind that."

Frank turned slowly, his head bent, his fingers massaging his temples. He had a headache and he felt lousy—was it the guilty verdict or a cold coming on? "So, the first thing we have to do is prepare for the penalty phase of the trial.

We've got ninety days, which puts us into September. God, I'm sorry you're stuck in here, Jack, but that's how long it'll take."

"It's not as if I'm going to walk out the front door a free man, Frank," Jack said. "The best I can hope for is life without parole."

Frank chopped the air with a hand. "I told you, we're going to get the decision reversed, but for now, for the next ninety days, we've got only one goal, and that's to convince the panel of judges that you don't deserve the death penalty. Then we'll have some breathing space."

"Okay, what can I do to help?"

"I've got the office on it. You know, Jack, you're the key in the penalty phase. You didn't take the stand in the trial, because we decided against it, but this time you will." Frank shook his head. "Maybe I should have put you on the stand. I don't know, Jack, maybe I should…"

"Frank, it's finished. No sense crying over spilt milk."

"Yeah, sure, and you're still in here, and I feel like hell about it."

"The Pitkin County Jail isn't so bad. There are worse places to be."

"Sure. Every jail in the country. This is the country club of them all, but it's still a goddamn *jail*, man."

"It *has* occurred to me," Jack said.

The lawyer acknowledged his client's quiet jab and sat down on the plastic chair provided for him. "What we have to do now is work on any angle that would convince the judges you deserve leniency. You're the perfect case, no priors, exemplary citizen, paid your taxes, the whole nine yards. Listen, I want you to realize this is no time or place for your damn pride. If I tell you to beg for your life, you'll beg, hear me?"

"It won't do any good," Jack said with the astonishing calmness and clarity he'd shown the past year, through his arrest, the trial, the guilty verdict.

"We'll get your friends to testify, your employers, the people you designed houses for, your mother..."

"*Not* my mother," Jack said in a hard voice. "This has practically killed my folks as it is. You leave them alone."

Frank regarded his client. "Like I said, this is no time for pride. Or privacy or dignity or any other goddamn civilized notion, Jack. This is your *life* we're talking about."

"Yes, it's *my* life."

"And I'm trying to save it, you damn fool," Frank replied in the low, gravelly voice he used to address juries. The sincere voice.

Jack Devlin stared at his lawyer without blinking. Frank couldn't tell whether he was mad or upset or scared or panicked or none of the above. The dark eyes gave away no information, the heavy-lidded, black eyes that drove Frank crazy. Goddamn unreadable eyes. And Jack's smooth, handsome face with its sparse whiskers gave away nothing more. Frank Iverson was the best defense lawyer money could buy. He'd dealt with hundreds of clients, mostly well-heeled celebrities, but he had never in his forty years of practice seen a man who possessed the utter composure of Jack Devlin.

Jack was the quiet sort, in his own head a lot. There was an old-fashioned formality to him. He was polite, soft spoken, unfailingly courteous. Grace under pressure, Frank often thought. He'd never known anyone on trial for murder who'd reacted like Jack. No one. And he admired his client for it, even envied him. He thought he knew where those admirable qualities sprang from, though Jack had never been very forthcoming about his past.

Frank had managed to pry a little information out of the forty-three-year-old architect over the past months. He knew he was half Hawaiian, that his great-grandmother on his mother's side had been one of the last queens of Hawaii. But Frank suspected it was Jack's relationship with his mainland American father that had turned him inward, given him that quiet drive. He knew Jack had fought with his father, who was a blue-collar worker and as strict as they came. Evidently Jack had left home at fifteen, gotten into a little trouble, then straightened himself out and faced life. He'd finished high school. Worked his way through college, sometimes carrying three jobs to do it. But Jack took nothing from anyone. Paid his own way. And that was why it was so ludicrous to think he'd murdered his wife for the money. Never. Not Jack.

"I still can't believe it," Frank said as if to himself.

"You said that."

"I mean, the D.A. went for all or nothing. Murder one, not even murder two or manslaughter. And he got it, by God."

"It's an election year," Jack reminded him. "This is a feather in his cap. He's a shoo-in now."

"I thought Aspen was a liberal town."

Jack shrugged. "I guess people here are fed up with violent crime, too."

"I always figured they were more concerned with getting reservations for dinner at the right place."

"You sound bitter."

"Damn right, and so should you."

"It's a waste of my energy."

Frank glared at his client. God, sometimes that everlasting calmness drove him up the wall. The man was facing the death penalty, and he never let down. "You shouldn't have been given a guilty verdict. The evidence was purely circumstantial. I'd like to call for a mistrial. I would, too, if I thought I had a chance."

"There wasn't another suspect, Frank. No one. I was the obvious choice. You had your investigators out looking for evidence for months. Were they all incompetent?"

Frank shook his head again. "They were the best money could buy."

"They didn't find anything, though. The police had me dead to rights. My fingerprints on the statue, my lighter there on the floor, the fight. The motive—Allison's threat to change her will. What do you expect a jury to think? And I had no alibi. Home alone." Jack stared out the window into the booking room, where a lady was waiting to go into the jail's common room to visit a prisoner. "It was real bad karma, that's all."

"I don't believe in karma."

"I didn't, either, Frank."

"We'll get you out. Sooner or later."

"Hope's a hard thing to live with. Sometimes I think it's easier to just exist, not think about it."

"Don't give up. I won't."

Jack leveled his dark gaze on Frank. "I'm out of money, Frank. Now that I've been convicted, I can't even inherit Allison's estate. I don't give a damn about that, but the point is, I can't pay you anymore. Now, doesn't that change your mind a little bit about not giving up?"

"Aw, Christ, Jack, I'm sorry. That's terrible."

Jack shrugged under the bright orange jail suit. Somehow he managed to keep his dignity in the garishly colored suit and prison-issue sneakers. "It doesn't seem to matter too much anymore, not in here. But I can't pay for your services."

Frank waved his words aside. "It doesn't matter. I'll do the penalty phase, I'll do it pro bono. It's my law firm, and I can do what I like. I owe you this. Don't worry about it."

"I can't accept your charity."

"It's not charity. Think of it as the best publicity I could ever ask for."

"Don't patronize me. I can't pay you and that's that. I'll use the public defender."

Frank Iverson glared at his client. "Your life's on the line, Jack. We're not going to argue over this. You retained my services for a flat rate, for the highest rate in this country, for God's sake. I'm seeing you through to the end. How the hell do you think *I* feel about the guilty verdict?"

Jack said nothing.

"I take it your silence means agreement. Allow me my

own pride here, Jack. You paid me to fight for your life, and that's what I intend to do. All right?"

Jack gave him a hard, assessing look. Then he nodded and said simply, "Okay."

Frank sighed in relief. "We've got a lot of work to do between now and the penalty phase. I'd like to get everything from your Sunday school attendance to your report cards in grade school. Teachers, professors, anyone you were close to."

"Character witnesses?"

"Yes."

"I can't ask people to do that, disrupt their lives to come here and testify. Hell, Frank, half of them are in Hawaii."

"So what? I'll send them tickets. If they're your friends, they'll do it." Frank pierced his client with his pale eyes. "This is your life, pal."

"So you keep telling me."

"Your attitude stinks, Devlin." Frank saw the hint of a smile, the barest lift of a corner of Jack's mouth, what was left of his dry humor.

"My situation stinks, Iverson."

"Hang in there. I'll be back tomorrow. I'm going to make some phone calls, get the ball rolling. Need anything?"

"No. But thanks."

Frank stood and waved to the jailer, Debby, to let him out of the interview room—the "hole," as he called it.

"Tomorrow."

Jack stood and flexed his shoulders as if to dispel tension. He waited for Frank to be let out the door to the small lobby. God, Frank hated to see him subdued like this, a prisoner, living according to the rules of prison life. Devlin shouldn't be in here at all. He should have been found not guilty and freed when his trial ended yesterday. Goddamn.

Frank walked out into the June sunshine of Aspen, leaving behind the hot, stuffy jail—a luxury jail, as Jack had said, where the prisoners were locked in cells only at night and

spent their days in a large common room with a television
set, a pay phone, a computer and even a kitchenette.

The detention officers who manned the jail were adamant
about the prisoners being classified by their behavior, not by
their crime, so even Jack had the run of the multipurpose
room all day. His behavior was exemplary. Frank suspected
that one of the lady jailers had a crush on him.

But it was still jail, and it bothered Frank a lot that he
hadn't gotten Jack off. He'd never lost a big case before; he'd
hardly lost any, even the unimportant ones. This was a
blemish on his record and he had to erase it. The truth was,
he had more money than he needed and he loved his work.
He'd have taken on the Devlin case from the start even if
Jack had been broke at the beginning.

Yes, he'd get Jack off the hook one way or another. If by
some outside chance the panel of judges gave Jack the death
penalty, he'd appeal all the way to the Supreme Court and
then some.

He walked up the slight incline from the jail to Main
Street, past the original Victorian courthouse, where the trial
had been held last month. It was a perfect June day, the sky
that particular sapphire blue exclusive to the dry western
states, the aspen trees green, their leaves shivering in a faint
breeze, the dignified old Victorian buildings of downtown
Aspen as picturesque as ever, the stony bulk of Aspen
Mountain like a verdant wave frozen over the town. Frank
drew in the thin, champagne-dry mountain air.

Thin, too goddamn thin. He was out of breath just walking to the Hotel Jerome, where he'd had a suite for the past
six months. This altitude, eight thousand feet, killed a guy.
Maybe he'd better start working out.

Frank could do anything he wanted. Freedom and enjoy-
ment of the good things in life were terrific, and Frank had
them in abundance, but in his line of work he'd seen too
many high rollers hit bottom. He'd seen the result of arro-
gance and too much money too fast. A man, or woman,
could be brought down so quickly it was shocking, and he

never took anything for granted. Look at Jack Devlin, a nice guy, damn good looking, a top architect in trendy Aspen with a rich, drop-dead gorgeous, blue-blood wife. Had the world at his feet.

But the marriage went sour, and he and his wife were separated, and then one May morning she was found dead, bludgeoned over and over again with a priceless African statue, and Jack was the only logical suspect....

Damn, it was hot. Frank loosened his tie, unbuttoned his collar. His stomach was upset—must have been lunch.

God, he had a lot of work to do before the penalty trial. He was thinking about all the details, all the digging into Jack's past he'd have to do, how he'd have to handle his client. He was feeling really sorry for Jack, and that niggling sense of guilt at having failed a client dug at him as he walked.

He was tired, too. Really tired. The trial had taken a lot out of him.

Frank stood at the corner of Mill and Main streets waiting for the light to change. He needed a rest, a long rest. Well, he wasn't going to get it, was he.

The light changed, and Frank walked across to the Hotel Jerome, thinking, weighing strategies, questioning where he'd gone wrong and how he was going to get Jack's verdict reversed. And then he wondered, as he had so many times in the past year, if Jack Devlin hadn't killed his wife, then who in hell had done it?

TWO

Jack never had many visitors at the jail. Of course, he was a pariah in Aspen and had been ever since his arrest over a year ago. The premise that he was innocent until proved guilty had never held true. He figured the good news was that he'd found out who his real friends were.

At first his parents had flown in from Hawaii—twice in three months. But Jack had asked them not to come. It was too hard. Both emotionally and moneywise. So they'd stayed away all during the autumn and winter, right up until the trial and the hot, dry summer. Then they'd sat in the courtroom, dutifully quiet and supportive. So had his sister, his married sister, Lorrie, who lived in Japan with her husband and their two sons.

They'd all been there for the trial. And that had pained Jack. The expense, the look of worry in their eyes, the tears when the verdict had been read.

Now there was the penalty phase. In three months. September. And they'd be here again. What if he *did* get the death penalty? How would they handle that?

Jack ate a late lunch after Frank left, ate it in his cell, the door open to the common area. He didn't want to be with people, didn't want to see the look of pity in their eyes. Most everyone in the twenty-five-cell jail was incarcerated for either petty crimes, drug use or second-time drunk-driving charges. He was infamous among them, and the prisoners who'd come and gone over the past thirteen months had kept their distance. He didn't blame them. For all anyone knew, he *had* killed his wife. So he stuck to himself, reading, watching the news. He'd even designed a few hypothetical homes on the computer—just to keep busy. One of the prisoners last winter, a guy in for drug possession, had printed out one of Jack's home designs and kept it.

"Hey, thanks, Devlin," he'd said. "If you want, I'll pay you for this."

"Keep it," Jack had replied. "On the house, so to speak."

The money didn't matter. Being broke didn't matter. Funny how the things that had once held importance paled when you were faced with forfeiting your life. That business with Iverson, though, grated on Jack. Sure, he'd paid the man a fortune—it had wiped Jack out. But the deal hadn't included the penalty phase. He thought about that and felt like hell. A charity case. And he knew then and there that he and Frank were going to have to work something out. Jack still had a few things in storage, some artwork, clothes, his prize Harley. Yeah, it wasn't much, not for a high-class lawyer, but at least Jack wouldn't feel like a total bum.

He got a visitor late that afternoon, someone he was always glad to see, his stepson, Ben. They'd always been close, even though Ben had mostly been raised by his real father, John Richards, the manager of the Aspen Mountain Ski Corporation. Ben had only been nine when his mother and father had divorced, and ten when Jack had met Allison while she was vacationing on Maui. She'd been staying at a friend's home, the first house Jack had designed on his own. And she'd hired him to design her house in Aspen. They'd been married that same year, when the huge glass-and-stone Red Mountain home was still under construction. Ben had been giving Allison fits, and he'd moved in with his father. But Jack and Ben had nonetheless grown close over the ensuing years. They'd hunted and fished and skied together, and Ben had opened up to Jack. Even when the boy had gotten into trouble in high school, he'd talked honestly to his stepfather about it. Now Ben was one of the very few people who still believed him innocent of Allison's murder.

After undergoing the usual police screening before entering the common room, Ben found Jack in his cell. "Hey," he said from the narrow doorway, "you're looking pretty low, man."

Jack had been lying on his bunk, staring at the ceiling, trying really hard not to relive yesterday's verdict. He sat up. "I'm feeling on the low end of things, all right. But it'll pass."

"Sure," Ben said, and they moved out to a private corner of the common room. Ben got a soda from the pop machine and sat down across from Jack. "What happens now? The papers said all sorts of stuff, but you know how they get everything screwed up."

Jack shrugged. He'd read the papers. "We get ready for the penalty phase."

"In September."

"Uh-huh. The trial's about three, four days. There's a panel of three judges who rule on the penalty. No jury this time."

"God, Jack," Ben said. "They can't really give you the..."

"The death penalty," Jack finished for him. "Sure they can." He knew he sounded nonchalant, resigned to that possibility, but in truth, a knot had formed in his chest. He'd never let Ben see it, though. Not Ben or anyone else.

"Shit," Ben said, hanging his head. "Ah, shit, Jack."

He was a good-looking young man. Not as tall as Jack, but well built, with a nice carriage and a handsome face. Although he was in no way related to Jack, Ben could have passed for his son. They both had dark brown eyes, short dark hair, smooth pale skin when they hadn't been in the sun. Other than the telltale tilt of Jack's eyes and something in his cheekbones, they really could have been related. When one of Ben's aunts had pointed that out, Venetia Wickwire had denied it emphatically. Jack was positive Venetia was endlessly grateful that he and Allison had never had children of their own. Jack would have had a couple—wanted to—but Ben was more than enough for Allison.

"God, kids," Allison had always said. "I love babies, but why do they have to grow up?"

Ben finally let out a deep sigh and glanced up. "I'm going to testify, Jack, at the next trial. You don't deserve this. And I talked to a guy at school before graduation. His father's a police captain and he knows some good private detectives in Denver. There's got to be a way to prove..."

Jack shook his head slowly and smiled. "Don't waste your money. Iverson's crew couldn't find a thing."

"But damn it, Jack, *someone* killed my mother. There's got to be a way, something everyone overlooked."

"Yeah," Jack said pensively, "I guess I've only thought about *that* maybe a thousand times by now." Then he reached over and punched Ben's leg playfully. "Hey, we'll talk about this stuff later, okay? Right now I want to know all about graduation. Hell, I didn't even make it down to the local drugstore to get you a card."

"Very funny," Ben said.

"So who was the speaker? The president?"

"Ha, ha. No, but we did have the CEO of Chrysler Corporation. He gave a real good speech—you know, a major pep talk."

"So what *are* you going to do with your life, kiddo?"

Ben shrugged. The truth was, the recent graduate from Denver University never had to work a day in his life if he didn't want to. As one of the heirs to the Wickwire family fortune, he received a modest monthly sum from a trust, enough to live on. But as the sole heir to Allison's estate, the young man had it made. His real father was no slouch, either, and someday Ben would inherit from him, too.

Frank Iverson had thoroughly checked out Ben from day one of his investigation. Jack had been livid.

"No way, Frank," he'd said in the interrogation room the

week he'd hired him. "Ben Richards would never be capable of murder. Don't waste your time."

But Frank had. He'd put a team of P.I.s on Ben and on every person who'd ever had access to Allison's Red Mountain home, because someone had either known the combination on the security pad, or Allison herself had known her murderer and let him inside.

Ben had checked out pretty clean, as Jack had known he would. Frank's people had found some college drug use, some overspending on Ben's credit cards. The live-in couple at the house had hinted at a few arguments about money between Ben and his mother.

"Hell, Frank," Jack had said, "what kid in the world hasn't argued over money with his folks? Give me a break."

And Ben had an ironclad alibi. He'd been in Denver at his apartment, down and out with the flu, and there were witnesses.

Jack sat back down on the couch in the common room and put his hands behind his head, staring at Ben. "So what *are* your plans?"

"I don't know," Ben said, "I really don't. This whole last year's been hell." Then he looked up sharply, embarrassed. "God, I'm sorry. I know what you've been through, Jack. My year's been nothing compared to yours. It's just that, well, losing my mother like that and trying to get through my senior year... And this trial. The verdict... Don't you feel you're just going crazy? I mean, if it were me..."

Jack gave his stepson one of his wry, crooked smiles. "Sure I do. I get mad as hell. But I can't let it take over."

"Tough guy."

"You know I'm not tough. Never was. I've just learned that if you keep your temper under control, things go a lot easier. People always think I'm introverted, but, well, you know that. The truth is, Ben, I try to think things out, not make any sudden moves. It's just my nature."

Ben laughed lightly. "Yeah, I remember when I first met you. You scared the hell out of me. You were so quiet, you know. And that look you give people, like when they're talking and you're just listening... I used to practice it in the mirror." He laughed again. "Yeah, I used to spend hours trying to get it right."

Jack shook his head.

"But you're okay, Jack. You know how I feel. I always wished you were my father."

Jack wasn't aware of it, but he gave Ben a long, inscrutable look. Finally he said, "We *are* family. We always will be."

Ben nodded and sighed. "I guess I'd better tell you. I'm thinking about listing the house."

"You are."

"I'd like to put it on the market, Jack. After what happened to Mom... Well, you understand. It's hard to be there. Sarah and I are staying there now, you know, because of the trial and all. But it's hard."

"How is Sarah?" Jack asked, steering Ben away from his discomfort. "Has she still got the most beautiful legs in the West?"

Ben smiled. "Sure does. She's been great this whole time, I'll tell you, Jack. She's been a real rock."

Jack really did like Ben's girl, Sarah Glick. Not only was she a long-legged, southern California blond knockout, but she had brains. Both she and Ben had been prelaw at Denver University, where they'd met as juniors, but Sarah's performance as a student had always far outshone Ben's.

"We'll probably do law school together," Ben was saying. "But maybe not until next year. I don't know. After this penalty trial in September, well, after everything's settled with you, we're going to take a trip. Europe, I guess."

Jack nodded thoughtfully. "But you've got to set your goals, Ben. A trip's fine, but don't put off grad school too long. And for God's sake don't go getting married too quickly. I like Sarah a lot, you know that. But give it time. There's no rush. Maybe if your mother and I hadn't rushed into things... Well, we didn't realize we had different dreams."

"Mom never did want you to work," Ben said.

"Yeah, well," Jack said, "that was a problem. A big one. Maybe my head got swelled with all the success. I don't know. But Allison was right. I was taking on too much. I didn't see it at the time, but marriage takes work, too. Lots of it. Believe me, I've had plenty of time to think about that."

Ben took a breath. "Jack? Did you...love Mom? I mean, did you still feel anything after she filed for divorce? Maybe it's none of my business, but..."

"It's okay," Jack said. "You have a right to know. Allison and I did love each other. At least, *I* still loved *her*. But it changed. There were things other than my work that got in the way. To be honest, kids were one."

"You wanted kids?"

Jack nodded.

"Wow, I never knew that."

"Neither did I. Not until after we were married. That's the thing, Ben. You've got to know all that stuff before you commit to a lifetime with somebody. Your mom had you. You were almost a teenager when we got married. Naturally she didn't want to start all over. I didn't blame her, either. I understood that."

"But, Jesus," Ben said then. "She was having an...an affair, Jack. I didn't know till the trial."

Jack whistled between his teeth. "I didn't think that happened till after I moved out, Ben."

"But you don't know. Not for sure."

"No," Jack said quietly, "I don't. Probably never will."

"Goddamn," Ben said.

They both carefully steered the conversation away from the subject after that, and discussed the possibility of Ben's eventually entering the family business.

"I've been thinking about corporate law, or maybe even tax law, I don't know. And Sarah's definitely going into estate planning. Big bucks there. But I'm still undecided. I'd really like to do a lot of traveling."

"Like I said," Jack put in, "traveling's fine. But someday you've got to look at the future."

Then Ben chuckled. "Hey, maybe I'll just be another Aspen trust-funder."

"Oh, swell," Jack said, and they both laughed.

By then it was time for dinner, and the prisoners who'd been lolling around the common room filtered off to get their trays. The jailer, Debby, let herself into the room and walked over to Jack and Ben.

"Time to go, Ben," she said.

Both men stood and Ben gave Jack a hug. "Hang in," he said. "And I still want to hire those P.I.s I told you about. Maybe even put up a reward for information…"

"Ben," Jack said in a stern voice, "we've been over this. Don't do it. You're only making this tougher on me."

"It's your pride," Ben said. "I may still be a kid in your eyes, but I know you. Now's not the time for pride."

Jack gave him a hard look. "We'll talk more about it. I promise. But for right now just let Frank handle things. Promise me you'll do that."

After a long moment Ben finally nodded. "All right. For now. But the subject's not closed."

"Okay, Ben, okay. Now get out of here before they keep you, too."

Jack planned on eating alone that evening, as he always did. His mind was still churning with the verdict. It had happened less than twenty-four hours ago and yet, oddly, he felt as if it had been years. *Guilty of murder in the first degree.* God.

He was thinking about that again after dinner when he was told he had another visitor. It turned out to be Brooke Goldsmith, a woman Jack knew well, as he'd designed her house. Jack met her in the interview room.

"Hello, Jack," Brooke said. "Listen, I just had to come down here. This has been driving me crazy. Well, I don't know if you really are guilty, Jack, I just can't imagine it. But there's something I've wanted to come forward with."

"Go on," Jack said.

"Well, maybe I should have told your lawyer, but it just seemed... Oh, what the hell," she said. "Look, you know that live-in couple of Allison's? Ray and Marnie Wade? Well, they used to work for me. When they first moved here, oh, maybe six, seven years ago. Anyway, there was a missing ring.... My *wedding* ring, for God's sake. I didn't really know, but I suspected they took it. I mean, I'd been to a party. I'd had a few, of course." She laughed self-mockingly. "Anyway, when I woke up the next morning, it wasn't anywhere to be found. The house was locked. The security was on. Now, I may have lost it at the party, but I seriously doubt it. The upshot is that I fired them. I couldn't prove anything, of course, but I figured I'd never trust them again. You know."

"Sure," Jack allowed.

"Well, I just thought you'd like to know that. I mean, if you didn't...do that to Allison, *someone* did. I feel sort of stupid telling you now, but..."

"I understand," Jack said. "And thanks."

"I'd say my pleasure," Brooke said, rising, "but it really isn't."

Jack mulled that information over all evening. While the other prisoners watched a rented video in the common room, Jack lay on his bunk and thought about Ray and Marnie, the live-ins Allison had hired about a week after Jack had moved out and taken a condo downtown. *Could* they have stolen something, been discovered by Allison? Could it have turned ugly?

He guessed he'd have to tell Frank about this, although he hated to get the couple into a fix if they were innocent. Which they probably were. Still...

Jack was thinking that over, trying to analyze all the ramifications, when Debby, who was supposed to be off shift by now, came into his cell and gently closed the door behind her.

"I need to tell you something, Jack," she said. "I was going to let it go till morning, but I thought you'd want to know right away."

Jack sat up.

"Ah, hell," she said, "I don't know how to tell you but just straight out. Frank Iverson... Shit, Jack, he keeled over this evening at the Pitkin County Courthouse. Heart attack."

"Jesus." Jack took a breath. "Is he...?"

Debby shook her head. "He's alive. They airlifted him to Denver about an hour ago. I guess the prognosis is guarded." She looked down at Jack. "I'm sorry. None of us wanted to tell you. We drew straws."

"And you lost," he said automatically, his eyes meeting hers.

"Yeah, I lost."

"I know how you feel" was all Jack could say.

THREE

Everyone who was acquainted with Deputy Public Defender Eve Marchand knew she was a crusader; some admired her for it and some thought she was crazy. But all admitted that she was very good at what she did, and that was defending the underdog. She was a woman of strong convictions, sometimes irritatingly so, and she had ruffled the feathers of more than one sitting judge and self-confident district attorney.

It was funny, a lot of people thought, she didn't look the part. She had a small face and a cloud of wildly curly honey-colored hair—she looked like a small, mischievous child at times, but when she was on the job, facing down a D.A. or a judge, negotiating for a man's life, she pulled her hair severely back, put on her eyeglasses and accepted the mantle and the power of the righteous.

On this particular June afternoon in Denver, the sky was its normal hard, hot azure, the spine of the Rocky Mountains rising like jagged teeth to the west of the city, and Eve was leaving courtroom 19 in the City and County Building.

She and another deputy public defender on this case had put fixed smiles on their faces before leaving the courtroom, knowing what awaited them. They pushed their way through the throng of TV and newspaper people, ignored the microphones and questions. She only said, once, clearly and mildly, "We'll be giving a statement outside the building in a few minutes. Please, everyone, can we clear the hallway?"

Eve was exhausted, but she knew she'd have to keep up her facade for a little longer. She was too weary at the moment to savor the enormous satisfaction she should be feeling; she'd keep that for later. Right now she had to deal with the media.

Outside, on the broad, colonnaded steps of the stately edifice that housed the Ninth Judicial District Court, facing the gilded dome of the state capitol, Eve and Howie Bernhard stopped, and she took a moment to frame the statement in her mind. She held up her hand, and the clamor died down, the only noise the muted traffic from Colfax Avenue across the beds of flowers that bloomed between the capitol and the City and County Building.

"Today," she began, "today justice has triumphed. A man who was in danger of being *legally murdered*—" she waited for the murmur to die down "—has been saved from that fate. You all know how the Public Defender's Office and I myself feel about the death penalty. We're against it for so many reasons I don't have time to go into them today, but I can tell you that the death penalty is used overwhelmingly against the poor and minorities, that it's imposed arbitrarily, that it's so rarely carried out that it cannot be considered a deterrent to crime and, finally, that it is unacceptable in an enlightened society.

"Mr. Bernhard and I are very happy that the court saw fit to give Joseph Lardner life in prison rather than death. We feel that justice has been done and we thank you all."

The questions began, the usual ones. Eve had fielded them all before. Sweat dampened her underarms and trickled down between her breasts in the afternoon heat. Howie was sweating, too. She hoped the cameras didn't pick up the sheen, because it would make them both look frazzled and nervous.

"What about the families of the victims?" the Channel 9 anchor asked.

She let Howie take that one—he knew what to say. "We all feel for the victims' families, but another death will not bring their loved ones back. This decision at least gives them closure."

Eve stood there and smiled into the cameras, swaying with weariness. She just caught the tail end of a question directed at her.

"A new trend in opinions about the death penalty?" she repeated. "No, I don't really see that, unfortunately. A majority of people in national polls are still in favor of capital punishment. But I truly believe that if the public were better informed, their opinion would change. Meanwhile, I'll just keep doing my job the best I can. Now, if you'll excuse me..."

"Miss Marchand, Miss Marchand! Is it true you're leaving the Public Defender's Office for private practice?"

She turned to the newsman. How on earth had *that* gotten out? "I have no comment at this time."

Howie handled the next question: was there going to be an execution in Colorado soon? But Eve barely heard the answer. These reporters were like piranhas with vicious appetites. She had to protect herself from them, she knew; any chink in her armor and they'd race in for the kill. She could never let them know what a price she paid for her unruffled surface, how much her job took out of her.

"Miss Marchand," one of them was yelling, "can you tell us how you feel personally about today's victory? Did you know they're calling you the new Mistress of Delay?"

Eve smiled. "Well, I'll take that as a real compliment, but I think that title belongs to Ms. Holdman in Florida." Charlotte Holdman was one of Eve's personal heroines, a brash, passionate woman who'd fought ferociously against the death penalty for years. Against her will, Eve felt flattered by the comparison. "And to answer the first part of your question, I feel very satisfied about Judge Caspari's decision today. It was the right thing to do."

"What's your next case?"

"I haven't got anything pending right now, gentlemen. I'm taking a vacation, a long overdue one."

"Where are you going, Miss Marchand?"

"That, sir—" she grinned "—is privileged information."

She and Howie extricated themselves shortly thereafter and went inside. She gave him a quick kiss on the cheek. "Good work, Howie."

"Yeah, we did well, didn't we?" He squeezed her arm. "You were great in front of the cameras."

"You weren't bad yourself."

"See you, when? In a couple of weeks?"

"Sure. After my vacation. Thank God I've got that to look forward to. I'm wiped out, Howie."

He regarded her soberly. "You really quitting, Eve?"

She looked down. "I don't know. I'm thinking about it. I've put a few feelers out, that's all. Nothing serious."

"Don't quit, Eve. We need you. All those poor saps in jail, on death row, they need you."

"Aw, Howie, don't lay that stuff on me. I *know*."

"Okay, I'll shut up. Have a great vacation."

"I'll do that. Thanks."

Eve looked at her watch. God, late again. Gary was waiting. She picked up her briefcase and made her way out a side door of the building, her sensible pumps tapping on the marble floor, her gray gabardine tailored suit wrinkled from the long day. She was exhausted, mentally and physically. She knew she wouldn't be very good company tonight, and there was that barbecue at Matt Nolan's. She'd have to go; she couldn't disappoint Gary again.

Why did she care so darn much? Why couldn't she just go to work and do her job and not get so emotionally involved? She let herself out of the building and saw Gary's bronze Lexus at the curb. Guilt stabbed her, and she hurried to him. Gary had asked her those questions more than once, and she'd always answered him evasively. The truth was that when she'd first gone into public defense after law school, she'd been practicing in the South, dubbed the Death Belt because of the many executions there. On the very first case she'd been assigned, she'd been unable to prevent the man's execution. Two weeks later, the actual guilty party had confessed to the crime—a deathbed confession. The state had executed an innocent man. Eve had left the South and returned to her native Colorado. She'd been crushed. Still, she'd gone right back into public defense, vowing to herself that never again—on her watch—would an innocent man be dragged to the death chamber.

Defending men destined for execution had become her passion and her Holy Grail. Her reputation had spread, and soon calls from all over the country had started coming in to her Denver office, desperate calls from public defenders for her expertise, her encyclopedic knowledge of the appeals process and prisoners' constitutional rights and trial tactics.

And so far she'd never lost a client.

She never told anyone about that first case, though. Not her parents or close friends or even Gary. It was her dark secret. Her private pain.

Now, victorious today, she hurried toward the Lexus and refused to think about the past.

"Hi, honey," she said, sliding into the front seat, leaning over and kissing Gary. "Sorry I'm late. Again."

"I'm used to it."

"I know. But I'm off for two weeks, don't forget."

"Free, oh Lord," he joked. "Free at last!"

Gary Kapochek was a great-looking man. Tall, slim, well built, with a resolute jaw. He'd been a star wide receiver for the Denver Broncos, a really popular player, signed for three more years at an unheard-of salary when he'd started having a little trouble with blurry vision and dizziness. The diagnosis had been multiple sclerosis, MS, a tragedy for Gary, for the team, for his friends, for Denver, for the entire state of Colorado. He'd been thirty years old, at the height of his career. The newspapers had covered his story in depth, following him for months, even years. And when he'd gotten a job as assistant offensive coach for the Broncos, his adoring public had been thrilled.

He started his hand-controlled car and pulled away from the curb. "Tired?" he asked.

"Totally beat," Eve said, leaning her head back against the seat.

"If you don't want to go tonight..."

"No, really, I said I'd go and I will. I'll be fine." She turned her face toward him. "You got the tickets and all?"

"Sure do. Everything's ready. All you have to do is pack."

"Um."

They were going to Maine, to fish and boat and walk the shore. Complete relaxation. And Gary could walk a mile now using only a cane. He'd improved so much on a new form of interferon beta that he'd thrown away his crutches. The debilitating periods of weakness and fatigue were practically gone, and his doctor was hopeful that he'd go into full and permanent remission.

Gary patted her leg and gave her his boyish grin. "Oh, man, am I looking forward to this trip," he said. "Our first, our very first trip together."

"Come on, we went to Durango once."

"Only because you had to interview a witness."

Eve loved Gary's humor, his outlook on life, his patience with her, his absolute optimism under trying circumstances. He'd handled his illness without self-pity, with a winning smile and a positive mind-set, and she admired him enormously.

She sat in his car as he drove her home and thought about telling Gary that she wasn't so sure about quitting the Public Defender's Office, not as sure as she'd sounded the last time they'd discussed it. He'd pressed her very hard about the decision, for once meeting her excuses with steely resolve, and she'd suddenly seen the intensely competitive man under Gary's easy ways. He badly wanted her to go into private practice.

"So we have a *life*, baby," he'd said.

"Your life, you mean."

"No, I don't. You're entitled to your life, your career, whatever you want. But, Eve, right now you have nothing but your obsession. It's bordering on sick."

She'd taken off her glasses and rubbed her eyes. "There's so much to do."

"Let someone else do it."

She'd been about to say, *Nobody can do it as well as I can*, but she shut her mouth and held it in. It did sound obsessive, she realized.

Gary had leaned close and taken her hand. "Look, we're engaged, right? We're going to get married, but first you have to take some time for yourself, for us. My God, Eve, you can't even set a wedding date with your caseload. It's been four years, and I've been patient, but now's the time to make the break."

"They need me," she'd begged.

"*I* need you, baby."

Eve had looked down at her hands.

"Look, if it's money that's worrying you, I have money," Gary had said gently. "No matter what happens to me, there's enough. You wouldn't even have to work at all."

"I *want* to work."

"Yes, I know, and I want you to, but you're going to have to take care of yourself, too."

She'd given in and promised to put out feelers for a position in a law firm. She could still be a defense lawyer; she could even do pro bono work to assuage her guilt if she wanted.

But now she had doubts.

She glanced at Gary as he drove, rested her gaze on his strong profile, the square, sculpted jaw, the muscular neck. He was a good man, and he deserved a wife who had time for him. They'd discussed his MS often. What if he had a relapse? What if he went downhill, couldn't hold a job? What if he wasn't able to make love to her anymore? What if he ended up in a wheelchair permanently?

"I'd always love you," she'd said fervently. "It wouldn't matter."

And gradually Gary had come to believe her—or had it been the improvement in his illness? Eve didn't care about the reason, she was so happy for him, for herself. Their marriage would be a true partnership, a loving, compassionate relationship. And children were out of the question, not an issue. Gary refused to have any in case he'd pass on the propensity for contracting MS. It did have a genetic link, and Gary had made the decision years before.

Eve had felt pangs at first when Gary had told her that, but she saw his side and agreed with him. She was far too busy to consider a family, in any case.

She had to tell him about her doubts, though. They discussed everything. And yet... It would ruin their vacation. They'd quarrel. No, she'd wait. There was plenty of time to talk about it later. And, besides, Eve wasn't sure what she was going to do. She wasn't sure at all. It was a very important decision, and she wanted to give it time. No need to tell Gary now.

"Hungry?" he asked.

"Not yet."

"Well, it's going to be a great feed. Matt's invited the whole team, all the coaches, wives, kids, the works. A barbecue. A country-western band, a singer. You know Matt, he goes whole hog on these things."

"Sounds like fun."

"Maybe you could take a quick nap when you get home." She gave a laugh. "I wish."

"You're driving yourself crazy, Eve. You're skinny. You don't exercise...."

"Honey, you're repeating yourself. We've got two weeks now, two weeks of nothing to do."

"About time."

"Amen to that," Eve said, and she folded her glasses, slipping them into their case, then she pulled out the pins holding her bun in place and shook her head, running her fingers through her tangled hair.

"That's better," Gary said, turning his infectious grin on her.

Matt Nolan, the owner of the Broncos, gave a party every June at his tract mansion in the Cherry Hills subdivision south of Denver proper. It was an affair the entire organization looked forward to every year, and Gary was no exception. And he loved to show Eve off to his cronies.

It was a casual party, shorts and tank tops in the ninety-degree heat. Faye Nolan always prayed that the usual afternoon thundershowers didn't crop up, because even though there was a big canopy in place, the wind could play havoc with tablecloths and hairdos.

Eve tried to hide her weariness; it would hurt Gary's feelings if he knew she'd rather be home resting. She said hello to all the wives, most of whom she knew from social events and games, got hugged by several of the huge warriors on the team, was introduced to two brand-new members.

She smiled and nodded and made small talk and sipped on a beer until it was warm. All around her were war stories and wives' gossip, and the smell of barbecued meat rising on the hot air. And Gary, smiling, leaning on his cane. It didn't matter to anybody that he had a handicap. He'd made his place with the team, a respected and beloved coach. A poster boy, he sometimes joked. And Eve watched him and smiled to herself. What a great guy Gary was.

They ate barbecued beef, corn on the cob, coleslaw, baked beans, watermelon, ice cream. The players could really put it away.

"Is that all you're going to eat?" Gary asked Eve. "You'll starve to death."

I'm too tired to eat, she wanted to say, but she bit back the words. "I'm fine. Howie and I had a huge lunch," she lied.

The band started after dinner. Lights came on as the sky

dimmed; a portable dance floor had been set up. Couples danced, kids ran between their feet, the Nolans' two golden retrievers rubbed against people's legs, panting, seeking food scraps and affection.

"Let's dance," Gary said.

She looked at him. They'd never danced; he wasn't able to.

"Come on," he said. "Chicken?"

It was a slow dance, a cowboy ballad, and Gary moved so easily, so well, Eve was astonished.

"You're a good dancer," she murmured.

"Didn't I ever tell you that?" he asked.

"No, you didn't, honey."

"Well, I am. I *was*. But I'm not so bad now, am I?"

"You're great."

"So are you, baby."

She left the Nolans' party at ten, too tired to stay another minute. She convinced Gary to remain—he was having such a good time—and offered to drive his car home. He could get a ride from one of his pals later.

"You're sure, baby? I can drive you home. I will, honestly."

"No, you stay. Gary, I'll be fine. I just need some sleep."

"I'll be there later, okay?"

"I'll be asleep," Eve said, smiling.

"You're beautiful asleep." He kissed her. "Drive carefully. That's a new car."

"I promise. Now, go on back to the party. They miss you."

Gratefully Eve let herself into her house, pulled off her clothes, left them where they lay, brushed her teeth and fell into bed. She clicked on the television set, caught the end of the news: a babble of voices, a crowd of cameras and reporters, the broad front steps—and her and Howie.

"Privileged information..." she heard herself say, and she judged her smile objectively. Yes, it was okay, not bad. But she looked like hell, thin and pale, bags under her eyes. Gary was right: she was killing herself with this job.

She yawned and nestled her head into a pillow and felt her body relaxing, falling into sleep. In Maine she'd eat a lot, get some muscle tone, some color in her cheeks. Make love a lot, talk about the future with Gary. There would be time, precious time, and they could really be with each other.

She imagined it—the charming seaside bed-and-breakfast, the damp, cool air, the ocean, the seagulls, the rocky shoreline. Lobster and Boston bluefish and clams. And Gary...

When Gary got home, the TV was still on, flickering onto the bed where Eve lay asleep. A talk show, some guy blabbing about something, a rapt studio audience. Quietly Gary turned it off, shed his clothes, laid his cane against a chair and crawled into bed. He'd had a few too many beers, which was dumb, lousy for his already impaired coordination, but, hell, he'd had a ball. He leaned over and kissed Eve lightly on her cheek. She murmured and her eyelids flickered.

"Good night, baby," he said softly.

"Um," she murmured, but he knew she wasn't really awake.

The next morning was Saturday. They were leaving for Maine on Sunday morning, and Eve was packing while Gary lay stretched out in bed, his hands behind his head.

"Do I need a parka or just a windbreaker?" Eve was asking. "Is it really cold there, or just rainy and cool?"

"Cool," he said. "Or it could be hot."

"That's helpful."

"If you don't have the right clothes, we'll buy you something. Don't they have all those factory outlet stores in Maine?"

"Um."

"I'm hungry."

"There's coffee made," she said, digging in a drawer. "Oh, God, this old bathing suit. It's awful."

"Buy a new one." Gary sat up, pushed himself to the edge

of the bed and got his cane. He wondered if he really needed to use it now, but sometimes he still lost his balance.

"I'll fix us something," he said. "Pancakes? Eggs?"

"Would you? That'd be great." She frowned, holding up an old T-shirt. "All I have is suits and blouses and heels. I don't have any clothes for a beach vacation."

"That's because you never take them."

He pulled on a T-shirt and shorts and made his way into her kitchen, which he knew as well as his own. They each left odds and ends of clothes in the other's place and spent the night together often.

He was frying some bacon when he heard the front doorbell. At ten o'clock on Saturday morning?

"Eve? You expecting someone?" he called out, but she was in the back bedroom and couldn't hear. It rang again.

"Damn," Gary said, taking his cane and going to the front door.

His heart sank when he saw who was standing there.

"Hey, Gary, sorry, man, but I need to talk to Eve."

"Bob, it's goddamn Saturday morning."

"I know."

"We're leaving for Maine tomorrow," Gary said in a hard voice.

"So I hear."

"You could have phoned."

"I thought this needed to be said in person," Bob said quietly.

"Shit." Gary turned away from the man and went down the hall to stand in the doorway of the bedroom. "Hey, Eve, it's Bob Calpin to see you."

She looked up, startled, her hair curling wildly around her face. "Bob?" She frowned. "What on earth?"

"He's waiting."

"It's nothing," Eve said.

"Right."

"It's *nothing*, Gary."

Gary followed her back into the living room and stood leaning on his cane.

"Hi, Bob," Eve said warily.

"Hello, Eve. Nice job you did yesterday."

"Thanks." She said nothing more, and the silence in the room mounted.

"I, uh, got a call last night," Bob said.

She cocked her head.

"From Marty Cohen in Glenwood Springs." Marty was the public defender in the office that covered three western counties of Colorado. "He was asked to take on the penalty phase of the Devlin trial in Aspen."

"Devlin?" she said. "He's got Iverson."

"Frank Iverson just had a heart attack."

"My God," Eve said.

"He was going to have to do the penalty phase pro bono, anyway, Eve. The trial left Devlin broke. And you know the D.A. is seeking the death penalty. 'Because of the particularly heinous nature of the crime' is how it's worded, I believe. It's right up your alley."

Gary could see Eve's reaction, and his heart sank.

"Eve." Bob Calpin leveled his gaze on her. "Marty Cohen wants you. The Ninth Judicial District wants you. The presiding judge wants you. They all want Devlin to have the best public defender in the state. They don't want Devlin claiming he was misrepresented. Eve..."

"Hold it, Bob," she breathed.

"And I've already rescheduled your caseload for the next three months. It won't be a problem."

"I'm going on vacation tomorrow. I'm exhausted. I need a break."

"I know."

Eve looked at Gary, as if begging for help, but he just stood there, his hands on his cane, his eyes on her.

"I can't do it, Bob. You'll have to find someone else. Howie, maybe. No, I won't do it," Eve said firmly. "No, I just can't do it."

FOUR

It was Saturday afternoon when Jack was told that the public defender from the district office in Glenwood Springs was waiting for him in the interrogation room.

Cohen, Jack thought, following the jailer through the security doors. *Marty Cohen.* A few years back, Jack had sat on a jury in a case where Cohen had defended that rarest of creatures, a local indigent, on a robbery charge. Jack remembered the attorney well. He was a slight man in his early forties, jittery, mouse-colored hair, thick spectacles. He was a good speaker, experienced, passionate. The judge had cautioned him a number of times for going overboard, but Cohen had been willing to take the heat. In the end he'd convinced the jury—Jack included—that the local cops had trampled all over the accused man's rights, botched evidence and lost a crucial file in a computer glitch. The guy was probably guilty of the theft, but they'd let him off. Now Jack entered the interrogation room and wondered if Marty Cohen was going to take his case. Getting a guy off for stealing a pair of skis and a wallet was one thing. Keeping Jack off death row was quite another. He'd bet Cohen had never handled a case like this before.

Marty stood and shook Jack's hand in the cramped, stuffy room. He was wearing a polo shirt and jeans, running shoes. His mousy hair was thinner than Jack remembered, and he

still seemed nervous. His handshake was strong nevertheless, and his manner confident.

"Didn't you sit on a jury a couple years back...?" Cohen
asked.

Jack nodded and sat down on the plastic-covered bench
against the wall. "You got the man off," he said. "It was a
nice job."

But Marty waved that aside. "In this valley, it's no big
deal. We're not real used to serious crime, and no one wants
to send someone to prison who could be rehabilitated. On
the other hand," Marty said, sitting, opening a file, "it's an
election year for our esteemed D.A. You probably know
that. And lately he's lost several high-profile cases that he
should have won. He's running scared, and you're his one
success, his ace in the hole."

Again Jack nodded.

"I won't lie to you. He's out for your hide, Jack. And the
panel of judges who'll be hearing the penalty phase... Well,
we've got a lot of work to do."

"You're assigned to my case, then?" Jack had to ask.

Cohen looked at him and laughed. "Did I forget to mention that?"

"Uh-huh," Jack said.

"Figures," Marty put in, shaking his head. "It's been kind
of hectic in my office since Iverson's heart attack. The
phone's been ringing off the hook, in fact. The Ninth Judicial
District judge went ballistic and made calls all over the
state...."

"I don't get it," Jack said.

"The state doesn't want you coming back with an appeal
that claims you didn't get proper representation."

"I still don't get it. Aren't you taking...?"

"Hey, I can handle the local stuff. But when it comes to a
capital felony trial...and one that's been getting national
coverage...that's another thing altogether."

"So you *won't* be taking my case."

"I'll be working on it." Marty smiled reassuringly. "A

whole team of state public defenders will be working on it. In fact, you may be getting the top gun from the Denver office. She's terrific."

It took Jack a moment, then he cocked his head. "She?"

Marty laughed. "That's right. Eve Marchand. She's got more experience than anyone in the entire state when it comes to death-penalty cases." He reached into the briefcase that rested under his feet and produced that morning's copy of the *Denver Post*. Then he set it down under Jack's nose and tapped the picture on the front page. "There she is. Just won a big one in Denver yesterday. Pretty lady, huh?"

"Ah, yeah, sure," Jack said, distracted, far more interested in the article than he was in her looks.

He read through the story quickly, then glanced up. "Will she definitely be working on my case?"

Marty let out a breath. "Well, I'm sure hoping so. She hasn't committed yet. I guess she was just about to take a vacation."

"Right," Jack said.

"But her boss talked to her this morning, explained about Iverson's heart attack. We're all hoping she can postpone her trip. I hear she's tired, though. The kind of work we're in, you know, and in Denver she's under a lot more pressure than us local yokels."

"I see," Jack said.

"Regardless of who leads the team, I'll be working for you, Jack," Marty put in. "Eve's not the only public defender in the state who can handle this."

"She's just the best," Jack said wryly.

"This is true," Marty conceded. "And I'll let you know as soon as she commits."

"Or doesn't commit."

"Right." Marty leafed through the file on the table. "We've already requested the trial transcript and all of Iverson's files and notes, and they should be available to us late this afternoon. We've got ninety days. If we need more, under the circumstances, we'll get a postponement."

"I see," Jack said, a part of him wanting to get the whole damn thing over with, needing to know: death row or life in prison. But another part of him railed at the injustice, and he wondered where he was going to find the courage to face another trial—one in which his life was literally at stake.

He shook off his thoughts and glanced up at Marty. "Any word on Frank's condition?"

Marty shook his head. "He's still in guarded condition. Intensive care. I understand they're talking bypass surgery but waiting to see how well the drugs are working."

Jack nodded slowly.

"If I hear any more, I'll sure call you."

"Thanks."

They talked awhile longer, and Marty explained that no matter who led the defense team now, he or she would have his own particular strategy, and Marty wasn't going to do a whole lot of preliminary work until the team leader was decided on. "We'll keep our fingers crossed that we get Eve."

"Sure," Jack allowed.

"We'll know in a day or so."

"Sure," Jack said again.

Later he lay on his bunk and stared at the ceiling, feeling nothing but frustration. Everyone was talking about his fate. The state and local papers covered it every day—lethal injection or life without the possibility of parole. But while they all speculated, he was stuck in jail, unable to do a god-damn thing about Allison's murder. Frank had put that team of P.I.s on it months ago, but they'd come up empty-handed. Probably, like everyone else, Jack thought darkly, they'd assumed he was guilty and hadn't looked all that hard. Hell, if he didn't know better himself, considering all the evidence, *he'd* think he was guilty.

This past year had been hell. It wasn't just being locked up; it wasn't just his loss of freedom or career or any of that. It was the anger, the pain, the sense of utter frustration that someone out there was guilty of his wife's murder. Guilty and walking away scot-free. It had driven Jack nuts, and it had taken a wellspring of inner strength to survive.

"You're absolutely amazing," Frank had told him countless times. But Jack could only take each day as it came. Had to tell himself over and over to stay calm, to stay focused. But mostly he'd had to believe that the nightmare would end one day.

He had stayed in shape, using the exercise facility at the jail. He'd kept up with the news, kept up with designing on the computer. And he'd read dozens of law books. Too many. He'd become far more knowledgeable in that area than he'd ever wanted to be.

For all the good it's done, he thought grimly.

And then Frank's heart attack. It was more of a blow than Jack let on to anyone. Again he had to swallow the panic that welled up inside him. But now it seemed they'd found someone to take Frank's place. Someone good. Very good. "The best," Marty had said. But, apparently, a reluctant best.

Jack sat up and scrubbed a hand through his hair. He picked up the paper Cohen had left with him and stared at the grainy newsprint photo of Eve Marchand. She was pretty, but in a harried sort of way. A small face. Glasses, some loose strands of curling hair escaping a severe bun. The photo revealed no hint of pride in her victory. Nothing, really, that told much about her. Marty, of course, had said she was due for a vacation, and Jack had to wonder if she was burned out. That would be just great.

He tossed the paper aside and let out a long breath. What did it matter, really, who defended him in this next phase? The truth was that the system was out for blood. His blood.

It was a bright Sunday afternoon when Eve drove along Interstate 70, approaching Glenwood Canyon.

She drove fast, as she always did, passing the heavy summer tourist traffic that had slowed when the highway narrowed, entering the eighteen-mile-long scenic canyon.

Millions of years ago the mighty Colorado River had begun to carve the canyon walls out of sheer rock. Now the thousand-foot-high walls were a map of the eons; some were twisted and spiraled, some were massive pinnacles of red rock that jutted up out of the river valley at crazy angles, the striated slabs slanted against the blue bowl of sky overhead. For the most part they were unclimbable. Too sheer. Too dangerous. But every so often a narrow trickle of water spilled down the walls, and stunted pines grew there, softening the cliff faces.

Eve could see that the canyon walls were forbidding to all but bighorn sheep, although the river below was man's playground. Dozens of rafts floated along the river, dipping and bobbing, overflowing with white-water adventure seekers.

She was still looking at the rafts when she approached the state-of-the-art tunnel that had recently opened. It ran above the river and the railroad tracks that had been laid down well over a hundred years ago when the Rocky Mountains were still a formidable barrier to frontier settlers and California gold seekers. She took her foot off the accelerator; cameras in the tunnel monitored everyone's speed. That was all she needed, Eve thought, a traffic ticket to complete a perfect day.

The decision to drive to Aspen and interview Devlin should have been a difficult one. She was tired, worn out. And the vacation to Maine...

Gary had not been happy. When her boss had left yesterday morning and she'd said she'd take a look at the case, Gary had really gotten in her face.

"Do you have any concept what the word *no* means?" he'd asked angrily. "It's just as easy to say no as it is to say yes. If you'd been manipulated into this, I'd understand. But you gave in awfully easily. I think you *want* this case, Eve. Maybe you want the publicity. Maybe you're bucking for a promotion. I don't know, and frankly I don't care. All I know is that you've got your priorities pretty goddamn screwed up."

"That's not fair," she'd said. "Is it my fault the district judge asked me to take the case? Is it my fault Iverson had a heart attack and Devlin's broke? This is what I *do*, Gary. This is me. I care. And it's not the publicity. How could you even say that? You know it's not. I didn't ask Bob to come over here and mess up our plans. And I didn't say I'd take on the case. I said I'd *look into* it. We can change our tickets, leave early in the week."

"Sure. You're going to drive to Aspen, then turn around and say you aren't taking the case? Bullshit."

"Gary, don't..."

"And I want to know what you're doing about private practice. You've had offers. Have you interviewed for any of them yet? Let me guess," he'd gone on irately. "You haven't had time."

"I'm going to," Eve had said in a small voice. "I really am."

That had been yesterday morning. She hadn't seen or spoken to Gary since. She'd left a message on his answering machine, told him she was driving to Aspen today and that by Monday she'd make up her mind whether or not to take on Devlin.

"We can still leave for Maine on Tuesday," she'd said to his machine. "I'm stopping in Glenwood Springs to pick up the transcripts from Marty Cohen, and I'll tell him what the score is. He can probably handle it himself with my office behind him." She'd paused, then said, "I love you. Please don't be angry. Call you when I get to Aspen."

A few miles after the ultramodern tunnel, Eve drove into another one, then came to an open valley and the city of Glenwood Springs. She was instantly assailed by the odor of sulfur—the world-renowned sulfur hot springs that bubbled up and spewed their gasses from natural vents that ran along the Colorado River. Supposedly the waters were therapeutic. When she was a kid, her parents had taken her into the mountains on weekends. Skiing, snowmobile riding and great swims in the Olympic-size pool filled with the hot sulfur waters. In the winter, steam billowed from the pool into the bitter air. Now it was warm in Glenwood Springs, and because it was a Sunday, and also the tourist season, the pool and adjacent hotel grounds were jammed with people.

Eve turned off the main highway into the city and began looking for Marty Cohen's address. She could have taken a shorter route from Denver to Aspen, driven the twelve-thousand-five-hundred-foot road over Independence Pass, but then Marty would have had to meet her in Aspen with the trial transcripts, and it was a Sunday, and his son had a baseball game....

She found Marty's house south of Glenwood Springs on the Roaring Fork River, the same river that flowed all the way from the summit of Independence Pass through Aspen, Basalt, Carbondale and on into Glenwood Springs, where it met the Colorado River.

Marty's house was large but modest, all the "right" mountain toys evident in the yard. Mountain bikes, a trailer with a kayak leaning against a battered Jeep, fishing poles and skis hanging neatly in the open garage.

Marty was mowing a patch of lawn that ran down to the riverbank. Eve parked and got out and wondered if he remembered meeting her at last year's convention in Denver.

When he saw her he turned off the mower, wiped his brow and waved. He was a lean man, thinning hair, glasses. A lot of energy. But then, in their business, you needed a lot.

After the preliminary greetings—Marty not only remembered her but was embarrassingly flattering—he said, "I can't tell you how much everyone in my office admires your work," and he pumped her hand, apologizing for his appearance.

He had the transcripts all ready for her in a cardboard storage box. "It's a lot, I know," he said. "But everything's here. The police files, depositions, lab reports, the entire transcript from Jack's trial. Iverson's notes and files should be here by Tuesday, and..."

Eve shook her head as Marty was putting the box in the back seat of her car. "Listen," she said, "I'm happy to look all this over. And you know I'll give you all the advice I can over the next three months. But I'm supposed to be heading to Maine. Right now, in fact. I'm only doing this because my boss twisted my arm. I'm not making any promises, Marty, really. I'll meet with Devlin and see if I can help get things rolling. But..."

"I understand completely," Marty interrupted. "I know how tired you must be. And, hey, any help you can manage will be greatly appreciated. I've never handled a penalty trial. I understand that I'd have the Denver office working right there with me, but, well, you *are* the best."

Eve laughed. "Thanks for the compliment, but right now I can barely keep my mind on what day it is. I need a vacation."

"Of course you do."

"No, really," she said, but all he did was smile. She gave up, got into her car and started it.

Marty leaned into the window. "I got you a room in Aspen at a place on Main Street. It's called the Christmas Inn. Can't miss it. Green, red, on your left before you get to downtown. It's old, but it's only a few blocks to the jail. I asked for a suite."

"What? No Ritz-Carlton?" she quipped.

"Not on the state's budget," he countered. Then his expression turned serious. "I know you aren't decided on this case yet, and I really do understand. I only ask that you don't make up your mind until you meet Jack—Jack Devlin, that is. He's... Well, he's not what you'd expect."

"Uh-huh," Eve allowed. The truth was, she'd met so many convicted killers in the past few years that their faces were beginning to run together. Devlin would only be another in a long line. *I need a break*, she thought as she drove back toward the highway. *I really need a break.*

It was forty miles up the valley to Aspen. As the road climbed in altitude, the valley narrowed. She'd been to Aspen as a child and a teenager, but not for several years now. And the valley... Once there had only been a scattering of houses breaking up the ranch and farmlands. Now homes and small shopping enclaves had popped up like mushrooms in a spring rain. And as the altitude climbed, so did the value of real estate. No longer did the homes look as if they could have been in Anywhere, U.S.A. The closer she got to Aspen, the more megahomes she passed. They dotted the banks of the Roaring Fork and climbed the green hillsides. She wondered if Devlin had designed any of them. Most likely. And then she recalled Marty telling her he wasn't what she'd expect. Well, she had no expectations. He was merely another guy in a whole lot of trouble. Maybe he'd once been a super architect for the rich and famous. But now he was just like all the rest of them—broke and desperate.

She drove into Aspen and down Main Street. Familiar. The outlying areas of town had certainly changed, grown, but Aspen was still Aspen: quaint, charming with its colorfully painted, gingerbread-trimmed houses, its turn-of-the-century street lamps and signs. The only thing that looked different was the height of the cottonwood and aspen trees that marched up and down the streets in full summer foliage.

Eve pulled into the side parking lot of the Christmas Inn and looked up at the mountain, Aspen Mountain, the ski hill known to the locals as Ajax. *That* hadn't changed, either. The mountain still seemed to loom over the town, massive, breathtaking, a giant green wall that protected Aspen from the rest of the world.

She got the keys to her suite and then carried in her suitcase, the box of transcripts and police evidence files. She decided not to change out of the jeans and lightweight blue sweater she wore. This was Aspen, after all, and unless a lawyer was in court facing a judge, you dressed down or stood out like a sore thumb.

The box of files. She cleared the coffee table in the living room and started taking the folders out, sorting and separating. Then she put on her glasses, sat cross-legged on the couch and opened one. It was three o'clock in the afternoon. She'd call Gary at five, she thought, when he'd be sure to be home. But when Eve looked up again it was well past seven.

She grabbed the phone, amazed, as always, at how easily she could lose track of time and place. *Damn*, she thought, rubbing her eyes and standing to stretch.

Gary was home. And, as he pointed out, he'd been expecting a call for hours.

"I'm sorry," Eve said. "I just thought that if I could get through a bunch of these files... Well, you know."

"Sure," he said. "Whatever."

Eve took a breath. "Listen, I made it very clear to Marty that I'm only here to look things over. I told him I'd give advice, that sort of thing."

"Why do I not believe that?" he said.

"Come on, Gary, I want that trip as much as you do. I can interview Devlin and be done with this by tomorrow afternoon. I'm sure going to try."

"And what if it's more complicated than you think?"

"I'll cross that bridge when I come to it."

"So we won't leave for sure on Tuesday." It wasn't a question.

"We'll talk tomorrow. First thing."

"Uh-huh."

"Really, Gary, I promise."

"Have you met with that Devlin character yet?"

"No, not yet. I'm going to grab a bite to eat and walk on over to the jail as soon as I hang up."

"You haven't eaten?"

"I had a late lunch."

"Liar."

"Well, I had a bag of chips when I gassed up the car."

"Eve."

"Okay. I'll do better."

"And you'll get a good night's sleep?"

His tone had softened and she smiled. "You bet. I'm done in."

They talked a few more minutes, then Gary said, "I really want you to think about private practice. We've talked all this out, and I won't hash it over. Not now, anyway. But you remember you promised..."

"I remember," she said, standing over the coffee table, Jack Devlin's mug shot staring up at her. "I remember the whole conversation."

"Okay," Gary said, "I'll let you get back to work. Call me. First thing in the morning, okay?"

"First thing." She hung up and went into the bathroom, washed her face and hands and brushed out her hair. Ordinarily she would have pulled it back into a bun, worn her glasses, dressed the role of the state's top public defender. But it was Sunday, and this was Aspen, and she'd bet not a single attorney visited the jail for an interview in anything but mountain casual. She did put a few of the files into a leather briefcase, though, because she'd need them at the jail. And pencils and legal pads. Always lots of those. Then she looked down one last time at Devlin's photo and the one lying next to it—a police photographer's shot of the murder scene. Blood everywhere. Soaking the body, the rug, the furniture. Splashed in an arc across wall and window. Gruesome.

She looked back at Devlin's picture. There was nothing his photo could tell her, and she wondered how he'd handle himself when his public defender had him plead for his life in front of the panel of judges. Some defendants were tough and defiant. Some were cool-headed sociopaths who merely mouthed words. Most choked up, fear overcoming what little pride they had left. Sometimes Eve could read them. But Devlin was a mystery so far. She'd know soon, however.

She left the inn and walked east on Main Street, the im-

pressive hundred-year-old brick courthouse already in
view. She did stop at a small, French-style café and sat outside, ordering a croissant sandwich, eating it while the evening crowds milled the streets and locals pedaled by on
muddy three-thousand-dollar mountain bikes.

It was a jewel of a town, she thought as she sipped on an
iced tea. The light was turning from evening gold to a soft
mauve, and in a nearby downtown street mall students
from the summer music school played chamber music.
Soothing. Peaceful.

She sat back and closed her eyes for a moment, breathing
in the clean, thin air, thinking that Aspen had indeed kept
its Victorian ambience, preserved its downtown buildings,
so that it was still like a town from the distant past, but with
all the raw edges removed. No more whorehouses from the
nineteenth-century mining days or beer tents or gutters running with filth. Although, Eve supposed, there were still
nights in the old mining town that might be wild and care-
free. Not that she'd see *that* side of the resort.

She didn't have time to savor the ambience now, either.
She got up and paid the check and walked across Main
Street, the broad thoroughfare bisecting the town, to the
courthouse and the new jail that sat directly behind it.

It was a low, neat brick building built into a sloping hillside. There were flowers planted in front. She went into the
small, empty lobby, where a surveillance camera watched
her as she lifted the phone on the wall to introduce herself.

While she waited to be admitted into the jail proper, she
noted a poster on the wall. It was bright red, and it quoted
Dostoyevsky: "The degree of civilization in a society can be
judged by entering its prisons." That was Aspen for you.

The door opened, and she was shown past the brand-new
communications room, past the holding room and storage
area and closets containing all those wonderful police de-
vices: leg and arm chains, restraints, handcuffs, leg braces
that could be hidden beneath a prisoner's clothes to keep

him from escaping when on trial. The way Ted Bundy had. From this very same complex.

The night-duty jailer, a woman named Debby, came out of the prisoner's lockup to meet her. "It's pretty late, Miss…"

"Marchand," Eve said with a pleasant smile.

"Yes, well, Marty Cohen said you'd be here this afternoon."

"I'm sure he did."

"We really don't allow visitors at this hour."

"I understand," Eve said, still smiling. "The thing is, Debby, Jack Devlin is on trial for his life. Why don't you telephone the district court judge and get an okay?"

"Call the judge on a Sunday?" Debby said.

"It's your choice. You can either call the judge or simply bring Mr. Devlin to the interrogation room. I assure you that the judge will want Jack Devlin to have access to his counsel at any time. In fact," Eve went on in a neutral voice, "I think the police here had better get used to it. We're talking about life and death, after all."

Debby stared at her for a moment, then finally nodded. "I'll go get Jack." She unlocked the door to the interrogation room and left Eve there to spread out her files and await her notorious client and wonder at the familiar, protective way Debby had said "Jack."

FIVE

Jack Devlin was nothing at all what Eve had envisioned. She supposed she'd been expecting an Aspen mover and shaker, slick and charming. But when he was let into the tiny interview room she had to revise her opinion so fast it left her off balance.

"Miss Marchand," he said, holding out his hand, "welcome to my humble abode."

"Mr. Devlin." She shook his hand and found it warm and strong. Oh, yes, he was very attractive—as all the newspaper articles covering the trial had stated—but the articles had left out so very much.

"You didn't have to come on a Sunday, Miss Marchand. I was very surprised when Debby told me you were here. I just talked to Marty yesterday."

"I, uh, have some personal scheduling problems, so I thought I better get up here right away."

"Yes, I heard. A vacation. I'm really sorry about them calling you. Terrible timing."

She smiled and pushed her hair back behind an ear. "It's never good timing with this sort of thing."

"No," he said, "I suppose not."

He *was* handsome, his face smooth, the subtle hint of the exotic in his dark eyes and cheekbones and the straight black hair aslant on his forehead, but it was his manner that impressed Eve. He had a quality of acceptance, of dignity, even in his orange jail suit. He was in no way diminished by his surroundings, so different from the usual cocky, blustering prisoner exuding foul language, ferocity, fear.

"Sit down, please," he said, strangely, endearingly formal.

She sat in the chair, he sat on the bench.

"I can ask Debby to get you something to drink," he offered, a concerned host.

"No, thanks. I just had something."

"You must be exhausted," he said, assessing her with a steady gaze.

"I'm here to discuss your case, Mr. Devlin."

"Jack. Please, call me Jack."

For some unfathomable reason, she did not respond with her own first name. "Okay, Jack. I've read some of your files."

"Already," he said thoughtfully.

"Yes, there are, as I said, some time constraints, so I..."

"Are you taking my case, Miss Marchand?"

She looked down at the file in her hands. "I'm not sure yet."

"I see."

His words plunged into her like a knife. Guilt filled the wound, and a strange, unsettling knowledge came over her that this was a very unusual case, a very unusual man. There was an air of decency about him, a solemnity unrelated to his circumstances. His real self was impossible to discern beyond the formal courtesy and stillness. There had to be more—Will the *real* Jack Devlin please stand up?—but she couldn't even guess at what lay behind his manner. *Inscrutable*, she thought, *inscrutable Oriental*. What an incredibly apt cliché.

"I can't commit right now," she said, too quickly.

"Listen, I understand. This was sprung on you. You don't have to feel you're letting anyone down."

But that was precisely how she felt. Marty Cohen couldn't

do this; he didn't have enough experience. Who could? Who? She racked her brain, but there wasn't anyone in the office who could handle this case with the skill it was going to take.

No one but her. Oh, God, Gary was going to kill her!

"You don't have to worry, though. Whoever represents you will be the very best," she said.

He eyed her for a moment, then there was a tiny quirk of his lip, and he said, "I thought *you* were the best."

She had trouble meeting his eyes. He was a disconcerting client; usually Eve was in total control, and that was the way it had to be. "I'm good, I'll admit, but there are plenty of others in the Denver office who are perfectly competent and experienced."

"Then I'd appreciate it if you'd recommend one to me."

"Of course. I'll want to review your files first, though."

"Of course," he echoed.

His face was serious, his brows arrowing down toward his strongly curved nose. His mouth was wide, with a deep indentation in the upper lip. Her eyes followed the smooth lines of his face, trying to decipher him, catch the signals he was telegraphing. There weren't any that she could see.

"I'm sorry about Frank Iverson," she offered.

"Yes, so am I, although, to tell the truth, he was so shaken up by the guilty verdict, I'm not sure he would have been particularly effective," Jack said.

"*He* was shaken up?" Eve had to ask. "Weren't you?"

"I was prepared for it."

"Why?" She was taken aback.

He shrugged. "There weren't any other suspects. No one else had a motive. It seemed very simple, very clear."

How could this man be so dispassionate about his own life?

"Let me ask you something, Jack. I need to know what you think, and I need you to be absolutely truthful—always."

He held her gaze, watchful.

"Do you think you received competent representation from Frank Iverson?"

"Yes," he said firmly.

"I have to ask, because that's the first line of appeal we use, incompetent representation. Unfortunately it's true far too often."

"Not in my case. Frank did his best."

"When I read the trial transcript I'll be able to judge that better," she said.

"You won't find anything," he said with maddening calm.

"Okay." She fiddled with a file, feeling the need to do something with her hands. It was close in the room, and it was so small their knees were practically touching. She shifted position.

"I'm sorry about this room," he said, noting her gesture with a nod. "If you'd come earlier in the day, we could have sat out there in the common room. It's more comfortable. Right now, all the guys are glued to the tube."

"Okay," she repeated, tapping her fingers on the file. Then abruptly she stood, walked the few feet to the concrete wall and leaned against it, her arms folded. She met his gaze and launched into her standard speech to a potential client. "*If* I represent you in the penalty phase, you're going to have to trust me. You're going to have to do everything I say. There's a lot of work to do, no matter who takes your case, and frankly, given the climate in the country these days, not to mention the D.A.'s reelection bid... What's his name again?"

"Bill Makelky."

"Uh-huh. Makelky. He's running on a law-and-order platform, and you're his number-one vote-getter. The odds are against you, I have to be honest, but if you *do* get the death penalty, despite everything, if you do, don't panic. Your counsel will simply go on to the next stage, which is the appeals process."

He nodded. "Frank told me."

"Good," she said, then she repeated herself. "Good." She took a breath. "There are six men on death row in Colorado, and no one's been executed since 1967. There's time, you understand. This state, thank God, is not in the Death Belt, where they're completely irresponsible, at least in my view."

"I've been reading," he said mildly. "I'm aware of the fight over the death penalty."

"The penalty phase comes up in ninety days, as I'm sure you know. It'll last, say, three days. A panel of judges hears the case, not a jury, which used to be the law. But you no doubt know that, too."

He nodded.

"And your counsel can deal with only one issue in this phase, and that is whether or not you receive capital punishment. It will be addressed two ways. First—" she unfolded her arms and ticked it off on her fingers "—the immorality of the death penalty in general, and second, the inappropriateness of it in your specific case."

He nodded again, his eyes on her like dark lanterns.

"Now, if the decision is against us...you...there are two ways it can be attacked. The first one, naturally, is the appeals process. That's a given. But there's another way...if there were, say, new evidence of your innocence." She held his gaze soberly, watching, judging. "*If* there were such evidence, your counsel can request a new trial."

"I've read the Colorado Rules of Criminal Procedure," he said. "I believe it's Rule 35(c)(2)(V). Is that it? The rule on newly discovered evidence." He looked up at the ceiling and quoted: "If there exists evidence of material facts that could not be known, et cetera, et cetera."

"Yes," she said, trying to cover her amazement.

"The court has to find that the facts could not have been discovered in the trial," Jack said. "And I suppose a judge could rule on that according to his own opinions."

"It happens," she admitted. "But a public defender's job is to see that the court is convinced." She smiled at him. He reminded her of one of her law professors. How bizarre, arguing points of law with a prisoner. A *smart* prisoner.

"And they say you're the best at it," he said.

"I'm good. The best? Who knows?" She pushed her hair back again. "Right now, Jack, all you have to concentrate on is the penalty phase, your sentence."

"I heard that they call you the new Mistress of Delay."

She felt herself flush. "The press. You know." She shrugged.

"Oh, brother, do I know the press," he said with self-deprecating humor. "Seriously, what do they mean by that?"

"We're talking about *your* case, Jack."

"Answer that one question. Humor me," he said, and she saw the barest hint of a smile form on his lips. *Oh, yes,* she thought, Devlin was indeed a charmer.

"Go on," he urged.

Again, Eve shrugged. "There was a woman in Florida who was called that because she kept so many men from being executed. She was quite famous, at least in legal circles."

"Ah, I get it now. And you're famous, too?"

"Not at all."

"If you got me off, you would be, though."

"I can't 'get you off,' Jack. I can only address the issue of your sentence for now. That is," she said hastily, "*if* I take your case."

"But you could—hypothetically, that is—try to get me off after the penalty phase is over."

"Hypothetically. But that would depend on time factors, budget for our office, a lot of things."

"For instance, whether you, or whoever represents me, believes I'm innocent," he said flatly.

She waited, expecting the usual protestations of innocence, the prejudice of the judge, the bribed jury, the rotten deal he'd gotten. Jack said nothing, though, only waited in that stillness that surrounded him like a shroud.

Eve put aside her professional skepticism and went on.

"Whoever takes your case, and I'm sure Marty Cohen will be on the team, you'll have to be very forthcoming. They'll dig into your past, subpoena people, ask you a lot of questions. You'll have no privacy."

For the first time, Jack's composure faltered. He flicked his gaze away and frowned, hitching his shoulders. "Not my mother," he said in a low voice.

"I'm in no position to discuss witnesses now."

He swiveled back to pinion her with a fierce look. "Not my mother. Not my father. Not my sister."

"As I said…"

"Okay, sorry. I just couldn't stand for them to be tortured anymore."

"It's an understandable reaction," she said coolly. So there *was* passion in him, buried deep, but it was there. Interesting. "I'd like to ask you a few questions." She moved to the table and opened the file, looked at her scrawled notes, then looked at him. "You have no idea who could have gotten into your house and killed, um, let me see, Allison?"

"None."

"No one who had a motive?"

"Nobody. Except me."

"Because of her money, is that so? If you were divorced, you didn't inherit a penny."

"Correct. But as I told Frank and everyone else who would listen, I didn't want Allison's money. I paid my own way. Yes, the house was Allison's, but I was completely independent financially. I never took a dime from her."

"So you actually had no motive?"

"No."

"Jealousy?"

Jack sighed. "Yes, I knew she was having an affair. We'd been separated for six months. I wasn't happy about it, but I didn't kill her over it."

"You did have a quarrel, you and Allison, that afternoon of, let's see—" she ruffled papers "—May 16."

"Yes, we quarreled. I refused to sign the divorce papers. I walked out. Hell, I would've signed them sooner or later. I couldn't hold on to Allison against her will."

"And you were where when she was killed, in the early hours of May 17?"

He waved a hand. "It's all in there."

"Yes, I know, but sometimes it's useful to hear it from the person's own lips. I'm sorry if this is irritating you."

"No, it's okay, it's fine. Where was I that night? I was in my rented condo, where I was living after we separated. I was listening to music and working on a design for a house. And when she was killed, I was asleep."

"And you were alone."

"Yes, I was alone. No alibi. I even had my phone on the machine so I wouldn't be disturbed. I spoke to no one, I saw no one. No one saw me."

He'd answered every question directly and succinctly, none of the usual bull, an odd and admirable quality in a prisoner.

She cocked her head. "Why didn't Frank put you on the stand? You have a very convincing manner. I'm a little surprised."

"He was afraid I'd get pissed off and blow up. He was afraid my pride would look ugly, arrogant, you know. Hell, he even had a psychologist in here asking me questions to see how I'd do. Guess I failed my exam."

"Um, I see. Yes, he was probably right."

"So, what do *you* think?" he asked.

"Me? My opinion doesn't count for anything, Jack. I'm doing a job, and I need to be impartial, completely objective."

"Right."

"Look, you don't need to worry about what I think, or what anyone else thinks, for that matter. Justice is supposed to be blind."

"She cheated and pulled down that blindfold," he said

dryly. "The circumstantial evidence made me look guilty and she never looked any further."

She smiled. "It may seem that way, but I assure you it isn't true."

"Don't patronize me, Miss Marchand."

Her smile faded. "I'm sorry if I appear to be..."

"What you appear to be, Miss Marchand, is a very attractive woman who can walk out of this jail and do whatever you want."

Eve swallowed.

He rubbed his eyes wearily. "Sorry. It's not your fault I'm in here."

"If I decide to take your case, Jack, I'll work very hard for you. Whoever takes your case will do the same. We all care, really we do, or we wouldn't be public defenders. We'll go over every ounce of testimony from the trial, we'll look for any hook to hang our hats on, any little glitch or weak spot, anything the jury might have heard improperly. We'll get out character witnesses, we'll go into your past. You have no criminal record, no previous arrests. We'll convince the judges you're not a danger to society. We'll do psychological evaluations. No stone will be left unturned, I promise you."

She gathered her files and snapped a rubber band around them. "I would also advise your counsel to risk contempt and fines by telling horror stories of death row and of executions. I would bring up the statistics that show how many innocent people have been executed. I'll quote the Bible if I have to, Jack. I've done it before."

"You're impressive," he said, "when you get on your high horse."

"It's my job." She returned the files to her briefcase and thrust her hand out at him. "I'll be in touch, Jack."

He stood, too, and they were face-to-face. He took her hand, gave it a brief shake, then dropped it. It was at that precise moment, when she stood looking into the depth of his eyes, that Eve was struck with an inexplicable explosion of knowledge: Jack was innocent. It hit her with the force of a blow, without rational explanation but with the absolute power of truth.

Jack Devlin was innocent of murder.

She left the jailhouse quickly then, her heart beating wildly, the memory of her first case—the execution— weighing on her.

Ross Grafton, the jailer on duty until lockdown at eleven-thirty, liked to play gin rummy. Jack had let him win at least half the time over the past thirteen months, keeping in his head a running tally of how many times each of them had won. He found it a challenge.

Ross was a middle-aged, ex-Aspen Mountain patrolman, a sixties dropout from a "good" family on Long Island, one of those free spirits who'd gravitated to Aspen before it had gotten trendy, back when one of the local redneck store owners had put a sign in his window reading No Hippies Allowed.

Ross was smart, educated, well read. He told Jack amusing war stories of the good old days in Aspen, when everyone was stoned all the time, but he was a lousy cardplayer.

Jack discarded, Ross studied the five of hearts as if he kept track of every card played. He squinted, his brow furrowed, and picked it up.

"So you've got a new lawyer," Ross said, rearranging his hand.

"Not yet. She hasn't decided to take my case."

"She will."

"Why do you say that?"

Ross studied his cards intently. "She won't be able to resist."

"What makes you think that?"

"Public defenders, they can't resist helping the underdog. It's in their DNA."

"And I'm the underdog."

"You sure as hell are."

"Hmm." Jack picked up a card.

Behind them, one of a group of inmates watching a box-ing match on TV yelled something at the screen. There was a burst of laughter and a few off-color comments.

"Hey, keep it down, you guys," Ross called across the room. "I'm trying to concentrate." He turned to Jack, shak-ing his head. "It's like a college dorm, this place, and I'm the hall monitor. Geez."

"It doesn't feel like college to me," Jack said.

"It will when you get to Super Max. You'll look back on this jail as a country club. It *is* a goddamn country club."

"Damn it, Ross, drop the subject, will you?"

"Sorry."

"Gin," Jack said, slapping down his hand, feeling a spurt of infantile satisfaction. For God's sake, his brain was turn-ing to mush in here.

"Son of a bitch," Ross remarked mildly.

"Deal," Jack said.

Ross discarded, then looked at Jack and grinned. "That lady sure was pretty. All that curly blond hair. I'm in love."

"Hard to believe she spends her life dealing with death."

"Hey, man, what a way to go," Ross said lightly.

"Very funny."

"I read about her in the paper. She was on TV last night, too. Boy, did she look different. I almost didn't recognize her today."

"Discard" was all Jack said.

Later, locked in his cell, lying on his bunk in the dark, Jack went over his meeting with Eve Marchand. Over and over it.

She was smart, knew her job, that was obvious. Business-like, efficient. He'd discerned no pity in her, no emotion, no reaction whatsoever to him. He was a client, that was all. A job. He guessed she had to view her clients that way or she'd go nuts. He wondered if she ever got emotionally in-volved with her work. A public defender couldn't, he sup-posed, or he wouldn't last long.

The Mistress of Delay.

She had hazel eyes, an unusual tawny color, and that head full of honey blond hair. In person she looked much younger than she had in the newspaper photo, early to mid-thirties, but maybe she'd looked older in the paper because of her severe hairstyle and glasses.

He wondered, briefly and irrationally, if she needed to wear glasses or if they were only a prop. He wondered where she came from, what her background was, how she'd ended up in the Colorado Public Defender's Office. If she was so damn good, why wasn't she in private practice?

He hadn't a glimmer of what she'd thought of him. It struck him abruptly that he wanted very badly for her to think well of him, that he wanted, ultimately, for her to believe he was innocent. But Jack knew that defense lawyers and public defenders didn't care about—or were not supposed to take into account—their client's guilt or innocence. They didn't ask, and they didn't react if their client protested innocence or confessed to guilt. Their job was simply to provide the accused with their constitutionally guaranteed right to adequate counsel.

Frank Iverson had never asked Jack outright whether he was guilty, and to this day, Jack didn't know if Frank believed in his innocence or not.

Eve Marchand. He saw her features, small and fine. He saw her reach up to tuck a curling strand of hair behind a perfect ear. And he wondered about that vacation she was supposed to take. Where? With whom?

He thought of her as he lay there, locked in his cell for the night, hands behind his head, staring up through the darkness to the ceiling that he knew so well. He thought of Eve Marchand eating a late dinner in a restaurant or in her nice hotel room. Or taking a walk. Or maybe she'd gone to a movie or a concert or the ballet.

Goddamn it! His jaw locked in frustration and despair, and he fought the emotions down, using every bit of mental strength he had until his calm was restored. It wasn't any easier after this past, endless year. He'd have thought it would be, but it wasn't.

He tried to distract himself by playing a mental game: he designed a house to match an individual. Eve Marchand, for instance. It'd have to be a light, airy house, not formal or heavy. He built it in his head, several levels, cool and open, with honey-colored wood and big windows and a spiral staircase in the entryway. Tiles on the floor. Saltillo, yes. And vaulted ceilings with log beams. He placed Eve in the living room, sitting on a long cinnamon leather couch. And there would have to be a greenhouse off the living room. A wild profusion of plants and flowers. He saw her bending over a plant, her hand cupping a bloom, drawing in its scent.

Allison had been beautiful, but in a more flamboyant way, petite and fiery, with huge dark eyes and glossy straight black hair. Like Cleopatra, he often thought.

Eve had a fire inside her, too. A banked fire, but it was still there, different from Allison's, which had been a thirst for adventure and passion and experiences. Eve's was the quiet fire of a crusader, a person with a purpose.

Jack tried to erase the images, to free his mind and go to sleep. He never slept well, lying there thinking and thinking. Funny how some prisoners slept all the time.

Shakespeare had called sleep "death's counterfeit." Maybe that was why Jack didn't sleep much. Maybe he felt the need to be awake, to savor his waking hours because they might end too soon.

What would it take to save his life? Did Eve Marchand have the skill to do it? Did anybody?

SIX

Gary Kapochek had always considered himself pretty damn lucky to be engaged to Eve Marchand.

Everyone agreed. "Isn't she that public defender wizard?" the Denver Broncos' star quarterback had asked last year. "God, I thought she'd be much older, you know. And real brainy."

They all commented on how attractive she was, how smart, how dedicated. And Gary appreciated her attributes more than anyone. There was something about her piquant beauty, her pride, the crusader-for-the-downtrodden aspect of her. She drew people to her. She'd sure drawn him.

Eve was the subject of a conversation Gary was having with his best friend Nelson Rourke, who was one of the talent scouts for the Broncos.

They were sitting in the Greeley, Colorado, training camp offices, going over stats on this year's rookies, when Nelson brought up the subject.

"I thought you guys were going to Maine before training camp started," Nelson said, his feet up on a desk.

Gary shook his head. "We were. Yesterday, in fact. Still might go."

"Don't tell me, Eve got a new case."

"Yeah, well, maybe. Don't know yet. She's up in Aspen...."

Nelson hit his head with a palm. "The Devlin case? She's on *that?*"

"Uh-huh. She hasn't decided to take it, though. I'm sure hoping she doesn't."

"But it would be the biggest case she's ever had."

"I know, I know. The trouble, as you've probably figured, is that we never have any time together. Like this vacation."

"I guess," his friend said. "In fact, being as how I'm supposed to be the best man at your wedding, don't you think you ought to give me a date?"

"Sure, if we'd only set one." Gary snorted. "Eve's supposed to be going into private practice. She's been promising to set up some interviews. Hell, every defense lawyer in Denver wants her in his office. But she still hasn't had time to look into it. And until she does... Well, I can't see trying to set a wedding date."

"So she really is going to quit public defense?"

Gary shrugged. "So she says."

"She will. No one stays in public defense for too long. They say the money sucks and the pressure'll kill you."

"You don't have to tell *me* that," Gary said grimly.

He left Greeley at five and drove south along the Front Range toward his home in Boulder. He used the hand controls on his car, annoyed by them. But maybe in a month or two he could have them taken out, have the car converted back to foot control. Back to normal. By the end of the football season, maybe he could even empty his garage of the wheelchair and walker, all the paraphernalia that reminded him of the months and years of physical decline.

There was a lot to look forward to. Now, if only Eve would get her own life in order. Of course, Gary was busy himself, one hundred percent dedicated to his team. But the Broncos were only physically active from mid-July to January, and then only if they made the playoffs. That freed Gary for at least five months of the year.

He hadn't cared so much about the private time when the MS had been robbing him of his active life every day. But the new treatment was so promising—and he could see improvement every week—that everything had taken on a new meaning. He saw himself with Eve at his side, sailing distant seas, climbing hitherto-unclimbed mountains. Fate had thrown him a terrible curve; the disease had cut his career short and totally dashed his dreams. But now there was nothing except hope and a real future to look forward to, and he had the perfect woman to share it with.

He cut through downtown Boulder, home of the University of Colorado. The traffic was light, but then it was summer, and classes were out.

He passed the stadium—*his* old stadium—and smiled. God, life had been great then. A college football star, his grades really good, coeds by the dozen chasing him. Then he'd been drafted into the NFL, to Houston. But after two years in Texas the Broncos had made a trade and he'd wound up back in Colorado, where he'd wanted to be all along. He'd had three good years with the Broncos, even made the Pro Bowl in Hawaii. Then the diagnosis...

Two miles outside of Boulder, he turned into a new subdivision that ran up to the foot of the mountains. He'd bought his house almost a year ago, bought it because he was going to be married.

He was thinking what a great investment that had been, wondering when he and Eve would get married, when he turned into his driveway and there was her car. He smiled. The fact that she was there had to mean she'd decided not to take on the Devlin case. Maybe she'd come to her senses at last.

He got out, using his cane, a little shaky from the long drive. When he went inside, Eve was in the kitchen, cooking something that smelled absolutely fabulous. Garlic, onions, basil, tomato.

"Hey," he called, "I'm here."

"In the kitchen," she called back.

He found her at the sink, chopping vegetables, wearing jeans and a sleeveless white blouse. He loved the roundness of her ass in jeans. Her hair was loose, and when she turned to smile at him, she pushed it off her face with a wrist.

Gary kissed her, wanting to feel her against him, the pressure of her firm, small breasts on his chest.

But she pushed him away. "Cut that out. I'm covered in food here. Later."

Reluctantly he moved back and shook his head at her. "I didn't expect you tonight. In fact," he said, "I didn't expect you at all for about three months."

"Um," she said, leaning over the cutting board again.

"Does this mean we leave for Maine tomorrow?" Gary propped his cane against a cabinet and opened the refrigerator door, searching for a soda. "I guess I'd better call the airlines, then, and the inn at Boothbay Harbor...."

"Ah," she said, "let's not do that just yet."

Shit, he thought.

After a long moment she finally put the knife down, turned and leaned against the counter. Her arms were folded. He knew that body language. "I'm going to take the Devlin case," she said.

Gary just stared at her, the unopened can of soda in his hand.

"I know what you're thinking," Eve went on, "and before you say a word, I want to explain. It's not the job. It's not the publicity, either, although I'm not a fool. I know that this will be the biggest case of my career whether I win or lose."

"You *will* lose this one, you know," he muttered.

But Eve merely shook her head. "Maybe. *Probably*. But that's not the issue. I'll fight like the devil, anyway. You know that."

"And put yourself in the hospital."

"No, I won't."

"You won't even be in Denver, Eve."

"I know that. I drove back this morning and packed for the long haul."

"You won't be here for the opening game."

"Sure I will. I'll drive down. It's two months away...."

"Don't," he cut in. "Don't kid yourself. And that's not even the issue. You're wrecking our trip. We planned this for months."

"I'm sorry. What else can I say?"

"That you'll call your boss right this minute and tell him you've changed your mind. And it wouldn't hurt to reassure me that you still plan on going into private practice."

Eve closed her eyes for a moment, then opened them. "I can't think about that until this penalty trial's over."

"And then you'll find another excuse to put it off."

"Gary, you're pushing."

"Of course I am," he said, getting hotter by the second. "When we met, Eve, it was *you* who talked *me* into going out."

She regarded him silently.

"And that was okay," he said. "I wanted to have a life. I needed you, Eve, I still do. But I need you to start acting and thinking like a wife...like a mate, for God's sake. We can't keep living separate lives. If I sound like a typical domineering male, well, I'm sorry. But that's the way I feel."

"You don't sound like that at all," she said. "And you're absolutely right. We *will* have a life together. We'll make it work. *I'll* make it work. I promise. But this Devlin thing came out of the blue. Gary, he's not... This isn't like any case I've ever had before."

Gary snorted in derision.

"I know. That sounds crazy. But he's so...different."

"Different."

"Not your run-of-the-mill criminal, that's for sure. Gary, he's educated, intelligent.... He's taking this whole thing in stride. No, that's not exactly it. It's that he's handling it using his wits and showing a whole lot more courage than anyone I've ever seen. It's very strange, but..." Eve looked up at him and shook her head. "Gary, I don't think he did it."

"Uh-huh."

"No, really. I've never felt this intuitive about a client before. I've always tried to remain completely impartial. It's better if you are. Believe me. But in Jack's case, well, I just somehow *knew* he didn't murder his wife. I can't explain it. I just know he's innocent."

Gary couldn't say a thing for at least a minute. He didn't know what to say. He'd never heard Eve so enthused before. She was no longer the worn-out public defender who'd gone to Aspen only yesterday morning. She was transformed. As if some invisible force had infused her with a renewed zeal for her work.

"Gary?" she said tentatively.

"I don't know what to say," he began. "I don't really know what you're trying to tell me. I guess it's that you want to do this trial because Devlin got to you."

"He didn't *get* to me."

"I'll rephrase that. Because you believe in a client's innocence."

Eve nodded. "I can't let them give him the death penalty."

"But you know they probably will. The odds are against you."

"I know. I do know. And it's hard, Gary. It's the knowledge that he's been falsely convicted and may end up on death row that's so hard." She took a breath. "Please try to understand and support me in this. I know I've disappointed you, the vacation and all. But Aspen's a wonderful place, and maybe you could come up on weekends. There's the music festival, fishing, hiking...*short* hikes, that is. But there's so much to do, and I'll have a room already." She looked at him imploringly. "Will you?"

He stared at her standing there so sweet and innocent and pretty and he couldn't help laughing. "Okay, all right. You win. But when this case is over..." But he never finished. Eve went to him and wrapped her arms around his waist and kissed him.

They ate dinner on his back deck in the warm June evening. Behind them the Flatirons jutted into the sky in geometric slabs, red in the setting sun. It was a peaceful time, and Gary couldn't remember when they'd last been alone like this. He wanted to tell Eve to stay in Denver, to forget Aspen and the Devlin case. He wanted to tell her to move in with him. She lived in the notoriously crime-ridden area of Capital Hill in Denver. And although her street was relatively safe, upscale, with a neighborhood watch and off-street parking, it wasn't nearly as safe as his suburban neighborhood. Sure, his was more or less a tract home, but there were kids and dogs playing on the streets, and you could park your unlocked car on the road for weeks and have nothing stolen.

He looked at her honey blond curls lifting in the warm breeze and wanted to tell her that they should set the date for the wedding. He wanted to tell her a whole lot, but he sensed her total preoccupation with this new case, and he know he couldn't pin her down until after the trial.

They stayed out on the deck till almost dark, when the nightly thunderstorms built up over the Flatirons and raced eastward to the great prairies. Lightning streaked the sky to the north, and strong gusts of cool air bent the cottonwood trees.

They did the dishes and watched the news together—ordinary stuff. Important things to Gary. If the MS had taught him a single lesson, it was that life was unpredictable, that you had to treasure each moment, hold on to it, look for its meaning. He'd never exactly voiced that thought to Eve, but she knew, she'd seen him change. If only she could seize those moments herself. Someday, someday soon, she would.

They went to bed at eleven, Eve showering, appearing from the steamy bathroom in a summer nightgown, her hair wrapped in a towel.

"God, that felt good," she said, drying her hair now, combing her fingers through the wet curls.

Gary watched her in the blue pulsing light from the television set. He was already in bed, naked except for boxer shorts, his usual sleeping attire. He felt himself harden as he stared at her breasts, the silk of her gown lying softly against them, her nipples little peaks on the fabric.

"Stop fooling with your hair," he said teasingly, "and come here."

Eve smiled, put the towel over a chair and slid in next to him.

He remembered the first time they'd made love. It had been months after their first date. He'd been so sick, on the decline when they'd met. His mind had been willing, but his body had not cooperated.

It must have been six or seven months, he figured, before he'd been able to hold an erection. Eve had been wonderful, so understanding. Then the new treatments had begun, and gradually he'd been able to have a normal sex life with her. Now it was Eve who was either too exhausted or too pre-occupied. That was another reason he longed for her to get into private practice. A big reason.

She moved against him, her damp hair on his cheek, and they kissed while he slid her nightgown off her shoulders. Then he drew a hand across her breasts, feather-light. He kissed her more thoroughly and she sighed, then he moved his head lower and drew a nipple into his mouth.

He suckled first one nipple, then the other, feeling the sharpness of her hipbone against his own. She tasted of scented soap and some sort of bath oil, her flesh still warm and supple from the shower.

"Oh, Gary," she whispered as he slipped a hand beneath her gown and touched her inner thigh.

She moved, but he felt a tension in her, something he'd never noticed before. It was as if she weren't quite there.

He kissed the hollow between her breasts and felt her more deeply with his fingers, but again there was that barrier, that tension.

He lifted his head. "Are you all right?" he whispered.

She took a breath and then laughed lightly. "I'm fine. Wound up, I guess."

He moved his hand to her hip. "You want to talk first? Relax a little?"

"No, don't be silly."

"It's just... Well, it's like you're not really with me."

"I'm sorry. You're right. I'll try, though. It's this new case."

Gary propped his head on his hand and looked at her through the semidarkness, a muted monologue from the television in the background. "Let's talk," he said.

"I really... Oh, Gary, you *are* right. I'm actually excited about this case. But I haven't felt this... Well, I haven't felt this energetic in years. It's always such a battle, and I always feel as if I'm trying to swim up out of a deep, dark hole. But this time... It's so different. That's all I know. I'm sorry. But I just feel so...challenged. Can you understand?"

"Of course I understand," he said. And he did. He was happy for her, happy to see the spark back in her. So what if she'd be frantically busy for the next few months? It was reassuring to see the Eve he'd first met.

"You know," she said, still resting against him, her damp hair on his chest. "You could come up this weekend. I could get tickets for a concert, whatever you want. Do you think you could? Maybe Saturday morning?"

"Sure," he said, and he kissed the top of her head. "Sure. I'll meet you at noon at your hotel."

"Um," she whispered. Then she turned her face up to him. "Sorry about a few minutes ago. My mind's just racing."

"I know," he said. "It's okay. You lie here and scheme away."

"I love you," she said, and she nestled against him.

Sometime later he thought she'd gone to sleep, but he wasn't sure. He listened to a couple of the guests on the "Tonight Show," though his thoughts kept drifting back to Eve. And he wondered what, really, had put the life back in the woman he loved.

SEVEN

When Eve was working a case she had the tenacity of a bulldog. She put on a professional face and wasn't afraid to draw blood if it was in the best interest of her client.

So it went with Jack Devlin's case. By Thursday of that week she was well into the thick of it. Not only was she hard at work, but she had Marty Cohen out of the Glenwood Springs office poring over legal precedents and conducting peripheral interviews.

Hank Thurgood was here, too. Hank was one of the investigators who worked out of the Denver office. In Eve's opinion, he was tops. In his early seventies, Hank was nowhere near ready for retirement. He had a better nose for his work than any investigator she knew. Often Eve would accompany Hank on an interview, sometimes playing good guy to his bad-guy routine. Occasionally, depending upon the situation, they would switch roles. Like two cops. They worked the gig as well as anyone.

Hank accompanied her to Jack Devlin's former architectural firm for the interview with the owner. The office was located in the heart of Aspen, a prestigious address on Galena Street, a fact that didn't get by Hank, even though he was new to town.

"Wonder what the rent runs here?" he commented to Eve

as they entered the Elks Building, which took up nearly an entire block smack dab in the city core.

Eve climbed the Victorian staircase to the second floor and shrugged. "A lot more than *we* make."

"So Devlin must have been good. File says he only moved here twelve years ago. And I'll bet the competition's pretty steep."

Hank stopped at the second-floor landing to catch his breath. "Phew," he said. "Did you know this goddamn town's at eight thousand feet?"

"The cigarettes don't help, Hank," she put in with a devilish grin.

"Ah, stow it," he said, and Eve shook her head at him, wondering how he still functioned so well after a lifetime of self-abuse.

Hank not only smoked incessantly, but he swilled booze like a college kid. He was tall and lanky, somewhat bent over now, and he had a long, narrow face that reminded her of a basset hound. His ears were darn near as big, too, and Eve swore they flapped in a strong breeze. As for his style of dress... She'd never seen him in anything but baggy old tweed sport coats, loose gray trousers and orange hiking boots. Nevertheless, she was terribly fond of him, and his expertise was legendary.

They walked down the hall together, searching for Young and Fitzsimmons, Architects. It was Young who ran the business, reportedly the number-one architect on the Western Slope of Colorado. His territory included Aspen, Vail, Crested Butte and Telluride, and his fees ran as high as twenty-five percent. When talking multimillion dollar homes, that was a bundle.

Sid Young greeted them in the reception area and showed them into his office. The view was terrific, overlooking the corner of Galena and Hyman Streets.

Eve glanced around. "Nice," she said. "Very nice."

"Thanks," Sid Young replied, pulling up chairs for them around a long worktable that served as his desk. Everywhere Eve looked there were piles of blueprints and models, miniatures of elegant homes, landscaping and all. On the thirteen-foot-high walls were framed artists' renditions of Young's buildings, everything from schools to minimalls to Starwood homes.

"Impressive," Eve noted. "Isn't that the new music school facility?"

"Yes, it is," Young said, folding his arms, meeting their eyes.

He was a nice-looking man, mid-fifties, Eve figured, on the yuppie side, very well turned out with thick graying hair, a perfect gray mustache and that must-have Aspen tan. He was tall and lean and fit and had eyes so blue they were startling. It crossed her mind that he'd had a face-lift, but then she decided it was his self-confidence and good bearing that made him seem younger than his years.

"I wonder," Eve began, putting on her glasses, taking her yellow notepad out of her briefcase, "if we might see Jack's former office when we're done here. I assume his position has been filled, but if it wouldn't be too..."

"No problem," Young said. "Anything I can do to help."

She smiled. "And that brings me to my next question. Who *did* replace Jack?" Her smile remained, but it was only skin deep. She knew it. And so did Young.

"Excuse me?" he said.

"Who replaced Jack Devlin in your office?"

Hank sat back, steepled his fingers and stared at Young.

Young cleared his throat. "That would be David, David Webster."

"Uh-huh," Eve said, writing down the name. "And was this David Webster with your firm before Jack's arrest?"

"Yes, he was."

"And what was his position then?"

"Why..." Sid Young cocked his head. "Is this leading where I think it is? My God."

Hank leaned forward. "Mr. Young," he said, pinioning the renowned architect with a flinty gaze, "a man's life is at stake. Miss Marchand isn't about to leave a single stone unturned. Now, if you could answer her…"

Eve repeated her question. "Did this David Webster take a step up in the firm when Jack Devlin was arrested?"

"Yes, he did." Young leaned forward and looked from Eve to Hank and back. "But you'd be barking up the wrong tree if you investigated David."

"Oh?" Eve took her glasses off and met Young's gaze.

"Let me try to explain," Young went on. "Jack was probably one of the best-liked guys in the office. He was unpretentious and never afraid to seek advice. He's the one who brought David here in the first place. And believe me, David appreciated it. He was quite wet behind the ears, and, yes, this has been a break for him, but he's headed for the top of his profession, anyway."

"Um," Eve said, and she tapped her pencil on her chin. "I'd like a client list from you—Jack's clients. Would that be possible?"

"I don't know why not."

Hank cleared his throat. "Did Devlin make any enemies through work?"

Young laughed. "Sure, you bet. Never met an architect who didn't. About a hundred percent of the time it's arguments and lawsuits between the architects and contractors. It's strictly an ego trip. You know. The general contractor doesn't like a particular design and changes it on site. Sometimes the change causes engineering problems, stuff like that. The changes always cost the homeowner, and you'd better believe there are plenty of lawsuits filed on all sides."

Hank nodded. "So Devlin had a few enemies."

"Sure. Like I said, we all do."

"Could I have a few names?" Eve asked.

But Young shook his head. "I haven't got a clue. That was Jack's business, and you'll have to ask him." Then he frowned. "Now, do you mind my asking something?"

"Go ahead," Eve said.

"Maybe I'm ignorant of how the law works, but if Jack's already been convicted, why the investigation?"

Eve slid her yellow pad into her briefcase and sat back, adjusting the hem of her beige skirt over her knees. "To save a man's life, Mr. Young, *Sid*, we have to start from scratch. Right now we're looking for something, anything, that can place doubt in the minds of the judges who'll preside over the penalty phase."

"But I read that there won't be any evidence presented, that all you can argue for is a life sentence over the death penalty."

Eve nodded. "True. But even though justice is supposed to be blind, sometimes she lifts that blindfold and takes a peek."

Young thought a moment, then he smiled. "I think I see. You find something not quite kosher, and maybe the press gets hold of it, prints it... The judges are human, after all. And they read, too. You're looking to influence them, make them lift that blindfold."

"It's a possibility," Eve allowed. "But we're also preparing for the appeals process. We're looking ahead. Frank Iverson, Jack's lawyer..."

"I met Frank."

"Of course you did. Anyway, he spent a lot of time looking for police screwups, evidence-tampering, whatever. Needless to say, he didn't find enough to convince the jury that Jack's case was mishandled. We're taking a different tack, looking for something that could prompt a new trial for Jack."

"Like finding the real murderer?"

"That would be nice," Eve said. "Very, very nice."

Young frowned. "The papers are saying Jack's going to get the death penalty. Is he?"

"He might," Eve said. "But we're still going to push the patience of the court to see that he doesn't."

Hank spent a few minutes trying to learn which contractors Jack had had run-ins with. Young was careful, though;

no doubt he still had to work with those local builders. Eve wasn't too concerned. She'd get all that out of Jack.

They'd been in Young's office for more than a half hour when he glanced at his watch. "If you don't have anything more...?"

"No, and thank you," Eve said, beginning to rise. But then she sat back down and asked in a quiet voice, "Did you know Allison Devlin very well?"

Young pursed his lips and sighed. "Yes, I knew Allison. She was a good friend of my wife's. They golfed together, played some tennis. You know."

"Uh-huh," Eve said. "And what was Allison like?"

"Headstrong comes to mind. Always a little flamboyant, kind of wild."

"Was she a...nice person?"

"Allison? I wouldn't say nice. She was fun, and she sure did a lot of charity work. But she could be tough if she thought she was being crossed. No, *nice* isn't a word for Allison. Honest, direct, those are better descriptions. She was a loyal friend, too."

"Did you know Ben? Her son, Ben Richards?"

"Oh, sure, I know Ben. He was in my oldest son's class at school here."

"And?"

"Well, I like Ben. He's really a lot like his mother was, more stubborn, though."

"Give me an example," Eve prompted.

Young thought a moment. "Well, geez, I guess I'm thinking about that motorcycle he wanted when he was in high school. A Harley. Allison put her foot down, said no way. But Ben bought it, anyway—on credit, no less. I recall that he made a few payments by working nights at a local restaurant. But then he quit. I think the Harley was history pretty soon after that."

Eve smiled. "I can imagine." Then she rose, and she and Hank shook Sid Young's hand. "I'm counting on you to testify at the penalty trial," she said.

"Testify?"

"It will merely be a character reference."

"But Frank Iverson never said anything..."

"Iverson would have, believe me. If he hadn't had the heart attack, he most certainly would have asked you to."

"I'd be happy to," Young said, and he led them out to the receptionist, instructing her to show them Jack's old office and provide them with a list of Jack's former clients.

Ten minutes later they were back on the street, the client list in Hank's hand. "I'm going to start checking out these names," he said, lighting a cigarette, his seedy sport coat flapping in the warm June breeze. "I'll go ahead and do the interview with Allison's first husband, the father of the kid, Richards. He's some big shot at the local ski company, right?"

"Uh-huh," Eve said.

"And that Mochlin character, the tennis pro..."

"Allison's lover," Eve mused aloud.

"Yeah, that dude. I don't know whether I should grill him or you should do it. What do you think? Or maybe we should do it together."

But Eve shook her head. "I'm going to do that one. I'd like him on the relaxed side. Iverson's files say he's a real womanizer and that he was hot for Allison's money. I guess he was chomping at the bit waiting for Jack and Allison's divorce to become final."

"Yeah," Hank said, suddenly coughing, then stomping out the cigarette on the immaculate sidewalk, "I read that, too. Iverson had a note in his file with a big star next to it. Said Mochlin was bragging to friends that he was going to be husband number three. Maybe they had an argument. Maybe he wasn't going to marry all that money, after all."

Again Hank coughed. "Goddamn," he said. "I gotta quit these things. But anyway, let's push Mochlin on the alibi thing for the night of the murder. Evidently Iverson thought it was solid, but I've never seen one that couldn't be shot full of holes."

"Okay," Eve said. "I'll try to talk to him this afternoon. But I think I'll see Jack first. I just can't get a feel for how he handled knowing his wife was having an affair. Jack keeps a lot of stuff from me. Actually, he's keeping it from himself. He's not making this easy."

"So it seems," Hank replied, then he waved Jack's client list in the air and said he wanted to get going on it. "See you for dinner?" he asked.

"Sure," Eve said. "Around midnight, if we even get to it at all."

Eve's car was at her motel, but since she was only two blocks from the jail, she walked. Her mind was on Jack and how to pry information from him. It was vital that he open up to her, trust her. She wondered if he'd fully trusted Iverson, but it was her opinion that there were things Jack simply never examined, even in his own heart.

Men, she thought, passing the old brick city hall and stopping at the pedestrian crosswalk on Main Street. Well, *some* men, anyway.

The noon whistle—actually the fire siren—sounded as she entered the jail.

She was becoming a regular and, as she'd told Debby, she kept odd hours. She'd been in to see Jack three times since her first interview with him. On this visit she met him in the common room. He was eating lunch, reading the Denver paper when she got there.

Automatically, without even asking, without thinking, she sat down, picked up half his sandwich and began to take a bite. She caught herself, and she laughed. "My God," she said, "I can't believe I just did that."

Jack sat back in his chair and stared at her, the hint of a smile lifting the corner of his mouth. "Go on," he said. "Obviously you're hungry."

"I must be."

"Do you ever eat regular meals?" he asked, still regarding her.

"Um, sometimes. I try to, but lately..." She shrugged.

"Anyway, I need to get some straight answers out of you today. I'm serious about this, Jack. It's very important. I'm going to talk to George Mochlin this afternoon." Eve paused, gauging Jack's reaction. Of course, as she'd expected, she got none whatsoever.

She took a bite of the sandwich, pulled out her legal pad and put on her glasses. Jack handed her his napkin. "Thanks," she said, swallowing. "Okay. Before we get on to Mochlin, there's something I need from you. It's a list of everyone you butted heads with in town. I just finished talking to Sid Young, and he mentioned some lawsuits and bad blood over a few of the houses you designed."

Jack nodded.

"Can you make a list of names?"

"I can do that, sure."

"And one other thing. David Webster. The man who's filling your shoes at your former office."

"You can't think…"

"Jack," she interrupted, "get used to it. I don't trust anyone. Anyone but you, that is. You're my client. The rest of these people are all suspect in my eyes. You understand?"

He nodded, albeit grudgingly.

"Now, I admit that the contractors you had disagreements with, even the ones who filed lawsuits, wouldn't have been likely to have murdered your wife in order to frame you. Nor would David Webster have been likely to do that, but stranger things have happened. Hank's going to check them all out."

"No stone unturned," Jack muttered.

"You're damn right," she said. "Now. George Mochlin. I've read his testimony from the trial and gone over Iverson's notes. The guy sounds like a real creep. Would you say that's true?"

Jack leaned back in his chair and put his hands behind his head, crossed an ankle over a knee. *Body language*, Eve thought.

"Well?" she prompted.

"I never really knew Mochlin."

"Come on, Jack, give me a break. The divorce wasn't final. Mochlin was...screwing your wife." She was sure Jack would show some emotion now. But she didn't get a reaction. He only stared at her with those unreadable black eyes. "I don't believe you didn't try to find out *something* about him. Surely you asked around town."

"Why does this matter?"

"Because Mochlin's a suspect. Iverson had a lot of questions about him, too."

"Yes, I know," Jack said. "Remember, I was at the trial. I heard the whole thing."

"So? Was Mochlin lying?"

"About what?"

"You're being evasive, Jack. Mochlin testified that he had no interest in Allison's money. But in Iverson's investigation, there was gossip around town that Mochlin was only waiting for the divorce to be final before he planned on asking Allison to marry him. She was a real catch."

"Then you tell me why he'd kill her."

"I don't know. I can only surmise that *if* he's guilty, Allison must have heard the gossip and confronted him. They argued. Maybe it got out of hand."

"Whatever," Jack said, as if disinterested.

"Goddamn it, Jack," Eve muttered, leaning forward, her mouth a hard line now, "don't give me that. Don't pretend it doesn't matter, because it does. I'm looking for anything I can leak to the press right now, something that at least one of the judges will read. Something that will give him serious doubts about the death penalty in your case. And I'm telling you," she went on in a harsh whisper, "if I don't find *something*, all the testimony about what a swell guy you are isn't going to mean a thing. They'll put you on death row. Now, help me here. Damn it, Jack, help me."

For a long moment he regarded her in silence, completely inside himself, unfathomable. Then, finally, he leaned forward, so that their faces were very close. "All right," he said. "Half the people Allison and I knew came to me and told me that."

"What?" she urged.

"That George Mochlin had bragged to just about anyone who'd listen that he was going to be husband number three."

"And how did you feel about that, Jack?"

"I told Allison not to be a goddamn fool."

"This was when you were separated?"

"Of course. Allison wasn't seeing him until then."

Eve wasn't so sure about that, but she let it pass. "And did you and Allison argue about it?"

"Yes."

"Did you ever get...physical with her?"

"You mean did I hit or abuse her? No. God, no."

"Okay. I believe you. Now, tell me how you feel about Mochlin."

"This has nothing to do with the case."

"It has to do with you being honest with me, Jack, with your opening up to me."

Jack swore then.

"*Tell me.*"

"All right," he finally said. "I wanted to break every bone in the man's body. Does that satisfy you?"

Eve sat back and smiled. "Yes, Jack, it does. That's the first time you've appeared human."

Eve took off her glasses and dropped them into her briefcase. She stood up. "It bothers you, doesn't it, that I'm a woman?" she said, and she leveled her gaze on him. "Frank Iverson never asked you questions like this, did he?"

"No," Jack said, "he didn't. Frank didn't have to."

"Because he's a man."

Jack shrugged.

"I see. But I'm *not* a man, Jack," she said, "and this is the way I work. If a client's mother beat the hell out of him as a kid, I want to know all the sordid details. If there was sexual abuse, I'm going to drag it out of a client. I'm dealing with life and death here, and I'll look for any angle I can to keep a man off the row. I don't care what that angle is."

"Sort of like dirty pool."

"Yes. It's a curious system of justice in this country. Usually it's the poor broke sucker who ends up on death row while the rich go free. And even then there's no rhyme or reason for who gets executed and when it happens. It's the Chaos Theory at work. And in your case, Jack, they're going for blood. It's an election year, and this is a high-profile murder case. You can't do this alone. You can't hide behind that proud facade and try to tough it out yourself. You need help. *My* help. We'll get through this trial somehow, and I'm going to search like the devil for some catch to keep you off the row. I need to know you."

She took a breath. "Now, I'm out of here to try to find this George Mochlin and push as many of his buttons as I can. When I'm done, I'm going to locate your stepson, Ben, and talk to him."

"He's out of town."

"Great. When will he be back?"

"Saturday, I think. But..." Jack paused. "Look, Ben's been through a lot. I wish you'd..."

"*Ben's* been through a lot? Yes, he lost his mother. That *is* tragic. But you're the one who's going through hell, Jack. And I do need to talk to the young man. If he's your friend, as you say he is, he'll understand. He'll want to help."

Jack nodded soberly.

"Okay," she said, picking up her briefcase, "I'll see you later."

But Jack stopped her. He stood, seemed almost as if he were going to take her arm, but he hesitated. "That was quite a speech you gave a minute ago," he said, standing over her. "I want you to know something, though. I'm not a chauvinist. I'm glad you're on my case. I figure I'm damn lucky, and I wish to hell I could somehow pay you. The point is, I'm not used to this sort of representation. The female approach, if you will."

"And it makes you uncomfortable," she said.

But Jack only laughed, that guarded half laugh that was very hard to read. "I don't think *uncomfortable*'s the word, Eve. It's more like...*baffled*."

"Um," she said. "I'll have to think about that. It seems to me that I'm an open book. Maybe I'm a little too passionate about my work, but that's hardly curious in my profession."

"No," Jack said. "It's not just your passion, Eve. There's something else."

"Well...?"

"I don't know. When I do, I'll tell you."

"Promise?"

"Uh-huh," he said, but she didn't believe him. She smiled, shook her head and left.

It was on the drive to the golf and tennis club that it struck Eve like a blow, a truth she hadn't seen before. In all the dealings she'd had with men—and she'd had plenty—never once had anyone tried to keep himself from her. Her dad was an open book. Gary was certainly forthcoming. All of the clients she'd defended over the years were so willing to talk about themselves, it had become rote to her. But Jack... He was so unusual, so different from anyone she'd ever dealt with, that he was driving her crazy. It was becoming a cause to her—she simply had to open him up and see what really lay inside.

The Castle Creek Golf and Tennis Club was Aspen's most elite private country club. It lay on the west end of town, the emerald green fairways stretching to the base of Buttermilk, the beginners' ski mountain, and all the way down to the Roaring Fork River. The clubhouse was nothing short of magnificent: an open, airy structure of stone and glass. Inside were elegant bar and dining facilities, the latest in sports equipment, men's and women's gyms and locker rooms and Italian marble whirlpools. The dining room overlooked five indoor tennis courts.

Eve told the receptionist she had an appointment with the tennis pro, George Mochlin. When she was shown into his small office above the courts, he was completely taken by surprise, and neither he nor the flustered receptionist knew quite what to do.

"Oh, did my secretary forget to call?" Eve asked, feigning innocence.

She liked taking people by surprise—some people, anyway.

"Well," he said, "I guess I could give you a couple of minutes. I've got a one-thirty lesson, though."

"Fine." Eve sat across his desk from him, pulling out her legal pad and eyeglasses.

He was blond and tan and had sharp green eyes. A hint of a beard showed on his face, and Eve knew he had that five o'clock shadow down pat. He was long, lean and sinewy, probably over six feet, she guessed.

"So you're the one," he stated, regaining some composure.

"The one?" Eve smiled in a friendly manner.

"Sure, the hotshot public defender. I've seen your picture in the papers."

"I'll take that as a compliment, Mr. Mochlin."

"George, please."

"Okay then, George. And I'm Eve."

"You know," he said, just when she was ready to launch in, "you're a whole lot prettier than the newspaper pictures."

Eve put her glasses on. "I hope you're not flirting with me, George."

He laughed, white teeth flashing. "No, I'm not. Just stating a fact."

"Good," she said. "Now, if we could get down to business?"

"Of course. But if you think I'll say one thing to help that murderer Devlin, you're nuts. He deserves the death penalty."

"Um," Eve said. "You're entitled to your opinion. But this really isn't about Jack receiving the death penalty. What I'd

like to know are specifics about you and Allison Wickwire
Devlin."

Mochlin looked confused. "I thought... Hey, I've talked to
the cops, to dozens of lawyers and investigators... I *testified*
to everything on the stand. I don't get this."

"It's quite simple. After the penalty phase of Jack's trial
we'll begin the appeals process regardless of the sentence he
receives. It starts all over again, George."

"God, it'll never end."

"Sometimes it seems that way," she allowed. "So why
don't we get this over with and you can go teach your les
son."

"Okay, sure," he said.

Eve wrote the time and date on her yellow pad, then
looked up to meet his gaze. "When did you begin to see Al
lison? Was it before or after Jack had moved out of their
house?"

"After. I've said this a hundred times. It was *after* they
separated."

"Okay. And how long did you see Allison before her
death?"

"You mean her murder." He paused. "It was four, five
months, I suppose."

Eve wrote for a moment, then looked up again. Mochlin
was openly staring at her legs. "Did you know the security
combination to her home?"

"Of course. But I was never there without her. She always
met me at the door or outside."

"Okay," Eve said. "That certainly matches your testi
mony. Now, how about your whereabouts on the night of
her murder?"

"I'm getting pretty tired of this." He lifted his eyes to hers

"I'm sure. But please, indulge me."

"God, all right. I was with an old girlfriend. We'd gone to
the J-Bar."

"The J-Bar?"

"It's the bar at the old Hotel Jerome. A local hangout."

"Were you seeing this old girlfriend?"

"Hell, no. But she was hard to get rid of. You know."

"So you felt sorry for her or something? And you had a drink or two?"

"That's about the size of it. Hey, Melinda testified to all this, too. You can read it."

"I have. I just want to get it straight. So, between eleven and two in the morning, when Allison was killed, you were still at this J-Bar?"

"Yes," he said, bored now, "we were still there. The bartender even testified."

"He did, yes. But he wasn't sure of the time."

"That's his problem."

"No, George," she said, "it's your problem."

He snorted. "Pretty tough, aren't you?"

"Yes, I am. Now, Melinda Hearst testified that she left the bar right before closing. You were still there?"

"That's right."

"But the way I figure it, George, you had time to get into your car and drive up Red Mountain...."

He laughed. "I didn't *have* my car downtown."

"Then you must have a taxi receipt or something...."

"They don't give receipts. Besides, I live about five blocks from the bar. I usually walk it."

"Interesting," Eve said. "Then you still would have had time to walk home, get into your car and drive to Allison's. Maybe you got there and she let you in. And maybe you had an argument...."

"Just hold on there. Goddamn it, I *loved* Allison. We were even hoping to get married."

"That's *your* story, George. Allison never told anyone that."

"Of course she didn't. She was afraid Jack would find out and try to hold her up for a huge divorce settlement."

"Then why did *you* tell anyone who'd listen that you planned to be husband number three?"

"That's bullshit."

"No, it's not. Frank Iverson interviewed several people who were willing to testify to exactly that."

"So why didn't they?"

"Because Frank all but eliminated you as a prime suspect. But I'm not going to be that hasty. I think you had plenty of motive for killing Allison."

He looked stunned. "Motive? What could I have gained?"

"It's more a matter of anger, George. I think Allison may have heard about your bragging to people that you were going to marry her. She had no intentions of marrying you. You drove up there. You got in an argument. She turned her back on you and..."

Mochlin flew out of his chair. "That's the biggest pile of crap I've ever heard in my life! *Jack Devlin* killed her. Everyone knows he was going to be taken out of Allison's will when they divorced. The jury found him guilty, for God's sake. Lady, you are really desperate. Now, I'm done talking to you. This is bullshit. Get out of my office. Hell," he said, his tan turning red, "you may be a real looker, but you sure are a number-one bitch."

Eve took off her glasses and smiled widely. "I'll take that as a compliment, too, George."

"Hey," he said. "Don't come back here. I'm done talking to you. You wanna talk to me, do it through my lawyer."

"Okay, George," she said, rising, "take it easy. You're too young to have a heart attack."

"Will you just please leave?" he said, the veins standing out in his neck.

On the way out, Eve ran into his one-thirty lesson. She was fifty or so—a few years older than Mochlin—perfectly coiffed in her little tennis dress and sweater, her face a surgically induced beauty mask. She must have heard part of the conversation through the window in Mochlin's office, because she was staring at Eve incredulously.

Eve passed her and smiled. "Sorry," she said. "I think George is off his game today," and then she walked straight out into the bright summer day, still smiling.

EIGHT

Melinda Hearst opened the door of her Mountain Valley home, which was perched on the mountainside east of Aspen. Her dog came running out, wriggling and whining until she saw her mistress was not alone. She let out a little yelp of surprise, then sniffed George Mochlin's jeans-clad legs.

"Hey, Maggie," George said as he leaned over and ruffled the mutt's ears. "Long time no see."

"How about a drink?" Melinda suggested.

George shrugged. "Sure. Why not?"

They left Maggie out to do her business. She'd been locked up since five that afternoon, and it was now a few minutes past 2:00 a.m.

Melinda switched on lights, then went to the small sideboard in the living room and found a bottle of Grand Marnier. She poured two snifters and handed one to George.

"The place looks great," he commented, glancing around.

"I painted it about, oh, two or three months ago."

George eyed her as he sipped his drink.

"Of course," she said, slurring a little after a long night in the downtown bars, "if you hadn't dumped me, you'd have known that."

"Let's not start that again," he said. "Okay?"

Melinda pulled open the glass sliding door to the wraparound sundeck and stepped outside. A cool night breeze lifted her straight brown hair off her shoulders. "Mmm," she said, pulling two lounge chairs together. "Isn't this great? Look at the stars tonight." She sat on one lounge, patted the other. "Come on. Sit and enjoy it. I swear, I always said I wouldn't pay a dime extra for a view, but look at this, George. Just look."

George sat on the lounge beside hers and gazed up at the stars, then to the town below. It *was* beautiful. All the houses in Mountain Valley had super views of the valley, though as Aspen went, the real estate was a bargain. George hadn't known that, however, when he'd first met Melinda two years ago. They'd started talking at a local disco, and she'd mentioned her house on the mountainside and how she was going to do some remodeling. George, new to Aspen, had assumed she meant Red Mountain, or even Starwood. But as it had turned out, even though Mountain Valley was far from cheap, it was discounted real estate because it was east of town, where locals and families could afford a small slice of the dream.

George had still dated Melinda. After all, she was a knockout, and he'd never had a better lay in his life—and George had had plenty. Then, about a year after they'd first gone out together, he'd given a tennis lesson to Allison Devlin. Allison *Wickwire* Devlin. And the rest was history.

Melinda put her snifter down and tugged her light summer sweater over her head, dropping it to the deck. She was wearing only a lacy chemise.

"You know," she said, manipulating the raised lounge into a flat position, "I did pretty damn good for you on the witness stand."

George cocked his handsome head, as if he didn't know what she meant.

Melinda slipped the chemise off. "Brr," she said. "It's cold out." She grinned, then began to strip off her blue jeans, lying down, raising her hips to do so.

George stared at her breasts in the dim starlight. Magnificent. And real. "You told the truth," he said, his voice growing husky as he watched her.

"How do I know? I was drunk on my butt the night that bitch was murdered. I have no idea what time I left the bar."

"Yeah, well," George said, watching first the jeans disappear and then her black panties, "the bartender knew exactly when you left. And I was still there. Remember?"

"If you say so."

She stretched out fully, her breasts pale mounds in the dimness, one leg raised, the knee leaning against a perfectly curved thigh. He'd never seen anything as sexy, and he grew hard as he reached out and touched her thigh, feeling the cool silkiness with a hand.

"It's not over, you know," he said, and he ran his fingers across her flat belly.

"What's not over?"

"Devlin's got a new lawyer who's asking questions."

"But I thought…"

"So did I. I was wrong. It doesn't matter, though. If anyone talks to you about it, just say what you did on the witness stand."

"Damn," she whispered.

"Don't worry about it." George stood up and undid his belt, the snap on his jeans.

"That's why you called me tonight, isn't it?" she said, stretching her arms above her head lazily.

"No. Hell no." George unzipped his pants and sat on the edge of her lounge.

"Liar."

George laughed lightly. "Are you telling me you don't want this?" He fingered a cold, raised nipple, then cupped the breast with his warm hand, lowering his head to her. "Tell me you don't want this, baby, and I'll stop right now."

She groaned as his mouth opened on her flesh and he drew her nipple inside, circling it with his tongue. "Just tell me what you need me to say," she murmured.

"Later," George said, "later," and he straddled her naked body.

It was Friday when Eve sat down in her suite with both Hank Thurgood and Marty Cohen, who'd driven up from Glenwood Springs with piles of notes he'd taken on legal precedents concerning crimes of passion and the death penalty. Nothing was much help. Nor had Hank found anything that might sway the panel of judges.

"If we could just find one thing," Eve said, sitting cross-legged on the couch, "just one thing to leak to the press."

"We might be able to do something with George Mochlin's alibi," Hank suggested. "When I talked to his old girlfriend yesterday, that Melinda Hearst, she was nervous. Squirrely about exactly what time she left the J-Bar. And the bartender's only about ninety percent sure that Mochlin was still there at two."

But Eve shook her head. "We can't crucify Mochlin in the press, not with the little we have. We'll keep looking, though." She glanced at Hank, then back to his notes on the interviews he'd done with Jack's client list. "No help here. They all seem to love Devlin. We can get a few to do character testimony, but that's it."

"I agree," Marty said. "What about Richards? Allison's first husband?"

Hank tapped a pen against his narrow chin. "Out of town. Haven't been able to reach him." Then he looked at Eve. "Did you talk to that David Webster character, the one who took Devlin's position at the architect's office?"

Eve nodded and went through sheets of yellow legal paper. "Ah, here it is. My impression of him is that he's heartsick over what's happened to Jack. He's a nice kid, well, *man*, in his late twenties. I can't imagine he would have murdered Allison and set Jack up on a murder charge just to advance himself. Plus he was in New York visiting his parents the night Allison was killed. He would have had to hire someone to murder her. It's just not very feasible."

"Hey," Hank said, "you got that list of contractors who were involved in lawsuits with Devlin?"

"Right," Eve said, shuffling more papers. "Ah, here it is. Got it from Jack this morning."

"There's no way any of 'em did it, committed murder because they had a fight with an architect," Hank said, "but I'll check 'em out, push a little. You never know."

"How about the kid, Ben? Allison's son?" Marty asked.

"He's out of town till tomorrow," Eve said. "I want to do that one myself. I have yet to see the crime scene, too. Maybe tomorrow afternoon."

"Good," Hank said. "And let's not forget the kid's alibi. His girlfriend."

"Sarah Glick," Eve said.

"Right. I'll do that one."

"She lives in Long Beach," Marty put in.

"Hey," Hank said, "this trial is big-time. I'm sure the Denver office will spring for the plane ticket. Economy class, of course."

"I'll okay it," Eve said. "And I'd like you to fly to Hawaii, too. Check out Jack's past."

"I don't know, Eve," Hank said. "I can't see where that will get us."

"Just do it," she said, knowing that he was right, but needing to learn as much about Jack as she could. She was sure it would come in handy in the end. She just didn't know how.

"Well," Hank said, standing, stretching his tall, skinny body so that the mismatched socks above his orange hiking boots showed. "I'm going to start to work on this enemies list here. This'll take a while."

"And I'll keep at the law books," Marty said.

Eve rose, too. "I'm going to do some more ferreting around town on Mochlin. His whole act stinks as far as I'm concerned."

Hank nodded. "And the kid, Ben. Sure you can handle that one alone?"

"Uh-huh. I can handle any twenty-four-year-old you throw at me."

"Okay, well, I'm off," Hank said, heading to the door. "Maybe tonight I'll take a few hours to mix and mingle with the beautiful people. Want to join me, Marty?"

"Nah," Marty said, "I'm too old for that stuff."

"You're never too old, my boy, never too old." Hank bowed to them and left.

"Where did you get *him*?" Marty asked Eve when he was out the door.

Eve managed to reach Ben Richards on Saturday morning, and she set up an appointment to interview him in Allison's house—his house now—at five that same afternoon. Then she got into her car and did something she'd been wanting to do since she'd first arrived in town—she drove up and down the valley, taking time to visit the buildings Jack had designed. She'd gotten the addresses from the client list Sid Young had provided.

A side of Jack she hadn't seen began to unfold as she studied the buildings. He was artistic. In a quiet way his structures blended in with the mountain scenery, almost a part of nature themselves. He'd designed everything from small, single-family mountain retreats to cliffside megahomes.

He used a lot of stone and logs and glass and always utilized the views. Many of the homes had steeply pitched roof lines, affording more window space high on the walls. Eve could imagine that if a person were standing in the middle of the living room, he could still take in the entire view of the mountains.

There were heavy, natural log entryways and more subtle approaches, depending upon the features of the land. Everything Jack designed seemed to have a stillness to it, a peacefulness that was inviting. Was that who Jack was inside, really, she wondered, someone at peace with himself? And with life? Was that what she'd missed?

It was nearly five o'clock when she drove back into town

and sailed past her hotel, heading toward Red Mountain for her appointment with Ben Richards.

Red Mountain sat to the north of town, not quite hovering over it, but embracing it in a friendly, steadying way.

Before Starwood was built, before all the old Victorians in Aspen's prestigious West End had been restored to their graceful, elegant states, Red Mountain was the place to live. The road led up the mountainside straight from the riverbed to switchbacks on the steep pitches, and the giant homes were sunken into the slopes among aspen trees and buck brush and sage.

The views were extraordinary. Lavish. Expensive. Eve passed one home that must have been thirty thousand square feet. There was a guarded gate in front of it. And just past that huge pile of copper roof and river rock was the Devlin residence, or so the sign read at the stone-columned entrance to the winding drive. *Devlin,* Eve thought. So neither Allison nor Ben had changed the sign. Not yet, anyway.

The house appeared around a bend in the drive, nestled among the aspen trees and surrounded by stone-banked gardens.

Lovely. Simple, understated and, of course, blending into the mountainside. Had Jack designed it to complement his beautiful wife?

Parked in front of the house, beneath a covered stone entry, was a split-polished red Saab. Ben's? *How nice,* Eve thought. And she imagined that in the adjacent three-car garage would be a Range Rover or two. If Eve had noticed only one thing about Aspen, it would have been the number of immaculate Range Rovers, all with custom license plates.

She parked and got out and walked to the entrance across wide flagstones. Next to the door was the security keypad. How many people knew the combination? It had been established that there had been no struggle when Allison was killed, yet the coroner's report had stated that she'd been struck repeatedly from behind. She had either known and trusted her killer so well that she'd turned her back on him or someone had used the keypad to let himself in. Allison had been awake—for whatever reason, in the living room. Her killer had sneaked up from behind. It was a possibility, however remote. Nevertheless, Frank Iverson—and Eve, as well—believed Allison had let her killer in.

A tall, nice-looking woman came to the door. She was wearing a white, sleeveless tank top that showed off an ample bosom. She also wore khaki hiking shorts, displaying very long legs. She had a perfect tan, and her medium-length brown hair was sun-streaked and swept back. She introduced herself as Marnie Wade. Eve was a little taken aback—Marnie looked more like a casually dressed houseguest than she did an employee.

"Hi," Marnie said, and she explained that Ben was just changing clothes. "He asked me to show you into the study."

"Fine," Eve said, dutifully following her past a curving staircase of pale wood, past more flagstones, past the sweeping living room.

"Ah," Eve said, "do you mind if I spend a moment in here?"

"Of course not," Marnie said, switching directions, leading Eve down a set of stone steps and onto the hardwood floor in the living room. "This is where... Well, where Allison was..."

"Murdered," Eve finished for her. "Yes," she said, "I know. I've read the reports and I've seen the police photos. Right over here, wasn't it?"

She walked past a wet bar, past two oversize white couches and several chairs, past the mammoth stone fireplace to another section of the huge room, also furnished with couches and lamps and heavy wood coffee and side tables. In the far corner was a piano. It was beneath the piano that Jack's distinctive lighter had been found—only three feet from Allison's body.

Eve stopped next to the spot where Allison had fallen, taken her last breath and bled to death from a savage beating. She'd been wearing a mauve satin negligee. It had been soaked with blood.

Eve stood there for a long moment and stared at the bare floor. There'd been a Navajo rug here. But of course it had long since been removed.

Allison must have been standing right here, right where Eve was, and the person, a right-handed person, had repeatedly struck her with a heavy two-foot-long ebony statuette, a fertility goddess from an Ivory Coast tribe. He—Eve was sure it was a man—had dropped the statue, which the police had tested for fingerprints, of course. Allison's fingerprints had been found, and Jack's and Marnie Wade's. Of course. The blows had crushed Allison's skull, and she'd died of a massive brain hemorrhage.

Right there, Allison's blue blood had left her body. Eve studied the pale wood floor and was sure she could see the faint remnants of the bloodstain.

Her eyes lifted to the huge plate-glass window, which afforded a remarkably beautiful view of Aspen Mountain. She could see the entire town below, too, almost as if she were hovering over it in an aerie. It took a lot of money to buy this view. A whole lot. And Jack had built this for the woman he loved. Every beam and window and stone. For Allison. Allison Wickwire Richards Devlin, heiress to a fortune, a true jet-setter, a darkly lovely woman who'd reportedly been somewhat flamboyant as well as headstrong.

Eve's eyes focused back on the glass. It, too, had been splashed with blood. The rug, the floor, the piano legs, the window, all splattered. Someone had smashed Allison's head five, six times, according to the coroner's report. An act of rage—of course. Most definitely an act of pure hate.

For a very long moment Eve closed her eyes, dispelling the images.

She was still thinking about Allison, thinking about Jack and Allison in this house together, when a movement in the window brought her attention back to reality. A reflected shimmer. A person...

She spun around, her thoughts racing—Allison *had* to have seen the murderer in the reflection of the glass. At night, the lights would have been on.... She had to have seen it coming.

"Ray, my husband..." Marnie Wade was saying, and Eve realized it was Ray Wade whom she'd just seen coming toward her in the window.

She caught her breath. "Eve Marchand," she said, putting out her hand, shaking his.

Ray was a big man, solid and well built with prematurely graying hair, a lot of it. He was quite attractive, a former California surfer type. He, like his wife, was dressed in tan hiking shorts and a T-shirt. The T-shirt had a slogan on it, something from a bar in the California community of Newport Beach.

They exchanged a few pleasantries, then Eve got serious. "I wonder—" she said, addressing Marnie "—the fingerprints on the African statue... The police found three identifiable sets. Allison's, Jack's and yours, Marnie. Plus a few unknown ones."

Marnie put her hands on her hips. "So? Jack bought that statue for Allison. Sure he touched it. Everyone else did, too. His prints could have been on there for years."

"You've never wiped or dusted the statue?" Eve asked.

"What are you insinuating, that I neglect my duties?" Marnie shot back. "Of course I dusted it, but that didn't get the prints off. And you know it came out in the trial that he must have worn gloves or wiped the base off after he..."

"*He?*" Eve interrupted.

"Jack Devlin," Ray said.

"Um," Eve said, then she went right on relentlessly. "And Jack's cigarette lighter. How was that overlooked, too?"

Marnie stared at Eve, speechless.

"It wasn't overlooked," Ray said angrily. "He dropped it that night."

"Very conveniently," Eve said dryly. Then she smiled at Marnie. "How did you get along with Allison?"

Marnie started to say something, but Ray cut her off. "Don't answer that," he said. "We're not on trial here. And in case Miss Marchand hasn't noticed, Devlin was convicted of the murder. We know he did it, too."

"Um," Eve said, unflustered, and that was when she noticed that Ben Richards had finally appeared at the head of the stone steps. He was fresh from showering, his dark hair, so like his mother's, combed back wetly. He was wearing a lavender polo shirt and acid-washed jeans. As he approached, Eve could smell Ralph Lauren aftershave. It struck her that although he was a few inches shorter than Jack, and although he did resemble his mother, he and Jack could still have been related. Ben's skin was smooth and fine, his mouth sensual, his nose straight and manly—but the eyes, though dark, lacked that slight Mongolian fold. He also lacked Jack's stillness.

He held Eve's hand for a moment longer than necessary, then said, "Sorry, I'm just so glad to meet you. I can't tell you how glad. I tried to talk Jack into letting me hire someone when Frank got sick, but as you must know by now, Jack wouldn't let me spend a cent. Then I heard that you were taking him on.... Well, I'm just very happy for Jack."

Eve nodded. "I'm only doing my job, Ben."

He led her into the den after explaining that he couldn't stand to be in the room where his mother was murdered. He also explained that as soon as Jack's fate was settled, he was going to place the house on the market. "It's too hard living here," he said, showing Eve into a comfortable burgundy leather chair.

"I can understand that," she said, and she went into the familiar routine of putting on her glasses and taking a legal pad and files out of her briefcase while Ben settled himself comfortably behind a handsome desk.

Eve took note of Ben's attempts at composure. He had a glib, mature manner, but his eyes gave him away; they darted and blinked. They glittered. This was a very nervous young man. Perhaps by sitting behind the desk, as opposed to the matching chair next to hers, he felt more in charge. He was an only child, though, and she'd found a certain maturity in children raised primarily around adults.

"What will you do when you sell the house, Ben?" she asked casually.

He shrugged. "I don't know. Travel, I suppose."

"What about going into the family business?"

"The textile business? I might. Someday. I thought after I took some time off I might go to law school. My girlfriend..."

"Sarah?"

"Right. Anyway, Sarah and I both thought we'd go through law school together."

"Well," Eve said with a wry smile, "I'd stay away from public defense. It's pretty grueling."

"I've heard that," Ben replied.

They talked about Jack and what a rotten deal Ben thought he was getting. "You know, there's no way Jack did it."

"Um," Eve said. "Tell me why you think that, Ben."

"My God, he loved Mom. Sure they had their differences, but..."

"Differences?"

"Well, yes. Mom really wanted Jack to be free to travel, that sort of stuff. But Jack was always busy. Like *always*. He was really becoming one of the most sought-after architects in the valley. I mean, everyone said so. Anyway, Mom was really sticking it to him, trying to force him to slow down."

"You sound as if you took Jack's side."

"Oh, I did. I really did. When Mom filed for divorce, I was shocked. She wanted Jack to live off her. She really had a control thing going, and she used her money as a lever."

Eve studied him. "How did you and your mom get along?"

"Fine. Oh, she kind of tried to control me, too, but I was away at school most of the time. Couldn't get me there," he said with a dry smile.

"You lived with your father, didn't you, during your teens?"

"My real dad, yeah. But I was over here a lot. Jack and I used to do all sorts of stuff together. Back then Jack wasn't as much in demand, you know, just getting started in his career, and we really saw a lot of each other."

"Skiing? Camping?"

"Sure, all that."

"Then I guess your real father must have been very busy."

"Always is."

"But why would you have gone to live with him, then?"

Ben sighed. "I don't know. Mom was away a lot before she and Jack built this house. And Dad's usually here in town. Mom didn't want me out of school so much, you know, traveling with her."

"Uh-huh," Eve said, knowing full well there was more to that story. At least, Frank Iverson's investigators had found out that Ben and his mother had been at each other's throats since he'd entered his teenage years. And they had always fought over money, apparently right until Allison died.

Now, with Jack's conviction, Ben had the house, Allison's trust fund and the Wickwire family trust, of which he received monthly sums. *Plenty of motive for murder*, Eve thought. On the other hand, all kids fought with their parents about money. Not to mention that Ben had some income in his own right and would have inherited Allison's someday, anyway.

She glanced up from her notes and made the decision to ask him about the night of Allison's murder.

"Ben," she said, "I want to get something straight for my files. You testified that you were in Denver the night your mother died."

He nodded.

"You were sick?"

"As they say, I was sort of living in the bathroom. The flu."

"Right. And Sarah visited you?"

"Yeah. We were supposed to go to the movies."

"Uh-huh. And I have the times all written down here. Let's see." Eve tapped her pencil on a piece of paper from her files. "Here it is. Sarah came over at six-forty-five. The movie was at seven. But you were sick.... Then she called to check on you around 10:00 p.m."

"No," Ben said. "I called Sarah."

"Oh," Eve said. Of course she already knew that. Frank Iverson had checked the phone records. "Why did you call her?"

"I think I'd promised to. You know, before I went to bed. She was worried about the fever I was running. There was a lot of the flu around school that spring, and a couple of students had even been hospitalized. Dehydration, or something."

"Um. So you called Sarah around ten and then went to bed?"

"Something like that."

"And then early the next morning, Jack arrived in Denver to tell you about your mother?"

Ben looked solemn. "Yes. I don't know what time. Sarah was there, though. I remember she came about seven or eight. But as far as when Jack got there...I really don't remember much."

"It must have been a terrible shock."

Ben let out a long breath. "Yeah, it was. Half the time I still can't believe it."

Eve gave him a moment. "Ben," she said then, "who would have done such a terrible thing? You must have thought about it a lot."

He shook his head. "I don't know. It couldn't have been a burglar, because there was nothing stolen. And Mom just didn't have enemies. I mean, she did all this charity work and everything."

"What about George Mochlin? Her...friend," Eve said carefully.

"That creep? What an ass he is. A real fortune hunter. And I've wondered about him, believe me. I've really given it thought. Trouble is, what did he gain if he did it?"

"Maybe nothing," Eve said. "Maybe he came up here and somehow they got into an argument. As they say, a crime of passion."

"I don't know," Ben said. "I guess that could have happened. Mom could be pretty tough when she wanted. Maybe they did argue. But how is anyone ever going to prove it?"

"Well," Eve said, "we're working on a lot of angles."

"Probably me, too," he stated levelly. "Oh, I know I was a suspect."

"Did that upset you, Ben?"

"Of course. I mean, Mom and I fought sometimes, but, my God, to...murder her?"

"It's been hard, I'm sure," Eve allowed.

"Harder than anyone knows," Ben said.

Eve gave him another moment while she flipped to a fresh piece of paper on her pad. She looked up. "Tell me," she said, "how did your mother get along with the live-in couple, the Wades?"

"Fine, I guess. I was away at school, which you know, so I really can't say for sure. They hadn't been here all that long before Mom...died."

"So as far as you know, there were no disagreements, no reprimands?"

Ben shook his head. "Mom was always a slave driver when it came to the help, but they either toed the line or she canned them. I assume the Wades must have been okay."

"Are they okay for you?"

"Sure. Fine. I'm easy."

"No problems at all?"

Ben bit a lower lip, thinking. "Not really. Marnie's kind of opinionated, sarcastic sometimes."

"And Ray?"

"You never know. He's quieter."

"And nothing's ever been missing from this house since their employment?"

"Not that I'm aware of."

They talked then about the procedures of the penalty phase of Jack's trial. Like most laymen, Ben hadn't realized that although she'd have limited arguments to present before the panel of judges, she was already conducting a full-blown investigation.

"The minute Jack is given his sentence," Eve said, "we begin the appeal process. Our goal is to generate a new trial, and that's going to require new evidence for Jack's defense."

"Look," Ben said, meeting her gaze steadfastly, "I'd like to help pay for some of this. Whatever it takes. I offered to help Jack, but he wouldn't hear of it."

"I can imagine." Eve laughed. "But the most important thing you can do for Jack is testify before the judges."

Ben nodded.

"You're our star character witness."

Again, he nodded. "I'll be there for Jack."

"Good."

"Will he be testifying, too?"

"Oh, yes. He's going to have to come out of that shell and plead for his life with the judges. You bet."

"Poor Jack."

"How's that?"

"Well, you know, he's got that tough, macho thing."

"I'm afraid I don't..."

"I don't know exactly how to explain it. It comes from his background, I guess. He was brought up real strict. He keeps everything close, that's for sure."

"I've noticed that," Eve said. "But we're going to get him to drop his guard for this trial. We have to. If he doesn't..."

"They'll give him the death penalty," Ben stated grimly.

Eve nodded silently.

She left the house soon afterward, promising to help Ben prepare for his testimony. She drove down the steeply curving road back into the heart of Aspen with her mind churning. So much work to be done, so little time. And thus far she still hadn't found that lure to drag for the press.

It was three minutes past 7:00 p.m. when she finally put her key in the lock and opened her door. She walked in, tossed her briefcase on a chair, kicked off her shoes. And that's when she saw Gary. He was sitting by the window, very still, his eyes on her.

"Oh, God," she gasped, startled, her hand flying to her heart.

"Noon," Gary said. "I told you I'd be here by *noon*."

"It's Saturday. Oh, Lord, it *is* Saturday. Gary... I'm so, so sorry." And then she noticed there was something in his hand. It was one of the police photos from the evidence files. It had been lying on the coffee table.

Gary followed her stare, then held the photo up for her to see. It was a picture of Jack, an eight-by-eleven black and white glossy. For a long moment Gary just held it toward her, then finally he turned it around and eyed it again. "Nice-looking guy, isn't he," he said evenly.

Marnie Wade stood at the kitchen sink and hugged herself, fighting back tears. "That goddamn Marchand. That bitch," she choked out. "She's going to dig and dig and find out that we got fired by Brooke Goldsmith."

"No, she's not," Ray said from the other side of the butcher block island. "If Frank Iverson didn't find out, this Eve Marchand won't, either."

"But what if she does? What if Brooke tells her we got fired?"

"So what?"

Marnie spun around to face her husband. "I'll tell you *what*. She might think we got fired because we really *did* steal Brooke's ring. Then she'll think we stole something from Allison and that *she* was going to fire us, too. You know how those people think, Ray!"

"We didn't steal anything," Ray said. "Brooke Goldsmith just wanted an excuse."

"But it looks bad for us if they find out. And that fight I had with Allison, what if someone knows? What if she told someone?"

"Stop worrying. It's no big deal. So Allison found out we'd been fired and confronted you. You had a spat. Big deal. We didn't steal that damn ring from Brooke and we didn't steal anything from Allison, either. She was just looking for trouble."

"But they might find out and think it's a motive," Marnie wailed.

"For murder? Get off it, Marnie."

But she couldn't stop. There were things even Ray didn't know about. Such as Brooke's diamond ring and who really took it. And there'd been more than one argument with Allison when she'd found out they'd lied on their application about being fired by Brooke. In fact, that bitch Allison had really reamed Marnie good one day when Ray had gone into town on errands. It had been an awful fight, and Allison had said she was going to start looking for new live-ins.

Marnie began to run water in the sink. Her fingers were shaking. What if Ray found out she'd taken Brooke's ring? What if that lawyer lady found out? What if someone knew about that terrible argument between her and Allison? But even worse than that, the fight had been the very same morning that Allison was killed. If anyone ever found out...

NINE

Sunday morning was lazy at the Pitkin County Jail. Men slept late, the Sunday papers were perused, cells were tidied up for the visitors who'd arrive later.

One of the prisoners was already hard at work on his one-thousand-piece jigsaw puzzle—he completed one every few days.

Jack sipped his coffee and read the *Denver Post*. There was an interesting section on a revolutionary style of design an architect from Brazil was using. Jack was already conjuring up plans when he heard the buzz of the door and looked up to see Eve entering the common room.

She couldn't have looked less like a defense lawyer. Her hair was loose, a floating golden cloud of curls, and she wore a gauzy summer print dress with a linen blazer over it. No glasses. Every eye in the place was on her.

She made her way past the jailer who sat behind a desk in the common area, lifted her hand in greeting to a couple of the inmates and stood before Jack.

"Hi," she said, as if visiting on a Sunday morning was normal behavior for an attorney.

"Hello." He cocked his head. "Anything come up?"

"Nothing new. I just have questions about a couple of things."

"On Sunday morning?" She was like a breath of fresh air

in the stuffy jail, a sunset-pinkened cloud, a warm golden beam of sunlight...

"Is there anything you need?" she was asking.

He shook his head.

"You know, you could get some of your meals sent in from restaurants in town if you wanted. I heard that Indonesian princess got her meals catered by the best restaurants the whole time she was here."

Jack laughed. "You're kidding."

"No."

"I'll consider it. I don't think I can afford it, though."

She sat down on the couch across from him. "Am I interrupting something?" She indicated the Sunday paper.

"Nothing that can't wait." He studied her. "Don't you ever take a day off?"

"No, do you?" she shot back.

He smiled wryly, conceding the point. "Some of us have fewer choices than others."

"Uh-huh. Well, I guess I've made my choices, haven't I?"

"I guess you have. The question is why?"

"It has no relevance to your case, Jack."

"Right," he said, but he saw her duck her head and fiddle with something in her briefcase. He'd never considered himself a great judge of character, but there was something Eve Marchand wasn't telling him, and Jack suspected it had everything to do with his case.

Eve finally glanced up. "I spoke to your stepson, Ben. He's quite a self-possessed young man."

"Not really. It's just his Wickwire training."

"Um, I guess you'd know a false facade if anyone would."

"What's *that* supposed to mean?"

"It means that you're a master of disguise yourself."

He leaned forward. "Look, *counselor*, I'm in jail. I'm dealing with it the best goddamn way I can. I don't need psychoanalyzing."

Eve waved a hand. "Sorry, let's not flay a dead horse,

okay?" She thought a second. "Oh, yes, I wanted to ask you about Ben's girlfriend, Sarah. Is she a dependable alibi?"

"Sarah's a smart girl. Yes, if she said Ben was in Denver, believe me, he was."

"I'm sending an investigator to Long Beach to talk to her."

"Good God, hasn't she been questioned enough?"

"Not when your life's at stake."

It always hit him with a painful thud—*his* life at stake—and Eve seemed to bring it up as often as she could. He guessed that was her job. Or was it the female thing again?

"I spoke to Mochlin, too. Good-looking son of a gun, isn't he?"

"Do you have to rub it in?" he asked mildly.

"You're not a bad specimen yourself. Allison had great taste."

"You're approaching tackiness, Miss Marchand."

She smiled. "I guess I am. I apologize." She didn't sound the least bit sorry.

"I'm having trouble with Mochlin's motive," she went on. "He seems too selfish for the crime-of-passion scenario. I wondered if you had any thoughts on that."

"I agree with you. So did the police. No motive."

"Opportunity, but no motive," Eve mused, "unless, of course, we only have part of the story."

Jack quirked a dark brow.

"Maybe everything between Allison and Mochlin wasn't hunky-dory. She could have heard he was bragging about marrying her and how rich she was. She might have confronted him, argued. You get the picture?"

Jack hung his head and expelled a slow, whistling breath. "Yeah, I suppose anything's possible."

"Aside from that," Eve went on doggedly, "tell me about Ray and Marnie Wade, the live-ins."

He looked up.

"Well?" she said.

And then he told her about Brooke Goldsmith coming to

see him a little while ago and telling him about her ring disappearing when the Wades worked for her. "But," Jack added, "Brooke admitted she was drunk and could have lost the ring herself. I don't think you can put too much stock in anything she says."

"I'll keep that in mind," Eve said, taking notes. "I just find some of the evidence against you a little too convenient, like the lighter."

Jack shrugged. "Maybe."

Eve scribbled a few more notes on her legal pad, unconsciously tucking hair behind an ear, tapping the pencil on her knee. He studied her. She *was* beautiful. Or was it just that he was starved for the sight, the sound, the scent of a female? But no, not any female would do. It was this sweet-looking, tough-as-nails public defender. And today she was all dressed up to go out. Where?

"You're going somewhere," he said, indicating her dress.

"Yes," she said, "I am."

He wanted to ask where. He sure wanted to know with whom. But he'd never pry. And, besides, Eve would never let him.

She busied herself pulling notes out of a file in her briefcase, pushing her glasses up on her nose when she leaned over. He couldn't help noticing that her curling hair parted in the back, baring the nape of her neck, and that beneath the gauzy print dress she was wearing one of those camisole things, off-white. Her breasts were enticing beneath the soft material, and her skin was white. He knew there'd be no tan line. She'd be pure, milky white from the hollow at the base of her throat all the way down—her breasts, her belly…

"Ah, here it is," she said, opening a file to a particular yellow page.

"A concert?" Jack said.

"What?"

He'd been musing aloud. Caught, he had to reply. "Oh, I was just thinking you're probably going to the concert today."

Eve looked at him for a moment, then nodded. "That's right," she said. "A friend and I are going to *Carmina Burana*."

"Hmm," he said. "That's something I miss."

She lifted a brow.

"Concerts. With friends."

"Oh, of course." She bent her head to find her place on a page.

A friend, Jack thought. Male? He couldn't imagine Eve without a man. Without dozens of men groveling at her feet. Oh, sure, she'd intimidate many of the male persuasion, but not him. Eve's beauty and intelligence and passion were magnets to him. *A friend,* he thought again.

"Okay," she was saying, "back to Ben. When I interviewed him yesterday afternoon he seemed a little...tense. Could he be on anything?"

Jack cocked his head a little and met her gaze squarely. "Are you asking if Ben's on drugs?"

"Yes."

Jack shook his head. "I seriously doubt it. He dabbled in them in college, but not anymore."

"I hope you're right," Eve said, "because he's our star character witness, and I'd like to believe he'll come off as a real straight arrow in front of the judges. I know he visits you here a lot. I'd like you to talk to him."

"Are you asking me to tell him to show up in court straight?"

"Yes, I am. He looks up to you. He'll listen."

"Screw it," Jack said.

"I understand your reluctance. Just think about it. It would help. Okay?"

But Jack didn't answer her.

Eve ignored him and took off her glasses, put her notes away. "Okay," she said. "That's it for today." She hesitated, then seemed to decide something. "I drove around to look at some of your houses, Jack. They're beautiful," she said.

"Thanks."

"I mean it. They're very special."

He shrugged. "It was my job."

"Oh, I think it was a bit more than that."

He looked at her from under his eyebrows. "Like your career, right? More than a job."

"Maybe so." She stood. "Goodbye for now. We'll talk again soon."

"Uh-huh. Enjoy the concert," he said, his voice utterly without inflection.

He tormented himself all morning nevertheless, dwelling on her, wondering, guessing, remembering every gesture, every expression, every word. He was ashamed to admit the truth to himself, but he had to—he spoke it in his head in silent words and rolled them around in his brain, worried them the way a dog worried a bone: he was attracted to Eve Marchand. He, a prisoner, a man headed for Super Max in Canon City, either for life imprisonment or death by lethal injection, a penniless, prison-pale guy in an orange suit, he had a thing for his lawyer. As if she saw him as anything more than another crusade. There had been lots like him before, and there'd be plenty more after him. He wondered if they all fell for their pretty lady lawyer. God, what a moron he was!

He couldn't stop wondering, though. Who was she really? What made her want to spend Sunday mornings in a jail instead of in bed with her boyfriend? What made her tick?

And most important of all, the question that reduced him to impotent, furious jealousy—who was this "friend"?

It surprised Eve that even in Aspen everyone recognized Gary. People knew him from his Bronco days, and they knew him from the media coverage of his disease, of his dealing with it with courage and humor. He had brought MS to everyone's attention, clearing up misconceptions, patiently answering questions on television programs, granting interviews when he was really too fatigued to do so.

The arm crutches and the cane Gary hated were like badges of honor, medals of valor, symbols of his battle, his survival, his victory.

It seemed to Eve that everyone, men, women and children, all felt they owned a part of Gary Kapochek, that they were in some strange way intimately connected to him. And yet he was whole and unflustered by the public's emotional possessiveness. She was terribly proud of him wherever they went, perfectly content to recede into the background, to accompany him undetected by his admirers.

Their waitress at the Sardy House, where they had brunch, was so nervous about waiting on the legend himself that she giggled every time she poured coffee. A man at the next table in the restored Victorian dining room recognized Gary, and despite his wife's admonitions, he leaned across and asked Gary about the new rookie they'd gotten from Florida State.

"Is he big enough?" the man asked. "Can he tackle?"

Gary replied, gracious as always, and left the man a die-hard Broncos fan.

At the T-shirt shop where they bought mementos for friends, the saleslady recognized him, and on the tree-shaded, brick-paved mall where they sat on a bench to people-watch, a young man approached him, apologizing profusely, wanting to know if their quarterback was indeed going to retire, as rumor had it.

An elderly lady came up to them in a jewelry store and said that her sister had MS and had been inspired by Gary's attitude. She'd started an exercise program and was feeling much better.

"That's great," Gary said, smiling, his dimple deepening. "Tell her never to give up."

"I will. Oh, I sure will," the lady said. "Thank you so much."

Eve shook her head and gave a rueful laugh. "It's kind of scary how they all adore you. Lord, you'll get a swelled head. You'll be unbearable."

"No, I won't," he said. "You're just jealous."

"Me, jealous?"

"Yeah, you. You wish they'd all recognize you, baby."

"God forbid," she breathed, but she grinned and took his hand and squeezed it.

It was a beautiful day, and they had all of it to spend together. There were tickets for the afternoon concert at the Aspen Music Festival's famous tent to see Carl Orff's *Carmina Burana*, a powerful masterpiece Eve was looking forward to. And reservations for dinner at Piñons, a five-star Southwest-style restaurant that had a fantastic reputation.

What a day.

The Silver Queen gondola ran endlessly on its cable, taking people up to the top of Aspen Mountain for nature walks or a free concert or lunch at the Sundeck restaurant or just to look at the spectacular view.

Eve and Gary considered going up in the gondola, but ended up eating huge chocolate-chip cookies, sitting in the mall, too lazy to even walk the block to the gondola station.

"We should do it," Eve said wistfully. "Who knows when we'll get another chance?"

"You'll be here all summer," Gary said. "We'll have plenty of opportunities."

"Um." She flicked a crumb from her lip with her tongue.

"You have chocolate on your chin," Gary said.

She wiped at it. "These cookies are *so* good."

"Don't spoil your appetite, baby."

They walked back to the Christmas Inn before the concert. Eve could see the signs that Gary was tired, and she told him to take a nap. Power naps, he called them.

"I'll do some work," she said. "Go on, get some rest."

Gary kissed her and retired to the bedroom while Eve put on her glasses, pulled out her notes and began making lists.

George Mochlin—motive?

Melinda Hearst—reliable alibi?

Ray and Marnie Wade—thieves?

David Webster—job advancement?

Then the enemies' list, contractors who'd sued Jack. But Eve didn't like any of them as suspects. She wrote down Ben's real father's name, too, though Allison's ex-husband had absolutely no obvious motive for murder. Still, you never discounted the ex. Hank had an appointment with him, so she'd know more soon. Underneath her list of names she wrote: *statue—fingerprints*. Then *lighter*. The gold lighter with Jack's initials on it, the one Allison had given him when they'd started dating. Jack had told Eve right up front that he'd smoked then but had given it up years ago, only keeping the lighter because Allison had given it to him.

How had the lighter gotten to the crime scene? Eve felt that Iverson hadn't pursued that line of inquiry hard enough. Jack thought he'd lost it some months before the murder, but he wasn't sure. If it hadn't fallen out of Jack's pocket while he murdered Allison, as District Attorney Bill Makelky had so successfully insinuated, then how had it gotten there, three feet from Allison's body, on the priceless Navajo rug next to the piano leg?

Assuming Jack was innocent, Eve had no choice but to conclude that the murderer had deliberately placed it there to incriminate Jack.

She sat at the Formica table in the living room of her suite, took off her glasses and thought about Jack. She still hadn't deciphered him at all. He was an unfailing gentleman, polite, usually even-tempered. She knew there had to be a volcano seething beneath his impassive surface—she'd seen rare sparks of it—and she was more curious about him than she liked to admit. She was going to have to probe a lot more into Jack's psyche, too, to find out what was there. It was part of her job, because she couldn't defend a man she didn't know.

Outside an open window, birds sang in the warm afternoon, and a breeze flowed in, lifting strands of her hair, tickling. It was never too hot in Aspen because of its altitude. Not like Denver, where summers could be hellish. Here, it was eighty degrees, with a blue sky and a mild breeze. Lovely.

A concert, dinner, Gary...

Jack Devlin.

What did she really know about the man? He'd been a successful architect, he'd married, according to his own admission, far above him. "Allison was slumming that year," he'd told her dryly. No, it hadn't bothered him or Allison, but it had sure mattered to her family. Except for Ben.

What else did she know about him?

He'd worked his way through school, was very bright, sexy as hell, had everything going for him. But his wife had wanted a divorce, took a lover, was murdered. Something in the Devlin story wasn't as perfect as it appeared. Was it his fault? Did Jack have a tragic character flaw of some sort?

She'd have to dig. She'd done a fair job of it today, little feints, nothing serious, but perhaps she and Jack were approaching a kind of understanding. He didn't like it. He'd snapped at her once or twice already. That was okay, though. Maybe it was healthy for Jack to unload some emotion for a change.

Eve put her chin on her hand and stared unfocused out the window.

Was all this merely rationalizing? Maybe what she truly wanted was to get under Jack's skin, to make him react to *her.*

Damn. She'd never had to ask herself these questions before. Her clients had all been human beings, but easily understandable, and she'd approached them with unfailing objectivity, doing her very best within the law to defend them. But Jack Devlin was different from any of them, and she wanted to know what he thought about her. Not only as a defense lawyer but as a person. As a woman.

She thought of the various sides of Jack she'd seen—the architect who'd created that soaring vision in stone and glass for his wife, the prisoner, the man in the police interviews, in Frank Iverson's notes, in the court depositions, the man who answered her questions patiently—but they didn't make a whole. She couldn't grasp the essence of the man, and it irritated her, challenged her, made her so damn curious.

And jealous in a perverse way, because surely Allison had known that essence and Eve didn't.

There was one thing about Jack that Eve knew with certainty, however, and that was the fact that he was innocent of his wife's murder. And she would never again allow an innocent man to be put to death.

"Problem?"

Eve glanced up at the sound of Gary's voice, jarred out of her musing. "No, um, it's nothing."

"You looked like you were up against a stone wall," he said.

"Only a legal one," she replied.

"We'd better get ready. The traffic will be pretty heavy going to the music tent, and I want to get good seats."

"Five minutes," she said, getting up, going to him, running her fingers over his bare chest. "Just give me five minutes."

The concert was wonderful, the huge tent packed for the event. Eve was aware of people nudging each other, staring at Gary. At the intermission, when most concertgoers went out onto the tree-shaded patio in front of the tent to gossip and remark on the day's music or buy cookies and lemonade at the stand, they remained inside. Gary disliked being jostled in crowds because he could lose his balance.

They sat and talked in the muted light that came through the multipeaked canvas roof, and the shadow of a magpie perched on a high support showed through; its coarse voice could be heard above the mutter of the crowd. Gary pointed up and laughed.

"Not too many places birds compete with the orchestra," Eve said, fanning herself with the program.

The concert was over at six, and there were two hours before their dinner reservations.

"Tired?" Eve asked, hating to keep reminding Gary of his illness but nonetheless wary of letting him push too hard and relapse.

"No, I'm fine. Let's do something on the spur of the moment."

They decided to drive the fifteen miles up the Castle Creek Valley right outside of Aspen to the restored mining town of Ashcroft. It was a breathtaking drive, the roads winding up between steep slopes. In some places the mountainsides were smooth and verdant, but in others huge swathes of fallen trees, rock and dirt swept from the heights down to the road.

"Avalanches," Gary said.

"Avalanches," she repeated, trying to picture the force that had stripped the mountain bare.

Ashcroft itself was a small settlement, once a roaring silver-mining camp. Its false-front buildings were being restored, and they huddled in a broad green meadow surrounded by peaks, some still crowned with snow this early in the summer. Tourists wandered among the buildings; the air was still and cool and clear, the river, narrow here, rushing between its banks, carrying snowmelt down the valley to eventually join the mighty Colorado River.

"My God, this is wonderful," Eve said, looking around.

"That was the whorehouse," Gary said, pointing with his cane.

"How do you know?"

"A man knows things like that."

"Oh, sure." She laughed.

"Happy?" he asked.

"Totally."

"You need to do this kind of thing more, Eve."

"I know."

"You're a different person."

She looked down. "No, I'm not."

"Okay, you're in a different mood." He took her hand.

"Thanks for letting me do this case," Eve said quietly.

"As if I could stop you."

"And thanks for yesterday, for not getting mad at me for being so darn late."

"Maybe I am mad but hiding it."

"I love you," she said.

They kissed, oblivious to the tourists, to the kids giggling at them, then they walked back slowly, hand in hand, to the car, and Eve felt at peace, relaxed and at peace, for the first time in ages.

Piñons restaurant was upstairs in a building in downtown Aspen. Its decor was understated Southwest elegance, its menu mouthwatering and original. *Ahi* sautéed in crushed macadamia nuts, game prepared in special sauces, blackened roast pork with apples and Calvados, rack of spring lamb, home-baked bread, an extensive wine list. And appetizers.

"Pheasant quesadillos?" Gary queried.

"Portobello mushroom salad," Eve suggested.

"Both," he said.

"The prices are awfully high," she said hesitantly.

"Don't worry, I don't have to live on a public defender's salary," Gary said smugly.

"Meanie."

"Yeah, sometimes it's fun."

The meal was fantastic, the service impeccable. They held hands across the table and sipped the last of their wine.

"Thank you," Eve said quietly.

"You're welcome. Anytime. How often have I begged you to go out at home? But you're always..."

"Too busy," Eve finished. "I know."

"My case rests."

"That's my line, honey."

The night air was chilly as they walked back to the motel. The stars were so clear, the moon full—huge and silver. From the mountainside a coyote yipped, was answered, then there was a medley of yips and sudden silence.

"It's so beautiful." Eve sighed.

"So are you."

"You're buttering me up."

"Sure am." Gary laughed softly to himself.

They undressed slowly, languidly. Gary propped his cane on the night table and held his arms out to Eve.

They kissed slowly, deeply. He pushed her hair back from her face and kissed her chin, her earlobe, the place where her pulse beat in her neck.

"I hope we can do this a lot," he whispered.

"We will," she replied, stroking his smooth, hard back.

"Promise?"

"Mmm," she said.

He pushed her onto the bed and lay above her on one elbow, tracing lines on her belly with a finger. "I hope, Eve, I really hope you won't get crazy with this Devlin thing."

"I know," she whispered. "I'll try not to.... It's so strange, this whole case. It's not like any I've ever done before. I told you, I'm positive Jack's innocent, not that he said so, but I know, and it's..."

"Will you shut up?" Gary said pleasantly.

"Sorry."

He leaned down and kissed her, and she loved the way his body felt on hers, so familiar and beloved. She held his head and kissed him back.

"That's better," he whispered.

"You'd like him, Gary," she said, looking up into her lover's eyes. "I wish you could meet him. Maybe you can, someday. He's different."

She felt Gary stiffen and wished the words had never left her lips. He rolled off her, and she felt the sudden cold where his body had warmed her.

"Jesus Christ, Eve," he said harshly, turning his back to her.

"I'm sorry," she whispered. "I didn't mean to. It's just... I'm sorry. Gary, come here, please." She put a hand on his shoulder.

He shrugged it off and punched his pillow with a fist.

"Gary?" she tried.

"I'm sorry, Eve, but tonight I have a real bad headache" was all he said.

Hank Thurgood arrived at John Richards's office exactly on time Monday morning. He was shown in by a secretary, and he took in every detail of the place, the plain, spare building, the World Cup posters on the wall, the blandness of the decor.

John Richards wasn't bland, though. He rose from behind his desk and pumped Hank's hand. A heavyset man, not fat, but broad and good looking in a blunt, masculine way. Hank figured he'd seem sexy to women. And he was a people person, all smiles and superficial warmth. Dark haired, dark eyes, like Jack Devlin.

"Good morning, Mr. Thurgood," Richards said. "Great day, isn't it? But I can't wait till the end of summer. Closer to the ski season, you know."

"Really," Hank said, blinking. Skiing was a bizarre suicidal impulse to him, and he couldn't imagine why anyone would look forward to it.

"Sit down," Richards said. "Ask away. I've got a meeting at ten, but no problem. There's plenty of time."

Hank was getting vibes from the man—impatience beneath the friendliness. "Well, Mr. Richards," he began, "as you know, we're preparing for the penalty phase of Jack Devlin's trial, and we're talking to everyone again. I know the police pestered you, and so did Iverson's investigators, but a man's life is at stake here, so we have to look at everything."

"Sure, I understand."

"So you were divorced from Allison Wickwire Devlin when?"

"Let's see, it must have been fifteen years ago."

"An amicable divorce?"

Richards grinned. "Not really. I'd had an affair. So had

Allison. We hated each other's guts by then. The usual thing."

"I see. Now, did you get anything in the way of a financial settlement from her in the divorce?"

"Not a red cent," he said, and his face tightened. "And I should have, considering what I put up with."

"Did you ask for money from her?"

"Jesus, what a question. No. The only thing in the divorce papers was that she'd pay for Ben's education. She could afford it, too, let me tell you."

"And Allison got custody of your son?"

"Yes, but he did live with me for a while. You know. He was a handful in high school. Teenage problems."

"I understand he was close to Jack Devlin."

"They got along okay, I guess."

"What did you think of Devlin?"

Richards shrugged heavy shoulders. "I felt sorry for the guy. I knew what he'd have to put up with. That is, until he killed her. Now I don't feel too sorry for him. Although—" Richards leaned forward "—I can almost understand him doing it. She could drive you crazy."

"So you're convinced Devlin did it."

"Sure, aren't you?"

Hank let that one pass. "You were in Las Vegas when the murder took place."

"I was. You've probably seen my alibi."

"We have. Sometimes, though, a person can take out a contract, and they don't have to be there in person, so we have to follow up every possibility." He waited for Richards's reaction.

The man laughed. Genuinely and loudly. "Me? Put a contract out on Allison? Good God, man, we'd been divorced twelve years. If I'd wanted to kill her, I'd have done it back when I found her in bed with the gardener!"

"Mmm-hmm," Hank said. "Well, thanks, Mr. Richards."

"So, am I a suspect?" Richards asked a little belligerently.

"Oh, I can't say. I'm only an investigator. Just a lowly employee."

"Yeah, right," Richards said.

TEN

Time had become an arduous journey to Jack, with Eve's visits green oases of exquisite relief.

The weeks of August dragged by, and he found himself continually aching for the sight of her at the security door to the common room. Nonetheless, a part of him dreaded the interviews. She was merciless in her efforts to get him to open up to her. As a boy, growing up in a strict family, and as a man, he'd learned to keep his feelings close. Even in his marriage to Allison, he'd kept a part of himself private. Now he wondered if his reluctance to bare his soul to his wife had been due to the disapproval of her highbrow family. Of course, he only wondered that because Eve had planted the seeds of speculation in his head, endlessly digging, probing, driving him crazy.

How many times had he asked her: "Why do you need to know this stuff?"

And how many times had she given him the same reply? "This is the way I work. I'm looking for an angle, *any* angle, to use in front of the judges. Now help me, Jack."

He tried. He really did. But it was damn hard.

He thought an awful lot about Eve's so-called "need to know everything." Was it only a search for that angle she wanted? Or was she curious about him? Yeah, he thought continuously about Eve and her endless questions, and he let himself fantasize that hers was an uncommon curiosity.

It was on one of her visits toward the end of August when he finally sat back on the couch, put his hands behind his head and spoke a little about his youth.

"I dropped out of high school when I was sixteen," he said.

"Why?" Her usual question.

Jack shrugged. "I was bored in school. Getting in trouble on a daily basis with this group of guys I hung out with."

"A gang?"

"Not a real gang, no, but we had the markings of one."

"You weren't getting along at home?"

"I've always gotten along with my mother. But my father... He's a tough son of a gun. I think he feels the world dealt him a rotten hand. His folks were pretty poor. His dad, my grandfather, was a minister at a small congregational church on Maui—he'd moved to the islands from Ohio, and I think he thought he was still converting the natives," Jack said with a half smile.

"Go on," Eve urged, her hazel eyes fixed on him.

"Not much to tell, really. Because my grandparents were poor, my father went to work quite young. Fourteen, fifteen or so. He spent his youth moving from crummy job to crummy job, mostly in the tourist industry on Maui. You know, kitchen help to hotel laundries. He wound up a maintenance man. Still is."

"And you dropped out of school, too."

"Like father, like son."

"But you ended up finishing, then went on to college."

"Yeah." Jack nodded, remembering. "It was rough. I always worked at least two jobs. And, hell, I never had my own place till I was twenty-six, maybe older."

"You had a trade, though, architecture. How did you decide on that?"

"It picked me. I was one of those kids who could always do cartoons, you know, on my notebooks. I guess I've got a knack for drawing. I began in graphic design and moved into architectural design from there."

"Iverson had in his notes that you had a rough time of it."

"I worked hard," Jack said. "I started on the bottom rung of the ladder."

"You must have gotten a break, though."

"I did. I was working as an apprentice in a firm in Honolulu. One of the architects was in the middle of a major project on Maui, a beautiful home overlooking the Pacific. Anyway, he got offered a job designing one of the huge new hotels, and he spoke to the clients with the project on Maui, recommended I finish the design for them. And the rest, as they say, is history."

"Is that about the time you met Allison?"

Jack let out a sigh. "Yes."

"Tell me about it."

"Eve, look," he said, "this is all irrelevant."

"No, it's not. Humor me."

"All right," he said. "All right. That was when I met Allison. The owner of the house on Maui threw a housewarming party. Allison knew him from Aspen and was invited. We met on the veranda."

Jack studied Eve's face. She'd stopped taking notes and the pencil was poised above the ubiquitous yellow pad. She appeared to be lost in thought, staring nowhere in particular over his shoulder. He could imagine what she was thinking, but he knew the image in her head couldn't begin to approach the sensuousness of that hot evening. The sweeping veranda overlooking the waves crashing on rocks below. The bite of salt and the caress of warm, damp air filled with the scents of tropical blooms spilling over the stone balustrade and overflowing from huge pots. The blaze of colors splashing across a dusky sky. The light, that golden hue that glittered just before the sun plunged into the tropical sea. Allison. The hot, damp offshore breeze lifting her dark hair off sun-browned shoulders. Her dress was long, strapless, a shimmery moss green.

And Jack. He'd been in a white dinner jacket and black trousers. Rented, of course. He'd been so young then, so full of youth and uncomplicated happiness. He'd been self-conscious, too—his first tux, his first major project, his first formal party. He could picture himself as he'd looked that evening—jet-black hair too long in those days. Smooth-skinned, a year-round tan and that hint of Oriental in the cheekbones and eyes.

Allison had told him later that she'd thought he was Buddha in formal clothes, spiritual, ascetic, removed. He'd laughed at her and kissed her.

But the party had been great. Everyone, all those rich, rich people, being nice to him, as if he were one of them.

And Allison Richards.

They'd both been milling with the guests, sipping champagne. Jack on a real high from all the compliments on his design. And Allison had been vacationing, the ink on her divorce not quite dry. It was April. Off-season in Aspen, so she and a friend had decided to take a vacation. Ben was living with his father.

Jack and Allison had made eye contact across the sweeping, blue-slate veranda, approached each other gradually, deliberately, and met among palm fronds and torchlight. If it hadn't been love at first sight, it had certainly been lust.

"Romantic," Eve said, breaking into his memories.

"Maybe," he allowed. "At the time I just felt...lucky." He paused. "I guess what I really turned out to be was naive."

"Are you bitter?"

"No." He met her gaze. "I must sound dumb as hell."

She shook her head. "Not at all. I can see why Allison was attracted to you. You must have been very different from what she was used to."

"Amen to that."

Eve never seemed to relent when it came to questions about his marriage. She wanted the graphic details—the good points and the bad. That was the hardest part for Jack. Talking about Allison hurt. It brought back all the pain of the separation, of Allison's betrayal, too many memories, and he was continually dragged under by anger and frustration over being stuck in this jail, unable to do a goddamn thing about her murder.

And on one of Eve's visits, early in September when the buck brush and aspens were turning red and gold on the mountainsides, Jack told her about his rage.

"I'm stuck in here," he said, "and someone's out there walking around scot-free. The longer I'm in here, the less chance there is anyone's going to find out who really killed Allison. It's driving me nuts," he admitted. "Sometimes I feel as if my guts are tearing apart. Stir-crazy. Now I know what it means."

"I know, and we'll find the murderer, I swear we will, but first there's the penalty phase," she said, and he thought she was going to reach over and touch his arm, but she hesitated, then scribbled something on her pad, but he wasn't fooled. He thought about that gesture, the caring he'd seen in those beautiful eyes. He thought about it day and night.

It was toward the end of the first week of September that Eve came in with Hank Thurgood. Jack had certainly heard about the investigator from Eve, but this was the first time they'd met.

"Hank," the tall, lanky man said, thrusting his big-knuckled hand out for Jack to shake.

"Nice to meet you," Jack said, and he couldn't help noticing the sagging face, the godawful clothes, the reek of cigarettes. And when they all sat down, Hank crossing his bony legs, Jack took in the work boots and mismatched socks.

Eve said, "I know. He's really a model for *Gentlemen's Quarterly*." She shook her head at Hank. "But his brain works pretty well."

"Why, thank you," Hank said.

They got down to business. "Hank's got some news," Eve said. "It's not as earthshaking as I would have liked. But I wanted you to hear it from him. I may leak this to the press, but let's first see what you think."

Jack looked from Eve to Hank and back. "Go on," he said.

Hank cleared his throat. "You remember that chick that gave George Mochlin his alibi? The one who was with him at the J-Bar the night your wife was murdered?"

"Sure," Jack said. "Melinda Hearst."

Hank nodded. "Well, I've talked to her a couple of times now, and it seems the local D.A. pressed her real hard to testify that she was with Mochlin till 2:00 a.m."

"I remember her testimony," Jack said.

"Now she's not so sure. Said she never really was. But between Mochlin and the bartender, and then the D.A. pressuring her, she felt she had no choice but to go along with the closing time thing."

"Uh-huh," Jack said, aware of Eve's eyes on him.

"Anyway," Hank went on, "I found out that the bartender had called a Tipsy-Taxi for her. The driver who picked her up in front of the J-Bar says it was more like midnight when he dropped her off at her home in Mountain Valley. His name's Bradley. And he's willing to swear Melinda was too trashed on what you locals call Agent Orange..."

Jack smiled. "Grand Marnier."

"Right, well, anyway, Bradley says you could smell it all over her. He says there's no way she'd remember the ride home, much less know what time it was. The chit that he turned in to the cops for reimbursement says he dropped her at approximately—" Hank checked his notes "—twelve-fifteen."

Jack nodded grimly. "That means Mochlin had plenty of time to get his car and drive up Red Mountain. Theoretically."

"Exactly," Eve put in. "It's not enough for me to go to the Ninth Judicial District judge and start screaming for a new trial. But I think the press would take it and run with it, and if any of the judges in the penalty phase read about it... Well, it's not going to hurt you. What do you think?"

"It's going to make a fool out of Melinda," Jack said. "On

the other hand, it's clear Mochlin lied. I've got to wonder why. Was he covering his tracks?" Jack shook his head. He didn't want to drag an innocent person down. But what if Mochlin really was the killer? "Shit," he muttered under his breath. "I don't know, Eve. It doesn't seem like a heck of a lot."

"It'll work for our purposes," she said. "I want to go with it. It's all we've come up with. Marty Cohen agrees."

"That's right," Hank said. "I finally got to Allison's ex, by the way, this John Richards. Smooth character. Real friendly."

"What did you think?" Jack asked.

"Well, Eve and I kinda decided he's out of the picture. My nose told me he was telling the truth, and my nose never lies," Hank said.

"He came right out and admitted they hated each other," Eve said, "but that was fifteen years ago. No motive."

"No motive," Hank repeated.

"No opportunity, either. A dozen people placed him in Vegas," Eve put in. "We don't think he's worth pursuing."

"Okay," Jack said.

"Now, to get back to the bit of PR I want to do. I don't need your permission to talk to the press," she said, holding Jack's gaze. "But I'd like it."

He let out a whistling breath. "All right. Go ahead. As long as you're positive about the time being midnight."

"I am," Hank said.

Eve smiled. "I'll talk to the reporters today."

George banged on Melinda's door so hard that inside the gentle mutt Maggie began to bark and growl. "Melinda!" George yelled through the wood. "Goddamn it, unlock this door!"

It took her a few minutes, but finally Melinda settled the dog down and opened the door. She blinked, rubbed her eyes and yawned. "What the hell?" she said as George swept past her. "It's 7:00 a.m. Are you crazy?"

George whirled and thrust the morning edition of the *Aspen Times* under her nose. "Read this," he said between clenched teeth. "Just goddamn read it, bitch, and then you better start explaining."

He watched Melinda as she pulled the lapels of her robe together and crossed to the couch, plumping herself down, snapping on a lamp. Then, still drowsy, she read the article.

When she was through, George walked over and grabbed the paper out of her hands. Furious, he swatted her on the head with it. He'd have liked to have done a whole lot more.

"Why in hell did you tell that bitch lawyer of Devlin's all this crap!"

"I... This isn't what I said." Melinda cowered against the couch. "And I never talked to Eve Marchand. Honest. It was some real funky-looking older guy."

"*Who?*"

"I... He said he was a private investigator or something. But, George, I swear, the paper's got it all wrong. I only said I wasn't positive about the exact time. That was all. I never said anything about midnight."

"You didn't have to!" George thundered. "That investigator took it from there. Now they've got the bartender changing his story, and the cabdriver... They even had the chit from the Tipsy-Taxi service! What are you trying to do! Get me arrested?"

A tear slid down Melinda's cheek. She brushed it away and tried to sit up, gathering herself. She took a breath. "They can't arrest you for something you didn't do, George."

He glared down at her. "My God," he grated out, "you are one dumb broad."

Melinda sniffed. "Well, you didn't, did you?"

"Didn't what?"

"You know, kill Allison," she whispered.

George just stared at her. Then, after a long, tense moment, he spun on his heel and stormed out, slamming her front door so hard the dishes in her cabinets rattled.

* * *

The next time Jack saw Eve it was snowing, one of those early autumn storms that swept across the Rocky Mountain states and coated the land in big wet flakes. Of course, no one thought winter had arrived. Everyone knew Indian summer would return, the mountainsides burning with color, the days warm and golden again. But when Eve walked in, her hair and shoulders were wet from the storm and her cheeks were red with cold. She looked like a little girl to him, her hair loose and windblown, heightened color in her face.

"Phew," she said, running her fingers through her hair when she sat across from Jack, and he could see the outline of her breasts beneath the cinnamon sweater when she raised her arms. He had the sudden urge to run his own fingers through that mass of damp honey-colored hair.

Goddamn it, he thought. Aloud, Jack said, "Yeah, it looks nasty out. But it'll pass."

"The weather report said it'd clear up by next week, so there shouldn't be any problem for anyone getting up here."

For the trial, he thought. Right. For the trial that was going to seal his fate.

Eve stared at him, understanding where his thoughts lay. "I know," she said softly. "It's getting close." Then she smiled. "Okay. All the more reason to get to work here."

"So what do you have for me today, counselor?" he asked, his tone matter-of-fact.

"Plenty. First, have you seen the papers?"

"I read them."

"Then you saw the articles on Melinda Hearst's testimony. The *Denver Post* even featured a picture of the Tipsy-Taxi chit the cabdriver handed in for reimbursement. I think this raises some doubts. At the very least, people have to believe that if one witness lied, then maybe others did, too."

"Do you think this will affect any of the judges' opinions?"

Eve sighed. "Hard to say. They're a tough lot. And with public sentiment and elections in November..."

"Right," Jack said, and all he could picture was death row, where he might very well be headed.

Eve pulled out her legal pad and put on her glasses. "By the way," she said, looking up, "Hank's back from California and Hawaii."

Jack knew Hank had gone to Long Beach to talk to Sarah Glick, but Hawaii...

"Now, don't blow a gasket. He went to Hawaii to interview former colleagues, friends from college and..."

"*And* my folks."

"Of course."

"I want them left out of this. They've been through too damn much already. It's not going to make any difference if..."

"*Jack*," Eve said firmly. "What you want is not going to stop your mother and father from being here for you. You aren't in charge of this. *They* are. Let's not waste any more time arguing about it. All right?"

"No, damn it, it's not all right," he said between clenched teeth. And then he rose and paced the floor. Finally, though, he had to sit down again and face Eve. He was still angry, and it was really hard to be civil.

"I can leave and come back if you want," Eve said after a strained silence.

Jack lifted his gaze to her. "No, no," he said. "That's stupid. What's done is done. I don't like it, but I'll try to live with it."

"Do that," she said.

They spent the afternoon going over every detail of the fight Jack had had with Allison the day before her murder, the fight that the Wades had so readily testified to at the trial. As always, it was hard for Jack to talk about it. He still couldn't believe the last words between them had been in anger. And he still was of no help to Eve, unable to recall a single thing other than what had already been testified to.

They were interrupted about four. Ben came in, toting a white sack of cookies from a downtown bakery.

"Oh, sorry," he said. "They should have told me you were with Miss Marchand." Ben shrugged in apology.

"Eve, it's Eve," she said. "And I'm afraid I'm nowhere near done here today. Do you mind?"

"No," Ben said, his hands in his jeans pockets, snow still visible on the shoulders of his leather jacket. "I can come back later."

Jack smiled at him. "You must have something better to do."

"Not really," Ben said. "Save me a cookie." He left then, Jack watching him exit through the security doors. To be free to come and go, Jack thought, what a luxury. And he wondered how he could have taken his former freedom for granted. How could anyone?

They ate some of the cookies, then Eve went doggedly back to her questions. Jack felt his head begin to pound. He'd been over and over and over this stuff.

"What time did the police knock on your door that morning?" Eve was asking.

"Four. Four-fifteen. I don't know exactly."

"You didn't check a digital clock or anything when they woke you up?"

"For God's sake," he muttered, "it's all in your notes from a month ago. It's all in Iverson's notes."

"*Jack.*"

"All right, all right. I *did* look at the clock. I've just never remembered what it said. When the cops told me Allison had been killed, I was so stunned I've never been able to recall. Okay?"

Eve nodded, scribbling away while Jack stared at the curve of her thigh beneath her blue jeans. He snatched his gaze away quickly, because fantasies of Eve were making his head pound all the worse. *This is what it's like to go out of your mind,* he thought. *This is the beginning of it.*

"So the police talked to you for...what? Fifteen, twenty minutes?"

"About that."

"And did they ask you your whereabouts for the approximate time of Allison's death?"

"They didn't know exactly what time she was killed yet." Jack leaned over and put his head in his hands.

"But they had an idea. Remember, the Wades thought they heard a car starting up. It was around one-thirty in the morning."

"No," Jack said, "no one asked me for an alibi. Not then."

"Okay. So you left for Denver to tell Ben the news in person. That was around...?"

"Five."

"And you drove over Independence Pass."

"Christ!" Jack snapped. "You *know* I drove the long way around. You know damn good and well that the pass wasn't open then. Still too much snow."

"Just seeing if you're paying attention," she said offhandedly.

"How could I not be? You, woman, are one relentless lady."

"Um," she said. "So you got to Ben's about eight-thirty in the morning?"

"That's right. There wasn't any traffic, the interstate was free of ice. Sarah was already there to check on him. How am I doing?" he asked dryly, his head still in his hands.

"Oh, fine," she said, ignoring his sarcasm. "And how did Ben look to you?"

"Before or after I told him his mother had been bludgeoned to death?" He looked up sharply.

Eve put down her pad and took off her glasses. She glared at him.

"Am I suppose to wither, counselor?" he said evenly. "Because if I am, forget it. Not going to happen. I'm damn sick and tired of the probing. You're wasting your time. What I need to do is get out of here. Every minute I spend in here puts more distance between me and Allison's murderer. And that's the bottom line."

Eve gathered her things and stood. "Tomorrow, when you're not so tired," she said, "we'll go over exactly where you stood financially when your wife was killed. The D.A. thinks money is the perfect motive for murder. I don't. And I want you to convince me, *again*, that Allison's money meant nothing to you. Now I'm going to leave. I hope you have a pleasant evening." He could hear the tension beginning to play in her voice. She started to go, but then she turned back to him. "I'm tired, too, Jack. Very tired. But I can't afford to show it. Nor can you."

She might as well have slapped him in the face. He took a long, deep breath and rose to face her. "I'm sorry," he said. "God, Eve, I know you're doing everything in your power to save my life. I'm being an ass. I've got no excuse, either. If you want to go on right now..."

"No." She shook her head. "Tomorrow. When we're both fresh."

Jack nodded, but he couldn't stop the question that came out of his mouth. "How was your weekend in Denver? Did you get any rest?"

She thought a moment. Then she shrugged. "Not much. I went to the opening Bronco game."

"We won."

"Yes, we did."

Jack looked down into her eyes. "Did you go with your friend?" he asked, instantly regretting the question.

She regarded him pensively, but finally she said, "Yes, I did."

"Who is he?"

"It's not important, Jack."

"Chalk it up to curiosity," he said tightly.

She sighed. "Gary Kapochek."

"*The* Gary Kapochek?"

"Yes."

"I see," Jack said. "He's quite the hero. A football great. The MS..."

"Yes, he's a wonderful person."

"I hope Kapochek knows how lucky he is," he said quietly.

Eve gave a strained laugh. "Right now, as busy as I am, I don't think he'd agree with you." Then she turned and left, Jack staring after her.

It was a long, long night for Jack. He lay on the narrow bed, the ceiling light on, and stared at the overhead pipes. He couldn't stop the images of Eve with Kapochek from banging around in his brain. He saw them together everywhere. Mostly he saw them in bed. He tried to erase the pictures, tried with everything in him not to see them like that, but the images persisted with a will of their own. It was almost as if he knew Eve's body intimately, every curve and hollow, the texture of her skin, the feel of her silky hair crushed in his hands. The taste of her. And yet they'd only touched that one time when they'd first met. A single handshake.

The minutes ticked by with agonizing slowness, and he wished a thousand times over that he'd kept his mouth shut and never asked about her friend. He didn't want to know. He shouldn't know. It only made it tougher and filled him with a terrible, deadening hopelessness, and he couldn't believe he'd allowed this enormous chink in his armor to open up. Eve. She'd gotten to him. He'd let it happen, goddamn it.

Eve, he thought over and over, picturing her, wanting her, aching inside.

Eve and Gary Kapochek.

PART II

The Sentencing

ELEVEN

The first time Eve saw Jack out of prison garb was the cool September morning when the penalty phase began. He looked so different, she blinked. Handsome, debonair, successful. A man at the top of an honorable profession, in the prime of life. He wore a navy blue, double-breasted suit with a pinstripe, one that Marty Cohen had picked up from Ben's house, where Jack's clothes were in storage. He also sported a white shirt with a continental collar and a blue-and-red-striped silk tie.

He looked great. Only the handcuffs spoiled the effect.

"We'll take them off once we're inside the courthouse," Debby promised. "No one in the courtroom will see them."

"Can I have a moment with him?" Eve asked.

"Sure," Debby said. "Take the interview room."

In the close confines of the room, Eve had a few last-minute instructions. "Try to look interested in the proceedings," she said. "Don't space out, okay?"

He nodded.

"It'll take two to three days. Your mother will testify last."

His lips thinned.

"I know, I know, but it's a done deal, Jack. You have to let her do what she can for her son, for God's sake." She smiled reassuringly. "You all set? You look terrific."

"So do you," he said.

"My trial uniform." She stood and smoothed her gray skirt, tugged at the tailored jacket. "I've got to go now. I'll see you in the courtroom. By the way, there's a full complement of media types."

"I figured."

"Gotta go. See you in a few minutes."

The third-floor courtroom was old-fashioned, Victorian, with oak woodwork and tall windows. It was packed. Eve and Marty arranged their notes on the defendant's table, exchanged a few suggestions and points of law. Eve felt the familiar adrenaline high that always took over when she walked into the courtroom. It was the challenge of pitting her skills and stamina against the prosecutor and the panel of judges. But this time it was more—the outcome was a man's life—Jack's life.

Jack was led in by two sheriff's deputies, as this was a district court case. No handcuffs, as Debby had promised. He stood over Eve for a moment, then pulled out the wooden chair and sat. The gallery whispered and murmured, pens scratched on pads, sketching the notorious wife-murderer. No cameras in *this* courtroom.

Eve turned to Jack and smiled, and saw the stoic expression on his face. It was terrible for him, for this fiercely private man, and she reached out and laid a hand over his, giving him a sympathetic squeeze. Big mistake. A sudden surge of electricity seemed to leap from his skin to hers. She snatched her hand away, too quickly. She'd felt it, and so had Jack, because he gave her a swift, unreadable glance that lasted a heartbeat too long.

She took a deep breath and leaned back in her chair, surreptitiously looking around to see who might have noticed the episode. Not the sketch artists, she prayed. And not Bill Makelky, the D.A. Please, not Bill.

The D.A. was at the prosecutor's table, though, with his assistant, and both were opening briefcases, pulling out legal pads, seemingly blind to Eve's shock. Thank God.

Then she saw him—Gary, in the back of the courtroom.

Gary, here? He *never* came to watch her in court, never. She couldn't fit her mind around his presence, and she didn't have the time to wonder, so she turned back to Jack and gave him a reassuring smile.

The familiar routine took her mind off Gary, the court clerk's announcement, the room rising for the judges, and she put aside everything but her strategy, her opening statement, her entire being focused on challenging the law so that it conformed to the ideal it was meant to uphold.

"Got those statistics I faxed you?" Cohen whispered.

"Uh-huh. They're good. I'll use them."

Eve gave her usual opening statement—over the years she'd honed it to perfection. It rarely persuaded anyone who believed wholeheartedly in the death penalty, but it shook some who straddled the fence. And she meant every word of it.

"Death penalty laws in this country," she said, peering through her glasses at the judges, "defy legal definition the way a blob of mercury defies capture. These laws try to embrace a dark, nebulous cloud that cannot be held or analyzed rationally. Ultimately, death penalty laws are hollow and always open to subjective interpretation. The courts' interpretation of these laws is like a mad dog, biting at whoever it can reach, randomly condemning people to death. The death penalty brings discredit to our whole legal system.

"I will therefore argue against the use of the death penalty in *any* case, as a general rule, as a tenet of a modern, enlightened society. But I will also argue against the death penalty in the specific case of my client, Jack Devlin."

Eve shot the first of her arrows brazenly, openly.

"Jack Devlin," she said in a clear, carrying voice, "is a man who's already been found guilty of a capital crime and now faces the possibility of state-directed execution. But Jack Devlin is also—" she turned and looked at him and let everyone in the courtroom wait a little too long for comfort

"—a completely innocent man whose trial was a total and utter travesty, and I hold that..."

"Objection!" shouted the D.A.

"Sustained," the middle judge said. "Miss Marchand, really, we aren't going to rehash Mr. Devlin's trial. It's over. Please address the issue."

"Excuse me, Your Honor," she said, "but this *is* the issue."

"Proceed, Miss Marchand," the judge said dryly. "And don't presume to preach to us."

Another judge spoke up. "Miss Marchand, please keep in mind that we are not here to debate the constitutionality of the death penalty. That's already been done for us. Please proceed."

"Yes, Your Honor, I will, but I beg to disagree with you. We *are* debating the death penalty here. Each and every time a man faces capital punishment, we have to search our hearts and souls all over again, and we must, we really must..."

"Proceed, Miss Marchand."

"Nothing more right now, Your Honors."

The day went well for Eve, despite the D.A.'s opening statement. He presented his case, handing out the gruesome photographs of the crime scene and intoning the coroner's report of Allison's injuries while the panel of judges studied the pictures, but this was only to be expected.

Bill Makelky set forth his theory that Jack had married Allison strictly for her money. "He was a handsome young guy," Makelky said. "He was from a blue-collar family, had to work all his life. Here was his chance, this rich society lady a couple of years older than him. Of course he jumped at that chance. And he got his reward. A lavish life-style, the best of everything. Then the marriage failed, and his wife wanted out. She even had divorce papers ready to be signed. She was going to name a new beneficiary in her will, not even give Jack Devlin a settlement. Well—" Makelky smiled grimly "—the rest is history."

"Objection," Eve said.

"Miss Marchand?"

"Jack Devlin never took a penny from his wife. I can prove that. So your motive of pecuniary gain is out the window."

"Overruled. Continue, Mr. Makelky."

She'd made her point, which was the best she could do right now. She smiled reassuringly at Jack, but his face was shut tight.

Then Makelky brought out his next witness, a psychiatrist who analyzed Jack's character, telling the court that the prisoner was indeed a dangerous criminal and should be executed. Hardened, no hope of reform. Bill sat, smiling, satisfied. Then it was Eve's turn.

"So, Dr. Weiss," Eve said, fist on her hip, glasses dangling from her other hand, "how long did you have Mr. Devlin in analysis?"

"Why, I...actually, I haven't interviewed Mr. Devlin."

"Excuse me? You're testifying that he's dangerous to society and should be put to death like a stray *dog*, Dr. Weiss, and you've never even *met* the man?"

"I had his records. He was interviewed by a psychologist in jail. I..."

"And you've made this judgment, this *professional* judgment, about a man, condemning him to death, on the basis of another doctor's report?"

"Objection, Your Honor. This is established procedure. Miss Marchand is badgering the witness," Makelky said.

"Sustained. Go on, Miss Marchand."

She asked a few more innocuous questions of the flustered Dr. Weiss, but she'd made her point and retreated gracefully. And all the while, as she sat at her table or thought on her feet, framed her questions, postured and made witnesses squirm, she was aware of Jack's eyes on her, his dark gaze on her back as she faced the judges, his eyes burning through the fabric of her tailored suit. And the bur-

den of proof was so heavy on her, the desperate need to exhibit his innocence, to make no mistakes, was excruciating.

The D.A. stood, trying for damage control, and Eve
tapped her pencil impatiently until it was time for her to call
her first witness, Samuel Thomas, a guard on Colorado's
death row, a man whom she'd gotten to know quite well on
her many trips to the facility. He was a black man, tall and
heavy, amazingly soft spoken and well versed in the intri-
cacies of his workplace.

By asking Sam Thomas her carefully prepared questions,
Eve brought out the facts she wanted the court to hear. "Has
it ever come to your attention, Mr. Thomas, that innocent
men are imprisoned on death row?" she asked.

His simple answer, "Yes, ma'am, it certainly has," en-
abled Eve to launch into her speech.

"Are you aware that between 1970 and 1993 there were
forty-eight people released from death rows across this
country because there was a strong showing of their innocence? This is from a congressional study, Your Honors. Innocent men condemned to die. In this century, four hundred and seventeen other cases existed in which the
condemned man appeared innocent. Nevertheless, twenty-
three of these were executed. Innocent men killed by the
state.

"How many more innocent men died by hanging, gas-
sing, the electric chair, that we don't know about? In the beginning of 1995 a man was executed when it was his sister
who pulled the trigger. She got ten years. He got death.

"My point is also that a smart, experienced criminal,
caught for a capital crime, will almost always plead guilty,
that is, plea bargain, because he knows he might get the
death penalty in a trial." She took a breath. "So what we
have in our country is a general population in prison of the
very worst criminals, while the ones who are naive or
poorly represented or *the ones who are really innocent*, well,
they end up on death row."

"Objection, irrelevant!"

"It is not irrelevant," Eve said. "It applies directly to my client, so I am required to present it."

"You've already been warned not to retry Mr. Devlin. You're risking contempt charges, Miss Marchand," said the lead judge, looking at her from under bushy gray brows, his half glasses pushed down his nose.

And so it went. Eve would fight to gain ground wherever she could. Sam knew the routine, as he'd been an expert witness for Eve several times. He worked on death row because of sincere convictions about the humanity of the condemned, and he was as dead set against the death penalty as she was. They made a good team.

From her seat behind the defense table, Eve cocked her head and spoke directly to the panel of judges in a very mild tone of voice. "If it pleases the court, I would like Mr. Thomas to give us some pertinent information. What I want him to do is to describe the execution itself so it's very clear what you will condemn this man to."

"Objection," the D.A. called out.

"*Miss* Marchand, is this truly necessary?" one of the judges asked.

"Yes, Your Honor."

She won that bid, but even if she hadn't, she would have gotten the information in somehow.

She walked slowly around to the front of her table, leaned back against it and looked down at her crossed feet for a moment, then looked up and took her glasses off, staring straight at Sam Thomas. And, as always, she felt Jack's eyes on her. Did he approve of her strategy? What did he think now that he'd seen her in court? Was he nervous, afraid, suffering? She took a deep breath and went straight for the panel's jugular.

"Mr. Thomas, please describe the process of execution for us."

He did, in his quiet, understated way: he described the last few hours of the condemned man's life; the meal; the desperate wait for the governor's clemency call that hung over the whole institution; the many guards it took to lead the shackled man to the small, white-tiled room. The gurney with its straps, all hospital-clean and antiseptic; the window through which spectators could watch the execution. The canisters of the three different drugs that would be injected into the man's arm by a hidden guard whose job it was to pull the switch.

"What are these drugs, Mr. Thomas?" Eve asked. "And what effect do they..."

"Your Honors!" Makelky leaped to his feet. "Miss Marchand is leading the witness!"

One of the judges peered at her. "Please rephrase your question, counselor."

"Certainly," Eve said, and she turned back to her witness. "Would you identify the drugs used in the execution suite, Mr. Thomas?"

"Well, ma'am, there's sodium Pentothal. That's the first, because it renders the person unconscious, so that he doesn't feel the pancuronium bromide. That's the stuff that paralyzes the diaphragm, stops a man's breathing. Then there's also potassium chloride, which causes cardiac arrest. That's a heart attack, ma'am."

"Thank you, Mr. Thomas." Eve turned to the judges. "This is what our society has decided is a humane death, this sick, barbaric suffering...."

"Objection."

"*Miss Marchand.*"

"I'm sorry, Your Honor." But there was one more thing Eve needed from Sam Thomas, and he waited, knowing it was coming. "Mr. Thomas, would you describe for us the actual placement of the intravenous needle? Who does it? Is it one of the guards?"

"Oh, no, ma'am. There's a regular nurse who does it. In a white uniform and all. She comes in after he's strapped down and swabs his arm with alcohol and..."

"Excuse me, Mr. Thomas, just why does she swab his arm?"

"Why, ma'am—" the punch line "—to avoid infection, of course."

She could hear the rustle and murmur behind her, a few "oh Gods," some groans. Two of the judges winced before banging their gavels. Eve felt a great surge of satisfaction as she excused Sam Thomas with a grateful smile.

"Objection!" Bill Makelky was saying, but the courtroom erupted into a horrified buzz, the sketch artists going crazy, the reporters scribbling, the judges banging away angrily.

"Quiet. Quiet in the courtroom! Silence," said the lead judge, and a hush fell over the throng. "I am calling a close to the day's proceedings, and, Miss Marchand—" again the furious glare "—we will see you in chambers. Right now."

Eve hid her smile, turned her back on the judges to give Jack a thumbs-up. "See you later," she mouthed, then she turned back to the panel, her face unreadable. She was completely unintimidated; she'd been here before, she'd be here again. She squared her shoulders and went to meet her fate.

"He's in love with you," Gary told Eve at La Cocina that night.

Her fork stopped halfway to her mouth, and she gave a short laugh. "Don't be silly. You know this happens all the time. It's call transference—ask any shrink." Then she ate the forkful of spicy chicken burrito.

Gary shook his head. "This time it's different. I can tell. I saw the way he looked at you today."

"You can't tell anything from Jack Devlin's face, Gary. He's one close-to-the-vest guy."

"Maybe *you* can't tell. *I* can."

"For God's sake, I'm the only woman he's seen in a year."

"What about Debby and Bev, the ladies at the jail? You've told me all about them. Does he look at *them* the same way he looks at *you?*"

"How do I know how he looks at them—or me?"

"You're in denial," Gary said.

"Hurry up and finish. I've still got work to do tonight," she replied.

The ate for a few minutes in silence, until Eve tried to lighten the mood by making conversation. "I met Jack's parents today. They just flew in. His mother must have been very beautiful when she was young. His father's one of those hard-nosed, intractable American blue-collar types. Now I know where Jack gets his reserve from."

Gary put down his fork. "Is this supposed to entertain me, all this talk about your case?"

"Sorry." Her tone was huffy.

"Listen, I feel bad for Devlin if what you say is true, but my life doesn't revolve around him. Jesus, I think you're a little in love with the guy. You two would make a great couple. What in hell do you need *me* for?"

"*Gary*. You know how I have to be when I'm on a trial. I have to be obsessed."

"Sure, you have to be obsessed with the trial, the process, not the defendant."

"I'm not obsessed with Jack Devlin."

"The hell you aren't."

It wasn't a successful dinner, and when they walked back to the Christmas Inn afterward, they didn't have much to say to each other.

Gary relented enough to kiss her good-night, a light brush of his lips, then he went to bed while Eve stayed up to review tomorrow's strategy.

She looked at her notes, took her glasses off and rubbed her eyes. She was having trouble concentrating. Gary's accusations haunted her. "*He's in love with you.*" Could Gary be seeing something she didn't? In love, Jack in love with her? Ridiculous. He respected her, sure, admired her, maybe. But *love*?

And yet, when Gary had said it, her heart had leaped, unbidden, thrilled: "*He's in love with you.*"

She was ashamed of her reaction, and she flushed, sitting there in the living room of the suite, Gary's even breathing coming from the bedroom. He'd driven to Aspen to see her, and once again she'd ruined it. Gary was busy with the team these days, too, traveling every other week, at practice every day, yet he'd taken time off to come up to see her.

Damn.

"I think you're a little in love with the guy." Gary was being childish. He knew she loved *him*. They were getting married, for goodness' sake. Eve tried to conjure up the image of herself as Gary's wife, living in his house in Boulder—or would they buy a new house together? But no matter how hard she tried, she couldn't picture herself there, doing the things wives do.

She closed her eyes and felt panic coil inside her, cold and insidious. No, it couldn't be true. She was Jack's attorney. She cared, that was all.

She wondered what it was exactly that Gary saw. How did she behave around Jack? Did she preen or pose or smile too much? Did she lean too close or touch him too often? No, absolutely not.

She rose and stood by the window, pushed the drapes aside and stared out into the dark September night.

It was always like this in the middle of a big case. Gary knew that. She was obsessed, yes. So how was it different this time?

She liked Jack. As she'd come to know him, she'd found him to be a man of absolute integrity. He spoke the truth always, and he tried to overcome his discomfort of discussing anything personal. She saw him struggle with his reticence every day and respected him for being so frank about himself. She knew a lot about Jack by now, and she liked what she knew, but still there was some essence of the man hidden from her. Maybe that was what Gary saw, her intense curiosity. Yes, she'd tell Gary that.

It had been three months since she'd taken the Devlin case, and she'd been driving back and forth to Denver, back and forth, two hundred miles each way and she'd seen so little of Gary, each of them with such heavy schedules, it was ludicrous. She saw much more of Jack.

The feel of his skin came back to her without a bridging thought, and she flushed again. He had smooth, perfect skin, despite his prison pallor. She could picture him in her mind's eye on a beach in Hawaii, lithe and brown, his skin satiny, gleaming in the tropical sun. His hand had been warm and smooth, and it had sent a shock through her, as if his own electrical nerve impulses had leaped from his neurons to hers.

Did she love Jack Devlin a little? Maybe. She knew she'd never before looked forward to seeing a client as she did Jack. Never had she delved so insatiably into a client's past, pushed so hard. Nor had she ever experienced the absolute certainty of a client's innocence. Did that constitute love?

Friendship, curiosity, fear of letting a client down, all those things. Not love.

A scene came back to her from a day early in the case, when she'd sat with Jack in the common room of the jail. He'd been answering her questions about Allison and their financial arrangements, about his work, when he'd suddenly leaned forward, resting his elbows on his knees. "Why do you do this?" he'd asked.

"Do what?"

"This. Sitting in jails. Defending criminals."

Eve had put her pad down on her lap and taken her glasses off. "Why do you want to know? Does it matter?"

"Yes, it matters. I want to know because I can't understand your motives, and it bugs me."

She'd smiled. "I feel that I'm doing something very important. The Constitution guarantees every person competent legal representation. Someone has to do it, and I'm good at it."

"But why? Why aren't you in private practice? And why defense? Why not prosecution?"

"You *are* full of questions, aren't you. Let's see." She'd leaned back and thought, playing with her glasses. "I'm in public defense because I saw the inequity in our system. You know what they say, Jack, that there are no rich men on death row. It's true. And I hate that about our society, our country. It shouldn't be that way. There are lots of prosecutors who are really tops, but the best defense lawyers work only for the people who can afford them. Does that make sense?"

"You're an idealist."

"Maybe." She'd laughed. "Wait till you see me in court. I use every dirty trick in the book. Legal but dirty. I'm very effective. You might change your mind."

He'd looked at her for a long time, until she felt a little uncomfortable, then he'd shaken himself and said, as if to himself, "I didn't know people like you existed."

"Well, we do, but you never meet us until you're in the court system, and most people don't ever get into that situation." She'd put her glasses on and picked up the pad again, a hint that the interlude was over. "Their loss, right, Jack?" she'd remarked lightly.

His mouth had twisted in appreciation of the jab, but he hadn't said a word. And now, standing by the window in her motel room, Eve wondered what he'd been thinking. And as she wondered, a sudden thought assailed her: never in her life had she wanted to tell anyone about that first case, the execution. But abruptly, without reason, she had wanted to tell Jack.

Eve stood for a long moment frozen in the thought. Finally she shook herself mentally. *Forget it.*

She had to work. She had to prepare for tomorrow. If she didn't do her utmost, if she didn't foresee every ploy Makelky might try, she could lose this case, and that would be unthinkable. The thought of Jack wasting away for years amid the animal brutality of death row tortured her. She had nightmares about it. And his execution, the snuffing out of his life, the needle in his arm, the people watching—no, it couldn't happen. She wouldn't let it happen. She couldn't even think about it.

If she lost the penalty phase, she'd just go on. She'd find evidence to prove him innocent; somehow she'd do it. It would take years to exhaust all the appeals, so she'd have time to find out who had really killed Allison, and she'd get Jack's verdict reversed. She'd do it.

She sat down again at the table piled with files and notes, and bent her head to read a deposition, but all she could see was Jack on death row in his claustrophobic cell, alone, waiting hopelessly.

My God, she was exhibiting her usual compulsive behavior, worse this time. Much worse, because her client was a good man who had so much to contribute to the world, a worthy man. An innocent man.

Her feelings were somewhat akin to those she'd felt for Gary when she'd first met him, when he'd been so debilitated by MS. He'd needed her, which she'd recognized somewhere deep inside her, a man brought low by fate, a man she could love and nurture and help. Was it sick to be attracted to men whose needs she could fulfill?

Jack needed her, too. Right now he needed her far more desperately than Gary, who was so much better, talking about vacations and adventures, marriage, a whole new life. With her.

But how could she leave her job, or even take time off, when there were so many others who needed her services? How could she turn her back on them?

Maybe she *was* sick.

She took her glasses off and set them on a pile of papers. She couldn't concentrate tonight—it was no good. She got up, went into the bedroom and looked at Gary, lying there so peacefully asleep. Getting ready for bed, brushing her teeth, she wondered if Gary understood *her* needs, if he ever had.

Jack did. She could tell by the questions he asked. He felt as strongly about his work as she did about hers.

Slipping into bed beside Gary, she tried to relax, felt her body sinking, heard the deep, easy breathing of her fiancé, and had one last thought before she sank down into the dark embrace of sleep.

Was she a little in love with Jack Devlin because he was so utterly dependent on her? What if he hadn't been? What if she'd met him in an ordinary situation? How would she feel about him then?

TWELVE

The second day of the penalty phase was tough: Bill Makelky put Allison's parents on the stand. Venetia Wickwire was imperious and full of the most vicious hatred for Jack. But Bill got her to cry—he was good, Eve had to admit. Trevor Wickwire's lips trembled and he couldn't get much out, but he begged for the death penalty, "So that the man who killed my daughter no longer walks this earth."

Eve countered with a friend of Jack's grandfather, a former minister, a white-haired man who spoke well of Jack. Then there was his high school drafting teacher and a college roommate and a woman he'd worked with in Hawaii. A woman was important.

Eve had them all testify to his good character, his honesty, his talent. She brought out his spotless past—not even a traffic ticket, no problems with drugs or alcohol or gambling. She had a local banker testify that Jack's account was separate from his wife's and that there were no deposits made into his account that were not earned by him. On and on.

And every chance she got, she managed to sneak in a sentence or two about the paucity of evidence against Jack: it was all circumstantial, there were no witnesses, he had no motive, Mochlin's alibi was shaky, and so on. The judges kept reprimanding her, the D.A. kept hopping out of his seat, righteously indignant, but Eve went on tenaciously.

She was saving Jack's mother for the end, and, of course, Jack himself. She'd rehearsed with him what he should say, something simple and dignified and heartfelt; she'd even written a speech for him, but she still wasn't sure how he'd come across or what he'd say. She knew now why Iverson hadn't put him on the stand.

There was Ben Richards, too, and she would put him on just before Jack's mother. The murdered woman's own son, speaking up for his stepfather. Yes, that would be effective.

She kept giving Jack sidelong glances to see how he was holding up. It was hard for everyone to listen to the victim's family, their anguish, their futile rage, their desperate need for retribution. It always was. But Jack hadn't killed Allison, and he was being blamed for it, which made it even harder.

She watched him all day; his face remained unreadable, and he sat upright, hands folded on the table in front of him. Eve knew he was inside himself, not in the courtroom, someplace else where he could bear to be, but she was afraid it would look to the spectators and the judges as if he were coldly indifferent.

Was she the only person in court who knew how much he really did care?

After the lunch recess, Eve was surprised to see Frank Iverson at the back of the courtroom. He looked thin and pale, still sick, but he was there. She pointed him out to Marty and Jack.

"I saw him," Jack said without inflection.

"It looks good for you," she said. "He obviously cares."

Jack turned his eyes away. "I'm flattered," he replied, and Eve winced at the pain his sarcasm concealed.

The day ended early when Eve was fined for bringing up the Tipsy-Taxi driver who'd driven Melinda Hearst home the night of the murder.

"It was midnight," Eve said, "when Bradley dropped her off, so there goes George Mochlin's alibi. He had plenty of time to..."

"Objection!"

"Sustained. That will be a five-hundred-dollar fine, Miss Marchand, and let it be a warning to stick to the issue in the future." The judge banged his gavel and said angrily, "Court's in recess until tomorrow at 10:00 a.m."

"You've really pissed them off now," Marty Cohen whispered.

"I got the point across. And tomorrow I'll be nice, I promise," she answered, gathering papers.

"Mochlin doesn't have the guts to kill anybody," Jack said.

"All I'm trying to do," she said, "is arouse doubt. That's my job."

Jack nodded. "I understand."

"A tiny seed of doubt in one judge's mind, Jack, that's all we need, and I'll do anything I can to put it there."

The deputies came up to lead Jack off. Apologetically.

"I'll see you tomorrow," Eve said. "You have the speech? No, not speech, the...whatever you want to call it?"

"The plea for mercy," Jack said in a tight voice.

She met his gaze. "Yes."

"I have it."

"Make sure you look good tomorrow, respectable. Well, you do, you look great in that suit. Anything you need? Have you seen your folks?"

"I've seen them."

"They're in the Hotel Jerome. They're very comfortable."

"I'll bet they are."

"Jack."

"I have to go now," he said.

Eve turned back to her papers, shaking her head. She felt for Jack, and she hated pitying him, but it wasn't solely pity—it was mixed with admiration and sadness and frustration.

"Tough nut to crack, isn't he?" came a voice from behind her.

She turned. "Mr. Iverson, it's great to see you here. How're you feeling?"

"Like hell. Listen, don't mind Jack. It's hard for him."

"I know."

"You probably don't know quite how hard. I probably don't know, either." Iverson smiled and put a hand out to pat her arm. "You're doing a super job. I couldn't do better. You're a real hellion. I like that in a woman."

She laughed. "Flattery will get you everywhere."

"I failed Jack in the trial," he said more seriously. "I feel bad about that. If I can help you, any way you think of, let me know."

"Thank you. I appreciate it, but there's only tomorrow morning left, and if that doesn't work, we're out of time."

"You're putting Jack on the stand." It wasn't a question.

"I have to."

"Yeah, I know, but he won't convince anyone. He's too damn proud to beg."

"I hope to God you're wrong," Eve said soberly. "I hope to God we both are."

Ben felt his girlfriend slip her hand in his as they approached the courthouse steps the following morning.

Sarah said in his ear, "Don't talk to them, Ben, don't even make any eye contact. *Please.*"

But the gaggle of reporters awaited his arrival, and before he and Sarah even reached the stone steps there were a dozen microphones shoved under his nose. He felt claustrophobic and sweat oozed from every pore of his body. Two local police officers hurried to his side to forge a path into the courthouse, but it did little good.

"Leave him alone!" Sarah pleaded as she was jostled right along with Ben. "Don't you have any decency?"

Ben made it about halfway up the steps before he broke. He whirled around and felt Sarah squeeze his hand tightly, but he couldn't help himself.

"You want a statement?" he asked, his voice breaking, his knees weak. "I'll give you one. You jerks have crucified my stepfather for over a year now. You haven't got a clue. The truth doesn't mean shit to you...."

"Damn," one of the reporters said, knowing that would have to be cut.

Ben was oblivious, however. "Jack Devlin's an innocent man, and not one of you has ever given him a break. Where did justice go? Isn't a man supposed to be innocent until he's proved guilty? Well, *you're* guilty. All of you. And..."

"Ben!" Sarah cried, and she began to yank on his arm. "Stop it! You're not helping."

He finally shut up, the sweat streaming off his neck and soaking his starched white shirt collar. Inside the courtroom, waiting for the proceedings to begin, he still couldn't stop feeling as if the room were closing in on him.

"You've got to calm down," Sarah whispered. "This isn't helping anyone, least of all Jack."

Ben tried to breathe. "I know, I know," he said. "It's just that none of them know Jack the way I do. He couldn't have done it, Sarah. And they're going to give him the death penalty. I know it. I just know it," he said, and then his father slid into the seat next to him.

"Dad," Ben whispered, surprised.

"Couldn't miss this circus," John Richards said. "Hi, Sarah."

"Hi, Mr. Richards. Will you please tell Ben to calm down? He's a wreck over this."

"Can't say I blame him," Richards said.

"What if they give Jack the death penalty?" Ben said.

"You won't be the one at fault, Ben. You're doing what you think is right."

"Do *you* think it's right?" Ben asked his father.

"Son, it's not something I can give you advice on. I don't know the guy. I *did* know your mother, though, and frankly..."

"*Dad.*"

The clerk of the court was telling them to rise, and the three judges entered the room. It was time to begin.

Eve called Ben to the stand first thing. He was relieved. Still nervous as a caged animal, but grateful that he was going to get this over with.

"Good morning, Ben," Eve said with a calming smile, and the questions began. About ten minutes into his testimony, she finally started to probe his relationship with Jack. "So the two of you were close during your teenage years?"

Ben cleared his throat. "Very. My real father's pretty busy, and Jack didn't have all the clients he got later on in his career, so we had time to do stuff together."

They talked about that for a minute or two, then Eve asked, "Before Jack's success as an architect, did you ever witness him taking money from your mother?"

"Never. He..."

"Objection, Your Honors," Bill said with a groan of boredom. "This is totally irrelevant and repetitious, not to mention hearsay."

The judges whispered among themselves for a moment, then one of them said, "We'll allow Miss Marchand a little latitude here. But, Miss Marchand, please do not tax the court's patience."

"Yes, sir," Eve said, and she proceeded along that line of questioning until Bill Makelky rose again.

"Never mind, Ben," Eve said then. "We'll move on. Now, were you ever witness to any arguments between Jack and your mother?"

Again the objections. Again the judges allowed a few questions.

"Did *you* ever argue with your mother?" Eve asked a few minutes later.

"Sure," Ben said.

"Over what?"

"I was in college, and it was hard to make ends meet sometimes."

"But you never heard *Jack* argue about money with..."

Makelky leaped to his feet. "Your Honors, this is so out of line..."

"Sit down, Bill," the lead judge said. "But Miss Marchand—" he peered at her over his half glasses "—the court gets the point. Let's finish up here."

"Yes, Your Honor." She turned back to Ben. "Did you ever hear an argument over money between Jack and your mother?"

"Yes."

A hush fell over the room.

"Go on."

"Mom wanted Jack to live off her trust fund."

"And?"

"And they argued about it. Jack wouldn't take a dime."

"I see. So in your opinion, the contention that Jack murdered your mother because she was cutting him out of her will is utterly ridiculous and…"

"*Miss Marchand,*" the lead judge barked even before Bill Makelky had gotten to his feet, "that will be quite enough. This court has allowed you all the latitude in the world due to the serious nature…"

Ben barely heard the rest of the exchange. He felt immense relief. He'd gotten his say in, and Eve Marchand had run with the ball. Surely his testimony would sway the panel of judges. They couldn't give Jack the death penalty. Not now.

Shortly after, he took his seat in the gallery again next to Sarah. She leaned close and whispered in his ear, "You were great."

He let out a long breath. "I hope so," he whispered back. "For Jack's sake, I sure as hell hope so."

It was after the morning recess that Eve called Jo Ann Devlin to the stand. Jack's mother was good; naturally she cried and begged for her son's life. She was his mother, after all, and everyone expected it.

It was when his mother was on the stand that Eve saw Jack show emotion for the first time. He leaned an elbow on the table, covering his eyes with a hand. His shoulders slumped. The body language was unmistakable—pure, unadulterated humiliation and anguish. She wanted to touch him, comfort him; her heart bled for what he was going through, but she had to do it—it was her job.

"Thank you, Mrs. Devlin," she said to the sobbing woman. She turned to the judge. "Can we have a recess, Your Honor? Mrs. Devlin…"

"There's no need for a recess" came a voice, and Eve spun around, surprised. It was Jack, standing, his face blanched, ravaged.

"Mr. Devlin, please," Marty Cohen was saying, putting a restraining hand on Jack's arm.

He shook it off. "I have the right to speak, don't I?" he asked, addressing the judges.

"Yes, Mr. Devlin, you have that right."

"Jack…" Eve began in a warning voice. "Mr. Devlin…"

He ignored her.

"Will you take the stand, Mr. Devlin?" one of the judges asked, frowning.

"No, I'll just say what I have to say and get this farce over with." Jack stood behind the defense table, proud and slim and straight, as if he were one of the attorneys, and he looked right at the judges. His face was expressionless now—he'd gotten himself back under control—and Eve felt her heart beating too loud, afraid for him, hurting for him, terrified of what would come out of his mouth to damn him, to condemn him.

"I am innocent," he said in a clear voice. "I did not kill my wife, Allison. And if you put me in prison for life or if you execute me, you'll be no closer to justice, because her real murderer is still out there. Free." Then he sat down and folded his hands on the table in front of him, turning back into a statue.

There was a hush in the courtroom for a long minute, then a murmur, a buzz and the banging of three gavels. "Silence! Silence in the court!"

The penalty phase was over.

* * *

She and Marty went to see Jack that afternoon. They tried to put confident smiles on their faces.

"How long will it take them?" Jack asked.

"Overnight, at least," Marty said. "The longer they debate, the better. It means they aren't finding it an easy decision."

"You don't have to hang around," Jack said. "They'll let me know when the decision's made, won't they?"

"They'll tell us when it's time to go back to court and hear the verdict," Eve said. "I'll call you instantly."

He nodded. He seemed resigned. She hated seeing him like this—anger, even the dry sarcasm, was better.

"They can't ignore your past," Marty said. "They can't..."

"Sure they can," Jack replied tonelessly.

"We're all very hopeful," Eve said, "Frank Iverson is, too."

"Don't lie to me," Jack said mildly.

Marty left to get himself a hotel room. He couldn't drive home to Glenwood Springs tonight, because the verdict call could come any moment. Eve was left alone with Jack. Even the other prisoners were uncomfortable, giving them wide berth. She wanted so badly to touch him, comfort him in some way, but she couldn't, didn't dare. She was afraid her skin would freeze. Or burn.

"I'm grateful for how hard you worked," he said.

"Listen, Jack, no matter what happens, it's not over. There's the appeals process. It takes years, and either way, if you get prison or...death row, I swear we'll keep fighting, we'll find some evidence, something, to get your verdict reversed. We'll be fighting on both fronts, no matter what it takes, I promise. Don't lose heart, don't give up hope, Jack."

"Who's this 'we'?"

"Me, the Public Defender's Office, all of us. Marty, Hank."

"Really? Does your annual budget run to that kind of investigation, Eve?"

"The appeals process, yes. The rest... Don't worry, we'll manage it somehow."

"You might at that." He actually smiled. "Your commitment is daunting, Miss Marchand. If I were facing you in court, you'd scare the pants off me."

"Thank you," she said, inclining her head mock-graciously.

"Don't hang around here, honestly," he said. "Go out, go have dinner...with Gary."

She looked at him.

"I saw him in court."

"Um. I was surprised to see him there."

"He's waiting for you, isn't he? Go on, get out of this place." He smiled mirthlessly. "Besides, my folks are coming, bringing me dinner. They got special permission."

"That's nice," she said. "That's good."

"A real picnic."

"Jack," she said gently, her heart breaking for him, "don't..."

"Go on," he said harshly, standing, looking down at her. "Get out of here."

She went to dinner with Gary, her cellular phone in her purse in case the clerk of the court called, but it was probably too late tonight. It'd be tomorrow, she was sure. Hours and more hours of waiting. Jack in that jail, wondering, waiting. How could he bear it?

"You're quite something in court," Gary was saying. "I barely recognized you. You're scary."

"Funny," she mused, "that's what Jack said."

"Did you tell him what to say, at the end, I mean?" Gary asked. "That stuff about the real murderer being free?"

"No," she whispered. "I didn't."

"It was pretty good," Gary said, "but he wasn't exactly begging for his life, was he?"

"No, he wasn't."

"You think he'll get the death penalty?"

Eve looked at him, and her eyes filled with tears. "Yes, I do. I'm afraid he will."

Gary leaned across the table and held her hand. "It's not your fault, baby. You were wonderful. You've been killing yourself for three months. You did your best. You can't win every game, Eve."

"I wasn't good enough. I should have..."

"Stop it." He smiled. "Eat your dinner."

Eve looked down at her plate. "I can't," she whispered.

"Damn it, Eve, I have to drive back to Denver right after dinner. Don't you care how *I* feel?"

"You aren't in jail, Gary. You aren't facing execution for a murder you didn't commit."

"Ah, Christ, you're fixated on this case. I shouldn't have bothered coming up here."

"I'm sorry, Gary, but I'm really preoccupied. There's a lot at stake here."

"Your career," he said bitterly, throwing some bills onto the table. "Come on, let's get the hell out of here."

It was cold out, the nights frosty now that fall was here, even if the days were warm. The town was quieter, reveling in its off-season lull, the streets almost empty at night, the brick-paved malls no longer filled with music school students and jugglers and tourists.

"Okay, Eve, let's have it," Gary said as they walked along the quiet streets. "What's going on here?"

"Nothing. My case, my work, the usual."

"Not the *usual*."

"This is an important case. And he's innocent, Gary." She stopped in the middle of the street. "Wait, we're going the wrong way."

"This is the way back to the motel."

"No, no, the jail's the other way. I have to go back, Gary. He's there waiting."

"For Christ's sake, baby, you gonna sit up with him all night holding his hand?"

"No, but I have to go back now, for a while."

Gary sighed. "I'll walk you over there. Then I have to leave."

"It was good of you to come. I'm sorry I haven't had much time for you."

"Well, it's over now. However it comes out, you're done."

She didn't say a word.

"Eve, listen, when the football season's over I'm planning a trip to Asia. A month. Japan, Hong Kong, Thailand. I want you to come with me."

"February?" she said as if she hadn't heard him right.

"A month. February. It won't be too hot over there, and it's before the monsoon season. I checked already. You'll be in private practice by then, so you can take the time off. You've got five months to plan ahead, baby."

Her heart lurched into her throat, blocking her voice, making her nauseous. She couldn't say anything; there was nothing to say.

"You *will* be in private practice by then?" Gary asked in a hard voice.

She kept silent, her head whirling, her heart lodged somewhere under her ribs.

"Eve?"

She stopped and looked up at him and shook her head, her eyes brimming.

"I see," he said, a wealth of knowledge in his tone.

"Please, Gary, I can't talk about it now, not now," she got out.

"You damn well better be prepared to talk about it soon," he said.

"I will, I promise, when this is over, when I'm back in Denver. Right now I can't think, I can't..."

"Here we are at the jail, Eve," Gary said. "Your favorite place, huh? Well, I'll leave you here, baby, 'cause I've got to drive back home."

"Be careful driving, Gary. There might still be some ice on the passes."

"I'll be careful."

She laid her head on his shoulder and felt his arms go around her reluctantly.

"I'll call you tomorrow," she said, "after the verdict's in."

"Okay." He gave her a quick kiss, and she tried to return it, although her thoughts were all on Jack and how he was faring, what to say to him.

"Bye, honey," she said, and she hugged herself, chilly. "Do drive carefully."

"Bye." Gary waved and began walking away, using his cane, one leg dragging slightly, yet so very much better than when she'd met him. Her heart went out to him, but then she turned around and headed toward the front door of the Pitkin County Jail, and by the time she was buzzed into the booking room, she'd forgotten completely about Gary and February and the trip he had planned for them.

Jack was waiting just on the other side of the door.

She came back just after seven-thirty, and he was surprised that it was so early. Frankly, he was surprised she was there at all.

"It's too late for them to convene court tonight," she said. "I'm sure they won't, but you never can tell."

She smelled of cold night air, and her cheeks were pink. She didn't meet his gaze.

"Is it cold out?" he asked.

"Pretty chilly."

They sat on a couch at the far end of the common room, a place that by now was theirs by default; they never met in the tiny, stuffy interview room anymore. The TV set was on, and Jack had been reading the newspaper, one eye on CNN.

"You don't have to be here," he said.

She ignored his words. "Did you have a nice time with your folks?"

"Oh, terrific. Dad said two words all evening, and Mom cried."

"I'm sorry, Jack."

"I wish you hadn't involved them."

"I know how you feel, but it had to be done."

"You and I both know it didn't do a damn bit of good," he said.

"I don't know that."

"Eve, spare me your condescension."

She rubbed her eyes. "You never know. I've been surprised lots of times."

She was worried, though. He could tell. He knew every nuance of her face, every expression, every gesture and smile and tap of her fingers. And she looked tired, done in, a different woman from the righteous firebrand in court. Trials did this to her, drained her. *His* trial had done this to her. He felt a sudden furious helplessness. Locked in here, under sentence of...

"Long deliberations are always good," she was saying. "They've been at it for—" she lifted a slim wrist and checked her watch "—six hours now."

He wondered where Gary Kapochek was. Waiting for Eve in their motel room? Out with friends? If he were Gary, he wouldn't let Eve out of his sight, not for a moment. How insane, as if Eve would ever be anyone's property, as if a man could possess her.

She had leaned back against the couch and rested her head, closed her eyes. He studied the long, white line of her throat. He wanted so badly to touch it, to run his fingers along the smooth, pale skin, that it was a physical pain in his belly. He had to look away. His hands were shaking, his groin tight.

Didn't she know what she did to him?

He wondered if she affected Kapochek this way. He couldn't imagine any man not reacting to her with some sort of passion—fear or love or resentment. He wanted to ask her about her relationship with Kapochek, but he couldn't. And if he did, she wouldn't answer.

"God, I'm beat," she said, opening her eyes.

"Go on back to your room and get some sleep."

"I'll wait till lockdown," she replied, pushing her hair

back behind an ear. In court she wore a severe bun and glasses. Intimidating, professional. Tonight her hair was loose and she wore a pale gray sweater and slacks, a different person. "I couldn't sleep, anyway. I'm too anxious."

"It's *my* sentence, Eve."

"It's *my* case."

He stretched out his legs. "What do you really think my chances are? No bullshit, now."

She gave him a long, assessing look. Finally she answered. "Fifty-fifty."

"I would have said sixty-forty against me."

"Maybe." She twisted on the couch to face him. "Whatever it is, don't panic. Even if they set a date, don't panic. It won't mean anything, it's..."

"It'll mean they decided to put me to death," he said quietly.

She closed her eyes for a moment. "It's only temporary."

"Uh-huh. *Temporary* death."

"Jack, we'll get the sentence vacated, I swear to God."

"Sure."

They sat silently for a time.

"They'll move me to Super Max in Canon City either way," he finally said.

She bowed her head.

"It's pretty bad, I hear. Not like this place."

She looked up. "We'll be doing everything we can, everything."

"It could be years," he said calmly. He'd had a long time to get used to the idea.

"Stop it," she hissed.

"And the worst part is, while I sit there rotting away, Allison's murderer is free."

"We'll find him. I told you, we'll find out who it was, and then you'll get a new trial, or even get released immediately on the basis of overwhelming evidence."

At nine-thirty the jailer told them the judges had retired

for the night and would resume deliberations in the morning. Eve stood to leave.

"I'll see you in the morning. I'll call if there's any word," she said.

She looked so tired, so worried, so young, he wanted to comfort her. Him, the prisoner, comforting his lawyer. Crazy. And then he couldn't help asking what he'd wanted to know all along. "Is Gary waiting for you? I'm really sorry if..."

But Eve was shaking her head. "No," she said softly, "Gary went back to Denver."

It was one o'clock in the afternoon when the call came through to the jail where Marty and Eve waited with Jack. The verdict was in. Court would convene in thirty minutes.

Jack went to his cell to change back into his "civvies," as he put it, and Marty called Jack's folks at their hotel. Eve went to the ladies' room near the booking desk and patted cold water on her face. Her mouth was as dry as cotton.

She accompanied Jack and his guards out of the jail, across the short, flower-lined path to the courthouse. He walked a trifle awkwardly, his hands cuffed in front of him. At the back stairs leading up to the district courtroom, Ross took the handcuffs off. "Good luck, buddy," he said. "I'll miss our card games."

"I let you win, you know," Jack said, giving Ross one of his rare grins.

"Hell, I know you did. What do you think I am, stupid?"

Then they were seated behind the defendant's table, and Bill Makelky and his deputy were at theirs, and the courtroom filled with people. Eve saw the Devlins come in. Jo Ann had been crying.

The whole mind-numbing, archaic legal routine had to be gone through, the clerk of the court, the black-robed judges filing in like solemn birds of prey. The command to rise. The familiar process of dispensing justice.

But not a single one of the judges looked at Eve or Marty

or Jack; not one spared a momentary glance for the defense table, and Eve knew.

She felt her heart close up in her chest like a fist, and tears burned behind her eyes. Blindly she reached out and took Jack's hand, not caring who saw—it was too late for that. And she held on to him through the awful routine of the presiding judge pronouncing the sentence of death for Jack T. Devlin, "to be carried out on January 2 of next year at Colorado State Penitentiary Maximum Security Lockdown by the use of lethal injection. And until then, said prisoner shall be remanded to the custody of Colorado State Penitentiary until his sentence is so carried out, and further that he will be removed from the Pitkin County Jail at the discretion of the Pitkin County Sheriff's Office as soon as possible." *Bang* went the gavel with terrible finality.

All through the terrible words, she held his hand so hard her knuckles were white, and when the sentence was read, she felt his hand grasp convulsively at hers. She looked up at his face, but it didn't change.

In the back of the crowded room, Ben couldn't stifle a sob, and Sarah wrapped her arms around him and cried, too. "Oh, Ben. Oh, Lord, I'm so sorry."

His father put a heavy hand on his shoulder. "Poor bastard," Richards said. But Ben couldn't say a word.

Two rows of seats behind them George Mochlin sat very still, feeling as if someone had stuck a million tiny, hot needles into his body. His bladder almost let down. Behind him, someone, an acquaintance, patted his back. "The prick got what he deserved."

George tried to say something, anything, but his lips wouldn't work. Oh, God, he thought. Oh God, oh God, oh God.

The entire courtroom was still in an uproar, the D.A.'s friends and colleagues congratulating him, slapping him on the back. By God, he hadn't lost *this* one—he'd get elected again without a hitch!

Jack sat straight and stiff in his beautifully tailored pin-striped suit, and he hadn't yet taken his hand from Eve's when Marty awkwardly patted his shoulder and said quietly, "I'm sorry, Jack. I'm real sorry."

Jack inclined his head briefly but said nothing, then he pried Eve's fingers off his, carefully, gently.

"Oh, God, Jack," she whispered, "I'm so sorry." Then she swallowed and straightened her shoulders. "Don't worry," she said with false bravado. "I'll file the Notice of Appeal right away. Tomorrow. I told you..."

"Hang in there," Marty said. "We'll be working for you. It's far from over."

"When will they move me?" Jack asked, and there was nothing left in his voice but ordinary curiosity.

"They won't tell anybody. Probably within the next couple of days. They'll most likely wake you up one morning early and drive you down there," Eve said. "But don't worry. They'll notify us, and I'll visit you. We'll work this out, Jack."

"Sure," he said, but his eyes were looking somewhere else, and he was gone, inside himself, to his place of refuge.

The sheriff's deputy came to lead him away, back to his cell to await the trip to Canon City. "Come on, Jack, let's go," the man said apologetically, politely. They all liked Jack Devlin.

"See you soon, Jack," Eve said. "Don't give up. I'll be in touch."

The deputy took him by the arm and began to lead him away, but Jack pulled out of the man's grasp and faced Eve. He looked straight into her eyes, and he was there, in his body again, completely there, and she saw all the passion and misery and hate and desperation that he'd held and stored all these long months, so powerful that she took a step back as if pushed, and her breath caught in her throat.

"I didn't do it," he said in a choked voice. "You believe me, don't you, that I didn't murder Allison?"

"Yes, I believe you," Eve replied gravely, and then the deputy took Jack's arm and led him out of the courtroom.

PART III

Escape

THIRTEEN

It was snowing on Independence Pass the afternoon they drove Jack to the state maximum security penitentiary in Canon City. The two deputies slated for the job waited as he put a winter jacket on over his orange Pitkin County suit, then they locked him in cuffs and ankle chains and led him, shuffling and clanking, to the sheriff's department van.

The trip would take about three hours, and the two deputies were worried about the return drive over the pass in bad weather at night. Jack heard them talking about it through the wire grill as he sat in the rear of the van. Well, he wouldn't have to worry about coming back in a storm; he'd never be coming back, he thought, over Independence Pass or any other damn way.

There were no side windows on the van, but he could look through the grill out the front, and he watched the scenery roll by, so familiar, the winding valley brushed by autumn's hand. The van's engine strained as it began the climb up the narrow, twisting road to the summit of the pass, rock walls on one side and a steep drop-off on the other. It was a cool, gray day, drizzling on the valley floor, but at the top of the pass, four thousand feet higher, the rain would turn to snow.

"You okay, Devlin?" Gleason, the deputy riding shotgun, asked, twisting in his seat.

"Yeah, I'm okay," he answered.

"My kids always get carsick on this damn road," Gleason said.

"Well, if I feel sick, I'll let you know," Jack said dryly.

The rain changed to snow at ten thousand feet, and the road was wet, starting to get slushy. Jack could hear the tires sloshing through it.

They reached the twelve-thousand-five-hundred-foot summit, a flat, barren, treeless tundra right on the Continental Divide. Not much was visible, the snow coming sideways, the roadway solid white.

The driver, Peterson, was hunched over the wheel, swearing a lot. The wipers could barely clean the windshield. Nasty, Jack thought.

Then they were descending, and the snow let up a bit. Jack leaned his head back, closed his eyes and tried to doze. He could hear Gleason and Peterson's desultory conversation.

"I'm not goddamn driving this in the dark tonight," Peterson said once. "We'll take the long route around through Glenwood Springs."

Jack was lulled into a half doze. His body swayed with the switchbacks automatically; he thought about what it would be like in Canon City, how bad it would be, how he'd have to train himself to stand it. He thought about Eve, the last time he'd seen her, the last thing she'd said, the last lingering scent of her....

For a time Jack drifted in his thoughts; then, abruptly, Peterson yelled something.

Gleason swore, "Christ almighty!" and the van swerved crazily.

There was a sudden noise. That's what Jack would recall, the noise, followed by a tearing, screeching impact, and he was thrown hard against the side of the van. He must have faded out for a moment then. He remembered the silence next, and when he tried to sit up, everything was tilted, the van on its side. He crawled toward the front. "Gleason? Peterson?" he croaked. Nothing.

God, what'd happened? An accident, but... The grill separating him from the front of the van had been knocked askew. Were they both dead? He yanked at the grill with his cuffed hands. It wouldn't budge. He lay on his back, kicked with both feet, popped the grill out. The effort sent a red flash of agony through his head. A warm dampness was seeping down his neck. Blood, he registered, but there was no time for that. He crawled through to the front seat. Peterson groaned. Gleason was hanging from his seat belt, unconscious, his leg bleeding.

Crouching awkwardly, Jack finally reached his manacled hands up to his own head. Wet, warm, the roughness of a laceration. How bad? He tried to think. Nothing came to mind but the desperate need to get out of the cuffs. He couldn't move in them, couldn't help himself or anyone else. He did it without thought, reaching into Gleason's pockets, feeling for the keys he knew were there.

His fingers touched them, yes, and he pulled them out, his hands shaking, trying to fit a key into his cuffs, awkward. Drops of blood fell from his head onto the cuffs, obscuring the lock. It took only a minute to do it, though, and the cuffs clicked open, his hands free, and he opened the ankle cuffs even more quickly. He could move now.

Peterson was stirring feebly, Gleason was still out. Jack's mind whirled with possibilities—wait there, help would come soon. *Run*, open the door and run.

Then he saw the other vehicle through the broken windshield, a camper, on its side, its front crushed. He could see two people inside. And snow piling up on both vehicles, whirling in eddies, hissing on hot metal.

He could run. How far would he get? His head was beginning to throb now, and his shoulder ached, too.

He could run. He was free. In an orange prison suit, with no money, no ID?

But if he stayed... Wasn't this what he'd always wanted,

what he said he wanted, a chance to find Allison's murderer?

He could run. What more could they do to him if—when—they caught him? Not a damn thing. And he had this chance now, this fateful opportunity....

He could run.

Scrambling out the door of the van, Jack limped over to the camper. A frightened face peered back at him through the smashed window, an elderly woman.

"Are you hurt?" Jack asked.

She shook her head mutely.

"Is your husband hurt?" he tried.

"I...I don't know."

"I'll help you out and I'll try to get at him, okay?"

He had to climb up on the camper and pull the door open from there. Agony shot through his right shoulder when he reached in to help the lady out.

Then the man. He was awake, dazed, seemingly unhurt except for some cuts from broken glass. Jack sat the two of them beside the camper, where they were sheltered from the wind.

"I'm going to try to get those guys out of the van. Will you two be okay?" he asked.

"Go ahead, young man," the woman said, holding on to her husband.

He dragged Peterson out from behind the steering wheel. The cold air seemed to revive the man a little, but he was still pretty dazed. Then Gleason. He was as heavy as lead. But Jack got him out, stretched him on the ground beside the van. He was breathing, but his pant leg was soaked with blood, and it continued to well out of the cut.

It occurred to Jack that he was crazy to be doing this, taking time to help these people when he should be running for freedom. Why? But all he knew was that he couldn't leave them, not yet, not quite yet.

He pulled a red bandanna out of Gleason's pocket and tied it tightly around the man's leg. He knew little of first aid, but he did know that you had to keep pressure on a wound. The trouble was, he couldn't stick around to do it that way, so he'd try a tourniquet. Someone would come along soon and find these people—the road was only twenty feet away.

He managed to drag Gleason over to where he'd left the old couple. Then Peterson.

"Is he dead?" the woman asked shakily.

"No, just unconscious. He's bleeding, though."

"So are you," she said.

"I know." He took a deep breath, felt his head pounding. "I'm leaving now. You'll be okay. Someone will come along soon."

"Leaving?"

But Jack had no more conversation left in him. He did only one more thing before he left; he removed the guns from the holsters of both deputies and threw them as far away as he could. Then he turned up the collar of his jacket, thrust his hands into his pockets and moved off, heading down the eastern side of Independence Pass.

How far, he wondered, would he have to walk before he could find a vehicle? No, clothes first. He was a marked man in the orange suit. Clothes first, then a ride.

It was cold, the wind and snow in his face, but he was descending, and it would warm up.

He just had to keep moving, not get stuck out here in the dark. Keep moving.

He came across the hunters' camp shortly before dark. A Jeep, a new Ford pickup and a battered old Chevy pickup. All sitting there waiting for their owners to return from a day's hunting. The Jeep was unlocked, but there were no keys, but the old Chevy... Jack felt a thrill when he saw the keys thrown carelessly on the floor under the front seat. Who'd want to steal an old truck, after all?

He picked up the keys and smiled grimly to himself in the growing dusk. Then he searched the truck, hoping he'd find some clothes, a pair of pants, something to replace the prison suit. But there was nothing except a few oily rags.

The Jeep. Yes, there was a rucksack in the back. He opened it, felt fierce elation burn in him. By God, fate had turned her good side to him this day. Worn jeans, a torn brown-and-yellow wool shirt, a battered jeans jacket, a baseball cap. And a wallet. A goddamn wallet!

He changed right there, shivering in the cold. The clothes were too big, but it didn't matter. He took all the cash there was in the wallet—seven dollars—felt a twinge of guilt, suppressed it swiftly. He'd remember this man's name, and pickup's owner, and somehow, someday, he'd make it right.

He pocketed the cash and climbed into the old Chevy, tossing the orange suit on the seat. It started instantly when he put the key in the ignition, and he silently thanked the truck's owner for keeping it in such good repair.

Clothes, a ride. Damn, he had both, and no one had seen him since he'd left the accident site. He felt his heart lift in a pure, fierce spasm of joy. He was free, for a little while, anyway, and he could allow himself the exquisite release of emotion he'd held in for so long.

Jack pulled out of the campsite and onto the highway. He barely felt the cut on his head or his banged-up shoulder, his hunger or thirst or weariness or the cold. He flipped on the heat in the truck, got the wipers going, and drove down out of the mountains.

He was free.

After the trial, Eve had stayed in bed for nearly two days. When she wasn't curled up dozing, she moved in slow motion. Only once did she venture out of her Capitol Hill home, and only then for ten minutes to pick up an order of Chinese food a half block away.

She thought about Jack continuously, about the appeals she'd file, about the two-hour drive south to Canon City where he'd be imprisoned. She'd make the drive every day, but she knew spending her time that way wouldn't be as productive as working through the lengthy and arduous appeals process.

That process was only one avenue she'd take. There were others. She'd already initiated one by talking to Hank Thurgood. Her office wasn't going to spring for another full-blown investigation of the case, but Hank had promised to do some more snooping on his own.

"You're a doll," she'd told him on the day she arrived back in Denver. "This means a lot to me."

"So I've noticed," he'd said.

She'd lain in bed that first night and worried herself sick about Jack being transported to the state prison. His life was going to be hell there. She couldn't bear to think about it. Not Jack. Not there. And then she'd slept, woken, slept again. And dreamed. She'd dreamed the same dream over and over again: Jack in his new prison greens alone in that eight-by-ten-foot cell. Isolated. No TV. No radio. No human with whom to converse. The death chamber only a few feet away.

Gary had telephoned her last evening and reminded her he was leaving for Miami and the Sunday game with the Dolphins. She'd agreed to cook him breakfast at her house. "But only if you stop at the store and pick up some eggs and stuff."

"Still done in?"

"One more night's sleep and I'll be fine," she'd said.

But she wasn't fine. She got up still exhausted and still anxious about Jack. She hoped to God Gary didn't talk about the trial, because she'd never be able to hide her emotions. How could she have allowed her guard to slip so low? She tried to convince herself it was because of Jack's innocence, but in her heart she was deathly afraid it was much more.

She brewed some coffee and padded in her long robe into the bathroom and brushed her teeth, then combed out her hair.

"You look like hell," she said to her reflection. It was lucky Gary had seen her dragged out before, she guessed. She'd get over it. She had to. There was a lot of work to be done if she was ever going to force a new trial for Jack. An awful lot of work.

She poured a cup of coffee, put in two sugars, no milk. She'd have liked milk, but there wasn't any. She'd also have liked to have her place clean. It wasn't messy. But it sure was dusty. Of course, she hadn't really been home for the past three months. Twice, maybe. And then only for a single night at a time.

Eve sat in her living room on the couch and found the TV remote control under a *Time* magazine that was ancient history. The rest of her mail was still stacked up on the hall table. She'd get to it. Someday.

She clicked on the news, the "Today Show," but she'd missed the top-of-the-hour updates. She felt as if she'd been completely out of touch with the world.

She clicked down to a local Denver station. *Ah, there, the weather.* It seemed there had been a storm in the mountains, snow dumped on the passes. The weatherman said, "Good news for the ski areas in Summit County, bad news for drivers. Up to six inches fell on Vail Pass and visibility was down to zero. The storm should move through the Denver metro area by early this afternoon. The commute home may find ice and a little snow on the bridges and viaducts. By morning..."

Eve half listened. She sipped her coffee and glanced out the living room window. It did look cold, and the sky was the color of slate. The trees in the small yard, though, were still just turning gold.

Some ads came on, so she got up and poured herself another half cup of coffee. She ought to shower before Gary got here.... Eve checked the clock on the stove. God. He'd be here in ten minutes.

"The summit of Independence Pass..." she heard an anchorman say, and her attention was drawn back to the set.

Independence Pass was right outside Aspen. In fact, the road that ran the length of the valley went up over the pass, which traversed the Continental Divide. Independence was only open in the warm months of the year. She'd just driven back over it herself on the way home to Denver.

She sat back down on the couch, put her feet on the coffee table, flexed her toes and listened. The camera was on a man and a woman now. They both looked to be in their late sixties.

Someone was holding a mike up to the woman. "We wouldn't have driven over the pass if we'd heard the weather forecast." The woman gave a strained laugh. "I'm scared to death of heights as it is."

So? Eve was thinking, everyone was a little nervous on the passes in Colorado, especially in a storm. Was this news?

And then a reporter came on. "It was at the summit of Independence Pass where the Norrises encountered the patch of ice. Mr. Norris believes he lost control of his camper and slid into the oncoming sheriff's van...."

Eve sat up straight.

Now the reporter's voice was being overlaid by newsreel footage, and there was a camper on its side, snow piling up on it—the Norris camper, presumably—and next to it was a van, also overturned. The camera panned in. Written on the side of the van, snow partially obscuring the lettering, was Pitkin County Sheriff's Department.

"Oh, my God," Eve breathed, and her heart began to beat furiously.

The scene switched back to the studio in Denver. An update.

"This just in from St. Anthony's Hospital in Denver where one of the Pitkin County Sheriff's deputies was airlifted late yesterday. News 4 has Tom Murphy there now. Let's go to him. Tom?"

The scene switched to reporter Tom Murphy, standing in

front of St. Anthony's emergency entrance. He was holding a tiny mike to his ear with one finger.

"Ah, yes, Renelda, I've just spoken to one of the nurses who attended to the deputy, and she confirms the report that it was Jack Devlin—" Eve stopped breathing entirely "—who placed the tourniquet on Deputy Gleason's leg and then dragged him to shelter next to the overturned van."

"Amazing," came Renelda's voice from the studio. "Was the nurse able to confirm that Jack Devlin used Deputy Gleason's keys to free himself?"

"No. That report has not been confirmed."

"Free himself" tore through Eve's brain.

The scene went back to the studio. "We have an update from our Western Slope reporter in Aspen. Let's go there now. Ken?"

"Yes, Renelda, I'm here with Sheriff Broadly. Sheriff—" the reporter held the mike out "—can you update us on the search for Jack Devlin?"

The sheriff, a big, dark-haired man, came on. "Ah, yes, Ken. We believe that the stolen pickup truck from the Twin Lakes side of Independence Pass was taken by Devlin. This would have been around 6:00 p.m. yesterday evening."

"But earlier reports from your office stated that it was not believed Jack Devlin could have made it down to that camp-site in that storm. Can you comment on that?"

Sheriff Broadly said soberly, "We now believe that's exactly what happened."

The camera panned to the reporter. "The Norrises told this news bureau that Jack Devlin appeared to be bleeding. Can you confirm that?"

Again, the camera panned to the sheriff. "Mrs. Norris did state that Devlin helped her husband out of the overturned camper before he assisted Deputy Gleason. She said Devlin was bleeding from the head, but of course we cannot confirm that."

"I see. And how is the other deputy? The one who was treated here in Aspen?"

"Deputy Peterson is fine. He sustained only minor bruises and a mild concussion."

"Thank you, Sheriff," the reporter said, and he stared into the camera. "To update you in Denver, at this hour convicted murderer Jack Devlin has escaped en route to the state penitentiary. The Pitkin County sheriff has asked for help from the state police and the Federal Bureau of Investigation, stating that the local sheriff's department has neither the manpower nor the resources for a statewide manhunt. Sheriff Broadly believes that Jack Devlin may already have crossed the border into New Mexico in a pickup truck stolen from a hunter's camp...."

A moment later the scene switched back to Denver. In the studio, Renelda said, "Ken, we know that Jack Devlin may have been injured in the accident, but any word as to whether he's armed?"

Ken's voice: "Not yet, Renelda. Mrs. Norris thought he may have disarmed the two deputies, but she believes she saw him toss what she called 'the objects' over the side of the cliff where the accident occurred. And then, according to Mr. Norris, Devlin disappeared."

"Interesting. And of course it was snowing."

"Yes, Renelda, the fact of which has only made this manhunt more difficult."

"Thank you, Ken, from our Western Slope bureau..."

Eve blinked, shook her head and sucked in a huge breath. For an instant she wondered if she'd somehow dreamed all this, but then she looked down; her fingers were wrapped around the coffee mug so tightly, they were white and hurting.

No, she thought, *I'm awake.* And out there, somewhere, was Jack. Alone. And injured.

Ben heard the news not twenty minutes after Eve did. It was Sarah, who'd been out for a jog on the steep Red Mountain road, who rushed into the master suite and shook him awake.

"Get up! Ben! Quick! You've got to see the news!"

"God, Sarah," he said, barely stirring, "take it easy."

She caught her breath. "It's Jack. Ben, he's escaped! I swear to God, it's on the news right now."

Ben sat bolt upright. "You're joking."

But she was shaking her head. "It's true. He escaped last night, up on Independence Pass."

Ben squeezed his eyes shut and felt a surge of joy rush through him. "Let it be true," he whispered. "Oh, God, let it be true."

On the other side of town, at the base of Aspen Mountain in an upscale town home belonging to one of George Mochlin's tennis students, a similar scene was occurring. The woman was in bed, though, and hadn't needed a jog. She'd gotten plenty of exercise sweating beneath George's perfectly honed body.

It was the woman who turned on the TV at the foot of the bed. "Look at this," she said, nudging the dozing tennis pro. "George, look."

He did. Half asleep, her scent covering him still, he rolled over and opened one eye.

"Devlin is believed to be unarmed, though extreme caution is urged should you come upon him. The sheriff's office has issued a statewide..."

George sat up slowly, aware of a terrible pain in his chest, as if someone had dealt him a hard blow.

"Wow," his lady friend said, but he told her to shut up as he tried to fit his mind around the news. Devlin, on the run. And his very next thought drove a stake of fear directly into his heart: Devlin was near, in town, hiding, and he was coming for *him*.

"More coffee?" The waitress stood over the booth, the coffeepot poised above his stained mug.

"Ah, sure. Thanks," Jack said, keeping his head bowed.

She poured the coffee and turned to leave. Then she hesitated. "You okay, mister?"

"I'm, ah, fine."

"You don't look so fine." She nodded at him, bobbing the pencil stuck behind her ear. "Is that blood on your hair?"

Jack felt a shot of adrenaline in his veins. *Think, think,* he commanded his brain. He reached up and touched the cut above his right ear. He'd thought the stolen baseball cap covered it. *Damn.* "I was getting out of a car...really cracked myself. It's okay."

"Oh," the woman said. "You might want to wash it off in the men's room. You know..."

"Sure," Jack replied. "I will." As hurt and exhausted as he was, he knew exactly what she meant. The diner he was sitting in on Denver's East Colfax Avenue was full of homeless characters. Probably the only washing up they did was right here in this rest room—or one just like it up the street.

After he'd abandoned the pickup truck outside of Denver, he'd chosen the avenue as a district he'd be least likely to be recognized in. The old Highway 40—Colfax Avenue—ran from east to west across Denver, right up to the foothills. Both sides of the street for almost fifteen miles were lined with sleazy motels, run-down diners, used-car lots, strip joints, bars, bikers and hookers. And bums. Jack knew he fit right in: dirty, banged-up, wearing too-big, greasy clothes. Now he was sitting in the diner trying to get warm, his head cut, his right shoulder maybe busted, a dollar and twenty-five cents to his name.

Jack bent over his coffee mug and felt a wave of dizziness. Pain shot down his arm and his right hand shook. He took a deep breath, tried to get a grip. He had to think; he had to form a plan before someone recognized him beneath the Colorado Rockies baseball cap and the day-and-a-half's growth on his face.

The waitress returned, warmed his coffee for the fourth time. She gave him a sympathetic smile, and he felt a rush of gratitude. If she only knew. But most likely no one in this dive watched TV, much less read a newspaper. The homeless on the street corners sold them, but Jack would bet his last quarter they didn't read them. Still, by now, his picture had to be plastered all over the front page of the morning editions. Hell, he'd bet CNN was covering his escape.

He left his coffee for a minute to use the rest room to wash the blood out of his hair, and when he stood over the stained sink in the urine-splashed bathroom, he was taken aback at how really bad he did look. Not only was his face grimy, his clothes unfit for the Salvation Army, but the pain he was in showed in his dark eyes, in the tight lines grooving his mouth. "Shit," he said.

Back at the booth, hunched over, he stared surreptitiously at the waitress wearing a once white uniform and little net cap. He *could* play on her sympathy. He could tell her how he was down on his luck and could she spare a meal? Maybe even ask her if he could sleep somewhere for a few hours—namely at her place. She might agree. She looked hard in the face and had clearly been around the block a few times, but her eyes were kind.

Almost as quickly as the notion came to him, Jack dismissed it. Even if she agreed to let him sleep at her place—wherever that was—eventually, sometime today, she was going to see his picture. On television. On a newspaper at a corner kiosk. Somewhere.

As hard as it was to think, Jack knew he had to get off the streets.

He could call Ben. Ask Ben to wire him some money. But to do that he'd have to have ID, and Jack had none. Plus, to involve his stepson in this mess was unthinkable. He wouldn't do it. Never.

Still, he had to lie low for a while. Let himself heal. Think things out. He was free. After all these long months of imprisonment, he was free at last. If only he could remain that way for a few weeks, do some sleuthing on his own. It was the only way.

Jack glanced outside. It wasn't snowing, but a cold wind whipped dust and discarded papers by the window. He couldn't stay outside in this weather. Not in this condition.

He had to get off the streets. Sooner or later, most likely sooner, he was going to be spotted. He needed time, he was thinking when a police siren sounded nearby.

Jack's heart banged against his ribs, and that wave of dizziness swept him again. But the cop car sped by, heading west on Colfax, away from the diner. He swore under his breath and tried to collect himself. And he knew what he had to do.

Jack realized he'd known all along. He realized she'd been in his head since the escape, the whole way down the ridge line of Independence Pass, snow tearing at him, the cold clawing into his bones. Even when he'd found the pickup truck in the campsite near Twin Lakes, he'd been thinking about how he was going to make it to Denver.

But he couldn't involve her in this. Not Eve. The thought of getting her in any trouble at all hurt damn near as much as his shoulder.

But he *could* borrow some money from her. A couple hundred dollars. Meet with her for a few seconds, that was all. And someday, somehow, he'd repay her. No one needed to know. Eve would do it. Despite his being an escaped...murderer, Jack thought, Eve would do this for him.

Jack paid the bill for the coffee, thanked the waitress for letting him hang out inside for so long and left the diner.

It was raw out. The same storm that had dumped an early snow in the high country was now whipping down out of the mountains and heading onto the high plains. He turned his collar up, grimacing at the stab of pain that shot through his arm from the movement. He realized he was actually staggering, and he headed into a nearby alley and leaned against a cold brick wall, trying desperately to clear his head.

Got to contact Eve, he told himself. But how? Earlier, it had occurred to him that there might already be taps on the telephones of those who'd been close to him: his folks, Ben, Frank Iverson. Certainly there'd be a tap on Eve's phone. He could find her house, though. Weeks ago, when they'd taken a break from one of her interviews at the jail, she'd told him she lived in the heart of Denver, not far from her office.

"In LoDo?" Jack had asked, referring to the new "in" place to live, Lower Downtown Denver.

But she'd shaken her head. "No, not on my budget," she'd said. "I live up around Capitol Hill."

He'd wanted to ask if she shared her place with Kapochek, but he'd kept silent, not really willing to hear the answer.

Jack dragged himself away from the wall and moved down the alley, the cold wind buffeting him. He wasn't too far from Capitol Hill. But even if he found her address in the phone book and managed to make it there, surely some police agency had her house under observation. He sure as hell wasn't in any condition to deal with that. He couldn't get caught. Not yet. Not until he had time to look into Allison's murder himself.

Jack moved in and out of the alleys trying to stay warm, trying to think rationally. Every so often he'd hear a police siren. Once he ducked behind a Dumpster when the sound came too close.

Think, he told himself. He wasn't going to last forever out here. He needed to get a room somewhere; he needed some money.

He looked up from behind the Dumpster. All clear. Another spear of pain drove through his shoulder, and sweat broke out on his neck despite the freezing temperature.

He saw it then, a dry cleaner's across the street. He thought a moment. Dry cleaning. And he fought to hold on to the notion as he pictured the suits Eve had worn to court. She had to get them cleaned somewhere.

Jack found a telephone booth partway down the same block of Colfax in front of an adult bookstore. The phone book was torn half to shreds, but the *M* section was intact. Hands shaking from cold and exhaustion, he thumbed through it until he found Marchand, E. And there was her phone number and address.

He knew that after the coffee and tip he had two quarters left, and he reached in the loose front pocket of his shirt and took one out. He dropped it and swore, retrieved it from the sidewalk and slipped it in the slot. He held the receiver to his ear. If she was there, he'd leave his message quickly, not let her respond. She'd think about it and she'd get it. She'd also know his voice. That could be a problem if she said anything aloud. Eve was smart, though. She'd have to know there was the possibility of a wiretap. If he got an answering machine, so much the better, really. No chance of her accidentally giving him away.

He dialed. The phone rang in his ear. Once. Twice. What if she'd gone away? Taken a rest? What if she didn't pick up her messages for days?

It rang a third time.

And then the machine answered.

He waited for the tone, his heart racing. He took a breath and fought the pain in his body. The tone ended. "This is Harry," he began, "from Central Dry Cleaners on East Colfax." Jack stared at the sign above the door to the cleaners. "Remember the stain you complained about on your suit? Well, we got it out for you. It's ready any time you want to pick it up, Miss Marchand. I'll be here all day, and tomorrow, too, till six. Just ask for Harry. Thanks," Jack said, and he hung up.

He looked down at his hand. It was trembling. He thought about Eve and prayed she was in town. Had she said anything to him about going away? But no. She wouldn't leave.

And then another thought struck him with the force of a blow. If and when she got his message, if and when she figured it out, would she help him? Or would Eve do the right thing, the lawful thing, and send the cops to pick him up?

Gary arrived at Eve's a few minutes before nine. He let himself in with his own key and heard water running in her bathroom. He was carrying a bag of groceries in one arm, using the cane with the other. He felt awkward, as he often did when trying to perform the most mundane tasks. And he was a little angry at Eve for not being there to open the door and take the bag from him.

He heard the pipes in the walls protest when she turned off the water, and he called out, "Eve, I'm here."

She answered from down the hall. "I'll be right out."

And that was when Gary noticed her TV was on. A local Denver anchorwoman was giving an update on Devlin's escape. "May be armed and dangerous... If you should recognize Jack Devlin or have any information regarding his whereabouts, the police urge you to use extreme caution and call the authorities at once."

Eve knows, he thought. She'd gotten up—he glanced at the coffeepot—made coffee and turned on the news. She couldn't have missed the reports. The question was, how was she taking it?

He put the carton of eggs on the counter next to the stove, poured two orange juices, opened the package of sausages and searched for her pans. She padded into the kitchen a minute later, back in her robe, her hair newly washed. On her tiptoes she kissed him and smiled and thanked him for picking up the groceries.

Gary cocked his head. "You look amazingly calm and relaxed considering..." He waited for a sign from her. Something to tell him how upset she was over the news of Devlin's escape. She gave none.

Gary leaned against the counter and put his hands on her shoulders. "Hey," he said, "come on. You heard the news."

Eve sighed and avoided his gaze. "Yes, I did," she said. "It's awful. He's going to get himself killed."

"I can't believe you're taking this so coolly. I'm not a fool, baby. I know the guy got to you."

"Don't be absurd. He's a client. You know I always get involved."

In the background there was yet another update on the television. "This just in on the Devlin escape," the anchorwoman intoned gravely. "Police report that Jack Devlin may have purchased gasoline for the stolen pickup truck in the mountain town of Frisco, which is near the Summit County ski resorts of Copper Mountain and Breckenridge. If the reports are true, this would lead police to believe that Devlin may not be headed toward a border at all. Keep in mind that this report is unconfirmed. We're told that the authorities are still concentrating their search in a four-state area. That would include Colorado, Utah, Wyoming and New Mexico. A spokesperson for the FBI urges that you exhibit extreme caution if..."

"For God's sake," Eve said, "Jack's *not* dangerous. The media will whip everyone into a frenzy. Don't they have anything else to talk about?"

"It's pretty incredible news," Gary said. "I'm surprised the media isn't beating down your door."

"Oh, they will," Eve said, "they sure as heck will."

Eve cooked the eggs and sausages and they sat in her kitchen nook and ate, the TV still on in the living room. Gary couldn't believe her control. No matter how much she protested that Devlin was merely another client, Gary knew better. She had to be roiling with anxiety. He ate and thought about that and felt jealous as hell. *Jealous,* he thought grimly, over an escaped convict.

Ignoring the continuous news updates, Eve deftly switched the subject to the Broncos-Dolphins game on Sunday. "How's that new wide receiver doing, you know, Hayden?"

"Coming along," Gary said, studying her.

"Um, didn't he drop two passes last week against the Raiders?"

"Uh-huh," Gary replied. "Of course, he was about to get creamed if he held on. Not a lot of rookies have the discipline to hold on to a pass when there're two defensive gorillas ready to pop them."

"So if they drop a pass, the gorillas go easier on them?"

"Pretty much so. It's like a little reward."

"But *you* always held on."

"Not always, not always," he said, his eyes still on her.

"What time's your flight today?"

"I told you last night on the phone. We're out of here at noon."

"Oh, right," she said, pushing the eggs around her plate. She glanced up and smiled. Not a care in the world.

"Look," Gary finally said, "I think it's damn commendable of you to show all this control, but, Eve, don't kid a kidder. I know you've got to be going nuts."

She laughed, waving aside his statement. "Hey," she said, "if Jack stays on the run, I won't have all those appeals to file. This will save me a ton of work."

"Right," Gary said. "And speaking of which, I really do want you to try to get back on track now with the private practice thing. I know Devlin's trial threw everything off, but it's over. Either he avoids apprehension or they catch him and he ends up on death row. Either way you've got to back off and take a hard look at what *you* want. What you want for us. I've got to be honest, Eve, I can't see living like this. It's absurd. We don't *have* a life."

"Gary..."

"No, wait, let me finish. I saw the doctor yesterday, and he says I can expect even more improvement over the next few months. Maybe even total remission. You can't imagine what this means to me. It's like getting a second shot at life. I want to go places, do things that were only dreams before. I'm not going to let anything get in my way, Eve."

"Gary, I..." She clutched the lapels of her robe together.

"No. Don't say anything right now. I want you with me. I want to set a date for the wedding. No more delays. I *love* you, Eve. If you really love me, then you'll live up to your end."

Eve looked at him for a long moment and then sighed. "I'm trying. I honest to God am trying to figure out where

I'm headed. Where *we're* headed. I do love you. I want to travel. I also have an obligation to my profession. I need..." She looked up and searched his face with those softly intelligent hazel eyes. "Gary, I need to know that I'm doing something really worthwhile. I believe in my work. I believe passionately in it. If I go into private practice..."

"You mean *when*, don't you?"

"Yes, of course. *When* I go into the private sector, I'm still going to work like the devil to educate the courts and the public about the absurdity, the brutality of capital punishment. You know that. You know *me*. I won't ever stop battling."

"I'm not asking you to. I only want you to slow down. You've got to back off, take a look at your life. That's all. Eve," he said, "I sometimes think you're only capable of feeling passion for someone who needs you desperately."

"Gary..."

"Let me get this said. It scares the hell out of me that you only fell in love because I was such a sad sack. And now...now that I'm getting better, I'm afraid you..."

She rose to her feet, shaking her head in denial. "That's bull and you know it." Then she picked up the plates and cleared the table.

Gary said nothing. He knew he'd pressed a nerve, and he was afraid to push any harder. Eve ran water in the sink, and he could hear the news in the background. Devlin, Devlin, Devlin. Hell, he wished they'd gotten the guy to Canon City and stuck the needle in him. It would be over then. Forgotten in a few days.

He checked his watch and picked up his cane, standing. "I've got to go," he said.

Eve turned off the water. Still she kept her back to him. Her shoulders were rigid. Yeah, he'd pushed her. But, damn it, someone had to.

"Don't be angry," he said.

"I'm not."

"Walk me to the door."

"Sure, okay," she said, and she finally turned, wiping her hands on the dish towel. She gave him a weak smile.

"And don't go off the deep end about this Devlin thing, either. Promise me you'll keep your objectivity."

Eve moved to his side and locked her arm in his free one. "I'm a real sensible girl," she said, and they walked toward her front door.

Once there, Gary leaned over and kissed her gently. Then he looked her squarely in the eye. "I want you to promise me something," he said, turning the doorknob. "If, and I only mean *if*, Devlin tries to contact you, I want you to use good judgment."

"Oh, Gary," she said, shaking her head, "don't be ridiculous. First of all, I'm no dummy. I'll bet my phone's already being monitored. And even if Jack did somehow contact me, which I very seriously doubt, I'm an officer of the court. I'd be obliged to turn him in."

Gary opened the door, then turned to her once more. "I hope you mean that, Eve, I really do," he said.

She laughed. "Oh, go on," she said lightly. "Get out of here before you miss your flight. And stop worrying. I'm not stupid."

But when he was in his car, driving toward Denver International Airport, Gary had a sudden mental flash—if Devlin actually contacted her, could Eve be the one to send him to death row?

FOURTEEN

Eve sat on her couch and flicked the remote control from one newscast to another like a junkie, desperate for any new tidbit on Jack's escape. Back and forth, local channels to national, back again, dozens of images crashing in her brain, the most prevalent of which was some rookie cop spotting Jack, pulling his gun, panicking...

She never knew exactly when it was that her eye caught the red blinking light on her answering machine. Still watching the TV, she got up, walked to the machine and pressed the message button. It had to be a reporter, a media hack, someone who'd called while she was in the shower.

She rubbed her eyes, half listening to the TV, half to the whirring of the tape as it rewound. She felt as if her life were coming apart at the seams. It was as if she were teetering on the edge of a precipice—one step and she'd be falling forever.

The message began, loud, absolutely clear and utterly shocking. "This is Harry," the voice said, "from Central Dry Cleaners on Colfax. Remember the stain..."

She knew his voice instantly and irrevocably, and her heart stopped in her chest, then beat again, a slow, heavy beat, while her mind raced. What should she do? Call the police? Call the office and send one of the investigators to pick him up? Colfax, somewhere on Colfax. Where? How?

Was he hurt? Several reports had said he was bleeding. Should she go herself and convince him to turn himself in? He couldn't last long out there alone, no money, hurt, the object of a manhunt. *My God, Jack*, she thought, *why didn't you run? Why did you come here?*

Her phone was most likely tapped; someone would figure out the message was a sham sooner or later. She was probably being watched. Her mind circled, questioned, calculated. A thousand new scenarios flashed through her brain. He was hurt, dying, desperate, dangerous. *He was free.*

Jack, she thought, *why did you call me?*

But she knew. Of course she knew.

Ten minutes later Eve was dressed, in her car and driving down the street before she remembered that someone could be following her. Glancing in the rearview mirror, her heart leaping like a mad thing, she searched the street, but she couldn't tell. Her palms were slippery on the steering wheel, and her nerves twitched like live wires.

Jack, hang in there.

She drove straight to the office and parked in her usual spot in the lot next to her building. She went inside the familiar foyer, got into the elevator. She'd look as if she were going to work.

But she got off on the third floor and ran down the back stairs, out the door, across the lot, striding, not running—that would draw attention to her—got into her car and pulled out onto the busy downtown street. She slid through a yellow light and drove away.

She prayed she'd shaken her tail. Closing her eyes for a moment, she felt panic bubble up in her, pressed it down. Jack was waiting; she had to hurry.

Stopping at a gas station when she reached East Colfax, she fumbled through a tattered phone book. Central Cleaners, Central Dry Cleaners. Her pulse pounded in her ears. Central Dry Cleaners. There it was, way out east, a lousy section of town. She ran to her car and gunned it out of the station, down Colfax, her fingers beating nervous tattoos on the steering wheel. *Hurry, hurry.*

The drive east on Colfax seemed to take forever, and yet it flashed by in no time at all. She drove and watched in her rearview mirror for anyone following, watched the address numbers, first one then the other, all the way down Colfax.

How long had he been waiting? Since she took a shower—hours. Would he still be there? Had he been apprehended already?

There it was, Central Dry Cleaners, a shabby place sitting on a cracked asphalt parking lot between a sleazy bar and a furniture-for-rent store.

She turned in and pulled up at the side of the building. Was he there? He didn't know her car. Would he see her? Looking all around, she bit her lip. What should she do if he wasn't there?

She considered asking inside, maybe even checking out the bar, but she didn't have time, because just then she heard a noise, swiveled around and there he was, crouching down at her passenger window.

She pushed the "unlock" button, and he pulled open the door and slid in beside her.

"Jack," she breathed.

"You came," he said. "I didn't really believe you would. I kept watching for the police...."

She stared, barely recognizing him. He had a baseball cap pulled down over his eyes, and he was unshaven. He wore baggy clothes, jeans and a rumpled flannel shirt and a Levi's jacket. "Jack," she said again, then she recognized something in the way he sat, the way he cradled one elbow in his hand, the taut set of his body.

"You're hurt."

"Some. I think it's okay." He eyed her. "Lend me some money, Eve." His tone was harsh, as if he hated himself. "A couple hundred dollars. I'll..."

"Money? Jack, I'm taking you straight to the hospital. This is crazy. You can't..."

"No hospitals," he said fiercely. "No goddamn hospitals or doctors. Now, don't make me beg. Some money, that's all I need."

Eve stared at him, thinking frantically. "Listen to me," she finally said. "They'll kill you, Jack. Some dumb cop will spot you and..."

Suddenly Jack grabbed her chin and forced her to look him in the eye. "Eve," he said sharply, "you're not in charge here. Not anymore. I'd rather die here and now trying to find out who the hell murdered Allison. I'm not going to rot for years in prison and then let them stick that needle in my vein."

"Jack..."

"No. Just shut up and listen. This is my gig now. All I need is some money, a little time, that's all. I know that by being here, you're putting yourself in jeopardy. I know you could be disbarred for this. Just lend me the money and drive off."

Eve took his fingers from her chin and shook her head. "No. I won't leave you. No," she said adamantly. "The system failed you once, *I* failed you. I won't do it again."

"Eve," he said, and she saw him grimace in pain, "now's not the time to argue. Please, for God's sake, just this once do as I say."

"No, Jack, no. I can't. I'd never be able to live with myself if I didn't help you right now. If we get caught together, well, I'll say you took me hostage. If that's what you're worried about, I'll tell them that."

Jack closed his eyes and leaned back in the seat as if suddenly drained. "Does anyone ever tell you *no*, counselor?" he asked.

Eve shook her head. "I'm the only one allowed to do that," she said. "Now, we'll go to my parents' house. It's up past Empire, a little place in the mountains called Pinecrest."

Jack swore under his breath.

"You're in no condition to argue," she said. She put the gearshift in Reverse and backed out of the parking slot.

"What will your folks say?" he asked after a minute.

"They're away."

"Neighbors?"

"Not close enough to even notice."

"I'll do this," he said. "A day. That's all I need. Then I want you out of it."

"Of course," Eve said, steering into the traffic.

"You're crazy."

She thought about that. "You know," she finally said, "I feel very sane right now. Saner than I've felt in a long time."

Eve drove west, out of the city, very sure of herself now. She'd buy Jack the time he needed. The consequences— she'd think about them later. This was the right thing to do, even up those unbalanced scales of justice for a little while, anyway. It was unethical. It was illegal. She could lose her license to practice law. It was a classic law school case of the greater-good dilemma. But in this case the greater good was absolutely clear to her: she was saving the life of an innocent man. Nothing else mattered.

She gave Jack a sidelong glance and saw that he'd put his head back on the seat again, shut his eyes. The long sinewy line of his throat was beautiful to her. This man, hurt, hunted, exhausted, still had such a grace and strength to him. He never lowered himself to what was around him, not jail, not this situation, either, but held his truths inside, untouchable.

She thought he must be asleep. His head lolled as she turned a corner, but he didn't stir. He probably hadn't slept since yesterday afternoon. And she wondered what he would have done if she hadn't gone to Central Dry Cleaners.

It was about an hour to Pinecrest, a small hamlet in the foothills west of Denver. A post office, a gas station, a motel, a grocery shop. Not much else except for the relatively new subdivision up the hill behind the town, several mountain-style houses of logs and stone and glass, each carefully screened from the others by the pine forest around them. Very private, very quiet.

Eve knew her parents were in Scottsdale playing golf. She wasn't sure how they'd feel about her using their house to hide an escaped criminal, but she was quite sure they'd never find out. It'd all be over before they were expected home.

She drove along the winding road behind the town, up the hill to the long, curving, climbing driveway of the house. Despite yesterday's storm, it was mostly dry, covered only by the golden coins of fallen aspen leaves. The tall trees cast shadows on the driveway, striped and dappled light and shadow. It was a peaceful house, totally surrounded by trees, set into the hillside, with a big deck on one side. Eve's mother loved it, her first new house ever, the first she'd okayed the plans for and chosen every fixture.

Eve pulled up in front of the garage. She thought momentarily of hiding her car, but Jack needed to get inside right away. Turning the ignition off, she laid a hand on his arm. "We're here," she said quietly.

He came awake abruptly, his face freezing into harsh lines, his whole body jerking convulsively. He gasped and swore, his face white.

"I'm sorry," she said. "Are you okay? Jack?"

"Yeah, give me a second. God, I was dreaming."

"Can you get out of the car?"

"Guess I'll have to, won't I?"

She got out and went around to open his door. He moved slowly and painfully, finally straightening, cradling his arm. "Guess I stiffened up sitting so long."

"Come on, let's get inside." She found the key where her folks always left it, in a flowerpot by the front door. The house was spotless, as her mother always left it, but cold. She turned the thermostat up first, tossed her jacket on the couch and turned to face Jack.

"Nice place," he said, standing there hunched over in pain.

"Sit down. God, you look awful. Hungry, thirsty?"

"All of the above," he said, sinking down onto a chair.

"Okay." She studied him for a moment, took a deep breath and held her hand out to him. "Let's go into the kitchen. The light's better. I'm going to take a look at your shoulder."

"You a doctor, too?"

"No, but someone's got to take a look." She took his good hand, wincing at the pain on his face when he got up.

"Funny," he said, "it didn't hurt so much yesterday."

"Adrenaline." She led him into the kitchen, setting him on a stool. "There. Can you get that jacket off?"

She was aware that she still held his hand in hers. She fought the urge to press his head to her breast, comfort him. She couldn't believe it. Jack. Here. The two of them all alone.

But he was hurt and she had to pull herself together and help him. She let go of his hand, avoiding those dark eyes that fixed on her, and slowly, carefully, began to pull at the left sleeve of his jacket. She freed that arm, then, with great care, she freed the right one, aware of his sudden intake of breath. She wanted to say it was okay, go ahead and yell, but she knew he wouldn't. Then she had to cut the shirt away with scissors, up under his arm, down the sleeve, so that she could pull it away.

"Oh, Jack," she said. His shoulder was terribly discolored, livid bruises staining his skin. She touched it lightly, afraid to press too hard. He sat as still as death, his head hanging now.

"Can you move it?" she asked.

"Yeah, if I have to. It hurts like the devil, though," he admitted.

"It could be broken. Oh, Jack, I don't know. You should be in a hospital."

"Don't waste your breath, Eve."

"Ice," she said. "My father always uses ice." She went to

the freezer and put ice cubes in a plastic bag, wrapped it in a dish towel.

"You want to take a look at my head?" he asked.

"Your head."

"I think it got cut. It was bleeding."

"You *think*..."

She looked at the place he was pointing to. She hadn't seen it with his hat on. Blood, dried blood, his hair stiff with it over his ear. She felt her knees go weak and her throat tighten. She swallowed. "Okay. Water, hot water. It's going to hurt. Here, hold the ice on your shoulder while I get what I need."

Sharp scissors, peroxide, hot water. She dabbed with a wet wash rag, dabbed and heard his barely muttered curse. "Sorry."

"No, do what you have to."

"I have to cut your hair away."

"Do it."

She snipped, saw the raw edges of the gash and closed her eyes for a moment, snipped some more. "It needs stitches, Jack."

He grunted.

"It's deep."

"It'll be fine," he said. "Just clean it up a little, whatever you can do."

She tried. Hot water, peroxide, her hands in his silky black hair, her face so close she could smell him, musky, a little sweaty. Her hands trembled with his nearness, the feel of his bare skin under her fingers, his warmth. His need.

"I'm afraid I've messed up your haircut," she whispered.

He gave a brief laugh.

She made a pad of gauze and taped it over the cut the best she could.

"There," she said. "That's all I can do. I hope it'll be all right."

"I'll live," he said dryly.

She got him on the couch, feet up, his bad arm resting on

cushions, the ice pack on his shoulder, one of her mother's blankets around him.

"Thanks," he said. "Eve, you didn't have to do this. I didn't mean to get you involved like this."

She put a finger on his lips and smiled. "But I couldn't help it, remember? You took me hostage."

"Yeah, I forgot for a minute there."

"Take it easy now. Relax. I'll fix us something to eat."

She found some frozen chili her mother had packaged and labeled. "Thanks, Mom," she whispered, heating it up. Crackers, a pot of tea, hot tea.

He was asleep when she brought him the bowl, his face so pale she was afraid for a moment, until she saw the faint rise and fall of his chest.

"Jack," she said softly, worried he'd awaken violently again from that terrible dream. "Jack, wake up."

His eyes flew open and he jerked, but that was all. "Hell of a houseguest, aren't I?"

"Here's some food. Can you eat with one hand? And tea. Tea's good for you. I know I read that somewhere."

He stopped her with a hand on her arm. "Eve. I can't ever repay you for this. I hope to God you won't regret it."

"I won't," she heard herself say, and she wondered where that certainty came from.

She held the bowl and he used the spoon himself. Watching him eat satisfied something inside her, watching the color return to his face, the lines of desperation relax. She could do this for him. Even if it only lasted a little while, she could do this.

He ate the last cracker and she poured him another cup of tea, liberally laced with honey.

"That was good," he finally said.

"My mother's a good cook."

"Will they have fits when they find out I was here?"

"Don't worry about it. They're my problem."

He searched her face. "I bet you want to know why I ran. I bet you're dying to ask."

"I'll admit to some curiosity," she said.

"I'm not sure myself. Partly it was instinct, I guess." He pushed himself up on his good elbow, grunting. "And then I figured, what more can they do to me? I'm a dead man to them."

"No," she said, "don't ever say that. There are appeals, new evidence. We talked about it, Jack."

He smiled sadly. "The average length of time until the appeals are exhausted is more than ten years. Ten years in Super Max. Eve, don't give me that hopeful crap. It's a pretty grim future."

She looked away, staring across the room. He was right, of course. It would destroy him.

"And then there's Allison's murderer. I want him. I want him to pay, to go through what I've gone through. Yeah, I want revenge. I want retribution and justice. But I'll tell you, Eve, I wouldn't wish the death penalty on anyone, not even him."

"I know," she whispered, "and we'll find him, I promise you. Whatever it takes. Hank's going to work on it. I'll work on it...."

"And *I'll* work on it. For whatever time I have. I owe Allison that."

"We all do, Jack." She sighed. "And we all owe you a pardon and a big apology. The system screwed up."

"I'm not holding my breath," he said bitterly.

He dozed off after that, and she did the dishes, tidied up the kitchen, keeping an eye on him. She pulled the down comforter off the bed in the guest room and settled it gently over him. Slipping away for a while, she turned on the TV in her parents' bedroom to the local news. She only had to wait five minutes before the story was on again, one of the Pitkin County deputies talking about what had happened, the sheriff telling everyone to stay calm, as they didn't believe the escaped man had a firearm. He'd discarded the deputies' guns when he could have easily taken them.

And then a photograph of Jack filled the screen, his mug

shot from when he'd been arrested. The sheriff gave his description: five-eleven, one hundred seventy pounds, dark hair, dark eyes. There was a possibility he'd stolen a '73 blue Chevrolet pickup, license plate number...

They didn't know anything more. Good. There was time. Eve turned the TV off.

She went back into the living room and stood over him, watching him sleep. She tried to imagine what he'd been through, but her mind couldn't encompass it. She wondered, looking down at him, how many people could survive this kind of ordeal and remain even vaguely human. And yet he remained the same slightly formal gentleman, honest, caring, intelligent.

At dusk Eve turned on a dim light, then went outside and parked her car in some underbrush near the road, where no one could see it.

Then she phoned her boss at home and told him she had the flu and was going to stay home for a few days.

"Stress," her boss said. "It's stress and exhaustion. Eve, I warned you to take it easier."

"I will, I swear I will. I'll sleep for the next few days."

She considered calling Gary, but she couldn't. She didn't want to lie, and she had no idea how to explain what she'd done. She'd call him in Miami later....

She heard a noise from the living room. Jack. Running in, she saw that he'd sat up and was flailing at the blanket with his good arm.

"Jack," she said, laying a hand on his shoulder, "what is it?"

He started violently, then fell back against the couch. His skin was putty gray and slick with sweat. "God," he muttered.

"What is it?"

"The dream." He rubbed his eyes with his hand. "They're killing me, and I can't breathe, and everyone is watching...."

Eve felt her eyes fill with tears. Falling on her knees beside the couch, she took his hand. "It won't happen," she said. "I swear to you. I won't let it happen."

He pinioned her with his gaze. "I almost believe you when you say that."

"Believe it."

"Eve, I can't let this hurt you. That would be the worst thing that could happen."

She shook her head.

"I shouldn't have involved you."

"Go to sleep," she said.

He lay back and closed his eyes. "I have to find the murderer," he said. "I don't have time to lie around like this. I need to be out there asking questions, pushing."

"Tomorrow," Eve said.

"There's not enough time. I don't have long. They'll find me. They'll find you. Damn it, they'll get me soon."

"Tomorrow," Eve said again. "Think about it tomorrow," and then she laid a soothing hand on his forehead.

FIFTEEN

Jack awoke confused, his head aching, every muscle stiff and sore. For a moment he wasn't sure where he was, until he recognized the raftered ceiling, the log walls. Eve's parents' house. He lay there quietly, taking in the mechanical sounds of the house, and then he saw Eve in the easy chair next to the couch, asleep, her cheek resting on the chair back, her legs curled up on the seat, hugging herself as if she were cold.

He watched her for a very long time; her face was averted, her hair lying in a mass of curls against her skin. So beautiful. He recalled with utter clarity the feel of her hands on him. She must have thought he'd shivered and cursed from the pain, and he had. But there'd been more to the ache inside him, more than he dared to think about.

Beautiful, brave Eve.

Two things concerned Jack now, though—the need to re-lieve his bladder and the question of how his shoulder would feel when he moved it.

He sat up with care, nearly groaning out loud. God, he was sore. Cautiously, he lifted his arm off the cushions. It worked. Very stiff, with a deep ache in the joint, but it worked. Maybe it wasn't broken, after all.

He pushed away from the down comforter and swung his

legs off the couch, stood shakily. A wave of dizziness swept him, but it passed.

He found the bathroom, and when he got back, Eve was still asleep. Good, she needed it.

He stood there, holding his bad arm, watching his hostage—that was a joke. Nevertheless, if he got caught, if she was still with him, he'd swear he'd kidnapped her. After all, what did he have to lose?

He had a little time now, and he was free. He looked around the rustic room, breathed in the fresh, untainted air. God, he could walk outside if he wanted to. No locks, no guards, only Eve asleep, watching over him, protecting him.

He felt a pang inside as he stood and looked down at her, because he could never have her, never hold her or love her or claim her love. He was a hunted criminal destined for death row, but beyond that she belonged to another man. Two attractive, successful people who loved each other, two people who would have a good life together.

She began to awaken then, shifted her position; her fingers closed, then released, she murmured, and her eyes opened, looking straight into his. Startled, she sat bolt upright. "Jack," she said in a sleep-husky voice. "What...?"

"I'm okay. Had to find the john."

"Oh." She rubbed her eyes and stretched. "I must have fallen asleep."

"I guess so."

"How are you feeling?"

"Like the cat dragged me in. Better, though. Better than yesterday."

"That's wonderful." She smiled, and he felt his insides squeeze again.

"Eve," he said, "we've got to talk. We've got to figure out what to do. I don't mean *we*, I know what I have to do. But you could be in a lot of trouble. I can't let that happen."

She got out of the chair and faced him. "Damn it, Jack, it's too early for that. I'm not even awake. I told you how I felt yesterday, and it hasn't changed. Now, let's get some food, showers, some clothes." She eyed him. "My dad's stuff should fit, a little big, maybe, but you're the same height."

"Eve..."

She turned her back on him and went down the hall. He heard water running, and he sank down onto the couch. God, he didn't have the strength to argue, and she knew it.

When she came out she'd showered and changed into a new sweater—it must have been her mother's. Her hair was wet and she carried a pile of men's clothes.

"Okay," she said, "I feel somewhat more human now. Here are some of Dad's clothes. Can you take a shower all right? Be careful of your head. You probably shouldn't wash your hair, the wound might open again."

"I think I can manage," he replied, "but if I couldn't, I'd like to know what you'd do about it."

She ignored him completely. "I think your arm should be in a sling. I bet I can fix you one. A scarf or something." She cocked her head and studied him. "Don't shave."

He felt the stubble on his chin. "Think it'll fool anybody?"

"No one who really knows you."

"I was afraid of that."

He could see she wanted to say something else. "What?" he pressed.

"I just wondered... Do you want to turn the TV on? Do you want to see what's happening?"

He averted his face as if he'd been slapped. "Christ, no."

"I think I might," she said quietly. "You know, just to find out what's going on."

"I'm not interested," he said harshly.

"Did you know... Jack, did you know the sheriff called in the FBI?"

"It figures." He closed his eyes. "My folks must be going crazy. Poor Mom. God, the police are probably all over them." He pounded his fist into the couch. "Goddamn it! And it makes it even worse for you, too."

"Not really. I'm still your hostage." Then she sat on the couch beside him, turning serious. "There's only one thing

I'm terribly afraid of. I just keep worrying that they'll find you...and they'll use violence, they'll shoot, and you might get hurt. I worry about that, Jack."

"I'd rather go like that," he said in a tight voice. "Quick and clean."

"Don't! Jack, don't talk like that."

"Fine. I'll take that shower, then. Give me the clothes."

The soap stung the cut over his ear and lots of other cuts he didn't know he had. His shoulder was too sensitive for the shower spray, but it felt good.

Here he was, taking a shower in the same place Eve had just been. He had spent the night with her, in a manner of speaking. Wasn't that what he'd dreamed and fantasized about for the past three months? Being alone with Eve Marchand? It was funny, if you had a sardonic sense of humor, because he couldn't take advantage of the situation. He was half crippled, hiding from the law, weak as a kitten. All those fantasies—what a waste.

He toweled his hair dry very carefully, wiped a spot off the fogged-up mirror with his good hand. He looked like hell. His hair was lopsided, there were lines in his face that'd never been there before and his eyes were sunken. He sure couldn't appear in polite society looking like this; he'd scare anyone he talked to. He felt a little like Frankenstein's monster, an object of terror and hate, a sick mirror image of society through no fault of his own.

No fault of his own. *Deal with it*, he told himself, *just goddamn deal with it.*

He managed Mr. Marchand's corduroy trousers, but the shirt was difficult. He kept trying to button it with his one good hand, fumbling, as he went into the kitchen.

Eve was stirring something in a pot. She looked awfully domestic with one of her mother's frilly aprons tied around her waist. He wanted to walk up behind her and put his arms around her, the way a man did with a woman he loved.

He couldn't, of course. She wasn't his to touch, and his right arm wouldn't go around her, anyway.

She turned and saw him working at the buttons. "Let me do it," she said. "I want to fix the sling up first, though."

Her mother's paisley scarf made a decent facsimile. "Is that okay?" she kept asking. "Does it hurt? Can you relax your arm?" Then she frowned. "We need one of those hospital slings. I can see they'd work much better."

Jack just stared down at her, his pulse too quick.

She pulled the shirt on his good arm, then around the bad one and began buttoning it up. Her head was bent, an inch from his nose, and he could smell the shampoo she'd just used. Her fingers moved up the shirtfront, buttoning, touching skin, trailing fire. He held his breath.

"Just two more," she said, and looked up.

Their eyes met and held. Jack could no more tear his away than stop his heart from beating. He saw something in her gaze that he couldn't name, didn't dare name. She swayed toward him, and he heard the swift intake of her breath. Everything inside him tightened, drew up into knots of pain and desire, and he became suddenly and acutely aware of all his senses. It was a strange, unsettling interlude, as if time had stopped, the room had emptied of air and sound, as if nothing existed except the two of them in a place where no one else could enter.

Finally he stepped back and the spell broke, shattered, and time continued. His lungs drew in air, and he felt irrational anger fill him.

"I'll do it," he said brusquely, turning his back on her.

There was a long silence, then he heard her say, "I made oatmeal. Is that okay with you?"

"Sure," he growled.

After breakfast Jack went out onto the deck that opened off the living room. It was cool after yesterday's storm, but the sun was bright and the sky was perfectly, brilliantly blue. He sat on one of the Marchands' wrought-iron chairs and put his head back, feeling the sun. God, it felt good. He hadn't been in the sun much for over a year. A Hawaiian boy, raised in the sun. It had put a shadow on his soul, he realized now. A simple thing like not being able to feel sunlight every day.

He sat there and tried to form a cohesive plan. Time was the key. He hoped he had enough.

One thing he knew: whatever there was to find, it would be in Aspen. Allison had been killed there, and her murderer was someone she knew, someone she'd either given her security code to or let in herself. Someone from Aspen.

He'd had a year to think about the crime, and although he was still no closer to solving it, he knew where to look. There was Mochlin, of course. Jack had never thought Mochlin much of a suspect, but the new information about his alibi put him in a different light. John Richards—he'd been in Las Vegas, had a dozen witnesses, an ironclad alibi, and both Hank and Eve felt he had nothing to do with it. It was true, if Richards had wanted to kill Allison, he would have done it years ago.

The Wades. Could Allison have been threatening them with the exposure of a theft? It would have been like her to do that; Jack was the first to admit Allison could be tough as nails. But would the Wades have *killed* her for that?

If he got to Aspen, talked to some of these people, pushed some buttons, maybe he could force someone's hand.

He'd gone over the evidence in his head a million times. All circumstantial. His fingerprints on the statue. Hell, he'd handled it dozens of times. So Marnie didn't dust too carefully. Big deal.

And then there was his lighter. How had the lighter gotten there? It had been driving him crazy for more than a year now. He'd lost it months before the murder, but he couldn't remember exactly when. He hadn't noticed, didn't even know how long it had been missing before he realized it was gone. Maybe he'd lost it right there in Allison's living room, and it had fallen or been kicked under the piano.

Maybe it was a coincidence and had nothing at all to do with her murder except in the eyes of the cops.

He sat there, feeling the sun warm his bruised body, gathering strength by the moment as if the rays were entering his body and healing him.

If the lighter's presence was *not* a coincidence, he thought, then someone had stolen it from him or perhaps picked it up where he'd dropped it or left it. They'd deliberately kept it, then placed it near Allison's corpse, planted it, as it were, and the only reason for that would be to frame Jack. If this were the case, then the murderer was close to him and to Allison, knew about their fight, the divorce, the money, everything. Either Mochlin or Richards knew enough, but so did the Wades.

Who was it, then? And *why*, why had this person killed Allison? No one had a motive—except the one attributed to Jack—and *he* hadn't killed her, that was the one sure thing in this whole rotten business.

Surprisingly, Jack dozed after a while, warmed by the sun, and he dreamed of Allison again, a light, happy dream of a time long past, a time when they'd first been in love and Jack had felt so very, very lucky.

He woke to the sound of footsteps and the brush of Eve's hand.

"Oh, I'm sorry. I didn't know you were asleep," she said. She held another ice pack. "I was going to give you this for your shoulder."

"That's okay. I keep dozing off like some old codger."

"You must need it," she said, arranging the ice pack.

"Listen, Eve, I'm going to get out of here today."

"Sure you are."

"I have to."

"What exactly do you plan to do?" she asked, sitting across from him on a chair. The sun was behind her; it made her features indistinct and created a shining halo of her hair. He wanted so badly to reach out and touch it.

"I think it's better you don't know."

"I see." She clasped her hands around one knee and leaned back. "And *how* are you going to do this, whatever it is?"

"I just need to borrow some money."

"And where would you go? How would you get there? You shouldn't drive like that, even if you could get a car. And you can't use mine, because there's probably someone looking for it. Oh, Jack, you're not being practical."

"*Practical.*" He moved restlessly, hating the fact that she was right.

"You're still a mess," she said softly. "You need some time to recover. Leave it alone for now."

"I don't have time to leave it alone, Eve. I only have *now.*"

She leaned forward and put a hand on his knee. "I know. You must be going nuts, but you really aren't in any shape to go anywhere."

"What about you?" he asked, suddenly realizing she had a job, friends who might be wondering where she was. And Kapochek. "Don't you have to go to work?"

"I called in sick. It wasn't hard to convince anyone. I guess I've been looking like death lately."

"You look just fine," he said.

"A gallant gentleman. Why, thank you, sir."

"What about your friends?"

"Gary's in Miami with the team," she said, "if that's what you were asking."

"It's not my place to ask."

She cocked her head, and he couldn't read her expression because of the sun behind her. "No," she said slowly, "I guess not."

She left then, telling him she was going to put the television on. "Someone has to keep up on the news," she said lightly.

He tried to think about what he was going to do when he got to Aspen, but he couldn't figure out how he was going to get there, and the same questions chased themselves around in his brain: Who? Why? And he felt the familiar anger and frustration rise in him. He couldn't afford to feel like that. He needed his wits about him, untainted by emotion. He needed all his powers of analysis.

Damn this useless arm!

He needed to be going somewhere, doing something, asking questions, forcing answers!

He got up and walked to the end of the deck, looking out over the valley, flexing his arm, closing and opening his fist in the sling, shrugging the shoulder to see how it felt. Sore, very sore. He cursed under his breath. Eve was right, he couldn't do a thing yet.

He wandered into the house and heard the muted sound of the TV set coming from the bedroom—she was listening to the news. Moving around the room, he noted architectural details—the angle of the rafters, the windows, the floor plan, a very good kitchen layout. He wondered idly who'd designed the house. It could have been Florio or Tom Jenkinson or maybe Cal Owens. Colleagues. Once his peers, now—what?—enemies? He'd lost their friendship, their respect, lost the right to breathe the same air as they did.

He studied the books on the shelves around the fireplace. The Marchands had wide interests, from the flora and fauna of the Rocky Mountains to spy thrillers. He stopped at the photographs of the family set in frames on the shelves. Eve in pigtails, Eve with friends, Eve on a horse, grinning from ear to ear. Eve skiing with a girlfriend. Eve at her college graduation in cap and gown, clutching her diploma. Her expression was serious. She'd known she was going to law school, he supposed, but had she known then that she'd be a crusader, a defender of the downtrodden?

It occurred to Jack that soon there would be new photos on the shelf, wedding pictures of Eve and Kapochek. She'd be dressed in white, holding flowers, happy, gloriously happy. They'd love each other and belong to each other. He was a good man, Kapochek, and he needed Eve. And they had a future together.

Jack had no future at all.

The day passed with agonizing slowness for Jack. Impatience gnawed at him, alternating with a sick exhaustion that caused him to doze and jerk awake.

"I'd go down to the store to get the newspaper," Eve said, "but I really don't want anyone to know I'm here."

"Your car's in the driveway," he pointed out.

She shook her head. "I parked it down by the road behind some bushes."

"Clever. You think of everything."

He slept that afternoon again, lying on a lounge on the deck. When he awoke he went inside to find Eve cooking dinner.

"Pasta," she said. "I couldn't find anything else."

"Sounds good."

"I'm not much of a cook. I never have time."

"I'm not fussy. Prison food is pretty boring, even in Pitkin County Jail."

He sat at the kitchen table and watched her. Every move she made was poignant to him, achingly so. It was as if they were a couple, doing normal, routine things, but he couldn't quite convince himself of that. This was special, this time they had together, fateful and rare, and it would have to last him the rest of his life.

Her narrow back, her hands holding and reaching and turning, her legs, jeans-clad, graceful. Her beautiful hair, her profile, her eyebrows pulling together as she searched in a drawer. The quick, shy flash of her smile as she turned to find him studying her.

"Don't watch, you make me nervous," she said.

They ate. He hardly tasted it, still watching her, sucking in every moment he could, to cherish and hold close, to remember for whatever time he was allowed.

The spaghetti kept sliding off his fork; his left hand was pretty useless. He made a mess, splashing sauce all over. Eve leaned across the table once and wiped the side of his mouth with her napkin.

"You need a bib," she said. "Maybe I should feed you."

"Maybe," he rejoined, still feeling her touch.

After dinner she watched the news again while Jack walked around the deck in the sharp evening air. Still weak but improving. Three circuits of the deck, clenching and unclenching his fist.

"Come in," Eve called from the doorway. "It's cold."

"Not yet."

"I'd turn the outside light on for you, but I don't want to draw any more attention than necessary."

"I'm fine."

"The FBI thinks you're in New Mexico. They have new evidence. A man saw you in Santa Fe."

"Good," he said. "I always liked Santa Fe."

"Um." She stood in the doorway, backlit, hugging herself. "You're making me nervous pacing like that, like an animal in a zoo."

He stopped short and looked at her. "Yeah, that's it, all right. That's what I am."

"Oh, Jack." Her voice was contrite.

"It's okay. That's what prisoners are, animals in a zoo."

She moved across the desk toward him, shadowy in the dusk. "You're not an animal," she said. "You're a man. A good man."

"How do you know?" he asked angrily. "What makes you so damn sure? How do you know I didn't bash Allison on the head?"

She was silent a moment, her eyes on him with absolute faith. "I know," she whispered. "I just know."

He wanted to grab her and yank her close, to kiss her mouth until she moaned, to tangle his fingers in her hair, to crush her and worship her.

"I've got to get the hell out of here," he said savagely. "I'm leaving tomorrow."

Eve only stared at him, as if in understanding, and somehow her compassion was more painful than anything else. He couldn't know it then, but things were only going to get worse.

SIXTEEN

F BI Special Agent in Charge Ralph Hawley banged the Devlin file on the conference table in the Denver branch office. Immediately his underlings put down their foam cups of coffee and sat at attention, military-style. They were scared to death of him. And that's the way he liked it.

"Devlin's been on the run for over forty-eight hours now, and so far you cream-of-the-crop agents don't have one single valid lead. What the hell is the government paying you for?" Hawley's shrewd blue-gray eyes met each of theirs in turn.

"Well?" he barked at Agent Krupp. "What about the sighting in Santa Fe?"

Krupp sat up even straighter. "I just got back less than an hour ago, sir, and I'm afraid it was a case of mistaken identity."

"You're positive? Willing to stake your career on it?"

Krupp swallowed hard. "Yes, sir, I am."

Hawley snorted. He was a tall man, straight as a blade, whipcord lean, his face prematurely lined, his hair completely gray despite the fact that he was only in his early forties. He wore his hair in a crewcut; he wished all his agents did, but regulations allowed for less severe styles. Nevertheless, none of his men sported a mustache, much less a beard. They wouldn't dare.

He stood at the head of the conference table, folded his arms and pinned Agent Morales with his famous glare. "Play that tape for us, please, Agent Morales."

Morales looked nervous. "The one from the phone surveillance at the Marchand woman's, sir?"

Ralph Hawley glared more fiercely.

"Yes, sir," Morales said crisply, and he popped a cassette into a player that rested on a table in front of him.

Hawley narrowed his eyes and listened. "Harry...Central Dry Cleaners on Colfax...stain on your suit..."

"Play it again, Agent Morales," Hawley said.

They all listened. When Morales finished playing the tape a second time, Hawley said, "Comments? Follow-ups?"

No one spoke for a long second. Finally, Agent Dent said, "Ah, sir, I'd like to follow up on this one."

"Oh?" Hawley said, pivoting to face him.

"Yes, sir."

"Well, let me tell you boys something," Hawley said ruthlessly. "I made a simple call to this dry cleaner's, and guess what?" He waited. You could have heard a pin drop on the gray carpet. "No guesses? Well, then, it's like this. There is *no* Harry there. Okay? And furthermore, has anyone here ever gotten a gander at Miss Eve Marchand?"

Morales cleared his throat. "I saw her at the federal courthouse once, sir."

"And?"

"She's, ah, very professional, sir. Ah, younger than you might think."

"And?"

"Ah, she's an attractive woman, sir."

Someone snickered but was instantly silenced by one of Hawley's withering glances. "Agent Morales is quite correct," he said. "Miss Eve Marchand is one fine-looking woman. Now, it occurs to me, as I'm sure it does to everyone here, that such a splendid example of the female of our species would be a bit hesitant to use a cleaner's in a district where she'd be certain to be molested. In fact," Hawley went on, his voice rising, "in fact, my dear agents, she'd be a goddamn fool to even consider it!" He waited a long minute, then pressed home his point. "So, that leads me to wonder—could this Harry have, in fact, been our boy Devlin leaving her a cryptic message?"

The agents nodded quietly in unison.

"Aha!" Hawley said. "What was so hard about that deduction? Nothing. Not a goddamn thing. So I'll tell you what. *I'll* check out the Marchand woman myself. And Morales..."

"Yes, sir?"

"You locate that defense attorney Frank Iverson and talk to him. And you, Dent, I want you on everyone in Aspen who testified for the defense. Devlin's got to seek help from someone, and I want that someone covered. And, Krupp, you'll check out that Santa Fe lead again. For God's sake, check in with the local authorities. Don't piss 'em off. Be sweet as pie. But find out if they're on to something we're not."

"Yes, sir."

Hawley picked up the Devlin file, turned to leave the briefing, then paused. Slowly he came back around to face his field agents. "I want Devlin," he said. "I don't care if it's dead or alive. I want him. What I *don't* want is for some penny-ante rural sheriff to beat me to him. Is that understood, boys?"

"Yes, sir," they chorused.

"Good, good," Hawley said, and he gave them a rare smile before his face settled back into the grim lines of his profession.

Eve didn't check her home answering machine for messages until well into the evening hours, when Jack had nodded off on the couch.

There were at least a dozen messages from media types, all wanting information on Jack, all asking her to please return the calls. *Fat chance*, she thought.

Her boss had called, too. Nothing that couldn't wait. And her mom had called, just checking in. "Your father and I are so sorry about the Devlin trial, honey. Hang in there and don't worry about the man. Everything always works out. Chin up."

"If only Mom knew," Eve said aloud.

Gary had telephoned, as well. And as she listened to his familiar voice, she was racked with guilt. She'd told him—*promised* him—she would turn Jack in if he contacted her. How could she have been so wrong? She listened to his message—tidbits about the upcoming game—and she realized that most likely the FBI was listening, too. Gary would hate that; even more than she did, he'd hate his privacy being invaded.

Then there was a call from Ben Richards. His tone was halting, as if he didn't know exactly what he wanted to say. But Eve got the gist of it if in any way, shape or form he could help Jack, she was to call him at once. It struck Eve that perhaps Ben had figured Jack would come to her, but she discounted the notion. All Ben meant to convey was his concern for his stepfather. She remembered how well he'd done on the witness stand and she smiled. At least Jack had one person on his side. No, she thought, he had two.

Then an unfamiliar voice came on the recorder. She couldn't figure out who it was for a minute, until he gave his name. Special Agent in Charge Ralph Hawley of the FBI. Her heart pounded against her ribs. *Oh, God*, she thought. *Oh, God.*

"Return this call at your earliest possible convenience..." he was saying, and he left his number in Denver.

The FBI. Special Agent Ralph Hawley. His call was not social. She knew that. She knew he'd heard the dry cleaner's message and picked up on it. He had to know. Any damn fool would have known!

"Okay," Eve whispered to herself, "okay. Calm down and think."

She had to return his call. If she ignored it, he'd be even more suspicious than he already was.

She thought for a moment and concluded that Hawley must have contacted her office by now. They'd have told him she was sick, resting. That might buy her a little time, but not much.

While Jack stirred restively with his own demons, Eve paced the floor. She had to play this smart. She could return the call from here, of course. But nowadays everyone in law enforcement had caller ID on their phones, and this Hawley would know instantly where she was. He might send someone here to check.

Damn!

Okay, so she'd have to drive to Denver in the morning and return his call from her house. There was no other choice. If he'd been having her place watched, he would realize she'd been gone. But so what? If he knew, if he asked, she'd say she'd stayed at Gary's or something, stayed there to avoid the incessant ringing of her home phone. He couldn't call her a liar. He couldn't *know* the truth.

She was still scheming when Jack sat bolt upright from another dream. Then he grabbed his shoulder, winced and swore. Even in the dim light from a single lamp she could see the sweat gleaming on his torso. Every fiber in her wanted to go to him.

"Bad dream?" she ventured, frozen near the plate-glass window.

Jack looked across at her; he scrubbed his good hand through his hair, carefully touching the bandage above his ear. "Is there any other kind?" he said.

Eve sighed and looked away.

"Sorry," he said. "I keep dumping on you."

"It's all right," she said. "I understand. This hasn't exactly been a picnic."

"No, it hasn't," he said dryly. Then he cocked his head slightly. "Why aren't you in bed?"

"Couldn't sleep."

"Uh-huh." Jack got up then, rising stiffly. She couldn't help staring at him, at the sweat still slick on the skin that showed through his open shirt, the button undone at the waist of his pants, the straight slimness of his body. He walked into the kitchen, snapped on the light and stood at the sink running water into a glass. She followed him despite the alarms sounding in her head. A knowledge lurked, not quite hidden, in a corner of her brain, a dangerous knowledge that was ready to pounce: she cared too much, far too much about him.

Oh, God, she thought as she watched him drink, *don't let him see.*

Sensing her presence, Jack turned. "Go to bed, Eve."

She held his gaze for a fraction of a second too long. "Yes," she finally said, "I will."

It was only six-fifteen in the morning when she awakened. She padded to the kitchen and put coffee on. As she was turning to go to the bathroom, Jack appeared silently in the doorway.

"Oh!" she gasped, and her hand went to her breast, and that was when she realized she was wearing nothing but one of her mother's lacy nightgowns.

She shrank inside her skin, feeling hot all over—she'd never expected him to be up so early—and turned her back on him. Too abruptly, she knew. "Coffee I put a pot on."

She busied herself at the counter, but   ld feel Jack's eyes on her, burning through the fli   n overwhelming urge built in her—to turn   fold herself in his arms—and it felt as if s
edge of a cliff and had to jump, ju
pation, to jump and get it over w

Finally she heard him move,
the hall, heard a door open th
quavering breath.

By seven Eve was showe
hide the dark rings of wo
on leaving for Denver to

fore seven, though she wasn't certain what to tell Jack. If he
knew the FBI was questioning her, he might flee, probably
would. A picture formed in her mind: Jack on the run again,
stealing a car, a cop spotting him, drawing his gun.... She
couldn't let Jack go off alone again. She simply *wouldn't*.

In the kitchen she poured herself a second cup of coffee
and found him outside, standing in the dawn. In the pearly
shadows of morning, she could see him drinking in his freedom. Suddenly she felt as if she were intruding on the most
intimate of moments. She turned to go quietly back inside.

"No," he said, "it's okay. Come and look at this."

Eve joined him at the rail on the deck. At the edge of the
pine forest, barely visible in the awakening day, was a doe
and her half-grown fawn. The mother raised her head from
the grass and sniffed the air, her big ears twitching while her
fawn grazed lazily, barely aware of the humans nearby.

"Pretty, huh?" Jack commented.

Eve nodded. "Do you hunt deer?"

He let out a low breath. "I have. With Ben and a couple of
friends. But right now, standing here like this, *free*, I'm regretting it. I'm regretting a lot of stuff. If I ever get to the bottom of my wife's murder, if I can ever be really free again,
my life's going to take a whole new direction."

"You mean your architecture? You aren't going to work
anymore...."

But Jack was shaking his head slowly as he leaned against
the rail, still watching the deer in the quickening light. "I
guess what I mean," he said pensively, "is that designing
spectacular homes for the rich has lost its glamour. Given
the chance, I'd like to spend my life...well, helping people.
Maybe people in jams like I'm in right now. I mean, I'm not
ackerjack detective like your pal Hank Thurgood, but
ot to be something I can do." He gave a low laugh.
out of this mess, that is."

is profile. The strength in him. The deter-
anything, she wanted to tell him it was
ake it okay for him. But Jack didn't

want that emotional support from her, and that frightened her a little. She was so used to being needed. Every man she'd ever known had needed her emotionally. But Jack was very different. He'd accepted her help as his public defender. *A lot of good that did him.* Now, though, he was keeping her at arm's length. Even if he got caught, she knew in her heart Jack would reject her efforts to save him from his fate. Eventually he'd turn completely inward and he'd be lost to everyone. She couldn't let that happen.

After a time they went back inside and shut out the cool September air. Jack took a shower while Eve fretted, knowing she had to leave within the hour for Denver to make the call to Agent Hawley. She didn't want to tell Jack the truth; nor did she want to lie to him.

When he emerged from the steamy bathroom, he'd put a new bandage on the wound over his ear—and done a bad job of it.

Eve nodded to him. "Come here," she said. "Let me do that right."

Jack grumbled something about his useless arm, then reluctantly sat down on a stool in the kitchen and let her fix the oversized Band-Aid on his head. She tried to be all business, but it was hard. Merely touching him was becoming more than she could handle.

She finished and stepped back, hands on her hips. "There. That should stay on okay for a while."

"Thanks," he said, fingering it lightly. "And thanks for everything. I'm not sure how I would have managed."

She took a breath. "Well," she said off-handedly. "I've got to make a run to Denver this morning. I'll be back as soon as I can."

"Denver."

"Uh-huh. Couple of errands."

Jack eyed her long and hard. "What is it?"

"Nothing."

"Come on, Eve. Don't you think I know you well enough by now to spot a lie?"

"Really, Jack," she said.

"Tell me. What errands?" he pressed, still pinioning her with that dark gaze.

Eve sighed. "All right. I've got to return a call to an FBI agent. It's no big deal. Routine, I'm sure."

Jack just kept staring at her, reading her. "And you have to call from Denver," he stated flatly. "Let me guess. You're afraid the FBI's on to you. Maybe they monitored my call to your house. Maybe they figured it out."

"Don't be silly."

"You're a bad liar, Eve."

"Jack…"

But he raised a silencing hand. "Go to Denver. Do what you have to do. But I suggest you tell them a whole lot of truth, even that I made you drive me here. Say you got away this morning."

"No."

"The matter isn't open for discussion."

Eve drew herself up. "You can't go this alone, Jack Devlin. You need my help. You're not even strong enough yet to…"

"I'm strong enough, Eve, and I want you out of this before it all comes crashing down around your ears. You're risking too much."

Eve swore at him. She rarely swore, but right now she was furious. "I know what you're planning. I know exactly what you're up to, Jack, and I'm telling you it won't work."

He laughed without humor.

"You're going to take off for Aspen, aren't you?"

He regarded her cautiously.

"Don't answer. You don't have to. I already know. It's crazy."

"I don't happen to agree," he said. "Aspen is where the truth is."

Eve sighed. "Let Hank do the ferreting. I'll call him and…"

Jack rose to his feet. "No. I'm the one who knows these

people. I'm the one they'll be scared shitless of. I've got to talk to them in person. I'll know who's lying. And that damn lighter of mine..." He paused, his brows drawing together, "the cigarette lighter. I'm starting to think it's the key. Someone planted it at the murder scene."

"You could have dropped it weeks before, Jack. We've been over this...."

But he was shaking his head. "No. Ray or Marnie should have found it. Allison was a stickler for housekeeping. I've got to talk to them, too. And Mochlin, that son of a bitch. I've got to see him face-to-face. There's only one way I'm going to clear myself, Eve, and that's if I go to Aspen and confront these people without shackles on my hands."

"You'll be caught."

"Yes, eventually I will. But maybe, just maybe, I'll find out what I need to know first. It's the only chance I have."

Eve looked at him. After a minute she finally had to nod. "There's no stopping you, is there." It wasn't a question. "I just want you to do one thing for me, okay?"

"Let's hear it first," he said.

"Wait till I get back this afternoon. Don't leave until we can talk this out a little more."

"I won't change my mind."

"I won't try to make you. I just think you should have a better plan. Please, Jack. Wait for me," she urged.

He finally had to agree. "All right. But how are you going to handle the FBI?"

Eve smiled. "That's my problem. I handle these guys every day, Jack. And if they're looking for a routine pattern in my behavior, well, they've got a long look ahead. The one thing I've never had is a routine."

It was at the front door, car keys and purse in hand, that Eve turned back to him, unable to stop the question from forming on her lips. "Jack, did you...at the end, did you still love Allison?"

He leaned against the far wall and folded his arms across his chest, wincing at the movement. After a long moment, he said, "Yes. Yes, I loved Allison. But now, in retrospect, I..." He hesitated and let out a whistling breath. "I guess it was based on all the wrong things. I never saw that before now."

"Why now?"

He shook his head.

"Tell me."

His expression closed, and she knew she couldn't press him anymore. But his words tantalized her: his love had been based on the wrong things. He'd never seen it before now. *Why not?*

The whole way into Denver she tore his words into shreds, analyzing each one, rearranging them, second-guessing, putting them back together. *Why now?* she kept asking herself. *Why now?*

Marnie Wade took her most defensive stance and faced Ben's girlfriend in the garage.

Sarah was nervous. At twenty-three years of age she'd never had a confrontation like this before. But Ben was being no help whatsoever. As far as he was concerned, his missing Rolex watch—the college graduation gift his mother had given him before her death—was of small consequence. Ben was far too preoccupied, glued to the television screen, sucking up every tidbit of news about Jack's escape. Sarah, however, had had enough of Marnie's laziness and sarcasm. And now the missing watch.

"Ben wants you packed and gone by this afternoon," Sarah said, facing her while Marnie put a lid on a trash can.

"*Ben* wants us out of here? Or *you* do?"

"It's Ben's watch. I know we can't prove you took it, but that's beside the point. Ever since Allison died, you and your husband have done nothing but take advantage of Ben. Don't you think he knows you charge all of your personal stuff on his accounts around town?" Sarah felt heat rising up her neck. "And when he got back from California last month there were seven hundred miles on the Range Rover that weren't there when he left."

Marnie swore, her eyes flashing. "You're full of it. No one drove that car. No one's driven it since Allison died. And as for that stupid damn watch of Ben's, hell, he's lost it six times since she gave it to him. Ask him, why don't you. And besides, *you* can't fire us, anyway. I'll bet Ben doesn't even know you're out here right now."

"Yes, he does. He told me to handle it," Sarah lied.

"Right," Marnie sneered, and she swept past Sarah, bumping her shoulder.

"By this afternoon, Marnie," Sarah called after her, furious. "This is no joke."

At the door leading into the utility room, Marnie paused. "We'll just see what Ben has to say about this." She went inside, slamming the door behind her.

SEVENTEEN

Special Agent in Charge Ralph Hawley rang the bell of Eve Marchand's Capitol Hill house at twelve noon sharp. He took in every detail as he waited for her to answer: the slightly seedy look of the place, as if she didn't fuss over it, the lack of flowers or any kind of landscaping. A busy lady. Oh, yeah, very busy.

He knew she'd heard from Jack Devlin as surely as if he'd been a fly on the wall when the conversation had taken place, and he'd pin her to that same wall with his knowledge. He was looking forward to it.

She opened the door, and he noted that she was younger looking than he'd expected, but cool, unflustered. She put her hand out. "Agent Hawley?" she said. "Come on in."

Her house was very plain, neat and serviceable, but with no frills, no personal touches. Very hard to read.

"Coffee?" she asked.

"No, no thanks. Had enough for today." This wasn't a social call.

They sat on chairs in her living room, looking directly at each other. She wasn't nervous—yet.

"So, Miss Marchand." Ralph rested his hands on the arms of the chair, tapping one finger on the fabric. "I don't have to tell you why I'm here."

"No, you don't." Her clear hazel eyes met his unflinchingly.

"Okay, let's not play games. I'm looking for Jack Devlin, and I figure he might have contacted you."

"Really."

"Look, I got a warrant three days ago to tap your phone, along with a whole bunch of others', and I know about that call from Central Dry Cleaners. I checked with them, Miss Marchand, and they don't have, and never have had, any Harry working there. They're all Orientals, one big happy family. And they never had any item of clothing belonging to you, not in the past six months, anyway." He pinned her with a hard glare. "It's a crime to aid and abet an escaped felon. And we could probably get you on accessory after the fact, too. You could be disbarred." He waved a hand. "Hell, I don't have to tell you all this. You're a *lawyer*." He put a heavy dose of scorn into the word.

She surprised him then. "Well, you're right. Jack did contact me."

Hawley leaned forward. "And?"

"I told him to turn himself in. He was hurt. I told him to go to a hospital."

"Where was he?"

"Somewhere in Denver."

"And then what?"

She shrugged. "Obviously he didn't take my advice."

"That was a really dumb thing you did, Miss Marchand. You should have called the police instantly. Goddamn it, we're not fooling around with a petty thief here. This man is dangerous!"

She looked at her hands and said calmly, "Jack Devlin is no more dangerous than I am. Probably less dangerous than you."

"Don't give me that baloney."

She leaned forward herself and fixed him with her gaze. "He's not dangerous and he's not guilty, either."

"Oh, sure, him and a hundred other convicted murderers."

"He's an innocent man, Agent Hawley, and he won't hurt anyone. He doesn't even have a weapon."

"He did a con job on you, lady." He shook his head. "Did he tell you where he was going?"

She was silent for a while, then she said, "I could invoke lawyer-client privilege, Agent Hawley."

"Go ahead, try."

She got up and walked to a window, folded her arms in a defensive gesture. "He talked about going back to Aspen. He wants to find the real murderer."

Hawley gave a short bark of laughter. "The *real* murderer!"

"Yes, that's what he said."

Ralph Hawley swore silently. She was lying. A good act, but he knew she was lying. No way was Devlin going back to Aspen where everybody knew him, where he'd be caught in a day, maybe in an hour. He might be heading to Mexico or to Canada, but he sure as hell wasn't headed for Aspen.

"Do you expect me to believe that?" he asked angrily.

She spread her hands. "Believe what you like."

He rose. "Okay, if that's the way you want it. I'd hoped you might cooperate, but I guess you're not going to."

"I'm worried about Jack. He's hurt, and I'm afraid you people will shoot him. He's not armed, he's not dangerous and he's not guilty."

"Nice speech, Miss Marchand, but save it for court." Hawley tried to stare her down, but she wasn't retreating one inch. A tiny spark of admiration flickered inside him.

"Look, if Devlin contacts you again, you call me personally." He handed her his card. "And if I find out that you're lying, I'll nail you to the wall."

She looked down at his card, then up into his face. "If he tries to contact me, I certainly will let you know," she said coolly.

Outside, on her porch steps, Ralph Hawley shook his

head in silent frustration. *She knows exactly where he is*, he thought. *The lying bitch.* And then, despite himself, he felt that ember of admiration flare. That was some woman, lawyer or not. He'd sure prefer to have her on his side—but she wasn't. She was on Jack Devlin's side.

The minute Hawley was gone, Eve stuffed some personal items into a bag, things she needed for a few days, and she thought as she did it that she must be crazy, putting herself at risk like this. She hadn't lied to Hawley, not technically, but he knew she wasn't exactly telling the truth, either. He'd warned her, and he was right. She was jeopardizing everything she'd worked for.

Why? For Jack, because he was innocent, a victim of the worst sort of injustice, and she couldn't bear for another innocent man to die. But there was more, because this time she was working outside the law, and her whole life had been spent working within it, respecting it.

She went out to her car and started it. There'd be someone watching her, she knew, maybe even Hawley himself. She'd be followed wherever she went. As she drove down the street she thought furiously, amazingly clear-headed.

She went straight to her office, parked in her usual spot, calmly walked into the building, went up in the elevator.

Nonchalantly she said hi to everyone and went straight to Chief Public Defender Bob Calpin's office.

"Eve," he said, surprised. "I thought…"

"I just needed a couple things from my desk, Bob. But I wanted to ask for a few more days off. I'm really done in this time."

Bob pushed himself back from his desk. "Sure, take whatever time you need."

"I'm sorry about this, but I'm a wreck over this Devlin thing. I'm going to hibernate, turn the phone off, the works."

"I understand, Eve. You did the best you could with Devlin. Don't torture yourself. And he's taken matters into his own hands now, running like that. It's not your problem anymore. Leave it to the authorities."

She thought about that all the way down the rear stairs and out onto the street, where she hailed one of Denver's infrequent taxis. *Leave it to the authorities.* If she did that, a lot of men would die; in this case, Jack Devlin. It just wasn't in Eve to give the authorities that kind of responsibility.

The taxi dropped her at a car-rental agency, where she rented a nondescript midsize car, and it wasn't until she was on I70 out of Denver that she started shaking.

She gritted her teeth, locked her hands on the steering wheel in a death grip and tried to stay at the speed limit. She'd been gone since eight that morning and she was worried about Jack. Had anyone found him? Was he okay? Could Hawley track her, trace her, locate them? How much time did they have?

She parked the car in the bushes, hidden from the road, and ran up the driveway, sweating, her heart beating like a drum, her breath short. She burst into the house.

Silence. Not a sound, not a sign of life. No blanket on the couch. No Jack.

He'd left. After she'd gone through all this he'd left, run off, disappeared again. Hurt, alone, no money, no car...

"Eve?"

Oh, God. He was there, coming in from the deck.

"Jack," she breathed. "I thought... God, I thought..."

"I wasn't sure who it was at first, so I went out on the deck around the corner. You okay? You look like something happened. Were you followed?"

She put a hand to her chest and tried to take a deep, cleansing breath. "I'm okay. A little shaky, though. What a morning."

She told him about Hawley while she ate a late lunch; she hadn't had a thing all day, and suddenly she was ravenous. He sat across from her, unconsciously flexing his hand in the sling, listening quietly.

"So he knows. I didn't tell him everything. He's a scary guy. Determined. Smart. He won't let this go, Jack."

He nodded.

"And then—" she took another bite of her sandwich "—I had to do some evasive maneuvers, get a rental car."

"Eve..."

She put her hand on his arm, stopping him. "They probably have an APB out on my license plate, or they will soon. This'll give us time."

"Us?"

"I'm going to Aspen with you."

"The hell you are!"

"Jack, tell me, how are you going to go alone? How will you get there? Where can you stay? Everyone in town knows you. You wouldn't last a day. I can do the legwork, I can get us a place to stay. I have it all figured out."

He frowned. He leaned his good elbow on the table and rubbed his temples. Then he looked up. "I can't let you do it."

"Why not? In for a penny, in for a pound."

"Goddamn it, Eve."

"Why not?" she asked again.

He looked at her, shook his head. "All my life I've fended for myself, and this sure as hell isn't the time to start asking for help."

"You're wrong, Jack. This is the time you need help the most." She reached out and lightly touched his arm. "Don't be afraid to ask, to accept help. Everyone needs it once in a while."

"No," he said stubbornly.

"It's time, Jack."

"You're out of your mind, Eve."

"Maybe," she said, "but I really don't think so."

While Eve cleaned up the dishes, her confidence bled away. She knew why—it had been coming for three days now. Hanging over her head, ready to fall like the slanted blade of a guillotine.

She had to call Gary.

She had to; there was absolutely no way around it. It wasn't fair to treat him like this, ignoring the fact that everything had changed, not telling him what she was doing. She owed him honesty. Oh, God, it was going to be awful.

It was much worse than she expected.

"Hi, baby," Gary said brightly. "You just got me in time. I have to meet Nelson for dinner soon. How's it going?"

"Gary," she said, then she swallowed. "Gary, um, there have been some developments here."

"What do you mean?"

"I, uh, I'm taking a few days off. I'm not at home. Gary, I..." She stopped, not sure what to say, trying desperately to come up with some kind of rationalization for her behavior.

"Eve? Where are you?"

It suddenly occurred to her that if she told Gary, he could call the police. Would he? She didn't know. Horrible, she didn't know if she could trust him. "Um, don't worry. I'm perfectly safe."

"Eve, what in hell's going on?"

She drew in a breath. "Jack called me."

There was a terrible silence on the phone.

"It's okay, Gary, I'm fine," she said quickly into the electronic void.

"My God, Eve." Gary's voice was low, hoarse. "He's there with you now, isn't he?"

She said nothing. Her heart beat so loud she could hear it inside her head.

"He's there with you," Gary rasped. "A convicted murderer, an escaped convict. My God, Eve, you're out of your mind!"

"It'll be okay. He's innocent. He's an innocent man. Gary..."

"Where are you?" he thundered.

"I'm safe, I'm fine. Don't worry. Please, don't worry."

"Don't worry? Eve, what's wrong with you?"

"I'm fine," she said again. "I'm going now, okay? I'll keep in touch."

"Eve, goddamn it, where are you?"

"Goodbye, Gary," she said quietly, and then she hung up.

When Gary got off the phone with Eve, he wasn't sure if he was furious or shocked. The only thing he was certain of was that she'd gone right off the deep end this time.

Harboring an escaped murderer.

He paced his hotel room, his limp more pronounced than ever. Under his skin, his nerves leaped erratically. Damn her honesty and damn her job. She was throwing away everything for this man—her career, her future. Throwing her life away on an escaped convict. Why was she so sure Devlin wouldn't murder her in cold blood?

Gary was so agitated that he forgot the time, forgot that he was supposed to be meeting his buddy Nelson Rourke for dinner to discuss one of the young college kids Nelson was scouting right here in Miami. All he could think was that he'd screw her up good, call the cops in Denver and tell them what he suspected. A moment later he scrubbed a hand through his hair and shook his head. He couldn't do that to her. As mad as he was, as much as he disliked Devlin, he couldn't do that to Eve. And he didn't know where she was, anyway.

At six-thirty the phone rang. He grabbed it, certain it was Eve calling back to tell him it was all a mistake.

It was Nelson. "Hey, I'm down here in the bar, pal. Did you fall asleep or something?"

Gary tried to fit his thoughts around reality. Nelson. Dinner. Hell. "Ah, no, sorry. I didn't realize what time it was."

"Want me to get a table in the dining room, meet you there?" Nelson asked, piano music playing in the background.

"Sure... No," Gary said abruptly. "Let's have a drink before dinner."

"Now, that sounds serious. A drink the night before the game? You've got me curious, pal."

"I'll be right down," Gary said, and he hung up, trying to collect himself. Tomorrow was the big game—he couldn't afford to be thinking about anything else. A drink, maybe two, and he'd calm down.

The two drinks, however, turned into three. Gary had eaten only a few pretzels and peanuts at the bar, and the alcohol was taking its toll on his empty stomach.

Nelson hung out with him, curious and concerned. It was when Gary ordered a fourth drink that Nelson said, "Okay. This is ridiculous. What's going on?"

"Nothing," Gary said.

"Right. When's the last time you got smashed? Are you trying to kill yourself?"

"Drop it, will you?" Gary sat back in the comfortable pastel chair, crossed his legs, automatically massaging his thigh.

"It's Eve," Nelson went on.

"I said drop it."

But his friend wasn't about to. "You know," Nelson said, leaning toward him, "a blind man could have seen this coming."

"I don't know what you're..."

"Ah, hell, Gary, Eve's one of the greatest ladies I know. But she's traveling a different road. She's not going to change."

Gary took a long drink of his margarita and then swore. "It's that goddamn Devlin."

"Figures," Nelson said. "Eve's got to be going nuts with the guy out there on the loose."

"Yeah, well," Gary said, almost telling his friend the whole truth. "I think she's gone crazy. I honest to God think she's lost it."

"How's that?"

"I think she's fallen for the guy."

Nelson sat back and whistled between his teeth. "No way," he said after a minute.

"Pretty damn hard to believe, isn't it?" Gary said, and he finished his drink, then waved the cocktail waitress over.

He remained at the bar after Nelson threw his hands up and went to a late dinner. By then Gary was feeling no pain and slurring his words, barely aware of the woman who'd taken the bar stool next to his. It wasn't until she tapped him on the shoulder and said hello that he took any notice at all.

"I don't know if you remember me," she said, "but we met last winter after a game in Pittsburgh. Donna Haverlund."

Gary peered at her, trying to focus. She looked vaguely familiar. A groupie? One of the women who followed the team wherever it went?

She seemed to read his mind. "I know what you're thinking," she said, her voice soft, pleasant, "but I'm not a groupie. My dad's one of the sports-medicine trainers. You know, Bill, Bill Haverlund. Sometimes he splurges for an extra plane ticket for me to go to the games. I'm quite a fan."

"Mmm," Gary said, turning toward her now, aware that she was a very attractive woman, a little young for him, midtwenties or so. Nevertheless, she *was* pretty, with big blue eyes and a mass of gold hair that hung below her shoulders in soft curls. She was wearing a flower-print coral-colored dress with a very short skirt, and high, high heels. She had bare shoulders and a super figure.

"I've always admired you tremendously, Mr. Kapochek."

"Gary," he said, his lips feeling suddenly numb. And that was when he knocked his drink over with his elbow. "Damn," he mumbled. "I guess I'm drunk."

"That's okay," Donna said, and she began to mop up the spill with cocktail napkins. "You should probably get some food in your stomach, though."

"Uh, yeah," Gary said, feeling a wave of dizziness.

"It's none of my business," Donna said, "but I've read all

about the medication you take, and maybe you really shouldn't be drinking."

Gary looked up and tried to focus on her. "Had a bad day."

She smiled and nodded. "It happens to all of us. Would you like me to help you to your room? I'm not flirting, Mr.... Gary. I'd just like to help if you'd let me."

He peered at her again and felt a hot rush of gratitude. "You might have to carry me," he got out.

"I don't know about that," she said, laughing, "but I've got a strong shoulder if you need it."

Gary did use her shoulder to lean on, and she wrapped an arm around his waist, steadying him, even carrying his cane. She got him to his room and into a chair, and that was when he got sick as the devil, grabbing a wastebasket and heaving into it. When he was done, lying back in the chair, sweating, dizzy, he was aware of her cleaning up the mess, pulling his shoes off, dampening a washcloth and holding it to his brow.

"God, I'm really embarrassed," he muttered.

But Donna shook her head. "Oh, we all do dumb things. This will be our secret. Okay?"

"Okay," Gary said, letting her pamper him, realizing how much he appreciated a woman's gentle touch.

After a time she helped him into bed, seeing that he undressed right down to his boxer shorts. She sat on the edge of the mattress and rubbed his back until he began to drift. He felt curiously good despite the beginnings of a headache, and he said drowsily, "You're very sweet, Donna."

"Oh, I don't mind," she whispered, still rubbing his back. "Now, go to sleep."

"Will you be here when I wake up?" he said, almost gone.

"If you want. I'll stay if you want."

"I want," Gary said, and he drifted off, her fingers warm and gentle on his bare back.

EIGHTEEN

"I'm going out," Jack announced just as Eve was getting ready to go to bed.

"What?"

"I'm going out. I need the keys to the car."

She stared at him. "But you can't even drive."

"Sure I can." He pulled his arm out of the sling and flexed it to show her. It hurt like hell, but it worked.

"Where are you going?" she asked in such an anxious voice that Jack had to smile.

"I've been thinking," he said. "Even with a rental car, they'll be sure to trace it sooner or later through your credit card. The FBI guy knows by now that you dropped the tail, so he's going to check around. I figure I can find an old wreck somewhere and take the plates off it. Switch them."

"I'll come with you."

"No, you won't."

"It isn't worth it, Jack. What if somebody sees you?" She was so worried for him, it struck him as ridiculous. *He* had nothing to lose—she had everything.

"How long will it take? Where are you going? Can your arm handle it?"

"Don't worry. I'll take care of it. Just go to bed."

"You need tools. I'll get them."

He followed her into the garage, where she found him a

couple of screwdrivers and some pliers. She handed them to him, but when he reached out to take them, she refused to let go.

"You're sure about this?"

"Stop babying me," he said, perhaps too sharply, because he saw her eyes cloud over.

"Sorry," she said.

He relented. "I'll be careful. I won't be too long. Get some sleep, Eve."

"I won't sleep a wink till you get back," she said seriously.

"The keys," he said, "okay?"

"You need a flashlight?" She rummaged around in her dad's tools until she found one.

"The keys?"

"Upstairs."

He left her, worried, sitting on the couch hugging herself. "I'll be careful," he said.

She nodded, biting her lip.

It occurred to Jack as he started down the driveway that he should get rid of the bloody, torn clothes Eve had cut off him. They were in the trash can in a bag; he'd seen her take the bag out. He'd dump them somewhere so they couldn't incriminate the unsuspecting Marchands. Lifting the trash can lid, he reached for the bag. *Ouch.* Wrong arm. He got it with his left arm and carried it down the driveway.

He thought about Eve as he backed the car out of its hiding spot in the bushes, and he thought about her as he drove down the road, savoring the feeling of being out alone, the night air hitting his face. It was such pleasure to be doing something as simple, as beautiful, as driving a car.

But Eve never left his thoughts. That call she'd made to Kapochek. Jack had gone out on the deck and closed the door, tried very hard not to hear. What had she said to him? Had she told him Jack was there? Had she trusted him that much?

And what had Gary's reaction been? If it were Jack, he'd have been livid, insane with fury. With jealousy.

What was Eve doing—burning her bridges? He drove, noting the route he was taking, and looked for parked cars, preferably abandoned. Out here the houses were widely spaced and surrounded by trees, and no one would notice him, especially in the dark.

Jack turned the radio on, and he listened to the music, smelling the night air. It was such exquisite freedom.

It took him an hour, but he finally found an ancient VW van, painted in faded psychedelic colors, sitting on blocks. It was parked by an old barn on what had once been a ranch, but the place appeared to be abandoned now.

It was awkward unscrewing the van's rusted plates with his bad arm. He couldn't hold the flashlight and screwdriver at the same time, but he managed. It took so long he started worrying about Eve—she'd be anxious. But he felt a great sense of accomplishment when he tossed the rental plates into the back seat, hid the bag of bloody clothes under the seat of the old van and drove off. He'd done it.

When he got back to the Marchands' house, he pulled into the bushes, doused the headlights and sat there a moment. If Eve was asleep, fine, he'd just go to bed, but if she'd waited up... It was hard to be so close to her; every moment of proximity was a kind of sweet torment. He had to constantly steel himself so as not to give himself away by touching her, saying something, looking at her a certain way. He was weak, staying with her like this, jeopardizing her future. Disgustingly weak.

He got out of the car and started walking up the driveway. It was steep, and he was in lousy shape, but he relished the darkness, the stars, the pine-scented air, the cold.

The lights were still on in the house. Damn her, she hadn't gone to sleep yet. But there was a new light—he peered through the darkness on the deck. A bright spotlight. The one she hadn't wanted to turn on in case the neighbors noticed.

He walked a few more steps, puzzled, and when he got closer, he saw Eve out on the deck, standing there in the light. She must have gotten too worried about him to stay inside, he thought; she must have gone out there to wait for him.

He could make out the pale oval of her face looking down the driveway at him, as if she knew he was there, but there was no way she could see him—it was too dark. And he was about to call out to her, to let her know he was back, when something stopped him, an intangible sense that something was wrong. Her stance, the light, the way she hugged herself against the cold…

The short hairs on Jack's neck prickled and he slowed down, watching Eve intently. She stood there like a statue, perfectly still, and then he could see her turn her head toward the house, and suddenly, shockingly, a man walked out onto the deck. Jack stopped short, frozen in the shadows of the tall pines along the driveway.

He didn't recognize the man, and he couldn't hear what he was saying, but he knew Eve had been out there on the deck for one reason only—to warn him of this danger. He took a careful step backward, his eyes locked on the brightly lit tableau on the deck, then he turned and quickly, quietly melted into the pitch-black forest, returned to the car and drove away.

Eve was out of her mind with worry. She shivered with a combination of cold and fear, and her mother's sweater did no good at all.

"You can come inside now, Miss Marchand," Ralph Hawley said. "We're through searching."

"I'd rather not," she said. "I like the fresh air."

"Have it your way." The FBI man shrugged. "We'll just hang around if you don't mind."

"I *do* mind."

Hawley smiled falsely. "Just a figure of speech, Miss Marchand. Devlin's coming back sooner or later. You know it and I know it. He has nowhere else to go. He's got your car, the one you rented, and he's not going to leave you here alone without it."

"A friend borrowed the car," she said. "I told you."

"Sure." He grinned again, a ferocious stretching of his lips. "And you also told me you rented that car because yours wouldn't start."

"That's right."

"Sure it is." He turned to go back into the house. "I'm patient, Miss Marchand. He'll be back, and I'll be waiting."

Eve walked to the edge of the deck and leaned her hands on the railing, staring out into the darkness. She drew the cold night air into her lungs and prayed that Jack saw the light, understood its significance, that he wasn't going to come up the driveway unsuspecting. Hawley had put his own car into the garage, so Jack wouldn't see it. Oh, God, she hoped Jack had noticed her warning!

Hawley and two other agents had arrived shortly after Jack had left. She'd almost dropped with shock, thinking, thank God Jack wasn't there.

Hawley had bragged about how easy it had been to find her. "All I had to do was go to your office and tell them I needed to talk to you. They were very cooperative, told me every place they thought you could be. You weren't hard to locate, Miss Marchand. Not hard at all."

The worst moment of the whole terrible ordeal had come when one of Hawley's henchmen had checked the trash can outside. Eve had watched from the living room window, watched the man walk up to the can and watched him lift the lid. Her heart had been in her throat.

It's all over now, her brain had screamed—he was going to find Jack's torn and bloody clothes.

But he hadn't. And it was a long, terrible moment before she'd realized that Jack must have had the presence of mind to get rid of those clothes. She'd almost fainted with relief.

Still Jack hadn't come back. It had been over two hours

now, two hours of terrible anticipation that he'd return and walk smack into the trap, that she'd be helpless to stop it.

It was past midnight before Eve went inside, chilled to the bone. Jack would have been back by now; he must have seen her. *He must have.*

She walked past the three agents, who were sprawled out on the couch and chairs in the living room, drinking cup after cup of coffee, waiting patiently, endlessly. She walked right past them, not saying a word, down the hall toward her bedroom, but she heard a muted comment, a riff of laughter, and Agent Hawley saying, "Good night, Miss Marchand. Sweet dreams."

Dozing, jerking awake, listening for sounds of Jack returning, of the agents moving around, Eve lay there, fully clothed, unable to sleep but exhausted at the same time. The hours crawled by, slowly, stubbornly. No Jack, no sudden noises. He must have been warned off, then. She hoped so. Oh, God, how she hoped so.

She lay there sweating, trembling, as tense as a coiled spring, and thought about Jack. Where was he? What had he done when he saw her? Was he all right?

At dawn, the pale light leaking from in between the curtains, Jack still hadn't returned. Eventually she got up and took a shower, washing away the night's cold sweat of fear. She felt weak and shaky, tired to death and as heavy as lead.

In the kitchen the coffeepot was full. She poured herself a cup and wandered into the living room. They were still there, ties loosened, jackets off, eyes red-rimmed, drinking coffee.

"Morning," Hawley said.

"You're wasting your time," Eve said. "He wasn't here. He isn't coming. I told you."

"Yeah, you told me a lot of things."

She took a sip of scalding coffee. "Don't you have better things to do?"

"Nope."

Eve closed herself in the bedroom, watching television.

Nothing was mentioned about the stakeout in Pinecrest, but Jack's picture was broadcast regularly, and one channel had even dug up file film of Allison's murder, Jack's trial, Frank Iverson being interviewed. The whole sordid story, repeated and repeated again.

Where was Jack?

At noon she went into the kitchen and made herself something to eat. Her stomach was so empty it growled, but nausea clogged her throat and she had to force it down. She looked up from the plate when she heard Hawley swear, a vicious mutter.

He stalked into the kitchen, his expression as black as thunder. "We're out of here, lady."

"Duty calls?" she said sweetly.

"I'll get him, don't you worry," Hawley snarled.

"Get who?" she asked coolly.

Hawley swore again, gathered his men together and went down to the garage. She sat there, head bowed, eyes closed, until she heard the garage door open, the car start, the door close, the car crunch down the driveway.

Gone! They were gone!

She almost went out of her mind then, pacing, waiting, wondering where Jack was, what he'd done all night. Time crept by, every minute an hour of anguished waiting. She tried watching the news, tried reading. She couldn't concentrate. By two o'clock pewter clouds hung over the peaks, the golden aspen leaves shivered in the wind, pinecones fell to the ground. A dark, bilious light closed down over the hillside, and then it began to rain, a cold, slanting rain that dashed against the windows.

Where was he?

She stood at the window and stared out through the rain, cold inside, afraid. Waiting until she couldn't stand to wait one more second.

He came then, slipping silently in the back door and moving up behind her. She heard a noise, the light sound of footfall, and she whirled around, and he was there, wet, his hair plastered to his forehead, his windbreaker soaked.

"Jack!" she gasped, sagging with sudden, dizzying weakness.

"I saw them leave," he said calmly, "but I waited, just in case."

She put her hand out blindly for support, her knees threatening to buckle, but he was there, holding her, his good arm around her waist.

"Hey," he said.

It was too easy to lay her head on his shoulder, to throw her arms around him, clutching at him convulsively. "Oh, Jack," she cried in a broken voice, "I was so afraid."

"Shh," he said, stroking her hair. "It's okay now. You did good, Eve. I just waited. It's okay."

But she couldn't control the rush of relief, the release of the fear that had consumed her, and she started to cry, her face against his wet jacket.

"Hey, take it easy," he said. "It's okay."

She shook her head, the tears still coming, sobs shaking her, holding on to him, feeling him there, really there. Safe.

She could smell him, the unique smell of his skin and his wet hair. His arm was strong around her, and he felt solid, lean and hard. This was what she'd wanted all these months, to be held by him, pressed up against him. She knew that now. She'd always known it.

He held her for a long time, stroking her hair, trying to calm her, and eventually she stopped crying, feeling empty and spent, her face buried in his shoulder. She sobbed once more, then felt him shift away from her a little.

"I'm sorry," she whispered, still looking down, embarrassed now. "It was just..."

"It's okay, Eve." He tilted her chin up with his hand. "You want a handkerchief?"

"Yes," she mumbled, sniffing. "Please."

He left her standing there for a minute and came back

with one of her father's handkerchiefs. She blew her nose, wiped at her eyes.

"Better?"

"You saw me?" she asked. "Last night."

"I sure did. Couldn't miss you."

"Thank heavens. You can't imagine how awful it was. Those men..."

"I'm sorry you had to go through that. You can't know how sorry."

"It's over now. It's over, Jack."

"No, it's not over. If Hawley found us here, he can find us anywhere."

"I hate him," she said between clenched teeth.

"He's just doing his job, Eve."

"But he *likes* it too much."

Jack smiled grimly. "Like you and me, a little obsessive, I'd say, and damn good at what he does."

"They told him at the office," Eve explained. "How could they know I didn't want to be found?"

"We don't have much time then."

She thought of the car. "Where did you park? They may still be around. It may be a trap."

"Don't worry. I watched them drive away. The car's hidden. I came through the woods."

"Did you find license plates?"

"Yes, all taken care of. Good thing, too, because now there'll be an APB out on the rental plates for sure. Hawley knows all about me, doesn't he?"

"Yes," she whispered. "He can't prove anything, but he knows, and sooner or later..."

"You'll be rid of me by then," Jack said cryptically.

"We have to go," Eve said in sudden panic. "We have to get out of here. He'll be back!"

But he only smiled. "I think we'd better wait till dark," he said, and he brushed her cheek with his fingers.

NINETEEN

Jack and Eve never did get out of Pinecrest that night.

They meant to. Eve straightened the house and wrote her parents a note to let them know she'd been there. But at five she sat down on the couch, said she was going to close her eyes for a minute, and she went out like a light.

At six, with the autumn dusk settling over the mountains, Jack unfolded a blanket and laid it over her. He sat in an easy chair on the other side of the coffee table, knees splayed, fingers steepled under his chin, and watched her.

At eight he was still staring at her, noting the way she curled up into a fetal position, how her fingers twitched now and again as she held the blanket to her chin, how she whimpered occasionally in her sleep, her mouth barely moving.

She had a beautiful mouth. And a beautiful nose, and those hazel eyes, her lashes resting on her cheeks like exquisite miniature fans. Her hair was spread out on an Indian-patterned pillow, a honey-colored halo of curls. He couldn't help remembering her as she'd been the other morning in the kitchen—in her mother's nightgown—the jutting of her hipbones beneath the silky fabric, the way her small, firm breasts had stood out with stark clarity, her realization and subsequent embarrassment. He'd turned around and left. He'd had to.

Nine o'clock came and went, and Jack jerked awake, realizing that he, too, had dozed off. He rubbed the four-day growth on his chin and stood, stretching, working his sore shoulder. Eve slept on. For a long minute he watched her again, fighting the pressure in his groin, telling himself it was only because it had been such a long time since he'd made love to a woman. He went quietly out onto the deck then, the bitter-cold September air a blessed relief. Still, he thought about her, only a few feet away. And Gary Kapochek—Jack thought about him a lot, too. Would Eve really be in Pinecrest if everything was all right between her and Gary? If she were Jack's woman, he'd be damned if he'd put up with it. Unless, of course, things had fallen apart between them.

Not your business, he told himself firmly, leaning against the rail as he stared at the black sky, the wind soughing in the tall pines. *Get over it.* And yet, he knew that if things were different, if he'd met Eve under different circumstances, he'd have given Gary Kapochek a run for his money.

Eve awakened at midnight and sat up in alarm, trying to orient herself. "Oh, oh wow," she said, lifting her hair off her shoulders. "What time is it? Jack? Jack, where are you?"

"Right here," he said. "I'm right here, Eve."

They waited till morning to leave, when there'd be plenty of traffic on the interstate and the rental car would be less noticeable if there were cops out and about.

Jack insisted on driving. It felt good, great, he thought, being behind the wheel again, flying down the highway, the sun on his left shoulder, the mountains beckoning.

His beard was five days old now, and with sunglasses and the baseball cap, he could have been just another guy cruising the mountains with his pretty lady by his side. He really was enjoying himself; despite Eve's case of nerves; despite the hellish situation he was in, he felt curiously alive, free.

Jack drove into the high country, past Idaho Springs, Georgetown, where the old narrow-gauge railroad still hauled tourists past gold and silver mines, up past Loveland ski area, where snow already covered the higher trails, up to the Eisenhower Tunnel that bored through the Continental Divide.

"You know," he said, slowing to enter the tunnel, "if a drop of water falls on the Divide, half flows to the Pacific, half to the Atlantic." It was a familiar Colorado adage. He laughed a little and glanced at Eve.

"Very funny," she said.

"Relax," he said. "I'm free. I don't know for how long, but right now it feels pretty damn good."

"Oh, God," she said, a hand on her stomach, "what if we're spotted? What if..."

"Eve," he said in a calming tone, "it's a rental car. There're hundreds of them on the road. And remember, I changed the tags. We even have tinted glass."

"I know, I know," she said. "I'm just so uptight."

He wanted to tell her to sit back and enjoy the ride, the golden aspen trees climbing the sides of the mountains, the white-capped, craggy peaks piercing the pellucid sky. He loved Colorado. Had loved it since his first trip here with Allison. No climate, no scenery could have been more different from his native island home. There was so much he'd like to tell Eve. But he wouldn't. He couldn't allow himself the luxury of intimacy. It was bad enough that he'd agreed to let her come along in the first place. Though, really, he'd had little choice, short of stealing her car.

He drove past Dillon and Frisco, then up to the summit of Vail Pass. In Vail, Eve ran into a fast-food joint and brought them lunch, which they ate in the car. Then they were off again, down the interstate along the Colorado River toward Glenwood Canyon.

As Jack approached the state-of-the-art tunnel in the canyon, Eve glanced at the speedometer. "God, slow down, Jack. That's all we need, a ticket."

She was right, of course, and he did slow to a few miles per hour below the speed limit. Just in case. Then, on the far side of the tunnel, a Colorado State Patrol car pulled out of a shoulder area and began to follow them.

"Oh, no!" Eve cried, turning in her seat. "Oh, no, Jack! What're we going to do?" Her face was as pale as a daytime moon.

But Jack wasn't too worried. "Look," he said, "it's no big deal. Cops always sit right there. I've been followed before, all the way into Glenwood Springs. Calm down. It's just routine intimidation."

"But what if he..."

"*Eve*," Jack said, "you're going to give yourself a heart attack. Don't you think he'd have his lights flashing if he'd recognized me?" Jack tried to sound matter-of-fact, even confident.

"I should have driven. I knew it," she said. "You don't even have a license. The court took it."

"Yeah, well," he said, keeping a close eye on the patrol car in the rearview mirror, "it wouldn't matter, anyway— the license plates are stolen. Remember?"

"Oh, God," she breathed.

The state trooper followed for about three miles, then moved into the passing lane, gaining on them. Jack didn't like it. Sure the glass was tinted, but not that much. If the trooper recognized him when he passed...

"Look," he said, "when the cop car goes by, lean over like you're putting a tape in the player or something."

"Distract him," Eve said, her voice trembling.

"Exactly. Believe me, the cop'll be looking at you. Who wouldn't?" Jack added, and he gave her a quick, reassuring nod. "We'll be okay." He looked in his side mirror. "Here he comes."

Eve went into action. She tossed her hair, laughed, pretended to be putting a tape in the player and then, just as the cop was abreast of them, slowing, staring through his mirrored sunglasses, she laughed again and gave him a casual wave.

The cop sped up, passing them, and Eve collapsed back against the seat.

"Oh, God, oh my God," she whispered. "It worked, Jack, it worked."

"Nice touch," he said.

"What?"

"Waving at him." Jack gave her a swift look. "You've got nerve. I'll say that for you."

They didn't see any more cops the whole way up the Roaring Fork Valley and into Aspen. Eve had settled down some, though she was still fidgety. She spent the time ticking off plans. "We'll go to one of those ritzy rental agencies, you know, one that caters to the rich and famous who want to stay anonymous in Aspen while they're on vacation. It's off-season. It'll be easy to rent a little house or condo.... No, a house. Someplace private. No questions asked. Then I'll get some groceries, you know, and I can start checking out some of the suspects."

"Eve," Jack said in a hard voice, "*you* won't be checking anyone out this time. It's my gig."

"But they'll turn you in. Jack, you've got to let me..."

"No. The only way I'm going to get anywhere is by doing it myself. We've been over this ground before. I'm not going to argue about it. Period."

He knew he sounded like a real ass after all Eve had done for him—but this was his show. He'd been waiting for it to start for a year and a half, dreaming about it, and he wasn't going to relent. Yeah, he thought, he was going to be caught. And probably in short order. But he'd bet he could rattle a couple of cages before the cops nabbed him. Maybe he could even get someone to crack under pressure. It was his only chance. And one thing was sure, he had nothing whatsoever to lose.

"That lighter," he said under his breath as they drove across the Castle Creek bridge.

"What?"

"My cigarette lighter. It's got to be the key." Jack hit the steering wheel with his fist. "If only I could remember what happened to it."

"You will, you will," she said confidently, but Jack wasn't so sure.

Eve had no trouble renting a small house in Aspen's prestigious West End. While Jack slumped down in the front seat of the car, behind the tinted windows and his sunglasses, she walked into Aspen's most exclusive rental agency across from the Little Nell Hotel. Five minutes later she reappeared, dangling a rental contract in one hand, a set of keys in the other.

She slid into the passenger seat, smiling. He hadn't seen that smile in quite a while. "It's a furnished two-bedroom house on Lake Avenue," she said. "Just head back to Main Street, and we turn right on First Street, then..."

"Eve," Jack said, putting the car in gear, "I do know where Lake Avenue is."

"Oh," she said. "Oh. Of course you do."

Jack found the address easily, because directly across the street was a new house he'd designed two years ago. It was one of the original mining-day Victorians, fixed up, of course, but structurally intact. It was one of the few houses in the West End that could still be called quaint.

He parked beneath the huge old evergreens that buffered one side of the house, which was hidden from the road.

"Wow," Eve said, opening her door. "Oh, Jack, it's...adorable."

"Yes, it is," he agreed.

"I always wanted my house in Denver to look like this. Just like this." Then she stood in front of the car, hands on her hips, and stared at it.

It was a bright yellow wooden Victorian with white gingerbread trim and delicate latticework leading into a rear garden area. There was a creaky front porch, tall, shuttered windows and an elegant front door with a beveled window.

By Aspen standards, it was a dollhouse: a kitchen, a breakfast nook, a living room with a fireplace, two bedrooms and a bath up a narrow staircase.

Eve fell in love at first sight. She checked out the rooms, the backyard that ran down to the nature preserve of Hallam Lake, then inside again, opening cupboard doors, touching the lace curtains, running her fingers along the carved molding bracketing the windows. She finally sat on a flowered window seat and sighed. "If it weren't for...well, you know...this would be heaven." She looked up at him, then seemed embarrassed. She stood up quickly. "Well, I'd better go to the store, get some supplies." She smiled tentatively.

Jack stared at her. "I can't pay you back right now for all this," he said. "But I will someday. This isn't...easy."

Eve took the car keys from him. "I know," she said. "I know you will, Jack," and then she averted her gaze and left for the store.

Jack sat out in the backyard while she was gone. It was completely private, surrounded by spruce and aspen trees, the leaves almost gone now from the aspens. Everything in the yard was autumn-hued, rusts and golds and umbers, the colors of the earth and mountains. Jack looked up toward Red Mountain, toward the house he'd built for Allison, and with the leaves mostly gone, he could make out the west wing of the structure far up on the mountainside. He recalled the first time he'd seen the completed house from the valley floor, the pride he'd felt, the trust he'd had in his future. It had been a long time ago. He'd been down many roads since then, some of which he'd seen coming, others, well, he guessed no one could really see round a bend.

He had to ask himself if his marriage to Allison had been a mistake from day one. Sure, they'd been compatible physically, but he was beginning to realize how ill-suited they'd been overall. Allison was spoiled, from one of the Fortune 500 families. She'd never had direction in her life.

Some had thought of her as reckless, but Jack saw her as undisciplined, living for the moment. She'd been strong, though, strong and stubborn and dissatisfied, while Jack had gone blindly along in his career, basking in his success, the one member of his family who'd made it.

Look where it had gotten him, he thought darkly. And it was his fault. Not the fault of his birth, and not Allison's fault, but his alone. He hated to admit it, but the glamour of Aspen and success had been too powerful a lure. If he ever got the chance—a real second chance—he'd spend his life doing some good. Building megahomes for the fabulously wealthy hardly fit that scenario.

Jack got up from the lawn chair where he'd been day-dreaming and went inside. He wasn't going to do anybody any good if he didn't clear his name. But even more, he owed Allison justice, and sitting around moping about his predicament and how he'd screwed up getting here wasn't finding the solution.

He found paper and a pen in a kitchen drawer, and he sat down in the breakfast nook and started a list. His time was going to be limited, and he intended to make the most of it.

Lighter, he wrote. *Lost it where? When?* Then he wrote down *George Mochlin. Find motive.* Then, *Ray and Marnie Wade—argument with Allison? Thefts?*

Surely, Jack thought, Allison would have told someone if she'd been having trouble with the help. She'd have at least told Ben on one of his weekend visits. Or Ben would have heard them arguing himself.

Ben, he wrote down. He could certainly go and see his stepson and ask a few questions. Or maybe Ben's girlfriend had been up for a weekend and heard something. Jack wrote down *Sarah Glick*.

He looked up then, hearing Eve's car pull into the drive-way. He still couldn't believe he'd involved her so deeply in this mess. Sure, he needed help, but this was above and beyond the call of duty. The one thing he knew with cold, hard certainty was that he had to get her out of harm's way. The trouble was, he was selfishly savoring every moment he spent with her.

Much to Eve's fascination, Jack insisted on cooking dinner. "I'm no gourmet chef," he said, "but I've been feeling useless for so long it's the least I can do."

"But your shoulder..."

He flexed his arm. "It's better. Really. Now, make yourself scarce and let me put something together."

Obviously she'd planned an eggplant casserole. There were noodles, jarred sauces, eggplant. Jack looked at it all on the kitchen counter, shrugged and went to work. Eve never did leave the kitchen, but Jack went about his business. "Sort of like building a house," he said, layering the ingredients.

"This is...nice," she ventured once, and he didn't question her. He didn't want to hear it, or to even dream.

They ate an hour later in the nook off the kitchen, the yard beyond the antique glass swathed in dusk.

It was so quiet, so peaceful that he could pretend it was real and that it would last. And he couldn't believe that after all those weeks of knowing Eve, but only knowing her within the confines of jail, he was here alone with her. It was a full-blown fantasy sprung to life. But a fantasy nonetheless. He had to remember that.

"This is delicious," she said, and their eyes met for a heartbeat too long.

He did the dishes and straightened the kitchen while Eve put on a jacket and went outside. He found her at the wooded bank that led down to Hallam Lake. She put a hand up and said, "Listen. The coyotes are yipping."

He stood there in the darkness and listened, and he heard them, a whole pack of them, warbling and keening.

Eve hugged herself. "It's so beautiful here. I was in town all those weeks and I hardly noticed a thing."

"You saw the jail. What more do you want?" he said softly.

"I sure did see that," she allowed. Then she turned toward him. "Jack, I...I don't ever want to see you behind bars again. Never. We've got to..."

But he silenced her with a finger on her lips. "Shh," he said. "We'll talk about it tomorrow."

"But, Jack..."

"Eve, no, don't. There's not going to be much time, not for this, anyway. Let's just enjoy the night, the freedom. Okay?"

"There will be time," she said quietly. "No one is going to find you here."

He laughed. "I hate to be a realist," he said, "but I have a feeling time's a lot shorter than we think."

He wanted to put an arm around her shoulder and tell her it would be all right. Somehow he'd make it all right. But he knew he didn't dare touch her. Not now. Not here. If he did, he'd never be able to stop.

TWENTY

Special Agent in Charge Ralph Hawley stood in front of the Marchands' house in Pinecrest and cursed, his breath pluming the chilly morning air. The house was empty. They were gone. Eve Marchand and Jack Devlin had flown the coop.

Of course. Hawley had begged for extra men to watch the house, but he hadn't been able to get them. Budget had been the excuse, the budget crunch. Frankly, he thought it was more likely plain old incompetence. Goddamn all moronic pencil-pushers!

His men had even found the spot where Marchand and Devlin had hidden the car in the bushes beside the road. There'd been an APB out for that rental car for days now, but no one had spotted it. Incompetence again.

He stood there in front of the pine-shadowed mountain home and thought, trying to subdue his frustration. He attempted to recall every word, every gesture, every reaction of the Marchand woman when he'd talked to her. He examined his memory, his excellent, well-trained memory.

She'd obviously driven back to Denver the morning he'd first talked to her and called him from there. Devlin had already been hidden in this house. Christ, she'd been cool. That spark of admiration for her ignited again. She was some woman. She'd been rattled as hell when he'd staked out this house, but she'd covered up well. How had they missed Devlin? Luck? It must have been luck, plain, un-adorned luck. Goddamn it.

He stood there and searched his memory, and it finally came to him. *Aspen.* She'd been evasive but hadn't lied about anything else, and maybe she hadn't lied about that, either. Devlin was going back to Aspen!

He was nuts, absolutely nuts, and he wouldn't last an hour. What was in the man's head? He should be hot-footing it to Mexico, for God's sake!

Aspen. That's exactly where the two of them were going.

Jack sat in the breakfast nook of the house on Lake Ave-nue, hunched over a cup of coffee. He'd slept restlessly, waiting in the dark emptiness of the night for the police to break in and arrest him, dozing and dreaming that he was in prison again. Dreaming of Eve, just across the hall in the charming, tiny bedroom with the flowered wallpaper and sloping ceiling. Dreaming.

He sat there and figured he had a day, maybe two, tops, and he had to make every second count. And when he reached the inevitable dead end, he couldn't be connected to Eve; he couldn't take her down with him. Some people might suspect what Eve had done, but no one would be able to prove it—Jack had to make sure of that.

Eve had just gotten out of the shower; he could hear her upstairs, moving around. The old floorboards creaked over-head. She'd be down soon, and he'd have to pull on his shroud of neutrality, guard against any weakness. It sapped his energy to keep up the facade in front of her, but he had to. If there was one certainty in this whole crazy situation, it was that there was no future for him with Deputy Public Defender Eve Marchand.

She came downstairs and poured herself a cup of coffee, then sat across from him. "Well," she said, "got any plans?"

"I've been thinking," he said, "and I have a few."

"I do, too. I thought I could..."

"Eve. I told you. This is *my* thing."

"But I can go anywhere I want. Jack, if you stick your face out of here, someone will recognize you, and that'll be that."

"I'll go to see Ben today," Jack said. "It's the Wades' day off, and Ben won't turn me in."

"You're sure?"

"Hell, yes."

"What are you going to ask him?"

"Mostly about the lighter. He may remember something I don't."

"You might give him a heart attack," she commented.

"Yeah, I thought of that."

"Then what?" She had her hands clasped around the coffee mug, and her brows were drawn together. It occurred to him that he could lean across the table and kiss her on the lips.

"Uh, Kent Lovett. I don't think he'll turn me in. I think he'll at least give me some time."

Her brow furrowed. "Lovett...?"

"A friend from the Cigar Bar. He might remember the lighter."

"He might not."

"I realize that."

"You'll be careful?" Eve asked in a worried voice. "Jack, I'll be a nervous wreck waiting here."

"No one'll recognize me. They won't be looking for me. Everyone figures I'm in Mexico." He smiled. "Don't you think this beard is a great disguise?"

"Not yet," she said dryly. "It just looks like you forgot to shave."

"I'll have to risk it."

"And if you don't come back here, what do I do then?"

He shrugged, keeping his face carefully impassive. "You return to Denver, to your job, to your life."

"I can't go back. It'll never be the same again. I can't just...forget you, Jack."

Something twanged inside him, but he ignored it. "Sure

you can. This was just an interlude, a bizarre interlude. When it's over, it's over."

"Not for you," she said softly.

He raised his coffee mug and sipped as if she hadn't said anything, but she leaned forward and put her hand on his arm. "I'll never forget you, and I'll never stop trying to get you released. You believe me, don't you? You trust me?"

He looked at her, at the earnestness, the passion shining in her face. She'd break her spirit trying to free him, he knew, ruin her life, kill herself with overwork. He put a hand over hers. "Let someone else do it, Eve," he said. "You can't be objective."

"Let someone else do it," she repeated angrily. "Not bloody likely, Jack."

He looked away from her and hardened his voice. "Let someone else do it. I don't want you on my case."

She pulled her hand from his, hurt.

"Look, let's not discuss this now. I've got more important things to do. I want you to stay here. Don't even poke your nose out. That FBI guy..."

"Hawley."

"Yeah, Hawley. If he finds out you're here, he'll know where I am."

"But, Jack..."

"*Listen* to me, Eve. For once, will you goddamn listen to me?"

Her mouth thinned into a hard line, but she kept quiet.

"I'm going now. It may take a while. I don't know if I can locate everyone right away. You stay put."

"I'll go nuts."

"No, you won't."

She took both coffee mugs and went to the sink, turning the faucet on. Her back spoke eloquently of her resentment.

Jack drove up the familiar Red Mountain road. He hadn't been there in eighteen months, and he took in every detail—the new house going up on the first switchback, the way the brush was turning bronze and red, the flocks of grosbeaks that were pecking at ripe chokecherries by the side of the road.

He hoped Ben was home; if not he'd wait. Surely Ben had been watching television, following his escape. Poor kid. What a way to step into adulthood—his mother murdered, Jack convicted of killing her. He prayed Ben was tough enough to pull through.

He reached the stone pillars; the sign still read Devlin. My God, hadn't anyone taken it down? Turning into the drive-way, he had a terrible flash of déjà vu. He'd done it so many times. But there was a difference this time. In front of the ga-rage was a red Saab. Must be Ben's, he thought. He'd always wanted one. Well, at least he had that to console him.

So Ben was home. Good. Jack parked and went to the front door. Instead of using his key and walking in as he used to, he rang the doorbell, then stood there, looking around. Allison's house, his design. It was still a great plan, fitting into the terrain as if it had always been there, as if it had grown out of the mountainside. His eye rested on every painfully familiar detail he'd designed for the woman he loved. Allison was gone, but the house was still here, like the gilded frame of a beautiful painting, empty.

Allison. His heart squeezed in his chest. But he didn't have time to indulge in self-pity. He heard footsteps, the door being pulled open. Ben stood there, hair tousled, sleepy-eyed, wearing a sloppy T-shirt and jeans, a question-ing look on his face. He hadn't been expecting anyone.

"Hi, Ben," Jack said.

The boy stiffened, took a step back and gasped. His eyes widened.

"Mind if I come in?"

"Jesus, Jack! Oh, my God, I was just watching the news, and they said…"

"I guess they got it wrong."

"I *knew* you'd show up!" Ben breathed. "I told Sarah."

"Sarah's here?"

"Yeah, yeah, but she's cool. Don't worry." He took Jack's

hand and pumped it, then threw his arms around him. "God, it's good to see you! You okay? They said you were hurt when the van crashed."

"I'm okay. I was beat up for a couple of days, but I'm okay now."

"Where have you been? How'd you get here? You hungry? You need some money?"

"Slow down, Ben." Jack smiled. It was good to be home. For a little while, it would be good.

Ben cocked his head. "You're crazy, you know. Why'd you come back here? Everyone knows you."

Jack stroked his beard. "You don't think this is a good enough disguise?"

"Hell, no." Ben pulled Jack across the floor. "Come on, we're eating breakfast. Sarah! Sarah, honey, look who's here!"

Sarah turned white as a sheet and sank back into the chair as if she'd been pushed. "Oh, no," she whispered.

"Yeah, it's Jack. Isn't this great?"

"I...I don't know, Ben."

"What do you mean?"

"What if...what if..." She swallowed convulsively.

"She's right, Ben. This is one of the first places they'll look if they get wind of me being in Aspen."

"Don't worry. Nobody knows you're here, not yet." Then he paused. "Where are you staying?"

"You don't need to know," Jack said.

"No, I guess it's better that way. God, I wish you could stay here, in your old room. Your clothes are stored there, and..."

"Ben," Sarah said in a choked voice, "I think it's better if he stays somewhere else."

"She's right. And I wouldn't ask it of you, Ben. I may be free now, but it won't last long."

"What do you mean?" Ben asked. "Aren't you going to go someplace and drop out of sight? Mexico, Brazil, Australia, someplace far away? Hell, Jack, I'll give you money, any amount you want. I can do that. I'd like to do that."

"No, Ben."

"What's wrong with you? You know where they'll send you? Come on, Jack, it's crazy to let them get hold of you."

"I can't, Ben."

"Why not? Why in hell not?" Ben cried.

"I know why he can't," Sarah said.

Ben whirled on her. "Well, why don't you clue me in, then?"

"Because," she said, "because if he runs, no one will ever find the real murderer."

Ben was struck silent for a moment, then he said, "So what? *So what*, Jack? Save yourself, that's all that matters."

"No, it isn't," Jack said calmly.

"Damn it, Jack!"

"That's why I'm here, Ben, in Aspen. I want to talk to a few people. I never had a chance to right after…"

"Mom was killed," Ben finished. "Okay, who? Who do you think did it?"

"I don't know, but I have a few ideas. You don't need to know the details."

"My God, Jack, you're so damn stubborn. I can't believe this!" Ben said.

Eventually Ben stopped trying to convince Jack to take money and leave. He and Sarah were awkward with Jack, not knowing quite how to react. Ben tried to behave as if things were normal, but it was pathetically obvious that they weren't.

"Want some coffee?" Ben asked.

"No, thanks. I'm not staying long."

"Well, come on into the kitchen, will you?" Ben said, trying hard, falsely jovial. "My coffee's getting cold."

They sat at the familiar table, not the formal dining room table, but the cozy one in the breakfast nook, the spot Jack had designed with the view in mind. But it wasn't like old times: it could never be like old times again.

Only the view was the same. The sun streamed in the window, golden leaves blew across it when the breeze picked up outside, the valley lay somnolent below them, robed in autumnal earth tones. A plane banked, caught the sun and winked at them, then descended for a landing at the airport. Yes, it was a two-million-dollar view.

Jack was aware of Ben and Sarah exchanging glances. He'd better get this over with and leave. "To tell the truth, I wanted to ask you something," Jack began.

"Sure, whatever."

Sarah rose and gave them both a shaky smile. "I'll leave you two alone, okay?"

"Sure, honey." Ben took her hand as she turned to go, let it slide out of his fingers. She gave him a tentative look, then turned away.

When she was gone, Ben said, "Don't sweat it, Jack. She's not going to tell anyone. She knows you're innocent."

"That's nice to hear."

"She does. We've discussed it. I'd trust her with my life."

Jack nodded soberly.

"So, what's up? Questions?" Ben leaned back, put his hands behind his head and stretched his legs out.

"It's that lighter of mine. I can't figure out how it got on the floor that night. It's been driving me crazy. I lost it, I'm pretty sure, sometime before your mom was…killed, but I can't remember how or when. The last time I actually recall having it was when we went fishing that March, last year, eighteen months ago. Remember? We went fly-fishing on the Fryingpan. It was cold out, I do remember that. And I gave you the lighter to light your cigarette. I remember being surprised you were smoking, because I thought you'd quit. I gave you some shit about it, too."

"I remember, sure. We froze, but we caught that super four-pound rainbow…"

"Do you remember the lighter?"

"Uh-huh. Yeah, you gave it to me because the wind kept blowing my matches out."

"After that day my memory is real fuzzy. I may have had it one other time. I'm going to check with someone else...."

"Who?"

"No one you'd know—not that I'd tell you. Better you don't know."

"Damn it, Jack, don't treat me like a kid!"

"I'm trying to treat you like an adult, but I don't want you getting into trouble over me."

"Okay, okay. I just don't want you back in jail. I can't stand the idea."

"It's not one of my favorite concepts," Jack said. "The lighter. Do you remember what I did with it? Did you give it back? Did I leave it there, on the river?"

"God, Jack, I can't remember."

"Think. Did you ever see me use it again after that?"

Ben thought. "You don't smoke anymore, and I never smoked at home, so I probably never saw you use it. But I'm sure I gave it back to you that day. I wouldn't have kept it."

"Did I ever take it out of my pocket, play with it? Maybe I used it at a party to light someone's cigarette?"

Ben shook his head. "Boy, I don't know. I have this hazy picture of you lighting Gena Wyman's cigarette at dinner one night. Maybe, I'm not sure."

"That would have been at that dinner we had here in April." He thought. "Easter dinner, was that it?"

"Maybe. Maybe that was it."

"So I still had it then." Jack frowned. "How in hell did it get under that piano next to Allison's body?"

"I don't know," Ben said thoughtfully. "Maybe you dropped it sometime earlier. Maybe it was just lying there."

"I thought of that, believe me. Maybe the damn thing doesn't have squat to do with the murder at all. Maybe it was just a coincidence."

"Or..." Ben began, then hesitated. "I forgot, you don't know."

"Don't know what?"

"The Wades, Marnie and Ray, they're gone. Fired. Sarah

did it. 'Course I backed her up. My Rolex watch was missing, and we think they took it."

"Jesus Christ."

"Hey, maybe *they* took your lighter. Maybe one of them dropped it by mistake...."

"Where'd they go?" Jack asked.

"No one knows. They just packed up and split. They were pissed, let me tell you."

"*Damn.*" He would have liked to ask the Wades some questions, by God. Had they taken his lighter? Had Allison confronted one or both of them over the previous firing? Had she taunted them with her knowledge, or threatened them? Allison could have done it; she sure could nail you where it hurt. And if she had, would they have been angry enough to kill?

The lighter was the key, though. He was still sure of that. He looked at Ben. "There's no way to trace them? A forwarding address?"

Ben held his hands out, palms up. "Not that I know of."

Jack got up and paced across the kitchen. God, this was frustrating, like trying to untangle a spiderweb. If you pulled too hard, a strand broke and you could no longer follow it.

"I don't have time to try tracing them, and I can't very well go to the post office myself and ask if they left a forwarding address. Goddammit!"

"I'll do it. I'll ask," Ben said.

"No. Absolutely not." He'd tell Eve, though. Maybe she could check them out. After he was back behind bars. *Shit.*

"I'll do it for you, Jack."

"No, Ben. Don't even consider it. I'll get it done by someone else."

"Who?"

"Never mind."

"Right," Ben said sarcastically, "it's better that I don't know."

"You got it," Jack said.

He left Allison's house that afternoon after changing into some of his own clothes. Clothes that actually fit him. A blue oxford shirt right off the hanger from the cleaners, a pair of jeans, a gray sweater, a pair of his own shoes, topsiders, a windbreaker. He felt vaguely human.

"You look better," Ben said as Jack bundled up Eve's father's clothes.

"Hey, I feel better. Thanks for keeping all this stuff for me."

"No problem."

"Tell Sarah goodbye for me."

"Okay."

"Keep in touch, Ben," Jack said.

"I wish to hell you'd take some money and run for it."

"Can't, Ben."

"Okay, do the right thing. I think you're nuts, though."

"See you, kid."

"See you."

He drove straight to Kent Lovett's office, which was upstairs in a Main Street building. He kept his sunglasses on, and the baseball cap. He looked like about seventy-five percent of the men in Aspen that cool fall day.

He gave a false name to Kent's receptionist, a false reason for seeing him, a false smile, and he was positive she didn't recognize him.

"Oh, I'm sure Mr. Lovett will see you when he gets back. He's having a late lunch today. I'll tell him as soon as he returns. Can you come back in, say, forty-five minutes?"

So he drove around, killing time, up the winding road toward Independence Pass, where he'd just been a few days ago, shackled in the sheriff's van, being transported to Canon City. That day the road had been icy; today it was dry as a bone.

He got back to Lovett's office and the receptionist gave him a big smile. "He's in. Go right on back there, Mr. Young."

Kent Lovett rose and started coming around his desk toward Jack. Abruptly, the smile on his face faltered, his out-stretched hand dropped. He sagged, his face freezing.

"Hello, Kent."

"God Almighty, Jack!" he rasped.

"Damn, I thought this beard was going to work."

"Jack, I can't... Wow, let me take this in. Give me a minute, man." Lovett put a hand to his head, almost comically. He was a small, dapper man, with grizzling curly hair, big nose and a tight, muscular body that he kept in top shape. "God, I can't believe this, you just waltzing in here like this."

"I don't have a lot of time."

"I bet."

"Listen, I'm not here to get you into any trouble. I just wanted to ask a few questions."

"They're after you, man, you know that? Your picture's on the tube every time I turn around."

"I know."

"So what in God's name are you doing here?"

"Trying to find out who murdered Allison," Jack said flatly.

Lovett studied him. "I never could figure out how you could do that, you know."

"I didn't do it. I may have been framed. The lighter, you remember my gold lighter, the one they found by Allison's body?"

Lovett nodded. "Everyone knew about your lighter. Fancy, with initials."

"That's the one."

Lovett looked around. "Wait a minute. Jack, come on, sit down. We're friends, right? Sit and we'll talk."

They sat on his leather couch as if they were business cronies. Kent even got two Cokes out of his office refrigerator.

"Okay, the lighter," Kent urged.

"I lost it somewhere. I'm trying to figure out when and where, who could have gotten hold of it, that kind of thing."

"Uh-huh."

"That night we closed the deal on the lots at Aspen Glen, we went to the Cigar Bar, you remember?"

Kent nodded.

"Did I have the lighter there? Did I light our cigars with it?"

"Wow." Lovett looked up at the ceiling, pursing his lips. "I'll tell you, Jack, all I can remember about that night is tits."

"Tits?"

"Yeah, the waitress had great cleavage. And I remember a match. She must have struck a match to light our cigars, because the flame, you know, it flared and lit up her cleavage. My eyes were glued to that."

"So I didn't have the lighter," Jack mused. "When was that, April of that year? May?"

"I think we closed May 1, but I can check with Gloria."

"No, that's fine, that's close enough."

"Is it any help?"

"Maybe. Maybe it is, Kent."

He left Lovett's office and drove away, circling around, just in case anyone was tailing him. It was unlikely, because if the law had found him, they'd most likely come at him guns blazing, with lots of backup. But he drove around for a while to be sure. He didn't want to inadvertently lead anyone back to Eve.

He needed to find Marnie and Ray. They could easily have taken the lighter, either one of them. And he still had to talk to George Mochlin. Tomorrow. He figured he had until tomorrow. That FBI agent would be on him by then, and it'd all be over.

Maybe he should resist arrest, he thought bitterly, and get shot. Quick and easy, like he'd said to Eve once. But then Allison's killer would still be walking around free.

Finally he headed back to the little yellow house on Lake Avenue. By now Eve would be going insane with worry and boredom. He hoped she hadn't done anything foolish. He hoped the FBI hadn't found her. He hoped...

But when he pulled up in front of the house on the quiet, leaf-strewn street and used his key to open the front door, he knew right away that the house was empty.

Eve left John Richards's office feeling a certain amount of satisfaction. Hank Thurgood had been right, the man had not killed Allison. He had neither motive nor opportunity, and he was too open about his dislike of his ex-wife. Hank's instincts had been right on.

She left Richards, feeling once again that Allison had had great taste in men. Richards wasn't handsome in the traditional sense—he was too broadly built and too rough-featured—but he had an undeniable animal magnetism. Eve had a feeling that he wasn't the nicest guy around, but he sure had charm and sex appeal.

And Allison had dumped him, then taken up with Jack. Then George Mochlin. Oh, well, two out of three...

She walked toward Lake Avenue, taking her time. God, she wasn't about to stay alone in that house a minute more than she had to—worrying herself sick, wondering where Jack was. She'd lasted until three in the afternoon, then she'd left. Anything to occupy the empty time, the minutes and hours till Jack returned.

Luckily she'd caught John Richards in. It had been a spur-of-the-moment decision, partly because she was curious about the man and partly because she so desperately needed to be distracted.

She walked down Main Street, idly looking in store windows, watching people. The big cottonwoods lining the road were golden, and leaves drifted down like confetti. Turning off Main into the grid of streets called the West End, Eve looked forward to strolling past all the beautifully restored Victorian mansions. One of the streets had been called Bullion Row back in the 1880s, when the owners of the grand houses had struck it rich in silver mines. The gaping tunnels still caught unwary skiers on Aspen Mountain.

Then there were the new Victorians, brash copies, built by

those who'd struck it rich in computers or land or some other modern-day endeavor. Imposing, lacking charm, they were monuments to their owners. Jack had never designed a house like that. He couldn't.

When she passed a drugstore on her way back to Lake Avenue, she took the opportunity to use a pay phone to call Hank in Denver. She dialed the number and waited impatiently. She didn't want to leave a message on his voice mail, but maybe if he was out, he had his cell phone....

"Thurgood," he answered.

"Oh, Hank. Boy, am I glad to hear your voice."

"Eve, is that you?"

"Yes, it's me."

"Where the hell are you?"

"Never mind. Listen, Hank, what's going on? Anything I should know?"

"About what, little lady?"

"You know what."

"I know he's there with you, or you know where he is," Hank said with great satisfaction. "That's what I know."

"No comment."

"Ain't that just like a lawyer." He went right on. "There is something, though, I've been dying to tell you."

"What?"

"I found out through a girlfriend of Allison's—I'll make a long story short—that Allison and George Mochlin had a big blowup. Over him bragging that he'd be hubby number three. I've been going nuts wanting to tell you."

"Well, well," Eve said.

"Yeah, interesting, huh?"

"When did this fight happen?"

"She couldn't remember exactly. Not long before the murder."

"Good work, Hank. *Great* work."

"Listen, Eve, they're crawling all over us here."

She knew who "they" were. "I bet. God, I'm sorry. What a mess."

"Officially you're on sick leave. By the way, some dodo told the FBI about your folks' place."

"I know. It's okay, though."

"Be careful, Eve. Real careful."

"I am. I will be. Hank?"

"Yeah?"

"Thanks. I owe you dinner and a movie. Thanks a million."

"Hey, it's us against them, right?"

She hung up, her heart lifting with anticipation. She had to tell Jack. This was exciting news, another nail in Mochlin's coffin. He must have done it; he must have killed Allison. He had both opportunity and motive. *It's got to be Mochlin*, she thought as she hurried out of the store.

George Mochlin had tried a couple of stiff drinks, then he'd tried some heavy-duty dope Melinda had given him, but nothing worked. His hands shook, his stomach had a fist in it, his chest was tight. He was a wreck, had been ever since Devlin had escaped. Days now. An eternity.

George sat in his condo, on his couch, his head between his hands, the TV set on. He'd had the news on all day, trying to keep tabs on Devlin's whereabouts, but no one knew where he was—or they weren't saying.

George knew where he was, though. Oh, yes, he knew. Devlin was on his way to Aspen to find him and kill him. Devlin was out for revenge. The man had nothing to lose, after all, not a damn thing. He'd kill George without a second thought.

George fought to get his head together, but all he felt was paralyzing fear and a buzz in his brain.

The thought came to him through the foggy miasma in his head—he'd leave. Sure, why not? He'd pack up and drive to Tucson. There was a big tennis tournament going on down there. He had friends; they'd put him up. He wouldn't tell a soul where he was going.

He'd leave right now if he weren't so screwed up. Although, he remembered, he had a couple of lessons tomorrow. Okay, he'd leave right from the club after he was done. Yes, he'd go tomorrow.

And then he stood up, his knees rubbery from the dope, and he went into the bedroom. Pulling open his night table drawer, he reached in and got his gun. He went into the living room and laid it right on the coffee table.

Then he sat down and watched the news again. He sat there and waited and watched, and every once in a while he'd pick up the gun and point it at the blinking TV screen and pretend to pull the trigger.

TWENTY-ONE

Eve knew she was in hot water the minute she walked in the front door. She avoided making eye contact with Jack, tossing her blazer and purse on the couch. Then she took a breath, straightened her shoulders and faced him. "Hi," she said.

Jack glared at her for a very long moment. "Do you *ever* listen to anyone?" he finally asked.

She shrugged. "One of my biggest faults."

"You never had any intention of staying in this house, did you?"

She shook her head and then smiled. "Forget all that," she said.

"Eve, look, if you won't..."

"No, *listen*, I've got news. Really good news."

Jack leaned a shoulder against the wall, folded his arms and stared at her.

"I called Hank, and he's come up with some very interesting information. It seems Allison found out that Mochlin was bragging about being her next husband. And they had a fight. A whopper. Jack," Eve said, "if you add Mochlin's lousy alibi to the fight..."

"Son of a bitch," Jack muttered.

Eve started dinner then, aware of Jack moving restlessly around the small house.

"Can I do anything?" he asked once, poking his head into the kitchen.

"You can set the table," she said, as if they were a normal couple getting ready for a meal.

After dinner they discussed what they'd learned that day, and Jack made a list: suspects, alibis, motives, the lighter.

Eve kept bringing up George Mochlin, to her mind the prime suspect.

"I agree," Jack said, leaning back in the wooden kitchen chair, folding his arms. "But I'd still like to find Ray and Marnie Wade, put some pressure on them. Keep in mind that Allison may have found out about that stolen...missing diamond ring. If Allison confronted the Wades, well, it could have gotten ugly. Ben told me that they just got them out of there. Some sort of trouble. I only wish I knew where they've gone."

"I'll put Hank on it. He'll find them."

Jack nodded, then seemed to retreat inside himself, to that place that she could never quite reach.

After a time she took her glasses off and rubbed her eyes. "We'll get to the bottom of this," she said. "We'll keep the pressure on till someone cracks. You've got to believe me."

"Time's short," he said. "Ben wanted me to take off, get out of the country... It was tempting. Still is."

A part of her wanted to tell him to do exactly that, but it wasn't a solution. They both knew it. She shook her head.

He nodded and smiled wryly. "You've done a lot," he said. "More than anyone should expect. I can never repay you, either. Not for this, anyway, for staying with me."

"Well, I wouldn't have done it for just anyone, Jack. Believe me." She almost said more, too much. She almost told him then and there that he'd become very special to her. More than special.

But Jack didn't want to hear that. Still, she wished she knew how he felt, what thoughts lay behind that neutral expression. Eve looked at him and wondered, did Jack's skin burn as hers did the few times they'd touched?

She glanced away, her chest hurting. If only things were different. "Time's short," he'd said, and she was so terribly afraid he was right.

They went to bed at eleven, in their separate rooms. Eve wasn't a bit sleepy, and she sat in her sleeveless white cotton nightgown in the chair by the window, staring out at the night, staring and thinking, wondering if this would be the last night. The last hours. And minutes.

She closed her eyes for a moment, trying to dispel the image of Jack on death row. There was no guarantee that she'd find the real murderer anytime soon. Find him—or her—and get a confession. That was what it was going to take to free him. All the circumstantial evidence in the world wasn't going to convince the court to vacate his sentence. There had to be hard evidence, an ironclad confession, the whole nine yards. And while she and Hank worked to get that evidence, Jack was going to be rotting away in that horrible, bleak prison. Innocent. Alone.

She realized then that Jack needed to know the whole truth about her past. She'd never told a soul, not since it had happened. But Jack had to know, he had to believe she was never going to let that happen again. He had to be told.

Eve stood, unhesitating. She felt suddenly as if she'd swallowed a poison all those years ago and had yet to purge it from her body. The toxin rose in her now, choking her. She took a sweater off the bedpost, wrapped it around her shoulders and opened her door, crossed the hall and tapped on his door. Her heart was in her throat. What would he think? That she might fail him, too? Or would he know in his heart, would he believe in her, trust her?

She opened his door a crack. "Are you asleep?" she whispered, peering in. But Jack wasn't in bed. He was standing in his jeans by the window, his torso bare, leaning against the wall. "Oh," she said, "I...Jack, I can't sleep, either. There's something..."

"Eve," he said, his face in shadows, "go back to bed. Please."

But she shook her head. "I have to tell you something. I have to do it now or I'll chicken out. Please, just listen. Don't say a thing. Just let me get this out."

He said nothing, but she could feel the tension radiating from him. Despite the darkness, she could make out the rigid set of his shoulders, the pitch of his head.

She moved toward him but changed her mind. Instead, she sat on the side of the bed, her hands clasped tightly in the folds of her nightgown. "I...I lost my very first case, Jack. It was in the South. I took the bar exam there because I wanted to help. And then they threw this death-row case in my lap. It was hopeless. Fourteen years of appeals and they'd all been turned down." Eve felt her chest tighten.

"You don't have to tell me this," Jack said.

"I do. Yes, I do have to tell you. They executed him, Jack. I begged and pleaded for his life, but I was so green...." She bit her lip. "They executed him and a month later someone else admitted he was guilty of the crime—a deathbed confession. Jack, my client was innocent. The state killed an innocent man."

She wiped at the tears spilling onto her cheeks. Somewhere in her mind there was surprise at how little she cared that she had broken down in front of him.

"Eve..." Jack said, but she had to go on.

"Let me finish. I quit. I just packed up and quit and came home. I took the bar here and got the job at the public defender's office in Denver. Oh, I thought I was so safe, that I could keep it from happening in Colorado. They haven't executed anyone here since 1967. But now... Now they've passed a new law. They're going to do it. And you'll be on death row.

"Stop it," he said in a hard voice. "Don't torture yourself. That execution wasn't your fault. How could you blame yourself?"

"I..." But she couldn't go on.

Jack swore under his breath and moved toward her. "For

chrissake, Eve, the bastards gave you a hopeless case...your *first* case, and you've blamed yourself all these years?"

"He was innocent!" she sobbed, and she was aware of Jack's weight easing onto the bed next to her, his strong arm going around her shoulder. She leaned into him, her face on his bare chest. "I had to tell you," she choked out. "You have to know that about me. I could have stopped the execution if I had just checked out one thing. But I didn't. I thought he was lying, and I didn't know how to go about it in the first place, and..."

Jack took her chin in his hand and turned her face up to his.

"I've never told anyone. No one. Not even Gary."

"But you told me. Why?" he whispered.

"I need you to know that I won't let it ever happen again." She sniffed and stared into his eyes. "I'm so afraid. If anything happened to you, I couldn't bear it."

He was still for a very long time, then finally he said, "Is that the only reason you told me, because I got the death penalty? Why me, why now?"

"Oh, God," she breathed, "I don't know. I don't know why I'm laying this on you."

"And you never told Kapochek...Gary?"

"I...couldn't," she whispered.

"Why not?"

But she only moved her head against him in denial.

He removed his arm from her shoulders. "I think you'd better go, Eve," he said, and she could feel his complete withdrawal.

Without thinking, she reacted, reaching up and taking his face in her hands, forcing him to look at her.

"Eve," he said, tensing, "don't..."

"No, listen to me. I can't live with a lie. I can't keep pretending. I... I want you. I think I've wanted you since the very first, since they brought you into the interrogation room and..."

"Don't do this," he said in a thick voice.

"If you don't want me, Jack, I'll go. I'll go right this second. All you have to do is say the word."

His reaction was sudden and explosive. He took her hands from his face and held them at her sides, held them firmly. He swore and said, "What about Kapochek? I want to know. I have to know, goddamn it. What about *him*?"

She met his eyes squarely through the shadowed darkness. "The truth is, it's been over for a while."

"Come on," he said sharply.

"It has been, Jack. Neither of us has admitted it, but we've been headed down different roads for a long time now." She explained everything to him, finally, everything she'd held close for so long. "And I'll never go into private practice. I'll never be the wife and companion he needs. A large part of me will always be dedicated to my work. Taking on your case was the last straw in our relationship. It's been coming. It's not your fault or Gary's. It's mine."

Jack stared at her for an endless moment, and her heart beat a furious tattoo in her breast. She could still feel the tension in him, the inner battle.

"Nothing's going to stop me from wanting you," she breathed. "So tell me now, Jack, tell me you don't want me that way and I won't say another..."

But she never finished. Jack crushed her to his chest and his mouth covered hers.

They came together as if a storm had erupted from a calm sky. Eve had never experienced such intensity of feeling or let herself succumb to such wild abandonment. He drew her nightgown off her shoulders and laid her back onto the pillow, his mouth hot on her breasts, his beard scraping across her flesh, painful yet eliciting a reckless need in her.

She grasped at him desperately, as if to erase the past year, all the months and weeks and days he'd been in prison, alone, without hope or love or human closeness. And she gloried in the feel of him, so familiar yet so new, his hot skin, rough hair, hard muscles. She moaned with the beauty of his body touching hers.

He moved his hand along her thigh, and she opened to him, burning inside, holding his head to her breasts.

"Oh, God," she said, "Jack..." and his fingers found her moistness.

They came together moments later, a rush of passion that was so instantaneous Eve cried out in surprise, the waves of fulfillment rushing over her. And then, a second later, he spilled into her, his lean body raised above hers, their eyes meeting.

For a long time afterward they lay together, Jack still inside her, Eve clutching him to her. She felt as if she knew every muscle and fiber of him, every nerve ending, as if somehow she'd always known. He moved his hand on her in a slow, gentle probing of her body, memorizing her curves and hollows. They didn't speak. Silence held them in a kind of magical enchantment in which nothing needed to be said. A word, a murmur, would break the spell. They slept that way, pressed together, and when one stirred, the other had to follow suit.

At dawn Jack awoke and kissed her neck and breasts and then her mouth, and the heat began to build inside her again, not a rush of fire this time, but a slowly mounting heat deep in her belly. They moved together in unison, wanting it to last forever, holding back, teasing, savoring the waves of sensation. And when it was over, Jack held her face in his hands and kissed her eyelids.

After all those hours, after so much passion, he finally spoke, a whisper in the quickening light. "It's never been like this before. Never," he said, and she knew it was the truth.

She kissed his face and sighed, no more words necessary. And yet as happy as she was that moment, Eve knew such joy carried with it a burden. Their pleasure seemed suddenly too fragile; like spun glass, it could be too easily shattered.

The day brightened over the mountains, and the sun slid down the yellow siding on the Victorian, warming it. Eve stayed in Jack's embrace but with a growing sense of apprehension and a singular sadness. Not knowing exactly how or why, she had already begun to suffer.

It was after ten when Eve opened her eyes, a golden spear of sunlight coming through the window.

She sat up, disoriented. Jack's room. His bed, she realized, and a hot flush rose up her neck. Then she smiled, a secret woman's smile.

Her happiness fled instantly, though, when she searched the house and yard and realized he'd gone. She knew where, too—Mochlin. He'd gone to confront him. And then fear and a sense of dread overcame her. Mochlin would turn him in. Without a moment's hesitation, George Mochlin would dial 911 and that would be it.

She stood in the kitchen for a long time, lost, afraid, Jack's scent still lingering on her flesh, and she couldn't believe he'd just left. Gotten up sometime after dawn and left her.

It wasn't until she was dressed and searching her brain frantically for a hint of what she should do next that she spotted the note on the table near the front door.

She snatched it up, her fingers shaking.

Eve,
Sorry I didn't wake you. I took the car. We both know what's going to happen. I only hope I can break Mochlin. I want you to know how much you've meant to me. Please understand that it has to be over now. I am sorry, for both of us.

			Jack

She stood there and read it again and again, her heart pounding, her brain telling her that he was lying—it couldn't be over—and a pain grew inside her, a tumor of fear and devastation. She put a fist on her stomach, as if she could force the ache down, and she fought the quick, hot burning of tears behind her eyelids.

Eve was still standing there when a sudden knocking tore her back to reality. She gasped, whirling toward the door.

Through the fine lace curtain at the beveled window, she saw them, men in suits, three of them. "Oh, God," she breathed. It was Hawley. FBI Special Agent Hawley and his men.

Her first reaction was to take a step backward, but at the same time something inside her clicked into action and she crumpled Jack's note in her hand. Moments later, after they knocked again, she finally let the men in. It took every ounce of courage she could muster to face them.

Ralph Hawley stood on the threshold and glared at her. "Okay," he said curtly, "where in hell is he? Goddamn it, woman, you're in enough trouble as it is! Now, where the hell is Devlin?" He nodded at his men, who pulled their guns out, shoved past her, and began to search the house.

"Well?" Hawley said.

Eve swallowed. "He's not here."

"Then where is he? Don't make it worse. Just tell me where he is and I'll go easy on you."

"I don't know where he is," she said, longing to back away but holding her ground. And Jack's note... It was still in her hand. She tightened her fingers around it until they hurt.

His men returned, shaking their heads. They holstered their guns, and all three stared at her.

"Okay," Hawley finally said, his flinty gaze locked on her. "Where's that rental car?"

"Car?" Eve said.

"The car you rented in Denver. The car you rented to throw us off the scent."

"Oh, you mean the car I rented because mine wouldn't start?"

He snorted in derision.

"Well, let's see," she said. "Isn't it parked out front?"

"Don't play games, Miss Marchand," one of the other men said. "You're in a lot of trouble here."

The third one spoke, too. "We all know you've been harboring Devlin. Now, where is he?"

"I told you." Eve moved to the couch and sat down. "He's not here."

"Oh, but he was," Hawley said.

Eve stared up at the three of them, then rested her gaze on Hawley. "Prove it, then, you son of a bitch, just prove it." Her mind turned back to Jack, fear for him knifing through her.

The agents sat down, too, and Hawley said, "We're staying until Devlin shows."

But Eve only laughed dismally. "Stay if you want," she said. "I'll guarantee you it's going to be a very, very long wait."

The instant Jack leaned his forearms on the receptionist's counter at the Castle Creek Golf and Tennis Club he knew he'd been made. The girl stared at him, swallowed convulsively and reached for the phone.

Jack reacted immediately. "Hi," he said. "I'm here to pick up my wife. She's got a tennis lesson."

The girl's mouth opened, but nothing came out.

"Not again," Jack said, his heart racing despite the smile he plastered on his face. "This is the tenth time this week."

"Wh-what?" she stammered.

"You know. That Devlin character. You're the tenth person who's stared at me this way. I never knew how much I looked like him." Jack surreptitiously glanced at the guest register on the counter next to his left forearm. There was a name—Roberts.

"But, you..." the girl was saying.

Jack laughed. "The name's Roberts, Bill Roberts," he said calmly. "My wife's just down there on the court right now with a member."

For a long minute the girl didn't seem to know what to do. Her hand hovered over the phone.

"Come on," Jack said, "do you know how silly this is?"

He could see the waves of uncertainty flow across her face, then, finally, she looked at the guest register, gave a choked laugh and seemed caught between confusion and embarrassment. "I guess," she began. "Well, it is silly. You *do* look a lot like him."

Jack leaned even closer. "I'll take that as a compliment," he said. "My wife always said Devlin was a good-looking guy. Now, can I go on in and find her? We've got a lunch date...."

"Oh, oh sure, Mr....Roberts, and I'm sorry, you know, if I..."

"No problem," Jack said, straightening. "It is ridiculous, though. I mean, what on earth would Devlin be doing back in Aspen?" And with that he beat a hasty path toward Mochlin's office, his heart knocking against his ribs.

He didn't locate the tennis pro immediately, but from the window in the man's office, Jack could see him finishing up a lesson on one of the indoor courts. It was a full ten minutes—a very long ten minutes—before Mochlin appeared in the doorway. Then, before Mochlin realized who he was, Jack closed the office door and twisted the rod that shut the blinds.

Mochlin whirled around, the blood draining from his face. "You..." he breathed.

"It's me, all right," Jack said, and he made sure he was blocking the pro's path to the door. "Sit down," he ordered. "We need to have a little chat, George."

Jack had seen men with cases of nerves before, but never to this extent.

"Take it easy." Jack looked down at Mochlin, who was sitting, stiff as a board, behind his desk. "I wouldn't want you to have a heart attack."

"I could yell, you know," Mochlin said, "yell for help."

"Don't bother," Jack replied. "I only want to talk. Is there some reason you don't want to talk, George?"

Getting anything out of Mochlin was like pulling teeth. The man's mind flitted from one subject to the next, answering questions Jack hadn't even put to him. "Melinda's just a lousy drunk! She didn't lie on the witness stand, I swear to God. She just never knew for sure what time she left the J-Bar. The bartender knows I was there till two. He swore to it!"

"Okay, okay," Jack said. "But what I'd like to hear about is the fight you had with Allison." Casually Jack sat on the corner of Mochlin's desk, his arms folded. He glared at the tennis pro.

"Fight?"

"Allison found out you'd been bragging about marrying her. She got pissed. You had a fight. Tell me about it."

Mochlin's eyes darted around the room. "We... It wasn't a fight, man, I swear...."

"Quit lying. Let's hear the truth."

Mochlin sucked in a breath. "So we fought. Big deal. Allison loved to argue. Hey, you have to know that. She argued with everyone. That live-in couple. *You*, man. And that kid of hers. It was no big deal."

Jack grinned. "This is the way I see it, pal," he said in an even voice. "You had a few too many that night. You left the J-Bar, picked up your car at your condo and drove up to talk to her. Yeah, sure, that's probably all it was going to be. A little talk. You let yourself in, or maybe Allison let you in. Doesn't matter. But the talk got ugly. You were loaded. Allison turned her back on you..." Jack shrugged. "The rest we know."

"No, no, no," Mochlin mumbled, running a hand through his thick hair. "No. I didn't go up there. No! Man, you're crazy, you're nuts...."

"You'll break," Jack went on relentlessly. "Maybe not today or tomorrow, but you'll break, George. They're not going to stop coming after you. Especially now. They *know* about the fight. It's all going to come crashing down around you. If you tell the truth, tell them it was a spur-of-the-moment act, you'll get off on murder two or maybe even manslaughter. You'll be free in eight, ten years...."

Mochlin leaped to his feet. His chair flipped over, hitting a file cabinet behind him. "You're crazy!" he yelled, and that was when Jack stood and grabbed the man's tennis shirt with one hand while his other formed a fist. "Go ahead! Hit me!" Mochlin cried. "They're still going to fry you, man! They'll catch you and fry you!"

And then Jack hit him. Mochlin went to his knees, sobbing, holding his jaw, his eyes wild.

Jack let go of his shirt and stood up straight, staring down at him. "That's for screwing my wife when we were still married," he said. He almost hit him again, but it wasn't worth it. Instead, he said, "Ah, hell," and he turned on his heel and walked out past the crowd gathering at the door.

Five minutes later, Jack was driving down Main Street. He knew someone—probably a dozen people—had dialed 911 by now. It no longer mattered. He parked the rental car on Garmisch Street and tossed the keys on the seat—Eve would deal with it, say the car was stolen, whatever. He walked along Hopkins then, avoiding the beaten track, heading toward the police department. Somewhere on Main Street a siren sounded, then another. He almost laughed. The cop cars were racing out of town, toward the tennis club.

He kept walking, his head ducked, hands in his pockets. He knew Eve was waiting for him, going out of her mind with worry, maybe not even alone anymore. Maybe they'd traced her.

He walked on, past the bank, the movie theater, the old firehouse, the thrift shop. More sirens sounded. Hell, he thought, this was the most excitement they'd had in this little slice of paradise since Ted Bundy escaped. He almost laughed to himself, but then he thought about Eve, about last night. It never should have happened. *He* should have stopped it.

He turned north on Galena Street and walked to Main, waited at the intersection for traffic to pass, then crossed to the courthouse. Another cop car streaked past, howling.

Death row, he thought, his steps slowing as he approached the police station; there were going to be endless days and unbearable nights ahead. And the only thing he had to keep him sane was the memory of Eve.

He stopped and looked at the sign that read Police. Then he sucked in a deep breath, set his shoulders and walked into the building to meet his destiny.

PART IV

Death Row

TWENTY-TWO

"You look like hell," Hank said tactlessly as he eased his lanky body into the chair across from Eve's desk.

"Why, thank you." Eve took her glasses off and rubbed the bridge of her nose. "You don't look so swift yourself."

Hank laughed, coughed, then took a cigarette out of the pocket of his shabby sport coat.

"Don't you dare light that in here," she warned.

"Wouldn't dream of it." He stared at Eve and shook his head, the unlit cigarette dangling from his lips. "Why don't you get away for a day or two? Drive down to the desert. You and Kapochek. Look at this mess on your desk." He thumbed through a stack of files. "How many times you gonna reread this? It's been almost a month since Devlin turned himself in. You're not going to get diddly-squat out of this stuff."

"There's got to be something," she said, "something we've missed."

Hank watched as she stood up and stretched in the cramped office. Then she went to the window, which overlooked the parking lot below.

He felt sorry for her. Of all the public defenders Hank had worked with, Eve had become very special to him. He'd never been married. Never had kids. If he had, though, he'd have wanted a daughter exactly like her. Someone upright and honest and moral, someone who knew where she was going. Often, when he was in town and Kapochek wasn't, Hank and Eve spent evenings together. They had dinner. Went to movies. Relaxed. He secretly hoped she never married, at least never moved out of the city. He'd miss those evenings.

He was worried about her now, though; he'd never seen her so frustrated or anxious. This Devlin case was one of the toughest nuts either of them had ever tried to crack. Ninety-nine percent of the time their clients were guilty, and all they were seeking was some glitch in the system to get their man off death row. The trouble with the Devlin case was that Eve believed the man was innocent. Hank wasn't quite as positive, though it was hard to see Devlin bludgeoning anyone to death.

Hank's money—and his efforts—were on Mochlin, and that's where he'd been spending his time, probing into the tennis pro's background, looking for any new lead, no matter how small.

Eve, however, still planned on grilling the former live-ins, the Wades. Hank had traced them to Southern California, the San Diego area, and Eve planned on paying them a visit as soon as both their background checks were complete. She also planned to speak to Ben Richards and his fiancée on the same trip, because Richards was spending most of his time in the Los Angeles area with Sarah now.

"Major waste of your time," Hank had told her more than once. "Trust me. I can smell a rat a mile away. It's Mochlin. Won't be easy to break him, though."

"We'll see," Eve always said. "Let's just finish the background check on Ben up in Aspen."

The thing was, they were going to need a miracle to break this case. They'd been down every avenue again and again, and it was beginning to look pretty damn grim. Hank didn't want to tell Eve that, but, really, she must know it in her heart.

"How about some spaghetti tonight?" he asked. "We

could go to that joint you like up in north Denver. They haven't had a drive-by shooting in over a week. We might make it in and out with our lives. Maybe we could even catch a movie. What do you say?"

"I can't." She looked apologetic. "Gary's back in town for a few days and we've got to see each other. It's been...a while."

Hank took the unlit cigarette out of his mouth and toyed with it.

"He ever say anything about your great adventure?"

Eve shook her head. "To be honest, Gary and I haven't really talked much since then. Couple of times on the phone."

"So tonight's the big heart-to-heart?"

"I guess it is." She sighed and gave him a weak smile.

"Confused?"

"Um."

"Is it Devlin?"

"Hank."

"Well, is it? It's real hard for this old boy here to believe nothing went on between you two. You're killing yourself over him."

"Over Gary?" she quipped.

"You know what I mean. I hate to ask, and you won't answer, but it's been on my mind."

"Don't ask."

"Did you? Did you sleep with Devlin?" he said, his flinty eyes pinning her.

Eve glared at him, tossed her hair, folded her arms and said, "That's privileged information."

"I thought so," Hank replied. "You're a goddamn fool, Marchand."

"Go to hell," she said.

It was a long drive up to Boulder that evening in rush-hour traffic. Eve's nerves were raw. It had been weeks since that phone call she'd made to Gary in Miami. Frankly, she was surprised he hadn't said something, picked a fight about it, bitched her out, something. But he hadn't. And it was this *thing* between them, a wall, an ugly lump of apprehension.

So this meeting was it, time for truth on both sides. She could have handled it if she weren't so confused about her feelings. She steered through the growing dusk and felt a stab of guilt. She had to confess what she'd done if their relationship was going to survive...and she wasn't even sure if it would survive, or could, or if she wanted it to. Or if Gary would want it to when he heard what she had to say.

They had so much invested in each other, years, successes, failures, so very much. And they *liked* each other, respected, admired each other.

But now she knew there was another kind of love. Passion. Ferocious, not comfortable. Unthinking, difficult. Maybe impossible. Yet once you'd felt it, the lesser emotion would not suffice, and she was so very afraid that's what had happened to her.

She hadn't wanted it or asked for it, but it had come to her, and she was everlastingly glad she'd embraced it. And so terribly sorry.

When she reached Gary's house it was dark out, a cold October wind whipping down out of the Flatirons. She hugged her wool coat to her throat and hurried to the door despite a mounting sense of dread. She only hoped they could keep this civil and behave like adults. Friends.

She let herself in with her own key and called out to him. "Gary, I'm here!"

"In the kitchen," he called back.

He looked good. As if he'd been taking excellent care of himself in spite of the grueling midseason football schedule.

Eve broke into a smile and he crossed to her, gave her a hug and then studied her at arm's length.

"You're barely limping, Gary," she said, pleased and happy for him. "I can't believe it."

"Taking my medicine, doing what the doctors say." He shrugged. "But you look sort of...done in, Eve," he said carefully. "I don't suppose you've even considered a short vacation?"

She shook her head.

"So that's out entirely?"

She looked for a sign of disappointment in his face. There was none.

"Well," he said, "I guess we were both dreaming all along, thinking we could just take off and leave everything behind us."

"Yes," she allowed, "we were. I'm sorry."

"I guess," he said, "it was too much to hope for."

"Yes," Eve repeated, "it was."

"And Devlin?" he asked, still holding her.

"I'm working on it."

"I'll bet you are." And then Gary let go of her and went to the oven, opening the door, checking on dinner—a ready-to-cook pizza from the local deli.

"Gary," she said, still standing there awkwardly. "Thank you for, well, for not saying anything to anyone when I helped...Jack. You could have called the police."

"I'd never do that to you, Eve. You know that."

"Yes, I do. But thanks, anyway."

"You were a fool."

She laughed humorlessly. "So I've been told."

"What about the FBI?" he asked. "Are they after you for it?"

"No. Not that I know of, anyway." She went to the cupboard where he kept his liquor. "I figure they got their man back and that was enough." She found the vodka. "Mind if I...?"

"No, go ahead," he said. "I'll have a beer."

They sat in the living room, feet up, and had their drinks with the pizza. Eve felt as if everything was surreal between them, every word spoken a means of skirting the issue. She was more confused than ever. Surely Gary wanted to know where they were headed. And so did she.

"I'd like you to come to the game on Sunday," he said.

"Sit with the wives, you know. The weather's supposed to be good, too. Reports say the storm's going to stay north of us."

"Sunday. Sure," she said. "I'd love to. It's with the Vikings, right?"

"So you *are* keeping up."

"Uh-huh. With the newspapers, anyway."

"Driving to Canon City a lot?" he asked then, too casually.

"Once a week." She felt tension in her neck, as if a hand had suddenly grasped her.

"And how is Devlin?"

"It's...depressing."

"Is he holding up?"

She shrugged. "As best he can." And then she felt that invisible hand tighten. "Gary," she began, "there's something I have to tell you."

His gaze rose to hers from across the coffee table where the remains of pizza and drinks sat. "I don't think I want to hear this."

"I need to tell you."

Abruptly he stood. He grasped his cane and began to walk the floor. "I don't goddamn want to hear this."

She shut her eyes for a moment, then opened them. She nodded. "Okay. Okay, I understand. Just so long as you know I wouldn't lie to you. I never have. And I never will."

He paced in silence for a minute, and then he stopped and faced her. "We have something special, Eve. We *like* each other. I think we should try. But... Well, you aren't the only one who screwed up."

She stared at him, bewildered.

"I... It was in Miami. After we talked on the phone."

"Yes..." she said hesitantly.

"I was out of my mind. I knew you were with...*him*, and I, well, I met someone."

"Oh," she said. "Oh."

"I won't go into detail, but..."

Eve let out a breath. "Don't say anything else. Please."

"I won't." He stood there, staring at her. "But I think we both have some soul-searching to do. Let's talk again after the game. We can have dinner. Someplace special."

"All right," she said, her eyes lifting tentatively to his.

"And let's both do some thinking before Sunday."

"All right," she repeated. "I suppose we'd better."

But by Sunday nothing had changed. She sat in the bright October sun with the football players' wives and cheered the Broncos on, but her heart wasn't in the game. She was thinking about Jack rotting away in that tiny cell on death row. She knew she should be weighing her situation with Gary—at least be mulling over his confession about some sort of tryst he'd had in Miami—but she couldn't muster the emotional response she should. The single thought in her mind was that she'd driven him to it.

The Broncos lost. A last field goal attempt by the Vikings hit the goalpost and bounced through the uprights.

Gary was on a bummer at dinner. He pushed his lamb chops around the plate and dwelled on the team's un-inspired showing on the field today. "The defense played well," he said. "You saw that. But the offensive line... Hell, we got sacked five times! You can't win a game if you're goddamn moving in the wrong direction."

Eve, too, had little appetite. "It was a tough loss," she agreed. It was never any fun to be around the coaches or players after a loss—especially one at home, and it was quite obvious that the discussion about where they were headed was on hold. It was just as well. She was as pre-occupied as Gary.

At her house, he only stayed five minutes. "I've got to be up early to go over the game tapes," he said. "We play in Dallas next week and we'd better be ready. I'm sorry. I know you wanted to talk."

Eve held his hand at the door. "We will talk," she said, "when we're both not preoccupied."

"Okay," he said. "And I love you, baby, I really do. I'll call you from Dallas."

"I'll be here."

"And promise you'll get some rest?"

"I will."

He kissed her goodbye. She closed her eyes and accepted his kiss. But later, alone in the darkness, she knew it was a lie. Even as Gary's mouth had covered hers, in her mind she was kissing Jack.

Life on death row wasn't hell—that was far too meaningless a cliché. It was purgatory: an endless waiting, neither dead nor alive, until one paid for one's sins. This limbo existed so the bureaucracy, the state, could kill a human being without the burden of sin. But first the bureaucracy had to distance itself from the act, and so the prisoner had to wait.

It was the isolation that was the worst. Each man was encased in an eight-by-ten-foot cell, all clean and new and sterile. The door was solid, not barred, with only a square opening through which food was passed. There was a prison-regulation window six feet up, a narrow aperture where Jack could see an oblong of sky, follow the patterns of clouds or clear blue. Or a plane.

He was allowed out of his cell one hour out of twenty-four, alone, to shower and to work out in the exercise room. He was allowed no contact with other inmates, ever, although they spoke to one another through the doors, their voices echoing out into the corridor. They never saw each other, though.

"What you in here for, man?" he'd been asked by the unseen occupants on either side of him when he'd arrived, shackled, always shackled except when he was locked in his cell.

"Killing my wife," he'd answered, unable, unwilling to start a conversation, which would mean a kind of relationship, however sick, a commitment to humanity. Jack wasn't in the mood for that—he was trying to survive, and for him that meant living inside his own head, where reality still made sense.

"Yeah," his neighbors had replied, "well, man, she probably deserved it."

"Oh, yeah," one had said. "I read about you. You're that rich guy, that architect."

"Not anymore," Jack had said.

The inmates on the row were treated like things, not people, spoken of in the third person. The guards took care not to grow too close, not to be friendly, not to be contaminated by the terminal illness that would eventually kill each of the convicts, one by one by one.

Jack saw this, lived in it, and as an intellectual exercise— and to keep his sanity—he tried to analyze it. The condemned man was trying to live, while the state was trying with legal sanctions to bury the corpse that insisted on moving and complaining and eating and talking.

The rules were strict. You ate at a precise time, the same every day. Your hour out was the same. You were awakened at the same hour and the lights went out at the same moment every night. When Jack thought about it, he could see how it was all organized for one purpose, a whole set of rules, a way of life—or existence—simply and purely to maintain a bizarre placidity.

Time was an endless string of lonely, empty moments, unbearable minutes and hours and days that marched toward an inevitable end. Unbearable time that had to be borne.

It was knowing the date and time and method of your own death that was so terrible.

One inmate had been on the row for fourteen years. Fourteen years. The scuttlebutt was that he only had a week or so more. His appeals had run out, and Colorado was about to execute its first prisoner since 1967. Of course, no one believed it.

The man in the cell next to Jack's kept saying, "It ain't gonna happen, man. No way." Jack wasn't so sure.

There were no TV sets, no radios. Some reading material was available, although it was censored, and inmates were allowed into the law library for an hour at a time. Alone.

Despite their belief that the execution wasn't going to take place, inmates spoke endlessly about how to go to death. They passed their conversations along by calling to one another down the line. If Jack kept his brain apart from it, he could have said it was interesting.

"I'll fight the bastards every step of the way," one man said. "They'll have to drag me. I'll hurt someone, yeah, I will. They won't forget me."

"You want to go with dignity, bro'. They'll remember you better for that. You go like a man. With pride. None o' that screamin' stuff."

The man whose execution was pending said absolutely nothing.

Jack was beginning to understand it. All men died. Some died young, suffering, maybe in a bloody accident or a war. All men died, but none knew the exact method and hour of his death, none but those incarcerated on death row.

They all had dreams and nightmares; Jack heard them at night, the prisoners' anguish echoing down the corridor. Screams, moans, curses. Whimpers. Animal shrieks of rage.

They all read the papers, too, hanging on every word of every article written about death row. About *them*. They knew all the gory details, how they would be strapped down, injected, what their bodies would do. It spilled out of them like vomit, the words telling what it would be like, how they'd react.

There was a solid bunk with a thin mattress in each cell, a sink, a stainless steel toilet. Some of the men rolled up their mattresses, put them in pillowcases and used them as punching bags. Some exercised constantly, mindlessly, hanging on the metal stanchions on the wall, chinning themselves until they sweated and their muscles bulged. Some didn't move or talk, only stared into space. Some cried. Some slept all day.

If it was purgatory, it was also bedlam.

No one had ever escaped. Every prisoner was monitored on screen all the time from the control center. Every hall was video monitored. Every door was opened and closed electronically from the control center, too.

Jack held himself together, drawing on his dwindling supply of inner strength and his ability to go inside himself. Sometimes it scared him to think that he might go inside so far, so deep, that he'd never come out, but then he thought, *so what?*

On one side of him was a man who'd murdered his business partner for an insurance claim. He was intelligent, and they talked some and played chess, each of them with a chessboard and the pieces, calling moves back and forth to each other, each moving both sets of pieces.

On the other side the inmate talked incessantly, even when no one listened, and only shut up when a guard came by and yelled at him. He'd killed several innocent bystanders when he was robbing a store, and he drove everyone crazy with his confessions.

"I did it, man," he'd say. "I shot the one in the chest. You shoulda seen his face. Then the old lady. The girl, in her neck. Blood everywhere. Screaming. Shit, how they screamed. And, I don't know, it was like someone else pulled the trigger, like I was looking down. Bang! Bang! I was so high on speed, I couldn't see, couldn't hear. I did it, yeah, I shot 'em. But, you know, man, they deserved it."

Half the night, he went on like that, jabbering, jabbering. Jack had asked Eve for one thing—earplugs.

He spent his time reading whatever he could get hold of, sketching houses, designing, incredibly detailed drawings, with appliances and furniture.

The worst, the very worst, times were when his attorney was allowed to visit. One hour once a week, by appointment with the superintendent, Friday afternoon at two o'clock. It took him half the week to brace himself to see her, then the other half to get over it.

"Hi," she always said, smiling through the glass at him. A patently false smile, but she got an A for effort. "How are you?"

"I'm okay," he'd say.

"Do you want anything? Can I bring you anything?"

No, nothing. Except those earplugs. And any articles on architecture she could locate.

Then they'd talk about his case, where she was in the appeals process, how hard Hank was working to check things out, on his own time, too, because the budget wouldn't cover all his hours. They'd move on to current events, news, anything to fill out the hour. They had curiously stilted conversations, each of them trying so desperately to spare the other pain. A complicity of misery.

He'd breathe a sigh of relief when she left, when he was led, shackled, back to his cell. And there he would pace, thinking of everything he'd wanted to tell her. How beautiful she was.

On Tuesday after lunch, at one o'clock, Eve had a standing appointment to phone him. He was shackled and led down the hall to the phone, handcuffed to a ring in the wall while he spoke to her.

"Hi," she'd say brightly, "how are you?"

"Okay," he'd say.

"It snowed today. It's really cold out."

"Mmm. Winter's coming."

"Do you need anything?"

"No, thanks."

"Ben called me from California last week. He wanted to know how everything was going. And he said he'd made an appointment to visit you."

"Yes, I know. I told him not to come."

"He mentioned that. Jack, don't push your friends away. He wants to see you."

"He's crazy to fly all the way from Long Beach to come here."

"He's not crazy, he's your friend."

"There is no such thing as friendship in here."

He'd hang up, his gut in knots, his throat aching, and he was led, shuffling and clanking, back to his cell.

Time was loneliness, the seconds and minutes and hours ticking inexorably away. And there was nothing Jack could do to halt the passing of time until his sentence was carried out.

Ben Richards was cold as he drove the rental car up to Canon City and parked in the visitors' lot. He'd had to make this appointment three weeks before, and he'd dreaded it every minute since then. But he owed it to Jack, God knew, he owed him that much.

It was a Saturday afternoon, a cold, windy day, with storm clouds gathering over the mountains, and it felt even colder to Ben, who'd been in California since Jack had been sentenced.

The security check took Ben by surprise. He'd expected to be checked, naturally, but not strip-searched. When the ordeal was over, and he was led deeper and deeper into the recesses of Super Max, he found he was nauseous and sweating profusely. Eve had warned him, but it was godawful, much worse than he'd imagined. By the time he was seated in the interview room, staring at the glass partition and the phone, he was swallowing bile.

They led Jack in on the other side of the glass, shackled, in a green prison suit, and he sat across from Ben, smiled and picked up his phone.

"Hey, Jack," Ben said, his voice quavering. "You look good." His fingers were white on the phone.

"Liar."

"So, how's it going?"

"As you see, Ben, as you see."

"You hanging in there?"

"Sure I am."

"Sarah says hello."

"You two living together in Long Beach?"

"Yeah, we are. After you turned yourself in, I bought a little place."

"Right on the water?"

"Sure," Ben said, "it's on the water." Then he shook his head, the nausea rising again. "Jack, man, this is bad. It's awful. How can you stand it?"

"Forget it," Jack replied, and he gave Ben a reassuring look. "Tell me about the house in Aspen. Have you got it listed yet?"

Ben shook his head.

"Got new caretakers?"

"Ah, sure, a really nice older couple. Sarah had them checked out thoroughly. After the Wades... Well you know."

"Eve told me about them."

"The creeps," Ben said. "I hope Eve's still working on that angle. I sure hope she's not letting them off the hook."

"She's not."

Ben glanced around at the sterile walls. "Jack, you've got to get out of here. Let me hire some top-notch detectives. Please..."

"Forget it."

"But, Jack, hey, you'll rot in this place!"

"Take it easy," Jack began, but Ben was losing it.

"I can't stand this. You know my real father was never a father to me. And Mom... God, Jack, you were my only real parent. I can't stand for this to be happening to you. Where the hell is justice? Let me..."

"*Ben*," Jack broke in. "Calm down. I know it looks bad when you first see it, but it's not as horrible as it seems. Everything's going to work out. It takes time. You could do me a big favor, though. Just don't come again. I mean it. Write. Or set up an occasional call. But don't come in person. It's too hard on you. Maybe on both of us. Do you understand?"

Ben took a couple of deep breaths and finally nodded.

"Okay. Now, go on and get out of here." Jack smiled at him. "And tell that pretty lady of yours hello for me."

"Okay," Ben said, taking another breath. "Okay."

"You all right now?"

"Sure," Ben said, "I'm fine."

But by the time he was led out to the bus that took him back to his car at the visitors' center, where he'd been processed through, the nausea overcame him. He vomited right in the center, all over the new tile floor.

One of the guards shook his head and said to another, "Musta been over at Super Max."

TWENTY-THREE

The drive to Canon City was all too familiar to Eve. Over the years she'd done it to visit clients dozens of times: south out of Denver on Interstate 25, southwest out of Colorado Springs, up to the rolling stretches of the Great Plains and foothills past Fort Carson to Florence. Just to the east of Canon City, where the old Territorial Prison still stood, she entered a stretch of dry, sage-dotted terrain she thought of as prison country.

There was a massive prison complex located there, consisting of many buildings, but Eve's destination was the new state-of-the-art Colorado State Penitentiary Maximum Security, known as Big Red or Super Max. It was the facility reserved for the real hard cases, the troublemakers from all over the state, and, of course, it housed death row.

Because she was an attorney, and her name was left at the guardhouse at the entrance to the complex, Eve did not have to go through the tedious processing at the visitors' center. Still, when she parked and entered the fortresslike red brick building, she was subjected to an electronic search by the "Eye," a walk-through unit similar to those used at airports. And then she had to sign a Consent to Search form, subjecting herself to a possible body search if there were any question as to her intentions. She knew the prison superintendent, however, and thank God she'd never had a problem visiting the clients she'd saved from death sentences, the ones who were serving life instead and whose appeals she was handling.

It was nevertheless a degrading, paranoia-inducing process; she was led through one security pod into the next, the prison gates clanging shut electronically behind her, going deeper and deeper into the complex. She'd told some of the rookie public defenders who'd never been to Super Max that it was like being entombed alive.

This was one of the most stressful trips she'd made. Of the three times Eve had been to see Jack, this was the hardest. Only a week and a half ago, Colorado had executed its first prisoner in over thirty years. The guard led her through the complex, past the security checkpoints, and she could feel the pervasive mood throughout the entire place. It was as if gray gloom oozed out of the walls. Even the experienced guards were still shaken, distancing themselves more than ever from the inmates, especially those on the row. She couldn't imagine how Jack was holding up under the weight of the isolation and hopelessness. And he knew, as they all did, that the appeals process in Colorado had been shortened dramatically. Time for the rest of the men on the row was running out, and they all felt it with a terrible immediacy.

Eve took her seat in the interview room and pulled out her files. She breathed deeply and worked at putting a smile on her face. They brought Jack in precisely as scheduled, shackled. The first thing she noticed was how very pale he'd grown. These men never saw the light of day, their only exercise an hour alone in a small room, and the lack of fresh air, of sunlight, was taking its inevitable toll.

When the guard seated Jack, handcuffing him to a bar in the glass booth, Eve picked up the telephone receiver. She smiled brightly and nodded to him to pick up his phone on the other side of the thick partition.

"Hi," she said in a cheerful voice.

He held on to the receiver and gave her a return nod.

"How are you?" she tried.

"I'm fine."

"Good," she said, "good. They feeding you all right?"

"Sure," he said, his dark eyes giving nothing away, and her heart clutched. She was losing him. Every day, every hour, every minute Jack spent in this place was taking him farther and farther away. She'd seen this before. But in Jack, who was already inside himself so much, the withdrawal was proceeding faster.

"Well," she went on brightly, "the judge should be reviewing the Notice of Appeal, Jack, and I should hear something by the end of next week. I'm very hopeful that..."

"Eve," he said, his voice so familiar, so close, and yet that glass barrier seemed a mile thick. "You don't have to pretend with me. All the appeals in the world aren't going to mean a thing."

"You're wrong, they're..."

"Look," he said, holding the phone to his ear, "what I need is for someone to confess to Allison's murder. But no one's going to do that. You know it and so do I."

"Hank's working on it," she said, her voice still ringing with confidence, "and so am I. Marty Cohen is also conducting some background investigations. It's only a matter of time before we get a break. And Hank's located the Wades. They're in the San Diego area. We're just waiting for a few more background details before we proceed. Things *are* happening, Jack."

"I appreciate it," he said woodenly.

She wanted to tell him so much, to share with him all the mundane details of her life, the way a person would to a...lover. She'd tell him how the neighbor's dog had tried to bite her ankle and how the battery had gone out on her portable phone. How she'd had a flat tire. How her mother and father had gotten home to Pinecrest and noticed that a few of her father's clothes were missing. They'd called Eve, wondering, but accepted her lame excuse.

She'd tell Jack what she had for lunch, how busy she was

at the office. She'd even tell him about her visit to Gary's, the mess their relationship was in. She'd tell Jack everything, share her life with him. She'd even confess her fears, her nightmares, how she'd sat up all night when they'd executed the prisoner only ten days ago.

The man had been two cells down the row from Jack.

She'd tell him how she'd thrown up the scanty dinner she'd had at the hour of the execution and that Hank had held her hand.

Oh, God, Eve thought, she so very much wanted to share it all with him.

"I heard from your mother," Eve said, trying desperately to maintain her composure. "I brought her up to date on everything."

Jack held her gaze and nodded slightly. "I wish she wouldn't bother. I wish she'd just wash her hands of the whole thing."

Eve sighed. "You mustn't give up, Jack. You've got to hold on to hope. I know we're going to beat this. I only wish... Well, I wish you'd have faith. I never felt so certain about anything in my life. Really."

"I appreciate your optimism," he said, his expression stoic.

"Oh, Jack." And without conscious volition she lifted her hand to the glass, met his eyes and waited for his response. He began to raise his hand, as if to press it to hers through the barrier, but instead he made a fist and lowered his hand.

"No," he said into the phone. "No, Eve. I've given this a lot of thought, a whole lot." He laughed without humor. "You remember what you told me? About the very first case you were assigned to?"

"Yes, I remember," she said.

"I believe," he went on, "I think that you've confused your sense of duty with something else. I want you to think about it."

She knew what he was getting at—that she was confusing her devotion to his case with love.

She felt her body tighten. "You're wrong," she said sharply. "I know the difference, Jack."

"Do you," he said. It wasn't a question. Then he leaned forward in his seat and looked her right in the eye. "I don't want you to come back here."

"What?" she said.

"Don't come back here. I don't want you here, do you understand?"

"But, Jack, I..."

"Send someone else. Send Marty," he said in a hard voice. "I don't want you. I'll refuse your visits if you try to come."

"But I have to see you. I need to see you. Your case..." she stammered.

He hissed into the phone. "Don't come back." Then he hung up and signaled the guard to return him to his cell.

Eve sat there, frozen, paralyzed. Eventually she realized that she still held the receiver to her ear, and she hung it up, very carefully, looked at it a moment, then rose, wavered a bit and walked out of the room.

She didn't remember the drive home to Denver. Somehow she got there in one piece, but she only snapped back to reality when she had to find the key to her front door.

She held it all together until she got inside, closed the door, threw her coat and purse on the couch and went into the kitchen for a glass of water. The tears started when she raised the glass to her lips. Silent tears at first, then wrenching sobs that came from deep inside. She leaned on the edge of the sink and cried as she hadn't done in years, until her eyes were swollen and her nose was running and she felt utterly empty inside.

"Don't come back," Jack had said. And she knew his resolve, his pride. What torment he must feel to say that to her.

Had she cried for Jack or for herself? she wondered. Had she cried for his suffering or for her own? Had she cried because he couldn't?

Finally she blew her nose in a napkin, rinsed her face and tried to think.

She had to eat; she hadn't had a bite all day. She felt weak, exhausted, and she had no appetite, but she knew she had to eat. And it was dark in her house.

The blinking light on her answering machine caught her eye as she was turning on the lights, and she pressed the button automatically.

"Call me," came Hank's voice. "ASAP."

She waited until she'd eaten and showered and recovered her equilibrium a little, then called his home number, because it was late.

"About time," Hank said.

"I haven't had a great day, either," she replied. "What's up?"

"This might improve your day, or then again, it might not, little lady."

"What, Hank?" she asked wearily.

"Marty Cohen called me today. He's been checking on Ben Richards's background up in Aspen. You know, like you told him to."

"Uh-huh."

"I think he found something very interesting." Hank paused. "There was an incident about seven years ago when Ben was seventeen. He was on the Aspen junior hockey team, and it seems he got into one of them hockey brawls, but he hit a kid so hard he broke his own stick and sent the kid to the hospital. And this wasn't even a game. It was a practice."

"Ben Richards?"

"Yeah, that sweet kid, that's the one."

"My God."

"I've got the name of the kid he hurt, the hockey coach, all that juicy stuff. You want I should check this out?"

"Wait, Hank, let me think." *Ben Richards.* "Marty's sure about this?"

"Yup. He spoke to Ben's hockey coach."

"My God. That could mean... No, I don't even want to say it."

"You don't want to say it *yet*," Hank replied. "I guess our Ben has quite a temper."

"Hank, do you realize what this could mean?" Eve felt energy flowing back into her in a great wave.

"Well, sure I do. That's why I called you. Okay, so do I go to Aspen and ask around or what?"

"No," Eve said firmly. "No. *We* go to Aspen and ask around."

"When?"

"Tomorrow. First thing."

"Christ, woman, you're a slave driver."

"Yes, isn't it great?"

Aspen was gray and windswept when Eve and Hank pulled up at the Christmas Inn. The last few yellow leaves were swirling off bare branches and spiraling to the ground. It looked as if it might snow.

Eve got on the phone the minute she was in her room. Buddy Perez, the hockey coach who'd told Marty Cohen about the incident with Ben, wasn't hard to track down. He was a real-estate agent, and Eve got him in his car, on his cellular phone. She met him at his office half an hour later while Hank tried to locate the father of the boy who'd been injured.

Buddy Perez was a good-looking man, athletic and darkly handsome. He sat behind his cluttered desk at the realty office and told Eve everything she wanted to know.

"Yeah," Perez said, "Ben had a mean streak. He didn't let it loose often, but when he did, it was nasty. That day, it was a big practice before the state play-offs. Everyone was pretty revved, and Larry got in Ben's face, kept trying to check him into the boards even though it was only practice. All of a sudden, Ben just exploded. I mean, we were all shocked. The kid snapped, turning on Larry and beat the hell out of him. Broke his stick over his back, punched him, kicked him. It took a second for the guys to realize what was happening and pull him off. It was pretty bad. Larry went to the emergency room and had some blood in his urine. Couldn't play in the state match.''

"What did Ben do when they pulled him off Larry?"

"He was like a madman for a minute. Took four of the boys to hold him. But then he calmed down. He even apologized. I had to suspend him for the rest of the season. So two players didn't go to state. We lost," Perez said dryly.

"Did you talk to Ben's parents about it?"

"Sure I did. His mother said she'd ground him. His father said he'd beat the shit—excuse me—out of him. The only one who sounded like he really cared was his stepfather.''

"Jack Devlin."

"Yeah, Jack. He told me he was going to talk to Ben, and he probably did, but I don't know what came of it, because I think Ben was sent away to private school back East for his senior year. I never saw him again."

Very interesting, Eve thought as she went back to the motel to check with Hank. No one had mentioned a word about Ben's mean streak, no one. Not even Jack, who knew, who certainly knew. If it had happened again, who else had Ben turned on in uncontrollable rage? *His mother?*

Hank hadn't been able to speak to the injured boy's father yet—they had to wait until he got home from work—but he had spoken to the Aspen High School principal, who remembered Ben Richards quite well.

"It's a small high school, so he said they really get to know the kids," Hank reported. "And he knew Ben. There were a couple of incidents he recalled. A fight Ben got into and a teacher he had an argument with. Nothing too serious, but he thought Ben might have some problems at home. He suggested counseling to John Richards once, but the man was insulted. Then they sent Ben off to private school."

"Hmm," Eve said, tapping a finger on her lips, "a pattern

seems to be emerging. Temper tantrums when faced with obstacles?''

"Could be," Hank said. "So, tell me, how come Jack never told you this stuff about Ben?"

"I don't know, Hank," she said thoughtfully. "I don't know."

They caught up with Larry Welberg, Senior, at his house at five o'clock. His son had left town years before, but Welberg remembered Ben very clearly.

"That little creep," he said. "He was a lazy hockey player, didn't try very hard. He might have been good if he tried. But if he was crossed, holy cow, watch out. The other boys knew and generally steered clear of anything physical with him in practice. In games he played defense. They called him the Enforcer."

"Did he ever beat up other kids like he did your son?" Eve asked.

"Not like that. A few tiffs, you know, like boys'll have." Larry Welberg shook his head. "Ben Richards was a dirty player. And he didn't get caught by the refs often enough. I hate to say it, but we were all glad when he went away to school. He was just trouble waiting to happen."

Eve and Hank discussed the new information over barbecued spareribs in one of the few restaurants that stayed open during the off-season in Aspen. Eve felt as if they'd made a big breakthrough, and she was high on the knowledge that she had a lead now. Something that might help Jack.

Hank wasn't so sure. "Wishful thinking," he said. "Be careful. A kid's hockey fight doesn't necessarily mean a thing. My money's still on Mochlin."

"It's a pattern," Eve said, licking barbecue sauce off her fingers. "And it's the first break we've had, Hank."

"What about Ben's alibi? He was in Denver, sick in bed."

"Like you've always said, Hank, alibis exist only to be broken, right?"

"You're dreaming, kid."

"Maybe," Eve said, but she had a feeling, a good feeling.

On the drive back to Denver the next morning, Eve was still excited about what they'd found out.

"Don't put all your eggs in one basket," Hank warned her.

"I'm not. We'll still pursue all the other leads."

"I don't think you're being objective about this," Hank said.

"Sure I am."

He shook his head lugubriously.

"Hank, give me a break here. This stuff about Ben, it's good. It's new and it's *good*. And Iverson never knew about any of it."

"He didn't know about Mochlin's cheesy alibi or the Wades' light-fingered habits, either," Hank said.

"I know, I know, but..."

And that was when Eve saw the state trooper's flashing lights in her rearview mirror.

"Shit," she said.

"I told you a million times you drive too fast," Hank said with a certain amount of satisfaction.

She pulled over just outside the new tunnel in Glenwood Canyon and waited impatiently for the trooper to complete his check of her plates. Finally he got out of his car and sauntered up to her.

"Excuse me, ma'am, but you were going ten miles over the speed limit in the tunnel. May I see your license and registration, please?"

"Are you sure I was going that fast?" she tried, smiling as sweetly as she could. "I really didn't think I was."

"I'm sorry, ma'am, but you were taped by our video cameras in the tunnel. There's no mistake."

"Oh," Eve said, and she took her ticket and drove well within the speed limit the rest of the way into Denver. Hank laughed when she asked dead seriously if he thought she could put the ticket on her expense account.

They made plans to fly to Los Angeles as soon as they could get bookings.

"You think Bob will okay the plane fare?" Hank asked.

"If he doesn't, I'll go, anyway. I'll just put it on my credit card. I don't care, Hank. I've got to talk to Sarah Glick about that alibi. And Ben, too—I have to talk to him."

"And the Wades? They're in San Diego, remember?"

"The Wades," she mused. "Maybe."

"Forget the Wades," Hank muttered.

"I'm not forgetting them. I just don't think they're as important. Look, Hank, you don't have to come with me. I'll go alone."

"And miss all the fun? Not on your life, little lady!"

When she got to Denver, Eve drove straight to the office, charged in to see Bob Calpin and put it to him. "I need plane tickets to L.A., a rental car and a couple of nights in a hotel. For me and Hank."

Bob leaned back and studied her. "Tell me about it," he said mildly, "and it better be good, Eve."

"Oh, it's good, all right." And she told him what they'd found out about Ben Richards.

She went home an hour later, reservations made, rental car waiting, tickets taken care of. She wasn't tired anymore, and she was starving, even after the burger and French fries and milk shake she and Hank had had for lunch in the fastfood joint on Interstate 70. She tried not to think of Jack, because she couldn't do him any good unless she was sharp, honed and focused. It was Ben's alibi she had to break—he couldn't have been sick in bed in Denver at the same time he was in Aspen committing murder.

She called Marty Cohen from home and told him about the new lead and that she and Hank were off to California tomorrow afternoon.

"Marty, will you call Jack and tell him?" she said, then she changed her mind. "No, don't. It'll only drive him crazy. I'll do it. Listen, Marty, Jack's in pretty bad shape. Maybe you could give him a visit, tell him, oh, I don't know, something to cheer him up."

"Sure, I'll do that, Eve."

"And, Marty, that was great work you did, finding out about Ben."

"My pleasure, Eve. Anything for the cause."

She ate a whole bag of potato chips, a hunk of cheese and two granola bars, then curled up on her couch in her most comfortable old sweats to watch her favorite police show. There was nothing to do now but mark time until she got to Ben's house in Long Beach.

She watched the cop show, trying not to think about Jack. If she started thinking about him, she'd spiral into a black hole. She couldn't let herself do that, because she had to stay sharp. She had to stay cool until she and Hank talked to Sarah Glick. Without Ben there. Alone.

It was about nine-thirty when she heard a knock on her door, surprising her. *Hank. It's Hank, she thought. This had better be good.*

She got up wearily and padded barefoot to the door, tucking her hair behind her ears. In her neighborhood, you left the chain on when you opened the door, and Eve followed the safety precaution. But it wasn't Hank standing there on her porch.

It was a woman, a young woman, maybe twenty-five, quite attractive, but cold, shivering and looking very nervous.

She introduced herself as Donna Haverlund, and Eve could only shrug.

"Do I know you?" Eve asked, the chain still on the door.

"I'm...I'm a friend of Gary's," the woman said, and it was a very long moment before everything fell into place in Eve's mind.

She invited Donna in, though her head was whirling. She felt a mild stab of indignation, too—Donna was not only very pretty, but she must have been ten years younger than Eve.

She offered the woman a seat on the couch and turned the television off. Then she sat down across from her and tried to clear her head. *Be civilized*, she told herself. *Be an adult*.

"Has Gary said anything about me?" Donna began, and Eve noticed the woman's fingers twisting her purse strap.

"He mentioned something," Eve replied. *Be civilized*, she reminded herself.

Donna nodded slowly, then raised her eyes to Eve. "I'm not real good at giving speeches, Miss Marchand. I'm not like you, you know, well educated, able to stand up in front of judges and juries and reporters. I'm a very simple person."

"Go on," Eve said, thinking that if this was an act—Little Miss Innocence—it was a darn good one.

"I guess I'd better just get all this off my chest," Donna said, "before I chicken out."

"Does Gary know you're here?" Eve broke in abruptly.

Donna shook her head.

Eve stared at her for a moment, then said, "I see. Well, then, why don't you say what you came to say and we'll take it from there."

Donna took a deep breath. "I love him," she said in a whisper.

Eve sat back as if pushed by an invisible hand. "Oh," she said.

"I love him and I can be with him all the time." The words came gushing out now. "I'd give up my job in a second, Miss Marchand. I can be at home or on the road with him. Whatever he wants."

"Oh," Eve repeated lamely.

"You see, Gary needs someone who can be there for him a hundred percent. I want to be that person."

"And I can't? Is that what you're saying?" Eve said tightly.

"No, you can't," Donna went right on. "The thing is, Gary's confused."

"*He's* confused."

"Yes. He doesn't know how to talk to you about this. He's letting it ride, you know, like men always do." She smiled anxiously. "And I know he still loves you, Miss Marchand, but not the kind of love you need in a marriage. He respects you and thinks you're wonderful and all that...."

Eve put up a hand. "Spare me, please," she said, her emotions in havoc, a part of her miserable and afraid, another part feeling as if a heavy weight were being lifted miraculously off her shoulders.

"Gary says you've met someone," Donna ventured in that quiet voice.

Eve said nothing.

"Well, that's none of my business. But I only wanted you to know that I'll be there for Gary. If you don't...love him anymore, I'll be there for him. It's just that you've got to tell him the truth."

Eve almost rose right out of her seat then, but she felt suddenly, curiously, ashamed. Everything this young woman had said was true.

"I'd better go," Donna said. "I'm sorry if I've upset you." She stood. "I only came here because I love Gary so much I can't stand to see him hurting like he is. Let him go, Miss Marchand, let him live his life. If you ever loved him, you'll let him go."

Somehow Eve showed Donna Haverlund to the door, and somehow she told her she'd think about all this and make a decision. The young woman left, no apologies. When she was gone, Eve leaned against the cold wood of the door and put a hand over her eyes. What had she expected? That she and Gary had some sort of a future? That she could...fall in love with Jack and still keep Gary dangling?

"You're a damn fool," she whispered.

TWENTY-FOUR

Eve awoke the next morning with thoughts about Gary racing around in her head. She knew in her heart that Donna Haverlund was right—Eve could never be there for Gary the way he needed, and Donna could.

The reality stung and, uncharacteristically, Eve had been hiding from it. In denial. Unwilling to give up the comfort and familiarity of Gary's companionship. Yet she was also aware of a curious sort of relief. It really was over.

But she had to put that aside and think about Jack. Jack needed her now; Gary didn't. And she had to confront Jack with what she and Hank had learned about Ben. The trouble was, she didn't have time to make the drive down to see him. And even if she did, he could very well refuse to talk to her.

Her mind flipped back to Gary then, spinning. Gary, Jack, Gary. Her life seemed to be hanging in limbo. Jack. How to talk to him? How to get him on the phone?

Eve sat there in her robe and schemed. Finally she picked up the receiver, took a breath and dialed the private line of the superintendent at Super Max. He'd helped her before. Maybe he'd do it again.

She cleared her head of everything but the problem at hand. When the superintendent came on the line, she launched in. "It's Eve Marchand, Jerry. I need a big favor," she began. "I want to set up a time to talk to Jack Devlin on the phone, but he can't know it's me."

"Come on, Eve," the man said, "what the hell do you think we're running here?"

It took some time, but finally Eve persuaded him that the call was vital. Jerry hemmed and hawed and gave in. "But don't ask me to pull this crap again. You hear?"

"I swear, Jerry," she said. "Never again."

Eve called back at the prearranged time. She waited, tapping her fingers on the kitchen countertop as the familiar clicks and switches sounded in her ear. Her heart pounded and her mouth was cotton-dry. What if Jack hung up on her?

At last he came on, a tentative "Hello?" and she could envision him standing there in his prison greens handcuffed to a ring in the wall, like a dog. Her heart broke for him all over again, but she steeled herself.

"Hello, Jack," she said calmly.

"Goddamn it, I told you…"

"I have news, Jack. Listen to me, will you."

There was a momentary pause, and she leaped into it. "*Listen.* We've been to Aspen, Hank and I. We found out about Ben attacking that boy in hockey practice. We talked to the high school principal and Larry Welberg's father."

"You *what?*"

"Why didn't you tell me? Why didn't you tell Iverson last year about Ben's temper? How did you expect us to defend you with our hands tied, Jack?"

She could feel his anger humming over the line—the silence pulsed with it.

"You don't listen, do you," Jack finally said coldly. "It doesn't matter what Ben did in a goddamn hockey practice all those years ago!"

"My God, Jack, it matters a lot. It means…"

He cut her off. "Ben was in Denver when Allison was killed, sick in bed. I saw him there with my own eyes early that morning. So did Sarah."

"You both saw him hours after the murder was committed. He had time to drive..."

He cut her off brusquely. "You're crazy. You're just looking for a scapegoat. You're obsessed."

"I'm obsessed with the truth, yes," she replied soberly.

"Let Ben alone," he warned.

"Not if it means leaving you on death row, Jack." Then she tried something else. "Your lighter...did Ben keep it that day on the fishing trip? Did he light his cigarette and slip it into his pocket? Did he forget to give it back to you?"

His answer was to hang up on her. Eve shut her eyes for a moment, then put the phone down. She wondered if she should have done that to him, adding to his torment. But his anger told her something: he was defensive about Ben. He knew there was a problem and he was trying to protect the boy. Apparently, he felt Ben needed protection.

And that was something worth knowing.

By that afternoon at four, Eve and Hank were in a rental car parked across the highway from Ben's new house in Long Beach. They had a supply of junk food and the understanding that Hank would not smoke in the car, and they were prepared to wait as long as it took to get Sarah alone. They could see Ben's red Saab parked in the driveway, and Sarah's old blue VW was there, too. At five, Sarah came out and drove away, and they discussed going in and tackling Ben first, but decided their original plan was better—get to Sarah alone.

She returned half an hour later with grocery bags and disappeared into the house. Then nothing happened for an hour.

Eve sighed. "We may have to come back tomorrow. How late should we stay here?"

"Late enough" was Hank's reply.

"If he did it, if he killed his mother, I'm not sure I understand his motive," Eve said.

"*If* he did it, and I'm not as convinced as you," Hank said, "but let's say you're right, I'd put my money on greed. You know, greed, control. Repressed anger. The classic reasons. From Lizzie Borden to the Menendez brothers, kids have killed parents for money. Sick, isn't it?"

"Talk about a dysfunctional family."

"If your theory's right, Ben would have been an old man before he inherited from his mother, given a woman's life expectancy. He couldn't wait. She must have said something to set him off. The straw that broke the camel's back. He thought about it, though. Premeditated murder. Look how well he planned it, right down to using Jack's lighter to incriminate him. He had to blame it on someone, and he knew the husband was always the prime suspect."

"I really think he was sorry the minute he saw what happened to Jack, though. He'd never let himself realize how bad it'd be. He was only thinking about how to turn suspicion away from himself," Eve mused.

"Sure, I bet he was sorry. But he would have been a lot sorrier if *he'd* been arrested."

"You know it was him," Eve said. "Your nose must be twitching by now. You just don't want to admit I'm right."

"Maybe. I can't figure out how you're going to prove it, though. Ben Richards isn't about to confess."

"I'll prove it somehow," she said fiercely.

They sat in silence for a time, then Hank unwrapped the container of French fries. "Want some?"

"Sure."

They munched companionably.

"I gotta pee," he said after a time.

"*God*, Hank."

"There's a gas station down the road. It'll take ten minutes."

So they drove to the gas station and Hank disappeared into the bathroom. Eve waited on pins and needles, desperate to get back to their stakeout. Hank smelled like cigarette smoke when he came out of the john.

They pulled up across from the house, and they both noticed simultaneously that Ben's car was gone.

"Oh, my God," Eve said.

"They could both have been in his car," Hank cautioned.

"Let's go—let's see if she's there," Eve said breathlessly. "You know what to do?"

Hank shot her a disgusted look. "I been doing this since before you were born, sweetheart."

"Okay, let's do it."

Eve rang the doorbell, heard it echoing inside the house. They waited, wondering if Sarah was home. *Let her be there*, Eve prayed.

Footsteps. Yes, someone was coming. Someone was fiddling with the latch, pulling open the door. *It'd better not be Ben*, Eve thought, and then she saw Sarah and relief washed over her, making her weak.

"Hello, Sarah," she said.

The girl stared, nonplussed. "Miss Marchand? What are you...I mean, we didn't know you were coming. Did Ben know? He isn't here right now...." Her voice trailed off.

"Can we come in, Sarah? This is my co-worker, Hank Thurgood. I don't think you've met him before."

"No, I...hello, Mr. Thurgood. Like I said, Ben isn't..."

"We want to talk to *you*, Sarah."

"Oh."

They sat on the brand-new furniture in the living room.

"Nice house," Eve said. "Ben bought it recently, I understand."

"He couldn't stand living in the Aspen house anymore. And I've started law school at UCLA."

"I see. Does Ben have a job?"

"No, he's taking some night classes. That's where he is now. U.C. Long Beach. Finances."

"Finances," Eve echoed. "He wants to manage his inheritance, I guess."

"Yes, he's very interested in that stuff now."

Sarah seemed relaxed. She had no idea, Eve realized.

"I heard Ben went to visit Jack. That was nice of him," Eve said.

"It was awful. It took him days to get over it. But he feels so terrible for Jack."

"Um," Eve said. "Guilty?"

"Yes, but I don't know why. It's not as if he could have done anything to get Jack off. I mean, he testified at the trial. His grandparents practically disowned him for that."

"I bet."

Hank spoke up for the first time. "Did Ben hate his mother?"

Sarah looked shocked. "No, of course not."

"Does he talk about her much?"

"Not much. He talks about Jack more. Why do you want to know? What are you...?"

"Oh, just routine questions," Eve said quickly. "The appeals process, you know."

"What else has Ben done with his money, besides this house?" Hank asked.

"I don't know. It's none of my business. And I don't think it's yours, either, Mr. Thurgood."

"I'm an investigator," Hank said. "I'm investigating."

"Ben? Why?"

"Routine," Eve repeated. "We have to do it."

"Well, you should talk to Ben," Sarah said. "Not me."

"You're sure he didn't have problems with his mother? I know he lived with his father earlier," Eve said soothingly. She was the good cop in this scenario.

"Well, they fought sometimes. Normal stuff."

"Has Ben ever hit you?" Hank asked.

"No! What are you asking? I don't think I'd better..."

"You're entitled to a lawyer, Sarah," Eve said. "You don't have to answer a thing without a lawyer."

Sarah went pale. "I can't believe this."

Eve spread her hands, palms up. "Well, if you have nothing to hide, you don't need to worry, do you?"

"Of course I...we...have nothing to hide!"

"Then you won't mind a few more routine questions," Eve said.

"What are Ben's plans for the future?" Hank shot at her.

"I don't know. Nothing special. He has to manage the estate. And he wants to travel."

"He doesn't plan on working?" Hank asked. "Or going to law school?"

"He *does* work. He manages the estate. It's very complicated, and it takes a lot of time. And his night classes..."

"That night of the murder, we want to get the timing right," Eve said, concerned, kind. "It's real important, Sarah. We'd really like your help."

"I told everyone. I testified at the trial. It's all in the records."

"I know, but we really do have to go over it again, okay?" Eve said.

"*God.* Okay."

"You went to see Ben that night. You were going to a movie, right?"

"It was six forty-five so we could get to the seven o'clock movie. I *told* everyone this already."

Eve made a point of writing the time down. She underlined it three times. "And Ben was sick."

"He had the flu. He was sweating and his face was bright red, then he'd get cold and shiver."

"Did you see him throw up?"

Sarah's eyes widened. "Of course not."

"Um," Eve said. "So you didn't go to the movie?" Eve was aware of Hank recrossing his legs, shifting one skinny ankle over a bony knee, his mismatched socks and orange work boots exposed.

"No, he was too sick. I went home. I said I'd call him later to see how he was. I made him take some aspirin. And liquids. I told him to drink lots of water."

"And did you call him later?"

"Yes, about eight-thirty or nine. I felt bad, 'cause I woke him up."

"And then he called you later?"

"Around ten. I'm not sure exactly, but I think it was close to ten."

"Where'd he call you from at ten?" Hank put in.

"From his apartment, of course. What do you mean? He was really sick."

"Right. Did you call him after that?"

"No. He said he was going to turn off the phone and try to get some sleep."

"And then," Eve asked, "when did you see him or talk to him again?"

"The next morning around, oh, seven-thirty. I was worried, and I knew he'd turned his phone off, so I drove over and let myself in with my key. He was asleep, so I waited. I didn't want to wake him up."

Hank spoke again. "So, from right round ten at night to seven-thirty the next morning, Ben was alone."

"He was asleep in his apartment, yes," Sarah said a little belligerently.

"How do you know?" Hank pressed.

"Because I know. Because he was so sick he couldn't have gone anywhere, and he called me, and he was there the next morning. What do *you* think he did?" Sarah asked angrily.

Hank leaned forward and pinned her with his pale gaze. "*I* think he drove up to Aspen, killed his mother and hot-footed it back to Denver before you got there. And then he used you for his alibi."

"Oh, my God," Sarah said. "You're insane!" She stood up. "I think you'd better leave. I won't talk to you anymore. I'll tell Ben. He's going to go ballistic. He'll sue you for defamation of character!"

"Sarah," Eve said, "I'm sorry if you're upset, but we do have to check everything out."

"Get out of here," Sarah said. She looked as if she were going to cry.

And that was when Ben walked in the front door.

"Eve," he said, surprised. "What are you...?" He turned to Sarah. "What's going on?"

"They came here to...to *accuse* you, Ben," Sarah sobbed. "They think, they think, they said *you* did it, that you drove to Aspen that night...."

"What?"

"We're only asking routine questions, Ben," Eve said. "For the appeals process."

"She's lying!" Sarah yelled. "They're not routine. They said you drove to Aspen and...and *you* did it, and you drove back, and when I came over that morning..."

"Shut up, Sarah," Ben said, then turned to Eve. "You come to my house, you come into *my* house and question *my* girl? How in hell do you dare to do that?"

A chill crawled up her spine at Ben's tone of voice. "Part of our ongoing investigation, Ben," she said.

"Get out of here," Ben yelled, and his face turned dusky red, a vein swelling in his neck. "I'll sue your asses to kingdom come, you stupid punks! Get out!"

"Take it easy there, young fella," Hank said.

"Get the hell out!"

"We're going," Hank said. "Just don't get your bowels in an uproar, pal."

Ben whirled around, his movements jerky. He grabbed a lamp, the nearest thing to hand, ripped the plug out of the wall and swung it toward Hank. "Get out!" he screamed.

Hank held up a hand, and Eve moved swiftly to his side. "Take it easy," she said. "We're going." And she and Hank backed quickly away, slipped out through the door and shut it behind them. From inside Eve heard a crash, the lamp, she guessed, and Ben's voice, screaming still, cursing, rising and falling in a paroxysm of rage.

"Is Sarah safe in there?" she asked Hank as they hurried away.

"Well, I'm sure as hell not going back in there to rescue her!"

"Should we call the police?"

"No, he might run. We don't want him to run."

"God, he was scary," Eve breathed. "And I thought he was a nice kid. Spoiled, maybe, but nice."

They reached the car and got in. Eve sat there, taking a few deep breaths.

"Holy cow, what a temper," Hank said. "My nose is convinced. It just smelled a rat."

"He did it," Eve said triumphantly.

"Yeah, he did it. But, little lady, you gotta get a confession from him to prove it beyond a reasonable doubt."

"I will," she said, driving away, away from Ben Richards's cozy beach house. "I have to."

At dinner they discussed making a morning trip to San Diego—only a couple of hours by car—to interview the Wades one last time. But the trip seemed a big waste of taxpayers' money now.

"What's the point?" Hank said, his mouth full of prime rib.

"I was only thinking about crossing all the *t*'s and dotting all the *i*'s."

Hank wiped his mouth. "We can always do it later if necessary. I say we got our boy. Now let's concentrate on how to nail his ass to the wall."

It was over coffee that Eve fiddled with a spoon and looked up at Hank. "Can I run something by you?" she asked.

"Sure," he said.

"And no wisecracks?"

"Not a one."

It took her a while to get it out, but finally she bent Hank's ear about Donna Haverlund's visit. "I've got to talk to Gary," she confessed. "As much as I hate to admit it, the woman—the *girl's* right. It's just that, well..."

Hank shook his head slowly. "A blind man coulda seen this coming," he said. "Trouble is, neither you nor Gary want to give up the comfort zone."

"Um," Eve said. "But what if Gary still cares? What if I hurt him and..."

"Ah, come on," he interrupted. "Gary's got a new babe and you're making up a million excuses. I thought you were smarter than that."

"I don't know." Eve sighed. "Maybe I drove him to it. I *did* drive him to it."

"Bull," Hank said, pouring another sugar packet into his coffee. That made four. "Face facts. It's over. It *was* over or you wouldn't have done what you did with Devlin."

"You sound awfully sure."

"I am. I know you. And trust me, our boy Gary wouldn't be involved with this Haverlund woman if his heart was breaking over you. Believe me, I know these things."

"So I should call Gary and level with him? Make him level with me, too?"

"You bet. And soon."

"He's in New England. I can't..."

"More excuses?"

"No, I just don't want to screw up the game for him."

"Eve, Eve, Eve," Hank said. "Come off it. Let the guy off the hook, for God's sake. It'll probably be the best he's felt in months."

Eve nodded, then she glanced at her watch. "It's after eleven in Boston. I can't..."

But Hank only laughed.

It was almost eleven-thirty, Boston time, when Eve sat cross-legged on the motel bed and called Gary's hotel—the hotel where the Broncos always stayed. Her stomach was in knots, and she wished she hadn't eaten dinner. Her palms were slick on the receiver. "Gary Kapochek's room, please," she said to the hotel operator, and she had to clear her throat.

The room extension rang once, twice. A third time. Then someone picked up. "Hello?" Eve's heart squeezed painfully. It was a woman. Donna?

For a long moment she couldn't speak.

"Hello?"

Eve took a breath. "Is Gary there?"

Silence. Then, "Ah, yes, he's, ah, right here."

There were muffled voices in the background, as if the woman had cupped her hand over the mouthpiece. A moment stretched out, an agonizing slice of time. Finally Gary took the receiver.

"Eve?" came his familiar voice, and in the background she could hear the distinct closing of a door.

"Yes, it's me," she said. "Are you alone now?"

He hesitated. "Yes."

"Oh, Gary," she said, her voice strangled, "I'm sorry. I shouldn't have called. I must have been crazy. I..."

"No, Eve," he said gently, "no. This isn't your fault."

"But it is."

There was a pause. "She," Gary said, "Donna, that is, told me what she did. God, Eve, I don't know what to say. She shouldn't have gone to you like that. I feel like hell. You can't imagine."

"I'm glad she did," Eve said abruptly. "I really am. She forced the issue. But what are we going to do now? Gary, I just, well, I'm so used to having you there. You know?"

"Yeah," he said quietly, "I do know. But I guess it wasn't meant to be. I've been giving it a lot of thought, believe me. I keep thinking we should have set that wedding date."

"Um," Eve said, and she shifted the phone to her other ear.

"I've got to know something," he said then. "Are you...in love with Devlin? Are you, Eve?"

It was some time before she answered. And even then it was terribly painful. "Yes," she finally said. "Yes, I am."

"God, Eve," he breathed. "You realize what a mess you're in? It's nuts."

"Of course. Of course I do. I'm a fool."

"You're going to get crushed, baby, you really are."

Eve sighed heavily. "I can't think about that now. So much has happened. My head's spinning."

"I'll bet it is."

"So is this it then? Are we just going to hang up and never see each other? Never speak again?"

He laughed ruefully. "No, I can't see that happening. And besides, my spare toothbrush and razor are at your house."

She managed a smile. "And my good nightgown's in your closet."

"So we'll have to get together."

"Yes. Soon." Then she said, "Are *you* in love, Gary? Will you be all right?"

"Yes and yes. She's...Donna's a good girl. A real homebody. She spoils me rotten."

"I'm glad," Eve said. "I really am."

"It's you I'm concerned about," he said. "I wish, well, I wish you'd find happiness."

"So do I," Eve said. "So do I, Gary."

They talked for a few more minutes, the way they used to talk, without recriminations, without all the hidden questions. The way they'd talked before she'd taken on Jack's case.

Before hanging up, Eve said, "Whip their butts on Sunday, will you?"

"We'll beat 'em. No problem."

"Take care," she said.

"I'll see you soon," he replied, and she believed him.

After the call she washed her face, cooling it, and went out onto the small balcony of her motel room. She leaned on the railing, looking out over the black ocean, smelling the saltwater. But what she wished, what she craved, was the sharp tang of autumn in Colorado and Jack next to her. Jack—free and happy—with *her*. And she could recall without effort how he felt, how he tasted and smelled, how he moved inside her, how they fit together as if they'd been torn apart eons ago and never quite healed except when they lay together, and then they fit perfectly, complete.

Oh, God, how she missed him.

Sighing, Eve went into her room and dialed her home phone to collect her messages. So boring, so humdrum after what she was trying to do here. After Sarah and Ben—and Gary. But life went on.

There was a message from her mother, one from a friend about getting together, two from companies offering her credit cards. And one from Bob Calpin.

"Eve, I guess you'll either pick this up or get it when you're back from L.A. But I think you'd better know. As of today, Jack Devlin signed the order designating Marty Cohen as his new defense lawyer. You're off the case, Eve. You've been fired."

She held the phone to her ear, closed her eyes and felt a bubble of hysterical laughter rise inside her. Jack had fired her.

TWENTY-FIVE

"Devlin."

Jack looked up from his sketch pad and saw the guard's face through the iron-barred window. The guy didn't look real happy.

"You've got a visitor, man. That's two in one day. It's against the rules, you know that."

"So tell whoever it is to go away," Jack replied, unperturbed by the prison guard's tone.

"Can't. It's another one of your lawyers. You got a fleet of them now, or what?"

Damn it, Jack thought. Marty Cohen had been in this morning. That left only one possibility. Eve. He felt that instant stab of longing and frustration.

"Come on, move it," the guard was saying, and the electronic door slid open. The man held up the handcuffs, rattling them. "At least this one's pretty," he said.

Jack wanted to refuse the visit. More than anything, he wanted to tell the guard he wouldn't see her. But in here, in Super Max, no one defied the guards, not unless you wanted even more misery in your life than you already had.

A few moments later, he was sitting down again in the interview room, his face set in implacable lines. Eve was across from him, the phone already in her hand. She nodded at him expectantly through the glass, urging him to pick up the receiver. He hesitated and refused to meet her eyes, trying to hold on to his anger. But anger was easy compared to his other emotions.

She nodded at him again and put the receiver to her ear. Finally he took his off the cradle and felt his jaw lock. He couldn't bear to be this close to her. Despite the thick glass, it was as if he could smell the scent of her hair, feel the smooth texture of her skin. Every aspect of her drove him crazy—the color of her eyes, the delicate bridge of her nose, her lips. He could almost taste her, and he realized he spent half his time thinking about how to save her from herself, how to keep her from ruining her life trying to get him off the row; the other half he tried to figure out how to save himself from seeing her, talking to her. Didn't she have any idea of the effect she had on him? Didn't she give a damn?

He lifted his gaze to hers, fighting for control.

"Hello," she said, and she smiled tentatively.

He said nothing.

"Jack, I know you fired me," she went on, "and I think I understand why. But things are happening and you've got to pull yourself together and help me here."

"If it's that business about Ben," he said tightly, "you can just forget it."

She took a breath, a sigh escaping her, and he felt a heaviness in his gut—she'd sighed like that, precisely the same way, that night in Aspen. In bed. In his arms.

"Hear me out, Jack," she was saying. "Don't hang up and run away. Just please hear me out." She waited, her gaze fixed to his. "All right. I saw Sarah and Ben yesterday. In Long Beach. Jack, it got ugly."

He swore, and then he hung his head.

"You don't understand. Ben...he's got one helluva temper. It's like watching a Jekyll and Hyde thing. But there's more."

"Eve, don't..."

"This is too important. We have to get at the truth. You've got to face it. Please just listen and try to be objective. Hank

354   *Lynn Erickson*

and I talked the whole way back from California. We went over and over the crime scene. Are you listening? Jack?''

"Yes, damn it, I'm listening."

"Okay. It's like this. Allison was struck from behind. She was facing the big plate-glass window. It was night and the lights were on in the living room."

"I know all this," he said woodenly.

"Okay, good. We figure she had to have seen her killer in the reflection. Now, if she were having a fight with, say, one of the Wades, would she have calmly turned her back on them? In the middle of a heated argument? We don't think so. And even if she had, she would have seen one or the other of them pick up the statue. She'd have turned around, probably tried to defend herself. There should have been at least one defensive wound. On a forearm. Someplace. Are you following me?"

Slowly, grudgingly, Jack nodded.

"Good. And Hank and I figure that the same scenario holds true for Mochlin. If he came up there, let's assume a little drunk, and we know Allison was ticked off at him for bragging about the husband-number-three thing, we think it's darn near impossible for her not to have seen Mochlin pick up that statue in anger. The thing is, Jack, if the murder happened in a moment of fury, Allison wouldn't have had her back turned. At the very least, she'd have seen it coming and spun around."

"What're you saying?"

"That we believe there was no argument. That Allison was perfectly comfortable with her killer in her own home. Enough so that her back was to that person. She never saw it coming, never spun around. It had to have been a very well-planned, premeditated act."

Jack sat there listening with his eyes closed, trying not to hear but unable to keep the images from forming in his head as Eve spoke. His heart felt like a sledgehammer, pounding against his ribs.

"We figure," she was saying, "that Ben thought the act

out thoroughly. He may even have called his mother earlier on his cell phone to say he was driving up late. Something simple, something reasonable. Or maybe he just showed up when he was sure the Wades would be in bed. He let himself in, found his mother, gave her some excuse for showing up. He had your lighter with him. He'd been keeping it for months, and maybe he planned all along to use it or maybe it was a spur-of-the-moment decision, but he ended up leaving it there to divert suspicion from himself. Okay, so they were in the living room. They were talking. Allison had no reason to be afraid. No reason not to turn her back on her own son…"

"And what the hell's the motive?" Jack threw out at her.

"Greed. Inner rage. It happens all the time. Just read the papers."

But Jack wasn't buying it. "It's a nice fairy tale, lady," he said. "I'm just not convinced."

"Try this, then," she went on. "There's nothing in Mochlin's background to even hint at overt violence. Same goes for Ray and Marnie Wade. But we know about Ben. Don't we, Jack? And you knew it all along. You just refuse to face it. Even now. Even when we're closing in on…"

Jack took the phone from his ear, held it and tipped his head back, trying to keep control. He took a few long breaths, then looked at Eve again. Finally he put the phone back to his ear. "You've had your say. Now it's my turn. And I'm telling you, Eve, I don't want you on this case anymore. I don't want you on the case and I'm not going to see you in here again. Ever. Have you got that? What I said the other day still holds. I think you've got this case mixed up with something else. Well, that's your problem. Whatever you think went on between us is all in your head. And it's skewing your judgment. Get over it."

"Jack," she said, a catch in her voice. "I only want you to concentrate on Ben, to think back…"

"No," he went on relentlessly, "no more bullshit. Just go. Get out of here and leave me alone. And leave Ben alone, too." He held the phone for another moment, unable to stop staring at her, and then finally he had to hang up and turn away. He never looked back. In his cell, though, alone with the beating of his heart, he knew that when they injected the poison in his veins, no matter how much time had passed, the look of pain in Eve's eyes would be the last thing he saw.

Eve got into her car and couldn't believe how calm she felt, especially after the way she'd reacted last time she'd been to see him. But this time was different. Did he think he was fooling her? After what they'd shared, did Jack think she didn't *know* him? And this business about protecting Ben—talk about denial.

She drove and she vacillated between love and respect for his integrity and anger at his stubbornness. He was an intelligent man. He should know he was making things worse by retreating into that place of his, that damn corner that promised him a curious sort of peace.

Halfway between Colorado Springs and Denver, she realized there was no way he was going to be able to stay in that private place of his for long. Eventually he was going to have to think about what she'd told him today. He couldn't hide from it forever. Every finger pointed in Ben's direction. Jack had to realize that. Maybe not right now. Maybe not even tomorrow. But sooner or later he was going to have to face it.

She turned off onto the Lincoln Street exit in Denver and drove toward Capitol Hill, frowning. Jack's denial was one thing—finding a way to set him free was another ball game entirely. How was she ever going to pin Allison's murder on Ben Richards?

She was concentrating on the problem at hand so deeply that when she parked in front of her house she didn't even notice the car right behind her, or the man sitting in it.

It wasn't until she was at her front door that she became aware of him, and only because he called out to her. "Miss Marchand, hold up there a minute!"

She turned around, startled. Then her heart sank. It was that FBI creep, Ralph Hawley. "Oh, brother," she muttered.

He strode up to her, and she saw a manila envelope in his hand. He was grinning, too, rather like the Cheshire cat.

"Mind if I come in?" he asked.

Eve sighed heavily. "Oh, sure, why not? It'll make my day."

They were no sooner inside, Eve barely out of her coat, when he opened the envelope and pulled out a black-and-white photo.

"Would you believe I've got proof that you were harboring a fugitive?" he asked, still grinning.

"Come off it," Eve said, and she took the photo he offered her, holding it up to the light. A long moment passed before she realized what she was looking at, and then, when she did, she swore. "Where...?" she said, still staring at the grainy blowup of her and Jack driving in the rented car.

"In the Glenwood Canyon Tunnel," he told her. "They videotape all the traffic. Time. Date. The whole ball of wax. And note the license plate."

Eve did.

"It was stolen off a car in Pinecrest. Did you or Devlin steal it, Miss Marchand? Oh, Well," he said smugly, "I guess it doesn't matter. I've got you dead to rights on this."

Eve leaned against her kitchen counter and felt all the wind go out of her sails.

"Well," Hawley went on, "what do you think I should do with this? Take it to your boss? Maybe to the state bar association or the attorney general. Let's see. Who do you think?"

Eve shrugged dully. "Whoever you want, I guess."

"And what a great career you had going. I almost hate to do it."

She just couldn't believe it. They'd videotaped them in the tunnel on their way to Aspen. Hawley must have sat and gone through those tapes for hours, staring at hundreds and thousands of cars before he spotted them. She should have

known. Hell, Eve remembered, she'd just gotten a ticket
there—the trooper said they had her on tape....

Videotaped all the traffic ran through her mind, and that
was when it came to her. "Oh, my God," she gasped.

"What?" Hawley said.

And then she broke out in a big smile, her heart racing.
"Where, exactly, did you get this?"

"State Police headquarters," he said, his brows drawn together.

"How long do you think they keep the tapes?" She was
practically breathless now.

He shrugged. "Couple of years at least, in case some
dumb ass wants to fight a ticket in front of a judge."

Eve beamed broadly. "A couple of years..." she said to
herself, and then she spun around and grabbed her coat.
"Come on," she said.

"Come on where?"

"To State Police headquarters."

Hawley frowned.

"You know," Eve said, taking his arm, half dragging him
out of the house, "I think I love you. Now, let's go use that
FBI pull of yours to do some good for a change."

Hawley frowned again, then shook his head at her.

"I'll explain on the way," she said, and then she laughed
out loud.

Eve jumped, knocking a foam cup of coffee right into
Agent Hawley's lap. "Stop!" she cried. "Back the tape up."

"Damn it, woman," Hawley muttered, "look at my
pants."

"I'll get them dry-cleaned for you. Now, back the tape
up."

Hawley pressed Stop then Reverse. Under his breath, he
said, "Probably at that dry cleaners of yours on Colfax."

But Eve wasn't listening; she was staring bleary-eyed at
the videotape machine at the Denver State Police headquar-

ters. It was ten minutes after nine. They'd been at it since five that afternoon.

"There!" She pointed and Hawley hit the Stop button. "That's Ben Richards's old Taurus! Look at the plates, ZG 440. It's him!"

"Are you sure?"

"I'm positive. And look at the time. It's 12:37 a.m. It fits like a glove. He talks to his girlfriend at ten, then dashes off, reaches the tunnel at 12:37, gets to Aspen around one-thirty. And I'll bet my career we find him on tape heading back in the eastbound lane sometime around 4:00 a.m. Can you print a still of this?"

Hawley nodded and stood, pressing a button on a printer next to the videotape player. He whistled between his teeth.

Eve sat back in her chair and smiled, folding her arms. "You know," she said, staring up at him, "if you hadn't caught us on tape, Ralph, I never would have thought of this. Never. Jack's going to owe you his life."

The blown-up photo of Ben Richards came out of the printer, and Hawley held it up, gazing at it. "Son of a bitch," he whispered.

Eve got special permission to sit in on Ben's interrogation. It took place in the Long Beach police headquarters, and Hawley explained to her that he'd be there, but he didn't want to step on local toes, so he was letting the Long Beach detectives do their thing.

"I get points, see," he said to her as they sat on straight-backed chairs against the wall of the monotone room. "No complaints for the head office."

"You're sure they know what questions to ask?" Eve wondered out loud.

"I prepped them as if they were learning catechism for church," he said. "They know the score."

An Aspen police detective watched from outside the room, too, through the one-way window, but they'd decided Eve should be inside the room—more pressure on Ben.

She was nervous, sitting there, waiting for Ben to be brought in. This was it—if Ben held out, if he was tough enough, they might never get sufficient evidence to force a retrial. There was the photo, yes, but was it enough?

"They're not arresting him," Hawley said, "just bringing him in for questioning. At least that's what they told him."

"He must suspect something's up," she said. "After Hank and I visited, he must know he's on the hot seat."

Hawley shrugged. "He figures he got away with it, just like you thought you'd gotten away with harboring Devlin."

"Um."

Hawley grinned. "I sorta like having a gun to your head, Miss Marchand. I feel safer that way."

"Please call me Eve now that we're practically partners," she said coolly.

Finally two detectives brought Ben into the room. Eve took a deep breath and tried to relax her shoulders. This was it; the show was about to begin.

Ben was dressed in shorts and a T-shirt that read Denver University Hockey. He was smiling, talking to one of the detectives, seemingly relaxed. When he saw Eve, a look of shock, then anger crossed his face. "What's *she* doing here?" he demanded.

"She requested that she be present," one of the detectives said, the one who looked like a California surfer. "And that's Special Agent Hawley from the FBI's Denver office. He's just sitting in."

"The FBI?" Ben asked.

"Just routine," the other detective said. He was Hispanic, darkly handsome, with a thick mustache.

"I'm not answering any questions until my lawyer gets here," Ben said. "He's supposed to meet me."

"Okay, that's fine. We're in no rush."

"Well, aren't you going to read me my rights?" Ben asked.

"What for?" the surfer said innocently. "You're not under arrest. You're not even a suspect."

"Not yet," Hawley muttered under his breath so only Eve could hear.

Ben's lawyer bustled in a moment later. He was a balding, dark-eyed man in an atrociously expensive suit. His eelskin briefcase must have cost what Eve made in a month. Well, she thought, Ben could afford it. For now.

Introductions were made. Ben's lawyer, Conrad Whelan, raised an eyebrow at Eve and Ralph Hawley but said nothing. He sat down at the table, folded his well-manicured hands and said, "Shall we begin, gentlemen?"

The two detectives began innocently enough: name, address, background, status as a student at U.C. Long Beach. Vehicle, driver's license.

"Oh, my," the Hispanic detective said, "you still have a Colorado license. Gotta get a California one real soon. It's the law."

"I just moved here," Ben said. "I may not even become a California resident. I don't know yet."

And on they went, asking detailed, unimportant questions, feeling Ben out, testing him, boring him, laying his suspicions to rest.

"Really, gentlemen," Whelan said. "Is this necessary? You're wasting my client's time, not to mention mine, and you know how valuable *that* is."

"Well, we're getting to it," the surfer said.

"What's *it*?" Whelan asked.

"Allison Wickwire Devlin's murder."

"Water under the bridge," Whelan sniffed.

"Just a few routine questions."

"Go on." Whelan waved a hand.

"Okay. Now, Ben, where were you that night?"

Ben rolled his eyes. "Not again! I've gone over this in

depositions, in trial, a million times. I was in my apartment in Denver, sick as a dog."

"Convenient," mused the surfer.

"I was *sick*. Sarah told everyone. I threw up. I had a fever. She saw me there."

"Mmm. Yes, she saw you at six forty-five, then you called her at ten at night."

"Yes."

"Then she came over about seven-thirty the next morning."

"That's correct."

"And between 10:00 p.m. and 7:30 a.m. you were sick in bed."

"Yes."

"Gentlemen, honestly..." Whelan said.

The dark detective held up a hand. "Please, be patient with us dumb public servants."

Whelan subsided with a disgruntled snort.

"But we have a problem," the surfer said, looking puzzled, "and we're having a hard time figuring it out."

"What's the problem?" Ben asked.

"Oh, it's just a little something Agent Hawley brought us."

"Well?" Whelan said.

"Well, here it is. You tell us what to think about it." The dark detective pulled a blown-up photograph out of a manila envelope and laid it on the table in front of Ben and his lawyer.

Eve saw Ben's shock. She saw his face go gray. She saw Whelan give him a surprised look.

"Can you help us out with this?" the surfer asked guilelessly.

Ben tried to speak, but nothing came out of his mouth.

"And we have this one, as well," the detective said, and he laid the second photo on the table, the one of Ben on his return trip.

"My client has nothing further to say," Whelan announced. "Come on, Ben, let's go."

But Ben couldn't, wouldn't move. He sat there staring at the pictures, his face putty-colored, his mouth moving soundlessly.

"Come on, Ben," Whelan repeated.

"God," Eve heard Ben whisper. "Oh, God."

"Not another word, Ben," Whelan warned.

"But, really, Mr. Whelan, you can see how we need some sort of explanation here. I mean, Ben Richards swore in court he was home in bed at these times." The surfer peered at the photos. "At 12:37 a.m. and 3:47 a.m. On the seventeenth of May. And yet, here he is, clear as day, videotaped in the Glenwood Canyon Tunnel. Now, how could that happen?"

"Jack did it," Ben rasped, so low it could barely be heard.

"Quiet," Whelan said.

"What was that, excuse me?" the Hispanic detective asked.

"*Jack did it.*"

"Shut up, Ben," Whelan said.

"I was sick. Sarah told you."

"But what about these?" the surfer asked.

Ben shook his head. "Jack did it. I was home sick."

"Ben, I'm warning you," Whelan tried again.

Ben shot up out of his chair, and the detectives' hands automatically went to their guns. So did Hawley's, Eve noticed. But Ben just stood there, shaking his head, trembling all over, drops of sweat standing out on his face. "Jack did it," he said again.

"Well, then, where were you going in these pictures? And why did you lie, Ben?"

Whelan stood and placed himself in front of his client. "Not another word, gentlemen. Either charge Mr. Richards or leave him alone."

Eve held her breath.

The surfer stretched his hands out, palms up. "All we

want is a few answers. You can understand that. A little co-operation.''

"We're leaving. Come on, Ben." Whelan took his arm, urging him toward the door, but Ben stood as if rooted. Shaking, sweating.

"Looks like your client is upset," the Hispanic detective said. "I wonder why."

An inhuman sound emerged from Ben's throat. Everyone stared. Tears stood out in his eyes, his chest heaved and an awful, tearing sob broke from his mouth. "Jack did it!" he screamed.

"Now, now, Ben," Whelan said, worried.

"Why don't you leave me alone?" Ben cried. "Jack did it. He was convicted. He's in jail. For God's sake, why can't you leave me alone?"

"Excuse me, Mr. Richards," the dark detective began.

"I didn't do anything! I was at home! Sick! Leave me alone."

"But the pictures..."

"They're all lies!"

"Pictures don't lie, Mr. Richards."

"Ben, let's go," Whelan said again.

"They won't leave me alone!"

"We can't leave you alone, Mr. Richards," the surfer said. "It could be that an innocent man has been convicted. Your stepfather, your friend. You don't want..."

"Make them stop!" Ben cried.

"Gentlemen, this is quite enough," Whelan said.

"They're driving me crazy," Ben moaned. "They come to my house, they keep asking and asking, and I can't stand it anymore!"

"*Ben*," Whelan said sharply.

Ben was crying now, wailing, his hands covering his face. Tears leaked between his fingers, and he rocked back and forth, awful sounds squeezed out of him.

The blond detective began reciting the Miranda warnings. "Benjamin Wickwire Richards, you have the right to remain silent. You have the right to have an attorney present. If and when you..."

Ben collapsed in his chair, head down on the table, still crying.

Finally, after what seemed like hours, he looked up, straight at the detectives. Mucus ran from his nose; his eyes were red and swollen. "I killed her," he said in a tortured voice.

"Shut up!" Whelan cried.

"I can't," Ben said. "I did it. I can't go on like this."

"Mr. Richards," the surfer said, "are you aware of the Miranda warnings I just read you?"

Ben nodded.

"He is not," Whelan said. "He's..."

"Shut up, Mr. Whelan," Ben said dully.

Hawley stood up and went over to Ben. "Ben Richards, I'm going to put you in custody of the FBI and return you to Aspen, where you'll be charged with the murder of your mother, Allison Wickwire Devlin. Do you understand?"

"I hit her and she fell down."

"Do you understand?"

"Yes."

"But first," Hawley said, "you'll write and sign a confession. Okay?"

Hawley pushed a piece of paper and pen in front of Ben. "Now."

Ben took the pen and began to write. Hawley met Eve's gaze over Ben's head and winked at her. She smiled weakly in return, then she closed her eyes, seeing only Jack—Jack in that lonely prison cell. *Hold on,* she thought, *just a little while longer.*

TWENTY-SIX

It all went quickly after that. Eve and Hawley flew back to Denver. Ben accompanied them, handcuffed to the Aspen detective. By the time they arrived, Marty Cohen and Howie Bernhard had already filed a motion with the Ninth Judicial District judge. It included Ben's confession and a report by the Long Beach detectives, faxed ahead, and it read in part, "The Public Defender's Office files this motion pursuant to Colorado Rule of Criminal Procedure 35(c)(2)(V), which states that there now exists newly discovered evidence of material fact that could not be known previously, and which requires that the court find Jack Devlin innocent of the murder of Allison Wickwire Devlin."

Eve read it quickly at the office, having come straight from the airport, nodded her okay, and they sent it off.

Of course, they had to wait for the judge to review it, and there was no guessing how long that would take. A day? A week? Months? Then the judge would—or would not—call for a hearing, which would take place in Aspen, where the original sentencing had occurred. They'd have to bring Jack to Aspen on a writ of habeas corpus, in other words, "bring the body back to court."

All these steps in the process were routine to Eve; she knew them well, but never before had they held such significance.

Marty had phoned Jack immediately upon learning of Ben's confession.

"How did he take it?" Eve asked anxiously, sitting in her office, which Marty was using while he was in Denver.

"Pretty badly," Marty said.

"Oh, God."

"It was hard, Eve. He was really broken up. He almost went nuts. I thought..."

"Oh, Marty," Eve whispered.

"Yeah, it was pretty bad. Then he just got real quiet, the way he does. Didn't say another word."

"He loves Ben," she said. "It must have half killed him."

"And sitting on death row, still sitting there, knowing Ben confessed... Jack asked if he could talk to the kid."

"He would."

"He's a good man," Marty said. "I hope the judge sees it our way, Eve."

"He *has* to."

"Well, not much we can do now," Marty said with a sigh, "but wait."

"Yes, now we wait."

Eve went home and slept for twelve hours. When she woke it was snowing out, one of those storms that hits the Rocky Mountains with maddening unpredictability in the autumn.

Slipping and sliding, no snow tires on her car yet, she drove to the office—better to wait there in company than to wait home alone. She would have liked to talk to Jack. She craved the sound of his voice, and she was very anxious about his mental state. All these months he'd been so desperate to find Allison's real killer. But now that the truth was out, knowing it was Ben, his stepson, the kid who'd loved him as a father...

Yes, she needed to see Jack. To be there for him. But she also knew it was better to wait, to give him time to adjust to the truth. She was the one, after all, who'd brought Ben to this final justice. And no matter how illogical, Jack was going to be in a lot of pain, perhaps even blaming her. So she'd wait.

Jack, she thought, driving through the snow, *please hang in there. It can't be long now.*

It wasn't.

That Friday afternoon word came from the judge in Aspen. He was setting a hearing for the following week. Arrangements would be made to transport the prisoner to Aspen.

"We did it!" Marty yelled.

Howie threw a brief in the air, letting papers flutter all over the office. Everyone, even Bob Calpin, went out after work to have a drink together.

Hank was there, of course, nursing a whiskey and smoking like a chimney. "So, little lady, you did it."

"It's not done yet," she said.

"Mere formality from here on out," he said.

"You know better than that."

"Yeah, well, I'm miffed. I'd hoped it was Mochlin. I still don't like the guy."

She laughed. Then her expression changed. "I've got another problem, too."

"Oh?"

"Hawley. Our FBI friend. I know he's going to file charges against me. He's just waiting, to make me squirm. But he'll do it. Harboring an escaped convict, accessory after the fact, obstructing justice. He can take his pick."

Hank sat back and shook his head. "No."

"No?"

"He won't do it."

"Sometimes you're really naive," she said.

Hank only smiled, then he deftly switched the subject. "So, what's up with you and Devlin?"

"Nothing's up, Hank. He fired me."

"Right. What happens when he's out, Eve?"

She averted her face. "Nothing."

"Okay, whatever you say."

"Hank."

"Just don't forget your old pal when you got six kids and a dear old hubby to take care of."

"You're dreaming, Hank."

"So are you, Eve, or I'll eat my hat."

"Start eating," she said lightly.

"Nah, I'll wait." He patted her hand. "You did good."

"So did you." She smiled. "Don't worry. Would I give up dinner together and those old movies?"

She drank two glasses of wine, then got into her car to drive home, happy and sad and a little drunk, and she prayed she wasn't stopped by a policeman.

On Saturday morning, the team got down to serious work, preparing their strategy for the hearing. They brainstormed, wrote and rewrote, tried to foresee every argument the judge might present. It could go either way, they warned one another. The judge might look at the pictures of Ben and say it was circumstantial evidence; he might hold that the confession was written under duress.

"He might," Howie said.

"He won't," Eve assured him. "He can't."

They worked feverishly all weekend, all Monday, and then Marty made plans to go home for the first time in a week. He'd be in Aspen for the hearing the next day, and Howie would drive up with him.

"I'm going, too," Eve said. "Wild horses couldn't keep me away." She smiled. "Don't worry, guys, I'll sit in back. Quietly."

She was as tense as a coiled spring. The worst scenario, she figured, was a new trial. Even better would be another hearing. Best would be a decision by the judge to vacate the conviction on the spot. Surely the judge would be reasonable and see that Jack was innocent. He had to.

Then doubts would assail her. What if the judge refused to accept the motion? What if he disbelieved the confession? What if...? Oh, God.

She slept badly and got up very early in the morning to

drive to Aspen for the hearing. This was the day. This was it. If things went well, if Eve and Howie and Marty had done their jobs well, Jack would be a free man. Maybe even today.

She packed a small bag—the hearing could last more than a day—and got ready to leave. It was still slightly dark out, and when she turned off all the lights in her house, she almost didn't see the manila envelope lying on the floor by the front door, pushed in through her mail slot.

An envelope. All by itself. No stamp. Only her name on it.

She set her bag down and picked up the envelope, opened it. At first she was puzzled by the contents, then she realized what they were: four neatly torn quarters of a black-and-white photograph—the one of her and Jack in the tunnel.

Hawley. She smiled, and then she laughed out loud. Hawley. What a piece of work! She walked out of her door, dropped the pieces into a trash can on the way to her car and got behind the wheel. She was going to Aspen. She was going to see Jack. She might just see him become a free man this very day.

Jack sat in the same Pitkin County courtroom in which he'd been tried and convicted of murder. They'd taken off the shackles, but he was in his death row green suit with his number stenciled on the pocket; this was only a hearing, after all. There was no press allowed in the room, no TV cameras, no jury, barely any audience, hardly anyone except the district attorney and his aide at one table and Marty Cohen, Howie Bernhard and Jack at the other. The judge was familiar to Jack: he'd presided over Jack's trial and had been one of the panel for the penalty phase. He was the man who now held Jack's fate entirely in his hands.

The judge looked at the gathered people over his half glasses, drew his bushy gray eyebrows together and began to speak.

"I reviewed your motion," he said to the defense table, "and I find it to be a very convincing piece of work."

Jack saw Marty grin openly. He himself felt numb—too

much had happened too quickly. Ben and the hearing and his trip back up here from Canon City. All he'd thought the entire drive was, stupidly, that he could see the sun, he could walk in the sun, feel it on his skin. Not about maybe going free, not about what Eve had done for him, not about Ben, but the sun. After so long within walls, he couldn't process all the stimuli being thrown at him. So he sat there, numb, half listening, half alive. It seemed far too difficult to be completely alive. Too hard.

And he was aware of Eve sitting silently in the back of the empty courtroom. But he couldn't think about her, either.

It was his life they were all talking about. And somehow he couldn't seem to make it matter.

But the judge was still talking. "I've reviewed the trial transcript, I've spoken to Mr. Richards, Ben Richards, and I'm convinced his confession was not made under duress. I've spoken to Miss Glick and the detective in Long Beach. I've consulted my colleagues." He paused here and cleared his throat loudly. "And I've discussed our options with Mr. Makelky—" he nodded at the D.A. "—and we have come to an agreement."

Silence. No one spoke, no one moved. The clinking expansion of the baseboard heaters broke the silence like pistol shots.

"I agree with the motion filed by the Public Defender's Office that we have before us irrefutable evidence that could not have been discovered previously. I agree that by the rule number...uh, what was that number?"

"Excuse me, Your Honor, rule number 35(c)(2)(V)," Marty said.

"Yes, the rule for newly discovered evidence, namely Mr. Richards's confession and the photographs. I am convinced that a retrial would serve no purpose and be of too great a cost to the taxpayers of this judicial district, and I therefore declare Mr. Devlin's conviction vacated." He leveled his gaze on Jack. "You are free to go, Mr. Devlin, and you have the apologies and good wishes of the court."

Jack had a hard time comprehending the words. His brain hung on "free" and savored it, but there was no reality to the concept. *Free.* Had he ever been free?

He felt Marty slapping him on the back, congratulating him. Howie hugged him. "Hey, man, we did it. You're free."

Bill Makelky came over to shake Marty's hand. He gave Jack a look that could have been apologetic, but Jack hardly noticed.

"We can go out the back door to the jail," Marty was saying, "because there's quite a crowd in front. Jack? Jack, I have your clothes over in the jail. Jack?"

He sat there, still numb. He was free. He was innocent of murder. He had the perverse urge to laugh.

"Jack?" Marty was saying.

"Yeah, okay," Jack roused himself to say, "let's get out of here."

He stood, his legs a little shaky, but they felt okay after a couple of steps. *Free.*

Eve was there, of course, waiting in the back of the courtroom. Her eyes were full of tears, her face blazing with emotion. She didn't try to stop him, though, and he only paused for a moment, looked at her, then passed on.

He managed to get into the jail without running into any reporters. They let him change into his own clothes, pants, a shirt, a sport coat, shoes. It didn't seem real. And they let him call his parents in Maui, where it was very early in the morning. In fact, he woke them up.

When he hung up, Debby was there, crying a little. "I knew it," she kept saying. And Bev and Ross Grafton, all congratulating him. Hell, he thought, this jail seemed like home. Almost.

"Look, Jack," Marty said, "the media are out there waiting. You want me to get you out of here in a cop car, or do you want to face them?"

Jack thought a minute. "I guess I'd better get it over with. You know they won't let up until I do."

"You're probably right. Can you handle it, Jack? They're brutal."

"Hey, Marty, don't talk brutal to me. I can handle it."

They descended on him like a lynch mob. "Mr. Devlin, Mr. Devlin... How does it feel to be free? To be vindicated? Mr. Devlin, did you know Ben Richards did it? Were you protecting him? Mr. Devlin, how do you feel about the death penalty now? Mr. Devlin, Mr. Devlin..."

Marty held his hand up and spoke into the microphones thrust at him. It was cold out, and wind whipped dead leaves around the crowd. Dark clouds scudded overhead.

"Mr. Devlin will give you a statement, and then we'd appreciate it if you'd leave Jack alone. Ladies and gentlemen, here he is."

Jack stared out at the gathered throng, at the video cameras on shoulders, on the satellite trucks parked in front of the courthouse, at the reporters crowding around him in a feeding frenzy.

"I appreciate all this attention," Jack began, "and I can only say I'm very happy that the truth came out and that I'm a free man. Unfortunately, another man will pay for the crime. It's a tragedy, and my heart is with Ben, no matter what he did. I want to thank the Public Defender's Office, Marty Cohen, Howie Bernhard, all of the men and the women who worked so hard on my case. I can't forget Hank Thurgood, or Frank Iverson either. And—" he paused and searched the crowd, found her far in the rear "—I'd also like to thank Eve Marchand. These people gave me back my life."

He took a deep breath, tried to gather his thoughts. "I want to take this opportunity to give you my opinion—*informed opinion*, mind you—on the death penalty." He looked around slowly, meeting as many eyes as he could. "I am against it. For anyone, anywhere, anytime, regardless of his crime. Killing is killing, no matter who's doing it. It does not solve any problems. I guess that's about it. Thanks and..."

"Wait, Mr. Devlin, a question!" someone called out. "Are you staying in Aspen?"

"I don't know," Jack said. "I honestly haven't thought about it."

"Are you returning to your career?" shouted another.

"I don't know. Perhaps. But if I do, I doubt I'll be designing starter castles for rich people. Whatever I do, I'll be speaking out against the death penalty, you can be sure of that."

"How do you see your future, Mr. Devlin?"

"I don't know. Until a few minutes ago I didn't have a future. Now, if you'll excuse me."

He retreated into the courthouse with Marty and Howie. A phalanx of police kept the crowd outside.

"Christ," Howie said.

"You were great, man," Marty said. "Impressive."

"What now?" Jack asked.

"I'll drive you home, I guess," Marty said. "You can do whatever you like."

"Home?" Jack gave a wry laugh. "I gave up my condo last year when I was in jail. Hell, I don't *have* a home."

"Your place on Red Mountain, I meant. It's yours now."

"Allison's house?"

"*Your* house," Marty said. "Ben can't inherit through murder, and you never signed those divorce papers. It's yours, man."

"I'll be damned."

"So I'll give you a lift."

"No," came a voice at Jack's elbow. "I'll give him a lift, okay, Marty?"

He turned and she was there. They were face-to-face and he couldn't escape.

"Sure, Eve, fine with me," Marty said.

"I'm so glad for you," she said, her eyes searching his face. "I'm so very glad for you."

He had to say something; they were all watching. Did his

shame and pain and love show on his face? "Thanks," he said. That was all. "Thanks."

"Go on," Howie was saying. "Marty can drop me at the airport on his way home."

"Listen," Jack said, "I appreciate what you did. All of you. I won't forget it."

"Our pleasure," Marty replied, and they left and he was alone with Eve.

"We'd better go," she said, "before the mob figures out where you are."

"I guess so." He was so reluctant, not wanting to be alone with her, remembering his cruel words, his rejection of her. He'd fired her, for God's sake.

"I wanted to talk to you, anyway," she said softly. "I know you were angry with me but..."

"Self-preservation," he said, and silence fell between them.

"I'm sorry. You were my client, and I did what I had to do. Jack..."

"So did I," he said coldly. If he let down now, he was a goner.

"Let's go," she suggested.

Her car was parked just behind the jail, down by the river. She unlocked the doors and they got in. She drove.

"What are you really going to do now?" she asked after a time.

"I don't know. I haven't had time to think."

"Um." Her fingers were white on the steering wheel, and it occurred to Jack that she was nervous.

He glanced at her profile. "I never thanked you properly for getting me off. You saved my life. I'm grateful."

"I'm sorry about Ben," she said softly. "I really am."

Jack nodded soberly.

"You didn't know, did you?"

"No, I didn't know. I still can't believe it."

"He won't get the death penalty, Jack. I won't let it happen."

"Thank God," he said, then, "Eve?"

"Um?"

"You belong in this work. Don't ever quit. It's important. But you already know that."

"Yes, I do. But thanks for the vote of confidence."

They were driving up the hill now, up, up, past the beautiful, familiar homes to the stone columns and the sign that still read Devlin.

"Marty spoke to the live-in couple yesterday," Eve told him. "Just in case. They're expecting you."

"I can't live in that house," he said.

"No, I suppose not. But just get your head straight for now, figure out what you're going to do."

She pulled up in front of the garage. "It's a beautiful house, Jack."

"For someone else, maybe."

They got out. A pale sun broke through the clouds, and wind rattled bare branches.

"Thanks for the ride," he said. This was agony. The things he wanted to say to her, the hopes, the dreams, the fantasies he'd created around her. If they could have met under different circumstances... If Eve could have loved him without her duty standing between them... Her duty and his need.

But he still needed her.

"You'll be okay here?" she asked.

"Sure, I'll be fine."

She moved closer to him, and he saw the tears in her eyes. His heart constricted. "Don't," he said hoarsely.

"I won't," she replied, trying to smile, and then she put her arms around him and laid her head on his chest. "Good luck, Jack. The best. You deserve it," she murmured, and he stood there like a post, quivering internally with anguish, his arms hanging down as if paralyzed.

She let him go and he breathed again. "If you're ever in Denver..." she started to say, then she shook her head, turned away and got into her car.

He watched her drive out through the stone pillars, and

then he walked to the front door of Allison's house—his house—and raised his hand to knock. He was free. A free man.

But strangely, his heart was empty.

Eve made her way back through Aspen, along Main Street fringed by the tall cottonwoods that were mostly bare now. Her heart felt bruised. She couldn't believe she'd let Jack go like that, saying nothing, not telling him how much she loved him. After all these months of fighting for Jack, she was incapable of facing this one last battle.

Where had it gone wrong? Or, better question, had it ever been right?

One night of passion—was that enough to base a relationship on? But then there were the weeks, the months of working with him, of seeing him every day under the most demanding circumstances, of coming to admire, then like, then love him.

What a coward she was.

She drove out of town, through the stoplight on the highway, not seeing anything but a blur of brown autumn scenery. Winter was coming. Dark, cold, lonely. She'd have her work, but she wasn't sure it was enough anymore. For the first time in her life, she wasn't sure it was enough.

She'd have to face the media over this case. She'd stayed in the background today, but she could use this case as an example of the evil of the death penalty—it was tailor-made for her crusade. But she couldn't muster up the enthusiasm she'd once had. The fire had gone out of her. Even though Jack had told her to continue her work, she felt her commitment slipping. She needed him by her side to keep her strong and focused, to infuse her with energy. She needed him for love and happiness and fulfillment. She needed Jack so desperately.

Didn't he deserve to know that?

It was too soon; he'd just been given his freedom. He didn't need her to dump another burden on him. Maybe he didn't want her professions of love, maybe he needed time to figure out what to do with his life. Maybe...

She drove past the airport onto the stretch of highway that wound between Shale Bluffs and the river. Traffic was sparse this gray October day; she'd make good time and be home by late afternoon. Home. That was a joke. It was just a place she lived.

It occurred to Eve at that moment that she had no life at all, no husband, no children, few friends, no hobbies or interests outside of the law. Nothing. She'd had Gary, but he was gone, too, because she'd had nothing to give him. Her life was empty.

She choked out a sob as forlorn as the cold gray hills that stretched away from the road in every direction. She was so alone.

Abruptly Eve pulled off the highway and stopped her car, leaning her head on the steering wheel. She couldn't go on like this, it was impossible. What a sniveling coward she was.

She sat there for a few minutes, head bowed, then she straightened, set her shoulders and put her foot down on the gas pedal. She turned the car, too quickly, spraying gravel from under her tires, squealing around, bumping onto the highway, driving back toward Aspen. Quickly. Speeding.

Dry-eyed, resolute, she flew past the well-known landmarks, down Main Street, waiting impatiently for a light to change to green. Up Red Mountain, up and around the switchbacks to the familiar driveway. Slamming to a halt, out of her car, not even closing the door, running breathlessly up to the elegant double doors, pounding on them.

"Jack! Jack!" Oh, God, he had to come, he had to.

And then he was there, opening the door, looking at her, just looking, his face smooth and unreadable, the face she'd seen so many times. The lie he displayed to the world.

"Goddamn you, Jack!" she cried, and all the pent-up anguish of the past few months was contained in those words.

She raised her arm as if to strike him, as if to hit him with her frustration and her passion and her need.

He caught her arm, stopping its trajectory, and for a moment they stood like that, an impassioned tableau, chest to chest, and then she made an inarticulate noise and she was in his arms, laughing, crying, clinging to him with all her strength. "Oh, Jack, I love you. Don't send me away, please. I need you, I need to be with you."

He held her fiercely and said things, too, things she could hardly believe, words that made her heart swell, and she covered his face with kisses. "Oh, God, Jack, I can't believe this. Oh, my God, how I love you."

He looked down into her eyes. "I loved you from the minute you walked into that jail. Didn't you know? Couldn't you tell?"

She shook her head.

"Stay with me," he said, holding her, standing there in the doorway of the house he'd built. "Stay with me."

"Always," she breathed.

He ran a finger along her cheek, then took her face in his hands. "I won't live here. I may try Denver. But wherever we go, you have to continue your work, Eve."

She nodded.

"I'll help you any way I can. I'll support your work. Your cause. It's my cause now, you know." He drew his brows together. "I've never had a cause before. I think I'm going to be good at it."

"I love you," she said.

He smiled, the first time she'd ever seen him smile openly, fully, and it was as if he were flying free, soaring, a young boy. "Dumb, weren't we?" he asked.

"Awful dumb."

"Hey, it's cold out here," he said. "Let's go in."

They turned, and, arm in arm, they went inside and closed the door on the world.

This April
DEBBIE MACOMBER

takes readers to the Big Sky and beyond...

MONTANA

At her grandfather's request, Molly packs up her kids and returns to his ranch in Sweetgrass, Montana.

But when she arrives, she finds a stranger, Sam Dakota, working there. Molly has questions: What exactly is he doing there? Why doesn't the sheriff trust him? Just *who* is Sam Dakota? These questions become all the more critical when her grandfather tries to push them into marriage....

Moving to the state of Montana is one thing; entering the state of matrimony is quite another!

Available in April 1998 wherever books are sold.

MIRA

MDM434

New York Times
bestselling author

Jayne Ann Krentz

will once again spellbind readers with

A Woman's Touch

When Rebecca Wade inherited land her boss, Kyle Stockbridge, considered his, she absolutely refused to sell out. Especially when he used a declaration of love as a way to convince her.

Despite Kyle's claim that their relationship—and his feelings for her—were independent of the issue between them, Rebecca knew that selling the land wouldn't solve all of their problems. For that to happen, Kyle would have to prove his love.

Available in April 1998 at your favorite retail outlet.

MIRA

MJAK315

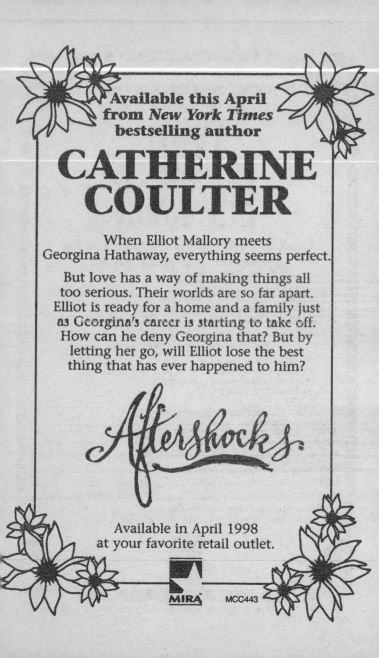